FIFTY POUNDS

AFTER tea Phillip Repton and Eulalia Burnes discussed their gloomy circumstances. Repton was the precarious sort of London journalist, a dark deliberating man, lean and drooping, full of genteel unprosperity, who wrote articles about Single Tax, Diet and Reason, The Futility of this that and the other, or The Significance of the other that and this; all done with a bleak care and signed P. Stick Repton. Eulalia was brown-haired and hardy, undeliberating and intuitive; she had been milliner, clerk, domestic help and something in a canteen; and P. Stick Repton had, as one commonly says, picked her up at a time when she was drifting about London without a penny in her purse, without even a purse, and he had not yet put her down.

'I can't understand! It's sickening, monstrous!' Lally was fumbling with a match before the penny gas fire, for when it was evening, in September, it always got chilly on a floor so high up. Their flat was a fourth-floor one and there was — O, fifteen thousand stairs! Out of the window and beyond the chimney you could see the long glare from lights in High Holborn, and hear the hums and hoots of buses. And that was a comfort.

'Lower! Turn it lower!' yelled Phillip. The gas had ignited with an astounding thump; the kneeling Lally had thrown up her hands and dropped the matchbox saying 'Damn' in the same tone as one might say good morning to a milkman.

'You shouldn't do it, you know,' grumbled Repton. 'You'll blow us to the deuce.' And that was just like Lally, that was Lally all over, always: the gas, the nobs of sugar in his tea, the way she . . . and the, the . . . O

9

dear, dear! In their early life together, begun so abruptly and illicitly six months before, her simple hidden beauties had delighted him by their surprises; they had peered and shone brighter, had waned and recurred; she was less the one star in his universe than a faint galaxy.

This room of theirs was a dingy room, very small but very high. A lanky gas tube swooped from the middle of the ceiling towards the middle of the table-cloth as if burning to discover whether that was pink or saffron or fawn — and it *was* hard to tell — but on perceiving that the cloth, whatever its tint, was disturbingly spangled with dozens of cup-stains and several large envelopes, the gas tube in the violence of its disappointment contorted itself abruptly, assumed a lateral bend, and put out its tongue of flame at an oleograph of Mona Lisa which hung above the fireplace.

Those envelopes were the torment to Lally; they were the sickening monstrous manifestations which she could not understand. There were always some of them lying there, or about the room, bulging with manuscripts that no editors — they *couldn't* have perused them — wanted; and so it had come to the desperate point when, as Lally was saying, something had to be done about things. Repton had done all *he* could; he wrote unceasingly, all day, all night, but all his projects insolvently withered, and morning noon and evening brought his manuscripts back as unwanted as snow in summer. He was depressed and baffled and weary. And there was simply nothing else he could do, nothing in the world. Apart from his own wonderful gift he was useless, Lally knew, and he was being steadily and stupidly murdered by those editors. It was weeks since they had eaten a proper meal. Whenever they obtained any real nice food now, they sat down to it silently, intently and destructively. As far as Lally could tell there seemed to be no prospect of any such meals again in life or time, and the worst of it all was Phillip's pride — he was actually too proud to ask anyone for assistance! Not that he would be too proud to accept help if it were offered to him: O no, if it came he would rejoice at it! But still, he had that nervous shrinking pride that coiled upon itself, and he would not ask; he was like a wounded animal that hid its woe far away from the rest of the world. Only Lally knew his need, but why could not other people see it — those villainous editors! His own wants were so modest and he had a generous mind.

'Phil,' Lally said, seating herself at the table. Repton was lolling in a wicker arm-chair beside the gas fire. 'I'm not going on waiting and waiting any longer, I must go and get a job. Yes, I must. We get poorer and poorer. We can't go on like it any longer, there's no use, and I can't bear it.'

'No, no, I can't have that, my dear . . .'

'But I will!' she cried. 'O, why are you so proud?'

'Proud! Proud!' He stared into the gas fire, his tired arms hanging limp over the arms of the chair. 'You don't understand. There are things the flesh has to endure, and things the spirit too must endure . . .' Lally loved to hear him talk like that; and it was just as well, for Repton was much given to such discoursing. Deep in her mind was the conviction that he had simple access to profound, almost unimaginable, wisdom. 'It isn't pride, it is just that there is a certain order in life, in my life, that it would not do for. I could not bear it, I could never rest: I can't explain that, but just believe it, Lally.' His head was empty but unbowed; he spoke quickly and finished almost angrily. 'If only I had money!

It's not for myself. I can stand all this, any amount of it. I've done so before, and I shall do so again and again I've no doubt. But I have to think of you.'

That was fiercely annoying. Lally got up and went and stood over him.

'Why are you so stupid? I can think for myself and fend for myself. I'm not married to you. You have your pride, but I can't starve for it. And I've a pride, too. I'm a burden to you. If you won't let me work now while we're together, then I must leave you and work for myself.'

'Leave! Leave me now? When things are so bad?' His white face gleamed his perturbation up at her. 'O well, go, go.' But then, mournfully moved, he took her hands and fondled them. 'Don't be a fool, Lally; it's only a passing depression, this. I've known worse before, and it never lasts long, something turns up, always does. There's good and bad in it all, but there's more goodness than anything else. You see.'

'I don't want to wait for ever, even for goodness. I don't believe in it, I never see it, never feel it, it is no use to me. I could go and steal, or walk the streets, or do any dirty thing — easily. What's the good of goodness if it isn't any use?'

'But, but,' Repton stammered. 'What's the use of bad, if it isn't any better?'

'I mean . . .' began Lally.

'You don't mean anything, my dear girl.'

'I mean, when you haven't any choice it's no use talking moral, or having pride; it's stupid. O, my darling' — she slid down to him and lay against his breast — 'it's not you, you are everything to me; that's why it angers me so, this treatment of you, all hard blows and no comfort. It will never be any different. I feel it will never be different now, and it terrifies me.'

'Pooh!' Repton kissed her and comforted her: she was his beloved. 'When things are wrong with us our fancies take their tone from our misfortunes, badness, evil. I sometimes have a queer stray feeling that one day I shall be hanged. Yes, I don't know what for, what *could* I be hanged for? And, do you know, at other times I've had a kind of intuition that one day I shall be — what do you think? — Prime Minister of the country! Yes, well, you can't reason against such things. I know what I should do, I've my plans, I've even made a list of the men for my Cabinet. Yes, well, there you are.'

But Lally had made up her mind to leave him; she would leave him for a while and earn her own living. When things took a turn for the better she would join him again. She told him this. She had friends who were going to get her some work.

'But what are you going to do, Lally? I . . .'

'I'm going away to Glasgow,' said she.

'Glasgow?' He had heard things about Glasgow! 'Good heavens!'

'I've some friends there,' the girl went on steadily. She had got up and was sitting on the arm of his chair. 'I wrote to them last week. They can get me a job almost any when, and I can stay with them. They want me to go — they've sent the money for my fare. I think I shall have to go.'

'You don't love me then!' said the man.

Lally kissed him.

'But *do* you? Tell me!'

'Yes, my dear,' said Lally, 'of course.'

An uneasiness possessed him; he released her moodily. Where was their wild passion flown to? She was staring at him intently, then she tenderly said: 'My love, don't you be melancholy, don't take it to heart so. I'd cross the world to find you a pin.'

13

'No, no, you mustn't do that,' he exclaimed idiotically. At her indulgent smile he grimly laughed too, and then sank back in his chair. The girl stood up and went about the room doing vague nothings, until he spoke again.

'So you are tired of me?'

Lally went to him steadily and knelt down by his chair. 'If I was tired of you, Phil, I'd kill myself.'

Moodily he ignored her. 'I suppose it had to end like this. But I've loved you desperately.' Lally was now weeping on his shoulder and he began to twirl a lock of her rich brown hair absently with his fingers as if it were a seal on a watch chain. 'I'd been thinking that we might as well get married, as soon as things had turned round.'

'I'll come back, Phil' — she clasped him so tenderly — 'as soon as you want me.'

'But you are not really going?'

'Yes,' said Lally.

'You're not to go!'

'I wouldn't go if ... if anything ... if you had any luck. But as we are now I must go away, to give you a chance. You see that, darling Phil?'

'You're not to go; I object. I just love you, Lally, that's all, and of course I want to keep you here.'

'Then what are we to do?'

'I ... don't ... know. Things drop out of the sky, but we must be together. You're not to go.'

Lally sighed: he was stupid. And Repton began to turn over in his mind the dismal knowledge that she had taken this step in secret, she had not told him while she was trying to get to Glasgow. Now here she was with the fare, and as good as gone! Yes, it was all over.

'When do you propose to go?'

'Not for a few days, nearly a fortnight.'

'Good God,' he moaned. Yes, it was all over then. He had never dreamed that this would be the end, that she

14

would be the first to break away. He had always envisaged a tender scene in which he could tell her, with dignity and gentle humour that . . . Well, he never had quite hit upon the words he would use, but that was the kind of setting. And now, here she was with her fare to Glasgow, her heart towards Glasgow, and she as good as gone to Glasgow! No dignity, no gentle humour — in fact he was enraged — sullen but enraged, he boiled furtively. But he said with mournful calm:

'I've so many misfortunes, I suppose I can bear this too.'

Gloomy and tragic he was.

'Dear, darling Phil, it's for your own sake I'm going.'

Repton sniffed derisively. 'We are always mistaken in the reasons for our commonest actions; Nature derides us all. You are sick of me; I can't blame you.'

Eulalia was so moved that she could only weep again. Nevertheless she wrote to her friends in Glasgow promising to be with them by a stated date.

Towards the evening of the following day, at a time when she was alone, a letter arrived addressed to herself. It was from a firm of solicitors in Cornhill inviting her to call upon them. A flame leaped up in Lally's heart: it might mean the offer of some work which would keep her in London after all! If only it were so she would accept it on the spot, and Phillip would have to be made to see the reasonability of it. But at the office in Cornhill a more astonishing outcome awaited her. There she showed her letter to a little office boy with scarcely any fingernails and very little nose, and he took it to an elderly man who had a superabundance of both. Smiling affably the long-nosed man led her upstairs into the sombre den of a gentleman who had some white hair and a lumpy yellow complexion. Having put to her a number of questions relating to her family history, and appearing to be satisfied and not at all surprised by her answers, this gentleman revealed to Lally the overpowering tidings that she was entitled to a legacy of eighty pounds by the will of a forgotten and recently deceased aunt. Subject to certain formalities, proofs of identity and so forth, he promised Lally the possession of the money within about a week.

Lally's descent to the street, her emergence into the clamouring atmosphere, her walk along to Holborn, were accomplished in a state of blessedness and trance, a trance in which life became a thousand times aerially enlarged, movement was a delight, and thought a rapture. She would give all the money to Phillip, and if he very much wanted it she would even marry him now. Perhaps, though, she would save ten pounds of it for herself. The other seventy would keep them for ... it was impossible to say how long it would keep them. They could have a little holiday somewhere in the country together, he was so worn and weary. Perhaps she had better not tell Phillip anything at all about it until her lovely money was really in her hand. Nothing in life, at least nothing about money, was ever certain; something horrible might happen at the crucial moment and the money be snatched from her very fingers. O, she would go mad then! So for some days she kept her wonderful secret.

Their imminent separation had given Repton a tender sadness that was very moving. 'Eulalia', he would say; for he had suddenly adopted the formal version of her name: 'Eulalia, we've had a great time together, a wonderful time, there will never be anything like it again.' She often shed tears, but she kept the grand secret still locked in her heart. Indeed, it occurred to her very forcibly that even now his stupid pride might cause him to reject her money altogether. Silly, silly Phillip! Of course, it would have been different if they had married; he would naturally have taken it then, and really, it would have *been* his. She would have to think out some dodge to overcome his scruples. Scruples were *such* a nuisance, but then it was very noble of him: there were not many men who wouldn't take money from a girl they were living with.

Well, a week later she was summoned again to the office in Cornhill and received from the white-haired gentleman a cheque for eighty pounds drawn on the Bank of England to the order of Eulalia Burnes. Miss Burnes desired to cash the cheque straightway, so the large-nosed elderly clerk was deputed to accompany her to the Bank of England close by and assist in procuring the money.

'A very nice errand!' exclaimed that gentleman as they crossed to Threadneedle Street past the Royal Exchange. Miss Burnes smiled her acknowledgment, and he began to tell her of other windfalls that had been disbursed in his time — but vast sums, very great persons — until she began to infer that Blackbean, Carp and Ransome were universal dispensers of largesse.

'Yes, but,' said the clerk, hawking a good deal from an affliction of catarrh, 'I never got any myself, and never will. If I did, do you know what I would do with it?' But at that moment they entered the portals of the bank, and in the excitement of the business, Miss Burnes forgot to ask the clerk how he would use a legacy, and thus she possibly lost a most valuable slice of knowledge. With one fifty-pound note and six five-pound notes clasped in her handbag she bade good-bye to the long-nosed clerk, who shook her fervently by the hand and assured her that Blackbean, Carp and Ransome would be delighted at all times to undertake any commissions on her behalf. Then she fled along the pavement, blithe as a bird, until she was breathless with her flight. Presently she came opposite the window of a typewriter agency. Tripping airily into its office she laid a scrap of paper before a lovely Hebe who was typing there.

'I want this typed, if you please,' said Lally.

The beautiful typist read the words of the scrap of paper and stared at the heiress.

'I don't want any address to appear,' said Lally. 'Just a plain sheet, please.'

A few moments later she received a neatly typed page folded in an envelope, and after paying the charge she hurried off to a district messenger office. Here she addressed the envelope in a disguised hand to P. Stick Repton, Esq., at the address in Holborn. She read the typed letter through again:

Dear Sir,

In common with many others I entertain the greatest admiration for your literary abilities, and I therefore beg you to accept this tangible expression of that admiration from a constant reader of your articles, who for purely private reasons, desires to remain anonymous.

Your very sincere
Wellwisher

Placing the fifty-pound note upon the letter Lally carefully folded them together and put them both into the envelope. The attendant then gave it to a uniformed lad, who sauntered off whistling very casually, somewhat to Lally's alarm — he looked so small and careless to be entrusted with fifty pounds. Then Lally went out, changed one of her five-pound notes and had a lunch — half a crown, but it was worth it. O, how enchanting and exciting London was! In two days more she would have been gone: now she would have to write off at once to her Glasgow friends and tell them she had changed her mind, that she was now settled in London. O, how enchanting and delightful! And to-night he would take her out to dine in some fine restaurant, and they would do a theatre. She did not really want to marry Phil, they had got on so well without it, but if he wanted that too she did not mind — much. They would go away into the country for a whole week. What money would do! Marvellous! And looking round the restaurant she felt sure that no other woman there, no matter how well-dressed, had as much as thirty pounds in her handbag.

Returning home in the afternoon she became conscious of her own betraying radiance; very demure and subdued and usual she would have to be, or he might guess the cause of it. Though she danced up the long flight of stairs, she entered their room quietly, but the sight of Repton staring out of the window, forlorn as a drowsy horse, overcame her and she rushed to embrace him, crying 'Darling!'

'Hullo, hullo!' he smiled.

'I'm so fond of you, Phil dear.'

'But . . . but you're deserting me!'

'O, no,' she cried archly; 'I'm not — not deserting you.'

'All right.' Repton shrugged his shoulders, but he seemed happier. He did not mention the fifty pounds then; perhaps it had not come yet — or perhaps he was thinking to surprise her.

'Let's go for a walk, it's a screaming lovely day', said Lally.

'O, I dunno,' he yawned and stretched. 'Nearly tea-time, isn't it?'

'Well, we . . .' Lally was about to suggest having tea out somewhere, but she bethought herself in time. 'I suppose it is. Yes, it is.'

So they stayed in for tea. No sooner was tea over than Repton remarked that he had an engagement somewhere. Off he went, leaving Lally disturbed and anxious. Why had he not mentioned the fifty pounds? Surely it had not gone to the wrong address? This suspicion once formed, Lally soon became certain, tragically sure, that she had misaddressed the envelope herself. A conviction that she had put No. 17 instead of No. 71 was almost overpowering, and she fancied that she hadn't even put London on the envelope — but Glasgow. That was impossible, though, but — O, the horror! — somebody else was enjoying their fifty pounds. The girl's fears were not allayed by the running visit she paid to the messengers' office that evening, for the rash imp who had been entrusted with her letter had gone home and therefore could not be interrogated until the morrow. By now she was sure that he had blundered; he had been so casual with an important letter like that! Lally never did, and never would again, trust any little boys who wore their hats so much on one side, were so glossy with hair-oil, and went about whistling just to madden you. She burned to ask where the boy lived but in spite of her desperate desire she could not do so. She dared not, it would expose her to ... to something or other she could only feel, not name; you had to keep cool, to let nothing, not even curiosity, master you.

Hurrying home again, though hurrying was not her custom, and there was no occasion for it, she wrote the letter to her Glasgow friends. Then it crossed her mind that it would be wiser not to post the letter that night; better wait until the morning, after she had discovered what the horrible little messenger had done with her letter. Bed was a poor refuge from her thoughts, but she accepted it, and when Phil came home she was not sleeping. While he undressed he told her of the lecture he had been to, something about Agrarian Depopulation it was, but even after he had stretched himself beside her, he did not speak about the fifty pounds. Nothing, not even curiosity, should master her, and she calmed herself, and in time fitfully slept.

At breakfast next morning he asked her what she was going to do that day.

'O,' replied Lally offhandedly, 'I've a lot of things to see to, you know; I must go out. I'm sorry the porridge is so awful this morning, Phil, but . . .'

'Awful?' he broke in. 'But it's nicer than usual! Where are you going? I thought—our last day, you know — we might go out somewhere together.'

'Dear Phil!' Lovingly she stretched out a hand to be caressed across the table. 'But I've several things to do. I'll come back early, eh?' She got up and hurried round to embrace him.

'All right,' he said. 'Don't be long.'

Off went Lally to the messenger office, at first as happy as a bird, but on approaching the building the old tremors assailed her. Inside the room was the cocky little boy who bade her 'Good-morning' with laconic assurance. Lally at once questioned him, and when he triumphantly produced a delivery book she grew limp with her suppressed fear, one fear above all others. For a moment she did not want to look at it: Truth hung by a hair, and as long as it so hung she might swear it was a lie. But there it was, written right across the page, an entry of a letter delivered, signed for in the well-known hand, P. Stick Repton. There was no more doubt, only a sharp indignant agony as though she had been stabbed with a dagger of ice.

'O yes, thank you,' said Lally calmly. 'Did you hand it to him yourself?'

'Yes'm,' replied the boy, and he described Phillip.

'Did he open the letter?'

'Yes'm.'

'There was no answer?'

'No'm.'

'All right.' Fumbling in her bag, she added: 'I think I've got a sixpence for you.'

Out in the street again she tremblingly chuckled to herself. 'So that is what he is like, after all. Cruel and mean! He was going to let her go and keep the money in secret to himself!' How despicable! Cruel and mean, cruel and mean! She hummed it to herself. 'Cruel and mean, cruel and mean!' It eased her tortured bosom. 'Cruel and mean!' And he was waiting at home for her, waiting with a smile for their last day together. It would *have* to be their last day. She tore up the letter to her Glasgow friends, for now she *must* go to them. So cruel and mean! Let him wait! A bus stopped beside her, and she stepped on to it, climbing to the top and sitting there while the air chilled her burning features. The bus made a long journey to Plaistow. She knew nothing of Plaistow, she wanted to know nothing of Plaistow, but she did not care where the bus took her; she only wanted to keep moving and moving away, as far away as possible from Holborn and from him, and not once let those hovering tears down fall.

From Plaistow she turned and walked back as far as the Mile End Road. Thereabouts, wherever she went she met clergymen, dozens of them. There must be a conference, about charity or something, Lally thought. With a vague desire to confide her trouble to someone, she observed them; it would relieve the strain. But there was none she could tell her sorrow to, and failing that, when she came to a neat restaurant she entered it and consumed a fish. Just beyond her three sleek parsons were lunching, sleek and pink; bald, affable, consoling men, all very much alike.

'I saw Carter yesterday,' she heard one say. Lally liked listening to the conversation of strangers, and she had often wondered what clergymen talked about among themselves.

'What, Carter! Indeed. Nice fellow, Carter. How was he?'

'Carter loves preaching, you know!' cried the third.

'O yes, he loves preaching!'

'Ha, ha, ha, yes.'

'Ha, ha, ha, oom.'

'Awf'ly good preacher, though.'

'Yes, awf'ly good.'

'And he's awf'ly good at comic songs, too.'

'Yes?'

'Yes!'

Three glasses of water, a crumbling of bread, a silence suggestive of prayer.

'How long has he been married?'

'Twelve years,' returned the cleric who had met Carter.

'O, twelve years!'

'I've only been married twelve years myself,' said the oldest of them.

'Indeed!'

'Yes, I tarried very long.'

'Ha, ha, ha, yes.'

'Ha, ha, ha, oom.'

'Er . . . have you any family?'

'No.'

Very delicate and dainty in handling their food they were; very delicate and dainty.

'My rectory is a magnificent old house,' continued the recently married one. 'Built originally 1700. Burnt down. Rebuilt 1784.'

'Indeed!'

'Humph!'

'Seventeen bedrooms and two delightful tennis courts.'

'O, well done!' the others cried, and then they all fell with genteel gusto upon a pale blancmange.

From the restaurant the girl sauntered about for a while, and then there was a cinema wherein, seated warm and comfortable in the twitching darkness, she partially stilled her misery. Some nervous fancy kept her roaming in that district for most of the evening. She knew that if she left it she would go home, and she did not want to go home. The naphtha lamps of the booths at Mile End were bright and distracting, and the hum of the evening business was good despite the smell. A man was weaving sweetstuffs from a pliant roll of warm toffee that he wrestled with as the athlete wrestles with the python. There were stalls with things of iron, with fruit or fish, pots and pans, leather, string, nails. Watches for use — or for ornament — what d'ye lack? A sailor told naughty stories while selling bunches of green grapes out of barrels of cork dust which he swore he had stolen from the Queen of Honolulu. People clamoured for them both. You could buy back numbers of the comic papers at four a penny, rolls of linoleum for very little more — and use either for the other's purpose.

'At thrippence per foot, mesdames,' cried the sweating cheapjack, lashing himself into ecstatic furies, 'that's a piece of fabric weft and woven with triple-strength Andalusian jute, double-hot-pressed with rubber from the island of Pagama, and stencilled by an artist as poisoned his grandfather's cook. That's a piece of fabric, mesdames, as the king of heaven himself wouldn't mind to put down in his parlour — if he had the chance. Do I ask thrippence a foot for that piece of fabric? Mesdames, I was never a daring chap.'

Lally watched it all, she looked and listened; then looked and did not see, listened and did not hear. Her misery was not the mere disappointment of love, not that kind of misery alone; it was the crushing of an ideal in which love had had its home, a treachery cruel and mean.

The sky of night, so smooth, so bestarred, looked wrinkled through her screen of unshed tears; her sorrow was a wild cloud that troubled the moon with darkness.

In miserable desultory wandering she had spent her day, their last day, and now, returning to Holborn in the late evening, she suddenly began to hurry, for a new possibility had come to lighten her dejection. Perhaps, after all, so whimsical he was, he was keeping his 'revelation' until the last day, or even the last hour, when (nothing being known to her, as he imagined) all hopes being gone and they had come to the last kiss, he would take her in his arms and laughingly kill all grief, waving the succour of a flimsy bank-note like a flag of triumph. Perhaps even, in fact surely, that was why he wanted to take her out to-day! O, what a blind, wicked, stupid girl she was, and in a perfect frenzy of bubbling faith she panted homewards for his revealing sign.

From the pavement below she could see that their room was lit. Weakly she climbed the stairs and opened the door. Phil was standing up, staring so strangely at her. Helplessly and half-guilty she began to smile. Without a word said he came quickly to her and crushed her in his arms, her burning silent man, loving and exciting her. Lying against his breast in that constraining embrace, their passionate disaster was gone, her doubts were flown; all perception of the feud was torn from her and deeply drowned in a gulf of bliss. She was aware only of the consoling delight of their reunion, of his amorous kisses, of his tongue tingling the soft down on her upper lip that she disliked and he admired. All the soft wanton endearments that she so loved to hear him speak were singing in her ears, and then he suddenly swung and lifted her up, snapped out the gaslight and carried her off to bed.

Life that is born of love feeds on love, if the wherewithal be hidden, how shall we stay our hunger? The galaxy may grow dim, or the stars drop in a wandering void; you can neither keep them in your hands nor crumble them in your mind.

What was it Phil had once called her? Numskull! After all it was his own fifty pounds, she had given it to him freely, it was his to do as he liked with. A gift was a gift, it was poor spirit to send money to anyone with the covetous expectation that it would return to you. She would surely go to-morrow.

The next morning he awoke her early, and kissed her. 'What time does your train go?' said he.

'Train!' Lally scrambled from his arms and out of bed. A fine day, a glowing day. O bright, sharp air! Quickly she dressed, and went into the other room to prepare their breakfast. Soon he followed, and they ate silently together, although whenever they were near each other he caressed her tenderly. Afterwards she went into the bedroom and packed her bag; there was nothing more to be done, he was beyond hope. No woman waits to be sacrificed, least of all those who sacrifice themselves with courage and a quiet mind. When she was ready to go she took her portmanteau into the sitting-room; he, too, made to put on his hat and coat.

'No,' murmured Lally, 'you're not to come with me.'

'Pooh, my dear!' he protested; 'nonsense!'

'I won't have you come,' cried Lally with an asperity that impressed him.

'But you can't carry that bag to the station by yourself!'

'I shall take a taxi.' She buttoned her gloves.

'My dear!' His humorous deprecation annoyed her.

'O, bosh!' Putting her gloved hands around his neck she kissed him coolly. 'Good-bye. Write to me often. Let me know how you thrive, won't you, Phil? And' — a little waveringly — 'love me always.' She stared queerly at the two dimples in his cheeks; each dimple was a nest of hair that could never be shaved.

'Lally, darling, beloved girl! I never loved you more than now, this moment. You are more precious than ever to me!'

At that, she knew her moment of sardonic revelation had come — but she dared not use it, she let it go. She could not so deeply humiliate him by revealing her knowledge of his perfidy. A compassionate divinity smiles at our puny sins. She knew his perfidy, but to triumph in it would defeat her own pride. Let him keep his gracious, mournful airs to the last, false though they were. It was better to part so, better from such a figure than from an abject scarecrow, even though both were the same inside. And something capriciously reminded her, for a flying moment, of elephants she had seen swaying with the grand movement of tidal water — and groping for monkey nuts.

Lally tripped down the stairs alone. At the end of the street she turned for a last glance. There he was, high up in the window, waving good-byes. And she waved back at him.

The Field of Mustard (1926)

THE OLD VENERABLE

Down in the village the women called him 'the dirty old man', the children did not seem to notice him, and their fathers called him 'the Owd Venrable', or old Dick, with a sigh as of vague envy. There was little cause for that, he living in a wood in a little old tent shanty built of boughs and string and tarpaulin, with a heap of straw to sleep on. Outside the tent was his fire, and he had dwelt there so long that the mound of wood ash had grown almost as big as his house. Seventy years old he was, an old venerable ragged crippled man using two sticks, with a cheery voice and a truculent spirit, but honest as spring water, sharing his last drop with the last man or the first — he invariably shared theirs. When he was drunk he sang, when he was not drunk he talked for evermore about nothing, to nobody, for his tent was in a wood, a little clearing in a great wood, and the wood was away, a long way, from anywhere, so that he lived, as you might say, on air and affability and primed his starved heart with hope. A man like that could hope for anything, and a mere anything — twopence — would bring him bliss, but his undeviating aspiration, an ambition as passionate as it was supine, was to possess a donkey. He had pestered many sympathetic people who had the means; often he had sent out that dove of his fancy from the ark of his need, but it had never returned, at least not with a donkey; and never an ass fell like a bolt from heaven. If it had done it would surely have taken no hurt, such a grand wood it was, miles of it, growing up and down the hills and hills, and so thickly bosomed that if you had fallen from a balloon into the top of that wood it would have been at the last like sinking into a feather bed. And full of birds and game. And gamekeepers. The keepers did not like him to be there, it was unnatural to them, but keepers come and go, the shooting was let to a syndicate, and he had been there so long that new keepers found him where the old ones had left him. They even made use of him; he swept the rides and alley-ways for the shooters, marked down the nests of pheasants and kept observation on rabbits and weasels and the flocks of pigeons which any-body was welcome to shoot. Sometimes he earned a few shillings by plashing hedgerows or hoeing a field of roots, but mostly he was a 'kindler', he gathered firewood and peddled it on a hand-truck around the villages. That was why he dreamed of donkey and nothing but donkey; a creature whose four feet together were not so big as one of its ears would carry double and treble the load of kindling and make him a rich man.

One day he tramped right over to the head keeper's house to deliver a message, and there Tom Hussey had shown him a litter of retriever puppies he was tending. They had a pedigree, Tom Hussey said, as long as the shafts of a cart; the mother herself was valued at fifty golden guineas, but the sire belonged to Lord Camover and bank-notes wouldn't buy that dog, nor love nor money — not even the crown of England. There they were, six puppies just weaned and scrambling about, beautiful bouncing creatures, all except one that seemed quiet and backward.

'That one?' Tom Hussey said; 'I be going to kill her. Sha's got a sort of rupture in her navel.'

'Don't do that,' said old Dick, for he knew a lot about dogs as well as birds and lambs and donkeys. 'Give it to I.' And Tom Hussey gave him the pup then and there, and he took it home to his tent and bandaged it artfully with a yard strip of canvas, and called it Sossy because it was so pert.

Every day the old man attended to that bandage round

Sossy's stomach — he knew a whole lot about dogs — and the dog throve and grew, and every night nuzzled in the straw beside him; and Dick rejoiced. They lived heartily, for Dick was a nimble hand with a wire, and rabbits were plentiful, and he was always begging for bones and such-like for his Sossy. Everywhere in that wood he took Sossy with him and he trained her so in the arts of obedience that she knew what he wanted even if he only winked one eye. After about six months of this he took off her bandage for the last time and threw it away. There she was, cured and fit and perfect, a fine sweet flourishing thing. What a glossy coat! What a bushy tail! And her eyes — they made you dream of things!

A while after that Tom Hussey came into the wood to shoot some pigeons. There was always a great flock of them somewhere in the wood and when they rose up from the trees the whirr of their thousand wings was like the roar of a great wave. Well, Tom Hussey came, and as he passed near the tent he called out the good of the morning to old Dick.

'Come here,' cried Dick, and Tom Hussey went, and when he saw that dog you could have split him with a lathe of wood he was so astonished. Sossy danced round him in a rare flurry, nuzzling at his pockets.

'She's hungry,' he said.

'No, she ain't. Get down, you great devil! No, she ain't hungry, she's just had a saucepan full o' shackles — get down! — that saucepan there what I washes myself in.'

When Tom Hussey shot a pigeon she stood to the gun and brought the bird back like an angel.

'Dick, you can swap that dog for a donkey whenever you've a mind to,' Tom Hussey said.

'An't she got a mouth? I tell you,' Dick cried joyfully.

'Like silk,' was the rejoinder.

'It's a gift.'

'Born,' chanted Tom Hussey.

'It's a gift, I tell you.'

'Born. She's worth twenty pounds. You sell that bitch and get you a donkey, quick.'

'No,' deliberated the veteran. 'I shan't do that.'

'Twenty pounds she worth, of good money.'

'I shan't have 'ee, I tell you.'

'You sell that bitch and get you a donkey. That's my last word to you,' Tom Hussey said as he stalked away.

But that 'Owd Venrable' was a far-seeing sagacious creature, a very artful old man he was, and when the time came for it he and Tom Hussey conjured up a deal between themselves. It would have been risky for Tom Hussey, but as he was changing to another estate he chanced it and he connived and Sossy was mated on the sly to one of his master's finest retrievers, as good as ever stepped into a covert, and by all accounts the equal of Lord Camover's dog that had begot Sossy. So when Tom Hussey departed there was old Dick with his valuable dog, looking forward to the few weeks hence when Sossy would have the finest bred puppies of their kind in the land. He scarcely dared to compute their value, but it would surely be enough to relegate the idea of a donkey to the limbo of outworn and mean conceits. No, if all went well he would have a change of life altogether. He would give up the old tent; it was rotting, he was tired of it. If things came wonderful well he would buy a nag and a little cart and a few cokernuts and he would travel the round of the fairs and see something of the world again. Nothing like cokernuts for a profitable trade. And perhaps he might even find some old 'gal' to go with him.

This roseate dream so tinted every moment of his thoughts that he lived, as you might say, like a poet, cherishing the dog, the source and promise of these ideals, with fondness and joy. The only cloud on the horizon of bliss was the new gamekeeper, a sprag young fellow, who had taken a deep dislike to him. Old Dick soon became aware of this animosity for the new keeper kept a strict watch upon his neighbourhood and walked about kicking over Dick's snares, impounding his wires, and complaining of his dirty habits and his poaching. And it was true, he *was* dirty, he had lost his pride, and he *did* poach, just a little, for he had a belly that hungered like any other man's, and he had a dog.

Early one morning as Dick was tending his fire the new keeper strolled up. He was a wry-mouthed slow-speaking young chap, and he lounged there with his gun under his arm and his hands in his pockets. Neither spoke for a while, but at last the keeper said:

'It burns well.'

'Huh, and so would you burn well,' grinned the old man, 'if I cut you atop of it.'

For fully two minutes the young keeper made no retort, he was a rather enraging young keeper. Then he said: 'Ah, and what do you think you may be doing round here?'

The old man flung a few pinches of tea into a can of boiling water.

'You get on with your job, young feller, and I'll get on with mine.'

'What *is* your job?'

The 'Owd Venrable' eyed him angrily.

'My job? I'll tell you — it's to mind my own business. You'll learn that for yourself later on, I 'spects, when you get the milk outer your mouth — you ought to, however. Wait till yer be as old as I.'

'Ah,' drawled the keeper, 'I don't mind waiting.'

'I met chaps like you before,' the old man began to thunder. 'Thousands on 'em. D'you know what happened to the last one?'

'Died of fleabites, I shouldn't wonder,' was the placid rejoinder

'I had him on the hop. When he warn't thinking,' the old man ruminating, grinned, 'I wuz! I give him a kick o' the stomach as fetched him atween wind and water, and down he went, clean as a smelt. D'you know what I did then?'

'Picked his pocket, I shouldn't wonder.'

'Yah! Never stole nothing from no man, 'cept it was my own. Clean as a smelt, I tell you.'

'Well,' the new keeper slowly said, shifting his gun from the left arm to the right, 'I can take a hiding from any man . . .'

'Ah, and from any old woman, too, I should say.'

'. . . from any man,' continued the imperturbable one, 'as can give it me — if you know of one.' He began to pick his teeth with a matchstick. 'Did you get my message?' he more briskly added.

'What message?'

'I sent you a message.'

'Then you sent it by a wet hen. I an't had no message.'

'I know you had it, but I'll tell you again. I've got orders to clear you out of this wood, you and your dog. You can take your time, don't want to be hard on you, but out you goes, and soon, you and your dog.'

'Well, we can go, my cunning feller, we can go.'

'That's right, then.'

'We can go — when we've a mind to. But who's a-going to look arter my job?'

'What job's that?'

'Huh, what job!' the old man disgustedly groaned. 'Why, who's a-going to keep an eye on things, and they poachers, thousands on 'em, just waiting for to catch I asleep! But they can't do it.'

'Naw, I shouldn't think anyone *could* sleep in a hole like that!'

'Yah, I could sleep, I could sleep a sack o' taters rotten! And who's a-going to clear up when the storms been shamracking about the place? I cleans up the paths, I cleans 'em for one and all, and I cleans 'em for you. Some I does it right for and some I does it wrong. If I did it right for all I'd be out of this world, seemly.'

'Who asked you to? Nobody asked you to, we can do without it, and we can do without you. So now I've told you.' With that the young keeper sauntered airily away.

'Yah!' the Old Venerable called after him, 'Clean as a smelt, I tell you, clean as a smelt', and as long as his adversary remained in view he continued to remind him of that excellent conclusion.

But despite his contempt the old man was perturbed; he knew the game was up, he would have to seek a lodging elsewhere. By the grace of fortune the blow had come just when it could least concern him; all he wanted was time for Sossy to rear her pups, and then he would go; then he would go gaily, driving his horse and cart like a man of property all over that Berkshire and that Oxfordshire, along with some old 'gal'.

A week later Sossy was safely delivered of nine puppies. Miracles are possible — they must be — but it is not possible to anticipate a miracle: a litter of nine! They were born in the tent beside the man, and they all — Dick, Sossy and the nine morsels — slept together, and in a few days, although Sossy, despite heroic feeding, began to grow lean, the pups were fat as slugs.

When they were seven days old the man got up one morning to go to a job of hedging. It was a bright, draughty March morn, and he noted the look of the early pink clouds. A fine day promised, though some of the cloud had a queer shape like a goose with its head turned backwards. That boded something! The blackies and thrushers sang beautiful. After Sossy had fed somewhat daintily from the same pot of 'shackles' as himself, old Dick hung the sack over the tent opening and left her mothering the pups. He limped off to work. The hedge he was laying was on an upland farm that overlooked his wood. At midday when he lunched he could sit and stare over the vast stern brownness that was so soon to unbend in unbelievable trellises of leaves. Already the clearings and banks were freckled with primroses, the nut thickets hung with showers of yellow pods, and the pilewort's cresset in the hedge was a beam to wandering bees. In all that vastitude there was one tiny hole into which he had crept like a snail for years and years, but it was too small to hide him for ever and ever. So now they would go, he and Sossy, driving about the land, he and Sossy and ... and some old gal. Just beside him was a pond and the barns of the farm. Two white horses were nuzzling each other in the croft, and a magpie watched them from the cone of a stack. A red ox at the pond snuffed in the water, and as it lifted its head to stare at the old man streams of water pattered back from its hairy lips. Deftly the ox licked with its tongue first one nostril, then the other, but water still dribbled from its mouth in one long glutinous stripe. A large cloud hung above the scene, brooding, white and silent as a swan. Old Dick rose and stretched himself; the wind had died. When the afternoon had worn on he ceased work and turned home. Half-way through the woods he came to a clearing full of primroses, and on a bank, with her muzzle in a rich clump of the blooms, lay his dog, shot through the breast. The old man knelt down beside his dog, but there was nothing he could do, she had been dead a long time. He recalled hearing the shot of a gun, hours ago, not a sharp report, but sullen. Perhaps she had gone out for a scamper and had been chasing a rabbit, or perhaps she had left her litter in order to come to him. The keeper had shot her, shot a poor man's dog, shot her dead. There was nothing he could do, the doom had come crushing even time in its swiftness.

'Fizzled and mizzled I am now,' he said forlornly, 'and that's a fact.'

He left her there and conversing angrily pottered home to his tent. Two of the pups were already dead. The others were helpless, and he was helpless; there was nothing he could do for them, they were too young to feed by hand, and he had nothing to feed them with. He crawled out of the tent to suck a long drink from the bucket of water that stood outside, and then he knelt there gazing without vision at the smouldering fire.

'I know, yes, I know what I can do,' he mumbled, picking up his long, heavy billhook. 'Just a smack o' that behind his earhole and he won't take no more hidings from e'er a man or a woman neither. Tipet, I says, and he'd be done, he'd be done in a couple o' minutes, ah, quicker, quicker'n you could say smoke.' He dashed the billhook to the earth and groaned. 'O, I be fair fizzled and mizzled now, I be, ah.' He sat up and pulled the bucket between his legs. Picking up one of the pups he plopped it into the bucket. 'There's your donkey,' he gurgled, 'huh, huh, huh! And there' — as he plopped the others in one by one — 'goes your cob and your cart and your cokernuts. And there' — as he dashed the last one violently in — 'goes the old gal. Huh!'

After a while the old man rose and emptied the drowned bodies into a heap of bushes; the clash of the bucket as he flung it back only fretted the silence of the wood for a few moments.

The Field of Mustard (1926)

THE FIELD OF MUSTARD

On a windy afternoon in November they were gathering kindling in the Black Wood, Dinah Lock, Amy Hardwick and Rose Olliver, three sere disvirgined women from Pollock's Cross. Mrs. Lock wore clothes of dull butcher's blue, with a short jacket that affirmed her plumpness, but Rose and Amy had on long grey ulsters. All of them were about forty years old, and the wind and twigs had tousled their gaunt locks, for none had a hat upon her head. They did not go far beyond the margin of the wood, for the forest ahead of them swept high over a hill and was gloomy; behind them the slim trunks of beech, set in a sweet ruin of hoar and scattered leaf, and green briar nimbly fluttering made a sort of palisade against the light of the open, which was grey, and a wide field of mustard which was yellow. The three women peered up into the trees for dead branches, and when they found any Dinah Lock, the vivacious woman full of shrill laughter, with a bosom as massive as her haunches, would heave up a rope with an iron bolt tied to one end. The bolted end would twine itself around the dead branch, the three women would tug, and after a sharp crack the quarry would fall; as often as not the women would topple over too. By and by they met an old hedger with a round belly belted low, and thin legs tied at each knee, who told them the time by his ancient watch, a stout timepiece which the women sportively admired.

'Come Christmas I'll have me a watch like that!' Mrs. Lock called out. The old man looked a little dazed as he fumblingly replaced his chronometer. 'I will,' she continued, 'if the Lord spares me and the pig don't pine.'

'You . . . you don't know what you're talking about,' he said. 'That watch was my uncle's watch.'

'Who was he? I'd like one like it.'

'Was a sergeant-major in the lancers, fought under Sir Garnet Wolseley, and it was given to him.'

'What for?'

The hedger stopped and turned on them: 'Doing of his duty.'

'That all?' cried Dinah Lock. 'Well, I never got no watch for that a-much. Do you know what I see when I went to London? I see'd a watch in a bowl of water, it was glass, and there was a fish swimming round it. . . .'

'I don't believe it.'

'There was a fish swimming round it. . . .'

'I tell you I don't believe it. . . .'

'And the little hand was going on like Clackford Mill. That's the sort of watch I'll have me; none of your Sir Garney Wolsey's!'

'He was a noble Christian man, that was.'

'Ah! I suppose he slept wid Jesus?' yawped Dinah.

'No, he didn't,' the old man disdainfully spluttered. 'He never did. What a God's the matter wid ye?' Dinah cackled with laughter. 'Pah!' he cried, going away, 'great fat thing! Can't tell your guts from your elbows.'

Fifty yards further on he turned and shouted some obscenity back at them, but they did not heed him; they had begun to make three faggots of the wood they had collected, so he put his fingers to his nose at them and shambled out to the road.

By the time Rose and Dinah were ready Amy Hardwick, a small, slow, silent woman, had not finished bundling her faggot together.

'Come on, Amy,' urged Rose.

'Come on,' Dinah said.

'All right, wait a minute,' she replied listlessly.

'O God, that's death!' cried Dinah Lock, and heaving a great faggot to her shoulders she trudged off, followed by Rose with a like burden. Soon they were out of the wood, and crossing a highway they entered a footpath that strayed in a diagonal wriggle to the far corner of the field of mustard. In silence they journeyed until they came to that far corner, where there was a hedged bank. Here they flung their faggots down and sat upon them to wait for Amy Hardwick.

In front of them lay the field they had crossed, a sour scent rising faintly from its yellow blooms that quivered in the wind. Day was dull, the air chill, and the place most solitary. Beyond the field of mustard the eye could see little but forest. There were hills there, a vast curving trunk, but the Black Wood heaved itself effortlessly upon them and lay like a dark pall over the outline of a corpse. Huge and gloomy, the purple woods draped it all completely. A white necklace of a road curved below, where a score of telegraph poles, each crossed with a multitude of white florets, were dwarfed by the hugeness to effigies that resembled hyacinths. Dinah Lock gazed upon this scene whose melancholy, and not its grandeur, had suddenly invaded her; with elbows sunk in her fat thighs, and nursing her cheeks in her hands, she puffed the gloomy air, saying:

'O God, cradle and grave is all there is for we.'

'Where's Amy got to?' asked Rose.

'I could never make a companion of her, you know,' Dinah declared.

'Nor I,' said Rose, 'she's too sour and slow.'

'Her disposition's too serious. Of course, your friends are never what you want them to be, Rose. Sometimes they're better — most often they're worse.

But it's such a mercy to have a friend at all; I like you, Rose; I wish you was a man.'

'I might just as well ha' been,' returned the other woman.

'Well, you'd ha' done better; but if you had a tidy little family like me you'd wish you hadn't got 'em.'

'And if you'd never had 'em you'd ha' wished you had.'

'Rose, that's the cussedness of nature, it makes a mock of you. I don't believe it's the Almighty at all, Rose. I'm sure it's the devil, Rose. Dear heart, my corn's a-giving me what-for; I wonder what that bodes?'

'It's restless weather,' said Rose. She was dark, tall, and not unbeautiful still, though her skin was harsh and her limbs angular. 'Get another month or two over — there's so many of these long dreary hours.'

'Ah, your time's too long, or it's too short, or it's just right but you're too old. Cradle and grave's my portion. Fat old thing! he called me.'

Dinah's brown hair was ruffled across her pleasant face and she looked a little forlorn, but corpulence dispossessed her of tragedy. 'I be thin enough a-summer-times, for I lives light and sweats like a bridesmaid, but winters I'm fat as a hog.'

'What all have you to grumble at then?' asked Rose, who had slid to the ground and lay on her stomach staring up at her friend.

'My heart's young, Rose.'

'You've your husband.'

'He's no man at all since he was ill. A long time ill, he was. When he coughed, you know, his insides come up out of him like coffee grouts. Can you ever understand the meaning of that? Coffee! I'm growing old, but my heart's young.'

'So is mine, too: but you got a family, four children

grown or growing.' Rose had snapped off a sprig of the mustard flower and was pressing and pulling the bloom in and out of her mouth. 'I've none, and never will have.' Suddenly she sat up, fumbled in her pocket, and produced her purse. She slipped the elastic band from it, and it gaped open. There were a few coins there and a scrap of paper folded. Rose took out the paper and smoothed it open under Dinah's curious gaze. 'I found something lying about at home the other day, and I cut this bit out of it.' In soft tones she began to read:

The day was void, vapid; time itself seemed empty. Come evening it rained softly. I sat by my fire turning over the leaves of a book, and I was dejected, until I came upon a little old-fashioned engraving at the bottom of a page. It imaged a procession of some angelic children in a garden, little placidly-naked substantial babes, with tiny bird-wings. One carried a bow, others a horn of plenty, or a hamper of fruit, or a set of reedpipes. They were garlanded and full of grave joys. And at the sight of them a strange bliss flowed into me such as I had never known, and I thought this world was all a garden, though its light was hidden and its children not yet born.

Rose did not fold the paper up; she crushed it in her hand and lay down again without a word.

'Huh, I tell you, Rose, a family's a torment. I never wanted mine. God love, Rose, I'd lay down my life for 'em; I'd cut myself into fourpenny pieces so they shouldn't come to harm; if one of 'em was to die I'd sorrow to my grave. But I know, I know, I know I never wanted 'em, they were not for me, I was just an excuse for their blundering into the world. Somehow I've been duped, and every woman born is duped so, one ways or another in the end. I had my sport with my man, but I ought never to have married. Now I'd love to begin all over again, and as God's my maker, if it weren't for those children, I'd be gone off out into the world again to-morrow, Rose. But I dunno what 'ud become o' me.'

The wind blew strongly athwart the yellow field, and the odour of mustard rushed upon the brooding women. Protestingly the breeze flung itself upon the forest; there was a gliding cry among the rocking pinions as of some lost wave seeking a forgotten shore. The angular faggot under Dinah Lock had begun to vex her; she too sunk to the ground and lay beside Rose Olliver, who asked:

'And what 'ud become of your old man?'

For a few moments Dinah Lock paused. She too took a sprig of the mustard and fondled it with her lips. 'He's no man now, the illness feebled him, and the virtue's gone; no man at all since two years, and bald as a piece of cheese — I like a hairy man, like . . . do you remember Rufus Blackthorn, used to be game-keeper here?'

Rose stopped playing with her flower. 'Yes, I knew Rufus Blackthorn.'

'A fine bold man that was! Never another like him hereabouts, not in England neither; not in the whole world — though I've heard some queer talk of those foreigners, Australians, Chinymen. Well!'

'Well?' said Rose.

'He was a devil.' Dinah Lock began to whisper. 'A perfect devil; I can't say no fairer than that. I wish I could, but I can't.'

'O come,' protested Rose, 'he was a kind man. He'd never see anybody want for a thing.'

'No,' there was playful scorn in Dinah's voice; 'he'd shut his eyes first!'

'Not to a woman he wouldn't, Dinah.'

'Ah! Well — perhaps — he was good to women.'

'I could tell you things as would surprise you,' murmured Rose.

'You! But — well — no, no. I could tell *you* things as you wouldn't believe. Me and Rufus! We was — O my — yes!'

'He *was* handsome.'

'O, a pretty man!' Dinah acceded warmly. 'Black as coal and bold as a fox. I'd been married nigh on ten years when he first set foot in these parts. I'd got three children then. He used to give me a saucy word whenever he saw me, for I liked him and he knew it. One Whitsun Monday I was home all alone, the children were gone somewheres, and Tom was away boozing. I was putting some plants in our garden — I loved a good flower in those days — I wish the world was all a garden, but now my Tom he digs 'em up, digs everything up proper and never puts 'em back. Why, we had a crocus, once! And as I was doing that planting someone walked by the garden in such a hurry. I looked up and there was Rufus, all dressed up to the nines, and something made me call out to him. "Where be you off to in that flaming hurry?" I says. "Going to a wedding," says he. "Shall I come with 'ee?" I says. "Ah yes," he says, very glad; "but hurry up, for I be sharp set and all." So I run in-a-doors and popped on my things and off we went to Jim Pickering's wedding over at Clackford Mill. When Jim brought the bride home from church that Rufus got hold of a gun and fired it off up chimney, and down come the soot, bushels of it! All over the room, and a chimney-pot burst and rattled down the tiles into a prambulator. What a rumbullion that was! But no one got angry — there was plenty of drink and we danced all the afternoon. Then we come home together again through the woods. O Lord — I said to myself — I shan't come out with you ever again, and that's what I said to Rufus Blackthorn. But I did, you know! I woke up in bed that night, and the moon shone on me dreadful — I thought the place was afire. But there was Tom snoring, and I lay and thought of me and Rufus in the wood, till I could have jumped out into the moonlight, stark, and flown over the chimney. I didn't sleep any more. And I saw Rufus the next night, and the night after that, often, often. Whenever I went out I left Tom the cupboardful — that's all he troubled about. I was mad after Rufus, and while that caper was on I couldn't love my husband. No.'

'No?' queried Rose.

'Well, I pretended I was ill, and I took my young Katey to sleep with me, and give Tom her bed. He didn't seem to mind, but after a while I found he was gallivanting after other women. Course, I soon put a stopper on that. And then — what do you think? Bless me if Rufus weren't up to the same tricks! Deep as the sea, that man. Faithless, you know, but such a bold one.'

Rose lay silent, plucking wisps of grass; there was a wry smile on her face.

'Did ever he tell you the story of the man who was drowned?' she asked at length. Dinah shook her head. Rose continued. 'Before he came here he was keeper over in that Oxfordshire, where the river goes right through the woods, and he slept in a boathouse moored to the bank. Some gentleman was drowned near there, an accident it was, but they couldn't find the body. So they offered a reward of ten pound for it to be found....'

'Ten, ten pounds!'

'Yes. Well, all the watermen said the body wouldn't come up for ten days....'

'No, more they do.'

'It didn't. And so late one night — it was moonlight — some men in a boat kept on hauling and poking round the house where Rufus was, and he heard 'em say "It must be here, it must be here", and Rufus shouts out to them, "Course he's here! I got him in bed with me!"'

'Aw!' chuckled Dinah.

'Yes, and next day he got the ten pounds, because he *had* found the body and hidden it away.'

'Feared nothing,' said Dinah, 'nothing at all; he'd have been rude to Satan. But he was very delicate with his hands, sewing and things like that. I used to say to him, "Come, let me mend your coat", or whatever it was, but he never would, always did such things of himself. "I don't allow no female to patch my clothes," he'd say, "'cos they works with a red-hot needle and a burning thread." And he used to make fine little slippers out of reeds.'

'Yes,' Rose concurred, 'he made me a pair.'

'You!' Dinah cried. 'What — were you . . .?'

Rose turned her head away. 'We was all cheap to him,' she said softly, 'cheap as old rags; we was like chaff before him.'

Dinah Lock lay still, very still, ruminating; but whether in old grief or new rancour Rose was not aware, and she probed no further. Both were quiet, voiceless, recalling the past delirium. They shivered, but did not rise. The wind increased in the forest, its hoarse breath sorrowed in the yellow field, and swift masses of cloud flowed and twirled in a sky without end and full of gloom.

'Hallo!' cried a voice, and there was Amy beside them, with a faggot almost overwhelming her. 'Shan't stop now,' she said, 'for I've got this faggot perched just right, and I shouldn't ever get it up again. I found a shilling in the 'ood, you,' she continued shrilly and gleefully. 'Come along to my house after tea, and we'll have a quart of stout.'

'A shilling, Amy!' cried Rose.

'Yes,' called Mrs. Hardwick, trudging steadily on. 'I tried to find the fellow to it, but no more luck. Come and wet it after tea!'

'Rose,' said Dinah, 'come on.' She and Rose with much circumstance heaved up their faggots and tottered after, but by then Amy had turned out of sight down the little lane to Pollock's Cross.

'Your children will be home,' said Rose as they went along, 'they'll be looking out for you.'

'Ah, they'll want their bellies filling!'

'It must be lovely a-winter's nights, you setting round your fire with 'em, telling tales, and brushing their hair.'

'Ain't you got a fire of your own indoors,' grumbled Dinah.

'Yes.'

'Well, why don't you set by it then!' Dinah's faggot caught the briars of a hedge that overhung, and she tilted round with a mild oath. A covey of partridges feeding beyond scurried away with ruckling cries. One foolish bird dashed into the telegraph wires and dropped dead.

'They're good children, Dinah, yours are. And they make you a valentine, and give you a ribbon on your birthday, I expect?'

'They're naught but a racket from cockcrow till the old man snores — and then it's worse!'

'Oh, but the creatures, Dinah!'

'You . . . you got your quiet trim house, and only your man to look after, a kind man, and you'll set with him in the evenings and play your dominoes or your draughts, and he'll look at you — the nice man — over the board, and stroke your hand now and again.'

The wind hustled the two women closer together, and as they stumbled under their burdens Dinah Lock stretched out a hand and touched the other woman's arm. 'I like you, Rose, I wish you was a man.'

Rose did not reply. Again they were quiet, voiceless, and thus in fading light they came to their homes. But how windy, dispossessed and ravaged, roved the darkening world! Clouds were borne frantically across the heavens, as if in a rout of battle, and the lovely earth seemed to sigh in grief at some calamity all unknown to men.

The Field of Mustard (1926)

'I WALKED out of the hotel, just as I was, and left her there. I never went back again. I don't think I intended anything quite so final, so dastardly. I had not intended it, I had not thought of doing so, but that is how it happened. I lost her, lost my wife purposely. It was heartless, it was shabby, for she was a nice woman, a charming woman, a good deal younger than I was, a splendid woman, in fact she was very beautiful, and yet I ran away from her. How can you explain that, Turner?'

Poor Bollington looked at Turner, who looked at his glass of whisky, and that looked irresistible — he drank some. Bollington sipped a little from his glass of milk.

I often found myself regarding Bollington as a little old man. Most of the club members did so too, but he was not that at all, he was still on the sunny side of fifty, but *so* unassertive, no presence to speak of, no height, not enough hair to mention — if he had had it would surely have been yellow. So mild and modest he cut no figure at all, just a man in glasses that seemed rather big for him. Turner was different, though he was just as bald; he had stature and bulk, his very pince-nez seemed twice the size of Bollington's spectacles. They had not met each other for ten years.

'Well, yes,' Turner said, 'but that was a serious thing to do.'

'Wasn't it!' said the other, 'and I had no idea of the enormity of the offence — not at the time. She might have been dead, poor girl, and her executors advertising for me. She had money, you know, her people had been licensed victuallers, quite wealthy. Scandalous!'

Bollington brooded upon his sin until Turner sighed: 'Ah well, my dear chap.'

'But you have no idea,' protested Bollington, 'how entirely she engrossed me. She was twenty-five and I was forty when we married. She was entrancing. She had always lived in a stinking hole in Balham, and it is amazing how strictly some of those people keep their children; licensed victuallers, did I tell you? Well, I was forty, and she was twenty-five; we lived for a year dodging about from one hotel to another all over the British Isles, she was a perfect little nomad. Are you married, Turner?'

No, Turner was not married, he never had been.

'O, but you should be,' cried little Bollington. 'It's an extraordinary experience, the real business of the world is marriage, marriage! I was deliriously happy and she was learning French and Swedish — that's where we were going later. She was an enchanting little thing, fair, with blue eyes, Phoebe her name was.'

Turner thoughtfully brushed his hand across his generous baldness, then folded his arms.

'You really should,' repeated Bollington, 'you ought to, really. But I remember we went from Killarney to Belfast, and there something dreadful happened. I don't know, it had been growing on her I suppose, but she took a dislike to me there, had strange fancies, thought I was unfaithful to her. You see she was popular wherever we went, a lively little woman, in fact she wasn't merely a woman, she was a little magnet, men congregated and clung to her like so many tacks and nails and pins. I didn't object at all — on the contrary, "Enjoy yourself, Phoebe," I said, "I don't expect you always to hang around an old fogey like me." Fogey was the very word I used; I didn't mean it, of course, but that was the line I

took, for she was *so* charming until she began to get so
bad tempered. And believe me, that made her angry,
furious. No, not the fogey, but the idea that I did not
object to her philandering. It was fatal, it gave colour
to her suspicions of me — Turner, I was as innocent as
any lamb — tremendous colour. And she had such a
sharp tongue! If you ventured to differ from her —
and you couldn't help differing sometimes — she'd
positively bludgeon you, and you couldn't help being
bludgeoned. And she had a passion for putting me
right, and I always seemed to be so *very* wrong, always.
She would not be satisfied until she had proved it, and
it was so monstrous to be made feel that because you
were rather different from other people you were an
impertinent fool. Yes, I seemed at last to gain only
the pangs and none of the prizes of marriage. Now
there was a lady we met in Belfast to whom I paid some
attention . . .'

'O, good lord!' groaned Turner.

'No, but listen,' pleaded Bollington, 'it was a very
innocent friendship — nothing was further from my
mind — and she was very much like my wife, very
much, it was noticeable, everybody spoke of it — I
mean the resemblance. A Mrs. Macarthy, a delightful
woman, and Phoebe simply loathed her. I confess that
my wife's innuendoes were so mean and persistent that
at last I hadn't the strength to deny them, in fact at
times I wished they were true. Love is idolatry if you
like, but it cannot be complete immolation — there's
no such bird as the phoenix, is there, Turner?'

'What, what?'

'No such bird as the phoenix.'

'No, there is no such bird, I believe.'

'And sometimes I had to ask myself quite seriously
if I really hadn't been up to some infidelity! Nonsense,

of course, but I assure you that was the effect it was having upon me. I had doubts of myself, frenzied doubts! And it came to a head between Phoebe and me in our room one day. We quarrelled. O dear, how we quarrelled! She said I was sly, two-faced, unfaithful, I was a scoundrel, and so on. Awfully untrue, all of it. She accused me of dreadful things with Mrs. Macarthy and she screamed out: "I hope you will treat her better than you have treated me." Now what did she mean by that, Turner?'

Bollington eyed his friend as if he expected an oracular answer, but just as Turner was about to respond, Bollington continued: 'Well, I never found out, I never knew, for what followed was too terrible. "I shall go out," I said, "it will be better, I think." Just that, nothing more. I put on my hat and I put my hand on the knob of the door when she said most violently: "Go with your Macarthys, I never want to see your filthy face again!" Extraordinary, you know, Turner. Well, I went out, and I will not deny I was in a rage, terrific. It was raining but I didn't care, and I walked about in it. Then I took shelter in a bookseller's doorway opposite a shop that sold tennis rackets and tobacco, and another one that displayed carnations and peaches on wads of coloured wool. The rain came so fast that the streets seemed to empty, and the passers-by were horridly silent under their umbrellas, and their footsteps splashed so dully, and I tell you I was very sad, Turner, there. I debated whether to rush across the road and buy a lot of carnations and peaches and take them to Phoebe. But I did not do so, Turner, I never went back, never.'

'Why, Bollington, you, you were a positive ruffian, Bollington.'

'O, scandalous,' rejoined the ruffian.

'Well, out with it, what about this Mrs. Macarthy?'

'Mrs. Macarthy? But, Turner, I never saw her again, never. I . . . I forgot her. Yes, I went prowling on until I found myself at the docks and there it suddenly became dark; I don't know, there was no evening, no twilight, the day stopped for a moment — and it did not recover. There were hundreds of bullocks slithering and panting and steaming in the road, thousands; lamps were hung up in the harbour, cabs and trollies rattled round the bullocks, the rain fell dismally and everybody hurried. I went into the dock and saw them loading the steamer, it was called s.s. *Frolic*, and really, Turner, the things they put into the belly of that steamer were rather funny: tons and tons of monstrous big chain, the links as big as soup plates, and two or three pantechnicon vans. Yes, but I was anything but frolicsome, I assure you, I was full of misery and trepidation and the deuce knows what. I did not know what I wanted to do, or what I was going to do, but I found myself buying a ticket to go to Liverpool on that steamer, and, in short, I embarked. How wretched I was, but how determined. Everything on board was depressing and dirty, and when at last we moved off the foam slewed away in filthy bubbles as if that dirty steamer had been sick and was running away from it. I got to Liverpool in the early morn, but I did not stay there, it is such a clamouring place, all trams and trollies and teashops. I sat in the station for an hour, the most miserable man alive, the most miserable ever born. I wanted some rest, some peace, some repose, but they never ceased shunting an endless train of goods trucks, banging and screeching until I almost screamed at the very porters. Criff was the name on some of the trucks, I remember, Criff, and everything seemed to be going criff, criff, criff. I haven't discovered to this day what Criff signifies, whether it's a station or a company, or a manufacture, but it was Criff, I remember. Well, I rushed to London and put my affairs in order. A day or two later I went to Southampton and boarded another steamer and put to sea, or rather we were ignominiously lugged out of the dock by a little rat of a tug that seemed all funnel and hooter. I was off to America, and there I stopped for over three years.'

Turner sighed. A waiter brought him another glass of spirit.

'I can't help thinking, Bollington, that it was all very fiery and touchy. Of course, I don't know, but really it was a bit steep, very squeamish of you. What did your wife say?'

'I never communicated with her, I never heard from her, I just dropped out. My filthy face, you know, she did not want to see it again.'

'O come, Bollington! And what did Mrs. Macarthy say?'

'Mrs. Macarthy! I never saw or heard of her again. I told you that.'

'Ah, yes, you told me. So you slung off to America.'

'I was intensely miserable there for a long while. Of course I loved Phoebe enormously, I felt the separation. I ... O, it is impossible to describe. But what was worst of all was the meanness of my behaviour, there was nothing heroic about it. I soon saw clearly that it was a shabby trick, disgusting, I had bolted and left her to the mercy of ... well, of whatever there was. It made such an awful barrier — you've no idea of my compunction — I couldn't make overtures — "Let us forgive and forget." I was a mean rascal, I *was* filthy. That was the barrier — myself; I was too bad. I thought I should recover and enjoy life again. I began

to think of Phoebe as a cat, a little cat. I went everywhere and did everything. But America is a big country, I couldn't get into contact, I was lonely, very
lonely, and although two years went by I longed for
Phoebe. Everything I did I wanted to do with Phoebe
by my side. And then my cousin, my only relative in
the world — he lived in England — he died. I scarcely
ever saw him, but still he was my kin. And he died.
You've no comprehension, Turner, of the truly awful
sensation such a bereavement brings. Not a soul in the
world now would have the remotest interest in my
welfare. O, I tell you, Turner, it was tragic, tragic,
when my cousin died. It made my isolation complete.
I was alone, a man who had made a dreadful mess of life.
What with sorrow and remorse I felt that I should soon
die, not of disease, but disgust.'

'You *were* a great ninny,' ejaculated his friend.
'Why the devil didn't you hurry back, claim your wife,
bygones be bygones; why bless my conscience, what a
ninny, what a great ninny!'

'Yes, Turner, it is as you say. But though conscience
is a good servant it is a very bad master, it overruled me,
it shamed me, and I hung on to America for still
another year. I tell you my situation was unbearable,
I was tied to my misery, I was a tethered dog, a duck
without water — even dirty water. And I hadn't any
faith in myself or in my case, I knew I was wrong, had
always been wrong, Phoebe had taught me that. I
hadn't any faith, I wish I had had. Faith can move
mountains, so they say, though I've never heard of it
actually being done.'

'No, not in historical times,' declared Turner.

'What do you mean by that?'

'O well, time is nothing, it's nothing, it comes and
off it goes. Has it ever occurred to you, Bollington,

that in five thousand years or so there will be nobody in the world speaking the English language, our very existence even will be speculated upon, as if we were the Anthropophagi? O good lord, yes.'

And another whisky.

'You know, Bollington, you were a perfect fool. You behaved like one of those half-baked civil service hounds who lunch in a dairy on a cup of tea and a cream horn. You wanted some beef, some ginger. You came back, you must have come back because there you are now.'

'Yes, Turner, I came back after nearly four years. Everything was different, ah, how strange! I could not find Phoebe, it is weird how people can disappear. I made inquiries, but it was like looking for a lost umbrella, fruitless after so long.'

'Well, but what about Mrs. Macarthy?'

Mr. Bollington said, slowly and with the utmost precision: 'I did not see Mrs. Macarthy again.'

'O, of course, you did not see her again, not ever.'

'Not ever. I feared Phoebe had gone abroad too, but at last I found her in London. . . .'

'No,' roared Turner, 'why the devil couldn't you say so and done with it? I've been sweating with sympathy for you. O, I say, Bollington!'

'My dear Turner, listen. Do you know she was delighted to see me, she even kissed me, straight off, and we went out to dine and had the very deuce of a spread and we were having the very deuce of a good time. She was lovelier than ever, and I could see all her old affection for me was returning, she was so . . . well, I can't tell you, Turner, but she had no animosity whatever, no grievance, she would certainly have taken me back that very night. O dear, dear . . . and then! I was anxious to throw myself at her feet, but you couldn't do that in a public café, I could only touch her hands, beautiful, as they lay on the white linen cloth. I kept asking: "Do you forgive me?" and she would reply: "I have nothing to forgive, dear, nothing." How wonderful that sounded to my truly penitent soul — I wanted to die.

' "But you don't ask me where I've been!" she cried gaily, "or what I've been doing, you careless old Peter. I've been to France, and Sweden too!"

'I was delighted to hear that, it was so very plucky.

' "When did you go?" I asked.

' "When I left you," she said.

' "You mean when I went away?"

' "Did you go away? O, of course, you must have. Poor Peter, what a sad time he has had."

'I was a little bewildered, but I was delighted; in fact, Turner, I was hopelessly infatuated again, I wanted to wring out all the dregs of my detestable villainy and be absolved. All I could begin with was: "Were you not very glad to be rid of me?"

' "Well," she said, "my great fear at first was that you would find me again and make it up. I didn't want that, then; at least, I thought I didn't."

' "That's exactly what I felt," I exclaimed, "but how could I find you?"

' "Well," Phoebe said, "you might have found out and followed me. But I promise never to run away again, Peter dear, never."

'Turner, my reeling intelligence swerved like a shot bird.

' "Do you mean, Phoebe, that you ran away from *me*?"

' "Yes, didn't I?" she answered.

' "But I ran away from *you*," I said. "I walked out of the hotel on that dreadful afternoon we quarrelled so and I never went back. I went to America. I was in America nearly four years."

' "Do you mean you ran away from me?" she cried.

' "Yes," I said, "didn't I?"

' "But that is exactly what *I* did — I mean, I ran away from you. *I* walked out of the hotel directly you had gone — *I* never went back, and I've been abroad thinking how tremendously I had served you out and wondering what you thought of it all and where you were."

'I could only say "Good God, Phoebe, I've had the most awful four years of remorse and sorrow — all vain, mistaken, useless, thrown away." And she said: "And I've had four years — living in a fool's paradise after all. How *dared* you run away, it's disgusting!"

'And, Turner, in a moment she was at me again in her old dreadful way, and the last words I had from her were: "Now I *never* want to see your face again, never, this *is* the end!"

'And that's how things are now, Turner. It's rather sad, isn't it?'

'Sad! Why you chump, when was it you saw her?'

'O, a long time ago, it must be nearly three years now.'

'Three years! But you'll see her again!'

'Tfoo! No, no, no, Turner. God bless me, no, no, no!' said the little old man.

The Black Dog (1923)

. . . and in the whole of his days, vividly at the end of
the afternoon — he repeated it again and again to himself — the kind country spaces had *never* absorbed *quite*
so rich a glamour of light, so miraculous a bloom of
clarity. He could feel streaming in his own mind, in his
bones, the same crystalline brightness that lay upon
the land. Thoughts and images went flowing through
him as easily and amiably as fish swim in their pools;
and as idly, too, for one of his speculations took up the
theme of his family name. There was such an agreeable
oddness about it, just as there was about all the lumin-
ous sky to-day, that it touched him as just a little remarkable. What *did* such a name connote, signify, or
symbolize? It was a rann of a name, but it had euphony!
Then again, like the fish, his ambulating fancy flashed
into other shallows, and he giggled as he paused, peering at the buds in the brake. Turning back towards his
house again he could see, beyond its roofs, the spire of
the church tinctured as richly as the vane: all round him
was a new grandeur upon the grass of the fields, and the
spare trees had shadows below that seemed to support
them in the manner of a plinth, more real than themselves, and the dykes and any chance heave of the level
fields were underlined, as if for special emphasis, with
long shades of mysterious blackness.

With a little drift of emotion that had at other times
assailed him in the wonder and ecstasy of pure light,
Jaffa Codling pushed through the slit in the back hedge
and stood within his own garden. The gardener was at
work. He could hear the voices of the children about
the lawn at the other side of the house. He was very
happy, and the place was beautiful, a fine white many-

windowed house rising from a lawn bowered with plots of mould, turreted with shrubs, and overset with a vast walnut tree. This house had deep clean eaves, a roof of faint coloured slates that, after rain, glowed dully, like onyx or jade, under the red chimneys, and half-way up at one end was a balcony set with black balusters. He went to a French window that stood open and stepped into the dining-room. There was no-one within, and, on that lonely instant, a strange feeling of emptiness dropped upon him. The clock ticked almost as if it had been caught in some indecent act; the air was dim and troubled after that glory outside. Well, now he would go up at once to his study and write down for his new book the ideas and images he had accumulated — beautiful rich thoughts they were — during that wonderful afternoon. He went to mount the stairs and he was passed by one of the maids; humming a silly song she brushed past him rudely, but he was an easy-going man — maids were unteachably tiresome — and reaching the landing he sauntered towards his room. The door stood slightly open and he could hear voices within. He put his hand upon the door ... it would not open any further. What the devil ... he pushed — like the bear in the tale — and he pushed, and he pushed — was there something against it on the other side? He put his shoulder to it ... some wedge must be there, and *that* was extraordinary. Then his whole apprehension was swept up and whirled as by an avalanche — Mildred, his wife, was in there; he could hear her speaking to a man in fair soft tones and the rich phrases that could be used only by a woman yielding a deep affection to him. Codling kept still. Her words burned on his mind and thrilled him as if spoken to himself. There was a movement in the room, then utter silence. He again thrust savagely at the partly open door, but he could not stir it. The silence within continued. He beat upon the door with his fists, crying; 'Mildred, Mildred!' There was no response, but he could hear the rocking armchair commence to swing to and fro. Pushing his hand round the edge of the door he tried to thrust his head between the opening. There was not space for this, but he could just peer into the corner of a mirror hung near, and this is what he saw: the chair at one end of its swing, a man sitting in it, and upon one arm of it Mildred, the beloved woman, with her lips upon the man's face, caressing him with her hands. Codling made another effort to get into the room — as vain as it was violent. 'Do you hear me, Mildred?' he shouted. Apparently neither of them heard him; they rocked to and fro while he gazed stupefied. What, in the name of God . . . What this . . . was she bewitched . . . were there such things after all as magic, devilry!

He drew back and held himself quite steadily. The chair stopped swaying, and the room grew awfully still. The sharp ticking of the clock in the hall rose upon the house like the tongue of some perfunctory mocker. Couldn't they hear the clock? . . . Couldn't they hear his heart? He had to put his hand upon his heart, for surely, in that great silence inside there, they would hear its beat, growing so loud now that it seemed almost to stun him! Then in a queer way he found himself reflecting, observing, analysing his own actions and intentions. He found some of them to be just a little spurious, counterfeit. He felt it would be easy, so perfectly easy to flash in one blast of anger and annihilate the two. He would do nothing of the kind. There was no occasion for it. People didn't really do that sort of thing, or, at least, not with a genuine passion. There was no need for anger. His curiosity was satisfied, quite satisfied, he was certain, he had not the remotest interest in the man.

A welter of unexpected thoughts swept upon his mind as he stood there. As a writer of books he was often stimulated by the emotions and impulses of other people, and now his own surprise was beginning to intrigue him, leaving him, O, quite unstirred emotionally, but interesting him profoundly.

He heard the maid come stepping up the stairway again, humming her silly song. He did not want a scene or to be caught eavesdropping, and so turned quickly to another door. It was locked. He sprang to one beyond it; the handle would not turn. 'Bah! what's *up* with 'em?' But the girl was now upon him, carrying a tray of coffee things. 'O, Mary!' he exclaimed casually, 'I . . .' To his astonishment the girl stepped past him as if she did not hear or see him, tapped upon the door of his study, entered, and closed the door behind her. Jaffa Codling then got really angry. 'Hell! were the blasted servants in it!' He dashed to the door again and tore at the handle. It would not even turn, and, though he wrenched with fury at it, the room was utterly sealed against him. He went away for a chair with which to smash the effrontery of that door. No, he wasn't angry, either with his wife or this fellow — Gilbert, she had called him — who had a strangely familiar aspect as far as he had been able to take it in; but when one's servants . . . faugh!

The door opened and Mary came forth smiling demurely. He was a few yards further along the corridor at that moment. 'Mary!' he shouted, 'leave the door open!' Mary carefully closed it and turned her back on him. He sprang after her with bad words bursting from him as she went towards the stairs and flitted lightly down, humming all the way as if in derision. He leaped downwards after her three steps at a time, but she trotted with amazing swiftness into the kitchen and slammed the door in his face. Codling stood, but kept his hands carefully away from the door, kept them behind him. 'No, no,' he whispered cunningly, 'there's something fiendish about door handles to-day, I'll go and get a bar, or a butt of timber,' and, jumping out into the garden for some such thing, the miracle happened to him. For it was nothing else than a miracle, the unbelievable, the impossible, simple and laughable if you will, but having as much validity as any miracle can ever invoke. It was simple and laughable because by all the known physical laws he should have collided with his gardener, who happened to pass the window with his wheelbarrow as Codling jumped out on to the path. And it was unbelievable that they should not, and impossible that they *did* not collide; and it was miraculous, because Codling stood for a brief moment in the garden path and the wheelbarrow of Bond, its contents, and Bond himself passed apparently through the figure of Codling as if he were so much air, as if he were not a living breathing man but just a common ghost. There was no impact, just a momentary breathlessness. Codling stood and looked at the retreating figure going on utterly unaware of him. It is interesting to record that Codling's first feelings were mirthful. He giggled. He was jocular. He ran along in front of the gardener, and let him pass through him once more; then after him again; he scrambled into the man's barrow, and was wheeled about by this incomprehensible thick-headed gardener who was dead to all his master's efforts to engage his attention. Presently he dropped the wheelbarrow and went away, leaving Codling to cogitate upon the occurrence. There was no room for doubt, some essential part of him had become detached from the obviously not less vital part. He felt he was essential because he was responding to the experience, he was reacting in the normal way to normal stimuli, although he happened for the time being to be invisible to his fellows and unable to communicate with them. How had it come about — this queer thing? How could he discover what part of him had cut loose, as it were? There was no question of this being death; death wasn't funny, it wasn't a joke; he had still all his human instincts. You didn't get angry with a faithless wife or joke with a fool of a gardener if you were dead, certainly not! He had realized enough of himself to know he was the usual man of instincts, desires, and prohibitions, complex and contradictory; his family history for a million or two years would have denoted that, not explicitly — obviously impossible — but suggestively. He had found himself doing things he had no desire to do, doing things he had a desire *not* to do, thinking thoughts that had no contiguous meanings, no meanings that could be related to his general experience. At odd times he had been chilled — aye, and even agreeably surprised — at the immense potential evil in himself. But still, this was no mere Jekyl and Hyde affair, that a man and his own ghost should separately inhabit the same world was a horse of quite another colour. The other part of him was alive and active somewhere . . . as alive . . . as alive . . . yes, as *he* was, but dashed if he knew where! What a lark when they got back to each other and compared notes! In his tales he had brooded over so many imagined personalities, followed in the track of so many psychological enigmas that he *had* felt at times a stranger to himself. What if, after all, that brooding had given him the faculty of projecting this figment of himself into the world of men! Or was he some unrealized latent element of being without its natural integument, doomed now to drift over the ridge of the world for ever. Was it his personality, his spirit? Then how was the dashed thing working? Here was he with the most wonderful happening in human experience, and he couldn't differentiate or disinter things. He was like a new Adam flung into some old Eden.

There was Bond tinkering about with some plants a dozen yards in front of him. Suddenly his three children came round from the other side of the house, the youngest boy leading them, carrying in his hand a small sword which was made, not of steel, but of some more brightly shining material; indeed it seemed at one moment to be of gold, and then again of flame, transmuting everything in its neighbourhood into the likeness of flame, the hair of the little girl Eve, a part of Adam's tunic; and the fingers of the boy Gabriel as he held the sword were like pale tongues of fire. Gabriel, the youngest boy, went up to the gardener and gave the sword into his hands, saying: 'Bond, is this sword any good?' Codling saw the gardener take the weapon and examine it with a careful sort of smile; his great gnarled hands became immediately transparent, the blood could be seen moving diligently about the veins. Codling was so interested in the sight that he did not gather in the gardener's reply. The little boy was dissatisfied and repeated his question, 'No, but Bond, *is* this sword any good?' Codling rose, and stood by invisible. The three beautiful children were grouped about the great angular figure of the gardener in his soiled clothes, looking up now into his face, and now at the sword, with anxiety in all their puckered eyes. 'Well, Marse Gabriel,' Codling could hear him reply, 'as far as a sword goes, it may be a good un, or it may be a bad un, but, good as it is, it can never be anything but a bad thing.' He then gave it back to them; the boy Adam held the haft of it, and the girl Eve rubbed the blade with curious fingers. The younger boy stood looking up at the gardener with unsatisfied gaze. 'But, Bond, *can't* you say if this sword's any *good*?' Bond turned to his spade and trowels. 'Mebbe the shape of it's wrong, Marse Gabriel, though it seems a pretty handy size.' Saying this he moved off across the lawn. Gabriel turned to his brother and sister and took the sword from them; they all followed after the gardener and once more Gabriel made inquiry: 'Bond, is this sword any *good*?' The gardener again took it and made a few passes in the air like a valiant soldier at exercise. Turning then, he lifted a bright curl from the head of Eve and cut it off with a sweep of the weapon. He held it up to look at it critically and then let it fall to the ground. Codling sneaked behind him and, picking it up, stood stupidly looking at it. 'Mebbe, Marse Gabriel,' the gardener was saying, 'it 'ud be better made of steel, but it has a smartish edge on it.' He went to pick up the barrow but Gabriel seized it with a spasm of anger, and cried out: 'No, no, Bond, will you say, just yes or no, Bond, is this sword any *good*?' The gardener stood still, and looked down at the little boy, who repeated his question — 'just yes or no, Bond!' 'No, Marse Gabriel!' 'Thank you, Bond,' replied the child with dignity, 'that's all we wanted to know,' and, calling to his mates to follow him, he ran away to the other side of the house.

Codling stared again at the beautiful lock of hair in his hand, and felt himself grow so angry that he picked up a strange looking flower pot at his feet and hurled it at the retreating gardener. It struck Bond in the middle of the back and, passing clean through him, broke on the wheel of his barrow, but Bond seemed to be quite unaware of this catastrophe. Codling rushed after, and, taking the gardener by the throat, he yelled 'Damn you, will you tell me what all this means?' But Bond proceeded calmly about his work un-noticing, carrying his master about as if he were a clinging vapour, or a scarf hung upon his neck. In a few moments, Codling dropped exhausted to the ground. 'What ... O Hell ... what, what am I to do?' he groaned, 'What has happened to me? What shall I *do* What *can* I do?' He looked at the broken flowerpot. 'Did I invent that?' He pulled out his watch. 'That's a real watch, I hear it ticking, and it's six o'clock.' Was he dead or disembodied or mad? What was this infernal lapse of identity? And who the devil, yes, who was it upstairs with Mildred? He jumped to his feet and hurried to the window; it was shut; to the door, it was fastened; he was powerless to open either. Well! well! this was experimental psychology with a vengeance, and he began to chuckle again. He'd have to write to McDougall about it. Then he turned and saw Bond wheeling the barrow across the lawn towards him again. '*Why* is that fellow always shoving that infernal green barrow around?' he asked, and, the fit of fury seizing him again, he rushed towards Bond, but, before he reached him, the three children danced into the garden again, crying, with great excitement, 'Bond, O, Bond!' The gardener stopped and set down the terrifying barrow; the children crowded about him, and Gabriel held out another shining thing, asking: 'Bond, is this box any good?' The gardener took the box and at once his eyes lit up with interest and delight. 'O, Marse Gabriel, where'd ye get it? Where'd ye get it?' 'Bond,' said the boy impatiently, 'is the box any *good*?'. 'Any good?' echoed the man, 'Why, Marse Gabriel, Marse Adam, Miss Eve, look yere!' Holding it down in front of them, he lifted the lid from the box and a bright coloured bird flashed out and flew round and round above their heads. 'O,' screamed Gabriel with delight, 'it's a kingfisher!'

'Where?' asked Adam. 'Where?' asked Eve. 'There it flies — round the fountain — see it? see it!' 'No,' said Adam. 'No,' said Eve.

'O, do, do, see it,' cried Gabriel, 'here it comes, it's coming!' and, holding his hands on high, and standing on his toes, the child cried out as happy as the bird which Codling saw flying above them.

'I can't see it,' said Adam.

'Where is it, Gaby?' asked Eve.

'O, you stupids,' cried the boy. '*There* it goes. There it goes . . . there . . . it's gone!'

He stood looking brightly at Bond, who replaced the lid.

'What shall we do now?' he exclaimed eagerly. For reply the gardener gave the box into his hand, and walked off with the barrow. Gabriel took the box over to the fountain. Codling, unseen, went after him, almost as excited as the boy; Eve and her brother followed. They sat upon the stone tank that held the falling water. It was difficult for the child to unfasten the lid; Codling attempted to help him, but he was powerless. Gabriel looked up into his father's face and smiled. Then he stood up and said to the others:

'Now, *do* watch it this time.'

They all knelt carefully beside the water. He lifted the lid and, behold, a fish like a gold carp, but made wholly of fire, leaped from the box into the fountain. The man saw it dart down into the water, he saw the water bubble up behind it, he heard the hiss that the junction of fire and water produces, and saw a little track of steam follow the bubbles about the tank until the figure of the fish was consumed and disappeared. Gabriel, in ecstasies, turned to his sister with blazing happy eyes, exclaiming:

'There! Evey!'

'What was it?' asked Eve, nonchalantly, 'I didn't see anything.'

'More didn't I,' said Adam.

'Didn't you see that lovely fish?'

'No,' said Adam.

'No,' said Eve.

'O, stupids,' cried Gabriel, 'it went right past the bottom of the water.'

'Let's get a fishin' nook,' said Adam.

'No, no, no,' said Gabriel, replacing the lid of the box. 'O, no.'

Jaffa Codling had remained on his knees staring at the water so long that, when he looked around him again, the children had gone away. He got up and went to the door, and that was closed; the windows, fastened. He went moodily to a garden bench and sat on it with folded arms. Dusk had begun to fall into the shrubs and trees, the grass to grow dull, the air chill, the sky to muster its gloom. Bond had overturned his barrow, stalled his tools in the lodge, and gone to his home in the village. A curious cat came round the house and surveyed the man who sat chained to his seven-horned dilemma. It grew dark and fearfully silent. Was the world empty now? Some small thing, a snail perhaps, crept among the dead leaves in the hedge with a sharp, irritating noise. A strange flood of mixed thoughts poured through his mind until at last one idea disentangled itself, and he began thinking with tremendous fixity of little Gabriel. He wondered if he could brood or meditate, or 'will' with sufficient power to bring him into the garden again. The child had just vaguely recognized him for a moment at the waterside. He'd try that dodge, telepathy was a mild kind of a trick after so much of the miraculous. If he'd lost his blessed body, at least the part that ate and smoked and talked to Mildred . . . He stopped as his mind stumbled on a strange recognition . . . What a joke, of course . . . idiot . . . not to have seen *that*. He stood up in the garden with joy . . . of course, *he* was upstairs with Mildred, it was himself, the other bit of him, that Mildred had been talking to. What a howling fool he'd been!

He found himself concentrating his mind on the purpose of getting the child Gabriel into the garden once more, but it was with a curious mood that he endeavoured to establish this relationship. He could not fix his will into any calm intensity of power, or fixity of purpose, or pleasurable mental ecstasy. The utmost force seemed to come with a malicious threatening splenetic 'entreaty'. That damned snail in the hedge broke the thread of his meditation; a dog began to bark sturdily from a distant farm; the faculties of his mind became joggled up like a child's picture puzzle, and he brooded unintelligibly upon such things as skating and steam engines, and Elizabethan drama so lapped about with themes like jealousy and chastity. Really now, Shakespeare's Isabella was the most consummate snob in . . . He looked up quickly to his wife's room and saw Gabriel step from the window to the balcony as though he was fearful of being seen. The boy lifted up his hands and placed the bright box on the rail of the balcony. He looked up at the faint stars for a moment or two, and then carefully released the lid of the box. What came out of it and rose into the air appeared to Codling to be just a piece of floating light, but as it soared above the roof he saw it grow to be a little ancient ship, with its hull and fully set sails and its three masts all of faint primrose flame colour. It cleaved through the air, rolling slightly as a ship through the wave, in widening circles above the house, making a curving ascent until it lost the shape of a vessel and became only a moving light hurrying to some sidereal shrine. Codling glanced at the boy on the balcony, but in that brief instant something had happened, the ship had burst like a rocket and released three coloured drops of fire which came falling slowly, leaving beautiful grey furrows of smoke in their track. Gabriel leaned over the rail with outstretched palms, and, catching the green star and the blue one as they drifted down to him, he ran with a rill of laughter back into the house. Codling sprang forward just in time to catch the red star; it lay vividly blasting his own palm for a monstrous second, and then, slipping through, was gone. He stared at the ground, at the balcony, the sky, and then heard an exclamation . . . his wife stood at his side.

'Gilbert! How you frightened me!' she cried, 'I thought you were in your room; come along in to dinner.' She took his arm and they walked up the steps into the dining-room together. 'Just a moment,' said her husband, turning to the door of the room. His hand was upon the handle, which turned easily in his grasp, and he ran upstairs to his own room. He opened the door. The light was on, the fire was burning brightly, a smell of cigarette smoke about, pen and paper upon his desk, the Japanese book-knife, the gilt matchbox, everything all right, no one there. He picked up a book from his desk . . . *Monna Vanna*. His bookplate was in it — *Ex Libris* — *Gilbert Cannister*. He put it down beside the green dish; two yellow oranges were in the green dish, and two most deliberately green Canadian apples rested by their side. He went to the door and swung it backwards and forwards quite easily. He sat on his desk trying to piece the thing together, glaring at the print and the book-knife and the smart matchbox, until his wife came up behind him exclaiming: 'Come along, Gilbert!'

'Where are the kids, old man?' he asked her, and, before she replied, he had gone along to the nursery. He saw the two cots, his boy in one, his girl in the other. He turned whimsically to Mildred, saying, 'There *are* only two, *are* there?' Such a question did not call for reply, but he confronted her as if expecting some assuring answer. She was staring at him with her bright beautiful eyes.

'Are there?' he repeated.

'How strange you should ask me that now!' she said ... 'If you're a very good man ... perhaps. ...'

'Mildred!'

She nodded brightly.

He sat down in the rocking chair, but got up again saying to her gently — 'We'll call him Gabriel.'

'But suppose — '

'No, no,' he said, stopping her lovely lips, 'I know all about him.' And he told her a pleasant little tale.

Adam and Eve and Pinch Me (1921)

THE HIGGLER

On a cold April afternoon a higgler was driving across
Shag Moor in a two-wheeled cart.

H. Witlow
Dealer in Poultry
DINNOP

was painted on the hood; the horse was of mean appearance but notorious ancestry. A high upland common
was this moor, two miles from end to end, and full of
furze and bracken. There were no trees and not a
house, nothing but a line of telegraph poles following
the road, sweeping with rigidity from north to south;
nailed upon one of them a small scarlet notice to stone-
throwers was prominent as a wound. On so high and
wide a region as Shag Moor the wind always blew, or
if it did not quite blow there was a cool activity in the
air. The furze was always green and growing, and,
taking no account of seasons, often golden. Here in
summer solitude lounged and snoozed; at other times,
as now, it shivered and looked sinister.

Higglers in general are ugly and shrewd, old and
hard, crafty and callous, but Harvey Witlow though
shrewd was not ugly; he was hard but not old, crafty
but not at all unkind. If you had eggs to sell he would
buy them, by the score he would, or by the long hundred. Other odds and ends he would buy or do, paying
good bright silver, bartering a bag of apples, carrying
your little pig to market, or fetching a tree from the
nurseries. But the season was backward, eggs were
scarce, trade was bad — by crumps, it was indeed! —

and as he crossed the moor Harvey could not help discussing the situation with himself.

'If things don't change, and change for the better, and change soon, I can't last and I can't endure it; I'll be damned and done, and I'll have to sell,' he said, prodding the animal with the butt of his whip 'this cob. And', he said, as if in afterthought, prodding the footboard, 'this cart, and go back to the land. And I'll have lost my fifty pounds. Well, that's what war does for you. It does it for you, sir,' he announced sharply to the vacant moor, 'and it does it for me. Fifty pounds! I was better off in the war. I was better off working for farmers; much; but it's no good chattering about it, it's the trick of life; when you get so far then you can go and order your funeral. Get along, Dodger!'

The horse responded briskly for a few moments.

'I tell ye,' said Harvey adjuring the ambient air, 'you can go and order your funeral. Get along, Dodger!'

Again Dodger got along.

'Then there's Sophy, what about Sophy and me?'

He was not engaged to Sophy Daws, not exactly, but he was keeping company with her. He was not pledged or affianced, he was just keeping company with her. But Sophy, as he knew, not only desired a marriage with Mr. Witlow, she expected it, and expected it soon. So did her parents, her friends, and everybody in the village, including the postman who didn't live in it but wished he did, and the parson who did live in it but wished he didn't.

'Well, that's damned and done, fair damned and done now, unless things take a turn, and soon, so it's no good chattering about it.'

And just then and there things did take a turn. He had never been across the moor before; he was prospecting for trade. At the end of Shag Moor he saw

73

standing back in the common, fifty yards from the road, a neat square house set in a little farm. Twenty acres, perhaps. The house was girded by some white palings; beside it was a snug orchard in a hedge covered with blackthorn bloom. It was very green and pleasant in front of the house. The turf was cleared and closely cropped, some ewes were grazing and under the blackthorn, out of the wind, lay half a dozen lambs, but what chiefly moved the imagination of Harvey Witlow was a field on the far side of the house. It had a small rickyard with a few small stacks in it; everything here seemed on the small scale, but snug, very snug; and in that field and yard were hundreds of fowls, hundreds of good breed, and mostly white. Leaving his horse to sniff the greensward, the higgler entered a white wicket gateway and passed to the back of the house, noting as as he did so a yellow wagon inscribed

Elizabeth Sadgrove
Prattle Corner

At the kitchen door he was confronted by a tall gaunt woman of middle age with a teapot in her hands.

'Afternoon, ma'am. Have you anything to sell?' began Harvey Witlow, tilting his hat with a confident affable air. The tall woman was cleanly dressed, a superior person; her hair was grey. She gazed at him.

'It's cold,' he continued. She looked at him as uncomprehendingly as a mouse might look at a gravestone.

'I'll buy any mottal thing, ma'am. Except trouble; I'm full up wi' that already. Eggs? Fowls?'

'I've not seen you before,' commented Mrs. Sadgrove a little bleakly, in a deep husky voice.

'No, 'tis the first time as ever I drove in this part. To tell you the truth, ma'am, I'm new to the business.

Six months. I was in the war a year ago. Now I'm trying to knock up a connection. Difficult work. Things are very quiet.'

Mrs. Sadgrove silently removed the lid of the teapot, inspected the interior of the pot with an intent glance, and then replaced the lid as if she had seen a black-beetle there.

'Ah, well,' sighed the higgler. 'You've a neat little farm here, ma'am.'

'It's quiet enough,' said she.

'Sure it is, ma'am. Very lonely.'

'And it's difficult work, too.' Mrs. Sadgrove almost smiled.

'Sure it is, ma'am; but you does it well, I can see. O, you've some nice little ricks of corn, ah! I does well enough at the dealing now and again, but it's teasy work, and mostly I don't earn enough to keep my horse in shoe leather.'

'I've a few eggs, perhaps,' said she.

'I could do with a score or two, ma'am, if you could let me have 'em.'

'You'll have to come all my way if I do.'

'Name your own price, ma'am, if you don't mind trading with me.'

'Mind! Your money's as good as my own, isn't it?'

'It must be, ma'am. That's meaning no disrespects to you,' the young higgler assured her hastily, and was thereupon invited to enter the kitchen.

A stone floor with two or three mats; open hearth with burning logs; a big dresser painted brown, carrying a row of white cups on brass hooks and shelves of plates overlapping each other like the scales of fish. A dark settle half hid a flight of stairs with a small gate at the top. Under the window a black sofa, deeply indented, invited you a little repellingly, and in the middle of the room stood a large table, exquisitely scrubbed, with one end of it laid for tea. Evidently a living-room as well as kitchen. A girl, making toast at the fire, turned as the higgler entered. Beautiful she was: red hair, a complexion like the inside of a nut, blue eyes, and the hands of a lady. He saw it all at once, jacket of bright green wool, black dress, grey stockings and shoes, and forgot his errand, her mother, his fifty pounds, Sophy — momentarily he forgot everything. The girl stared strangely at him. He was tall, clean shaven, with a loop of black hair curling handsomely over one side of his brow.

'Good afternoon,' said Harvey Witlow, as softly as if he had entered a church.

'Some eggs, Mary,' Mrs. Sadgrove explained. The girl laid down her toasting fork. She was less tall than her mother, who she resembled only enough for the relationship to be noted. Silently she crossed the kitchen and opened a door that led into a dairy. Two pans of milk were creaming on a bench there, and on the flags were two great baskets filled with eggs.

'How many are there?' asked Mrs. Sadgrove, and the girl replied: 'Fifteen score, I think.'

'Take the lot, higgler?'

'Yes, ma'am,' he cried eagerly, and ran out to his cart and fetched a number of trays. In them he packed the eggs as the girl handed them to him from the baskets. Mrs. Sadgrove left them together. For a time the higgler was silent.

'No,' at length he murmured, 'I've never been this road before.'

There was no reply from Mary. Sometimes their fingers touched, and often, as they bent over the eggs, her bright hair almost brushed his face.

'It is a loneish spot,' he ventured again.

'Yes,' said Mary Sadgrove.

When the eggs were all transferred her mother came in again.

'Would you buy a few pullets, higgler?'

'Any number, ma'am,' he declared quickly. Any number; by crumps, the tide was turning. He followed the mother into the yard, and there again she left him, waiting. He mused about the girl and wondered about the trade. If they offered him ten thousand chicken, he'd buy them, somehow, he would. She had stopped in the kitchen. Just in there she was, just behind him, a few feet away. Over the low wall of the yard a fat black pony was strolling in a field of bright greensward. In the yard, watching him, was a young gander, and on a stone staddle beside it lay a dead thrush on its back, its legs stiff in the air. The girl stayed in the kitchen; she was moving about though, he could hear her; perhaps she was spying at him through the window. Twenty million eggs he would buy if Mrs. Sadgrove had got them. She was gone a long time. It was very quiet. The gander began to comb its white breast with its beak. Its three-toed feet were a most tender pink, shaped like wide diamonds, and at each of the three forward points there was a toe like a small blanched nut. It lifted one foot, folding the webs, and hid it under its wing and sank into a resigned meditation on one leg. It had a blue eye that was meek — it had two but you could only see one at a time — a meek blue eye, set in a pink rim that gave it a dissolute air, and its beak had raw red nostrils as though it suffered from the damp. Altogether a beautiful bird. And in some absurd way it resembled Mrs. Sadgrove.

'Would you sell that young gollan, ma'am?' Harvey inquired when the mother returned.

Yes, she would sell him, and she also sold him two dozen pullets. Harvey packed the fowls in a crate. 'Come on,' he cried cuddling the squalling gander in his arms, 'you needn't be afeared of me, I never kills anything afore Saturdays.'

He roped it by its leg to a hook inside his cart. Then he took out his bag of money, paid Mrs. Sadgrove her dues, said 'Good-day, ma'am, good-day' and drove off without seeing another sign or stitch of that fine young girl.

'Get along, Dodger, get along wi' you.' They went bowling along for nearly an hour, and then he could see the landmark on Dan'el Green's Hill, a windmill that never turned though it looked a fine competent piece of architecture, just beyond Dinnop.

Soon he reached his cottage and was chaffing his mother, a hearty buxom dame, who stayed at home and higgled with any chance callers. At this business she was perhaps more enlightened than her son. It was almost a misfortune to get into her clutches.

'How much you give for this?' he cried, eyeing with humorous contempt an object in a coop that was neither flesh nor rude red herring.

'O crumps,' he declared, when she told him, 'I am damned and done!'

'Go on with you, that's a good bird, I tell you, with a full heart, as will lay in a month.'

'I doubt it's a hen at all,' he protested. 'O what a ravenous beak! Damned and done I am.'

Mrs. Witlow's voice began indignantly to rise.

'O well,' mused her son, 'it's thrifty perhaps. It ain't quite right, but it's not so wrong as to make a fuss about, especially as I be pretty sharp set. And if it's hens you want,' he continued triumphantly, dropping the crate of huddled fowls before her, 'there's hens for you; and a gander! There's a gander for you, if it's a gander you want.'

Leaving them all in his cottage yard he went and stalled the horse and cart at the inn, for he had no stable of his own. After supper he told his mother about the Sadgroves of Prattle Corner. 'Prettiest girl you ever seen, but the shyest mottal alive. Hair like a squirrel, lovely.'

'An't you got to go over and see Sophy to-night,' inquired his mother, lighting the lamp.

'O lord, if I an't clean forgot that. Well, I'm tired, shan't go to-night. See her to-morrow.'

II

Mrs. Sadgrove had been a widow for ten years — and she was glad of it. Prattle Corner was her property, she owned it and farmed it with the aid of a little old man and a large lad. The older this old man grew, and the less wages he received (for Elizabeth Sadgrove was reputed a 'grinder'), the more ardently he worked; the older the lad grew the less he laboured and the more he swore. She was thriving. She was worth money, was Mrs. Sadgrove. Ah! And her daughter Mary, it was clear, had received an education fit for a lord's lady; she had been at a seminary for gentlefolks' females until she was seventeen. Well, whether or no, a clock must run as you time it; but it wronged her for the work of a farm, it spoiled her, it completely deranged her for the work of a farm; and this was a pity and foolish, because some day the farm was coming to her as didn't know hay from a bull's foot.

All this, and more, the young higgler quickly learned, and plenty more he soon divined. Business began to flourish with him now; his despair was gone, he was established, he could look forward, to whatever it was he wanted to look forward, with equanimity and such pleasurable anticipation as the chances and charges of life might engender. Every week, and twice a week, he would call at the farm, and though these occasions had their superior business inducements they often borrowed a less formal tone and intention.

'Take a cup of tea, higgler?' Mrs. Sadgrove would abruptly invite him; and he would drink tea and discourse with her for half an hour on barndoor ornithology, on harness, and markets, the treatment of swine, the wear and tear of gear. Mary, always present, was always silent, seldom uttering a word to the higgler; yet a certain grace emanated from her to him, an interest, a light, a favour, circumscribed indeed by some modesty, shyness, some inhibition, that neither had the wit or the opportunity to overcome.

One evening he pulled up at the white palings of Prattle Corner. It was a calm evening in May, the sun was on its downgoing, chaffinches and wrens sung ceaselessly. Mary in the orchard was heavily veiled; he could see her over the hedge, holding a brush in her gloved hands, and a bee skep. A swarm was clustered like a great gnarl on the limb of an apple tree. Bloom was thickly covering the twigs. She made several timid attempts to brush the bees into the skep but they resented this.

'They knows if you be afraid of 'em,' bawled Harvey. 'I better come and give you a hand.'

When he took the skep and brush from her she stood like one helpless, released by fate from a task ill-understood and gracelessly waived. But he liked her shyness, her almost uncouth immobility.

'Never mind about that,' said Harvey, as she unfastened her veil, scattering the white petals that had collected upon it; 'when they kicks they hurts; but I've been stung so often that I'm 'noculated against 'em. They knows if you be afraid of 'em.'

Wearing neither veil nor gloves he went confidently to the tree, and collected the swarm without mishap.

'Don't want to show no fear of them,' said Harvey. 'Nor of anything else, come to that,' he added with a guffaw, 'nor anybody.'

At that she blushed and thanked him very softly, and she did look straight and clearly at him.

Never anything beyond a blush and a thank-you. When in the kitchen, or the parlour, Mrs. Sadgrove sometimes left them alone together Harvey would try a lot of talk, blarncying talk or sensible talk, or talk about events in the world that was neither the one nor the other. No good. The girl's responses were ever brief and confused. Why was this? Again and again he asked himself that question. Was there anything the matter with her? Nothing that you could see; she was a bright and beautiful being. And it was not contempt, either, for despite her fright, her voicelessness, her timid eyes, he divined her friendly feeling for himself; and he would discourse to his own mother about her and her mother:

'They are well-up people, you know, well off, plenty of money and nothing to do with it. The farm's their own, freehold. A whole row of cottages she's got, too, in Smoorton Comfrey, so I heard; good cottages, well let. She's worth a few thousands, I warrant. Mary's beautiful. I took a fancy to that girl the first moment I see her. But she's very highly cultivated — and, of course, there's Sophy.'

To this enigmatic statement Mrs. Witlow offered no response; but mothers are inscrutable beings to their sons, always.

Once he bought some trees of cherries from Mrs. Sadgrove, and went on a July morning to pick the fruit. Under the trees Mary was walking slowly to and fro, twirling a clapper to scare away the birds. He stood watching her from the gateway. Among the bejewelled trees she passed, turning the rattle with a listless air, as if beating time to a sad music that only she could hear. The man knew that he was deeply fond of her. He passed into the orchard, bade her good morning, and lifting his ladder into one of the trees nearest the hedge began to pluck cherries. Mary moved slimly in her white frock up and down a shady avenue in the orchard, waving the clapper. The brightness of sun and sky was almost harsh; there was a little wind that feebly lifted the despondent leaves. He had doffed his coat; his shirt was white and clean. The lock of dark hair drooped over one side of his forehead; his face was brown and pleasant, his bare arms were brown and powerful. From his high perch among the leaves Witlow watched for the girl to draw near to him in her perambulation. Knavish birds would scatter at her approach, only to drop again into the trees she had passed. His soul had an immensity of longing for her, but she never spoke a word to him. She would come from the shade of the little avenue, through the dumb trees that could only bend to greet her, into the sunlight whose dazzle gilded her own triumphant bloom. Fine! Fine! And always as she passed his mind refused to register a single thought he could offer her, or else his tongue would refuse to utter it. But his glance never left her face until she had passed out of sight again, and then he would lean against the ladder in the tree, staring down at the ground, seeing nothing or less than nothing, except a field mouse climbing to the top of a coventry bush in the hedge below him, nipping off one thick leaf and descending with the leaf in its mouth. Sometimes Mary rested at the other end of the avenue; the clapper would be silent and she would not appear for — O, hours! She never rested near the trees Witlow was denuding. The mouse went on ascending and descending, and Witlow filled his basket, and shifted his stand, and wondered.

At noon he got down and sat on the hedge bank to eat a snack of lunch. Mary had gone indoors for hers, and he was alone for a while. Capriciously enough, his thoughts dwelt upon Sophy Daws. Sophy was a fine girl too; not such a lady as Mary Sadgrove — O lord, no! her father was a gamekeeper! — but she was jolly and ample. She had been a little captious lately, said he was neglecting her. That wasn't true; hadn't he been busy? Besides, he wasn't bound to her in any sort of way, and of course he couldn't afford any marriage yet awhile. Sophy hadn't got any money, never had any. What she did with her wages — she was a parlourmaid — was a teaser! Harvey grunted a little, and said 'Well!' And that is all he said, and all he thought about Sophy Daws then, for he could hear Mary's clapper begin again in a corner of the orchard. He went back to his work. There at the foot of the tree were the baskets full of cherries, and those yet to be filled.

'Phew, but that's hot!' commented the man, 'I'm as dry as a rattle.'

A few cherries had spilled from one basket and lay on the ground. The little furry mouse had found them and was industriously nibbling at one. The higgler nonchalantly stamped his foot upon it, and kept it so for a moment or two. Then he looked at the dead mouse. A tangle of entrails had gushed from its whiskered muzzle.

He resumed his work and the clapper rattled on

throughout the afternoon, for there were other cherry trees that other buyers would come to strip in a day or two. At four o'clock he was finished. Never a word had he spoken with Mary, or she with him. When he went over to the house to pay Mrs. Sadgrove Mary stopped in the orchard scaring the birds.

'Take a cup of tea, Mr. Witlow,' said Mrs. Sadgrove; and then she surprisingly added: 'Where's Mary?'

'Still a-frightening the birds, and pretty well tired of that, I should think, ma'am.'

The mother had poured out three cups of tea.

'Shall I go and call her in?' he asked, rising.

'You might,' said she.

In the orchard the clappering had ceased. He walked all round, and in among the trees, but saw no sign of Mary; nor on the common, nor in the yard. But when he went back to the house Mary was there already, chatting at the table with her mother. She did not greet him, though she ceased talking to her mother as he sat down. After drinking his tea he went off briskly to load the baskets into the cart. As he climbed up to drive off Mrs. Sadgrove came out and stood beside the horse.

'You're off now?' said she.

'Yes, ma'am; all loaded, and thank you.'

She glanced vaguely along the road he had to travel. The afternoon was as clear as wine, the greensward itself dazzled him; lonely Shag Moor stretched away, humped with sweet yellow furze and pilastered with its telegraph poles. No life there, no life at all. Harvey sat on his driving board, musingly brushing the flank of his horse with the trailing whip.

'Ever round this way on Sundays?' inquired the woman, peering up at him.

'Well, not in a manner of speaking, I'm not, ma'am,' he answered her.

The widow laid her hand on the horse's back, patting vaguely. The horse pricked up its ears, as if it were listening.

'If you are, at all, ever, you must look in and have a bit of dinner with us.'

'I will, ma'am, I will.'

'Next Sunday?' she went on.

'I will, ma'am, yes, I will,' he repeated, 'and thank you.'

'One o'clock?' The widow smiled up at him.

'At one o'clock, ma'am; next Sunday; I will, and thank you,' he said.

She stood away from the horse and waved her hand. The first tangible thought that floated mutely out of the higgler's mind as he drove away was: 'I'm damned if I ain't a-going it, Sophy!'

He told his mother of Mrs. Sadgrove's invitation with an air of curbed triumph. 'Come round — she says. Yes — I says — I 'ull. That's right — she says — so do.'

III

On the Sunday morn he dressed himself gallantly. It was again a sweet unclouded day. The church bell at Dinnop had begun to ring. From his window, as he fastened his most ornate tie, Harvey could observe his neighbour's two small children in the next garden, a boy and girl clad for church-going and each carrying a clerical book. The tiny boy placed his sister in front of a hen-roost and, opening his book, began to pace to and fro before her, shrilly intoning: 'Jesus is the shepherd, ring the bell. O lord, ring the bell, am I a good

boy? Amen. O lord, ring the bell.' The little girl
bowed her head piously over her book. The lad then
picked up from the ground a dish which had contained
the dog's food, and presented it momentarily before
the lilac bush, the rabbit in a hutch, the axe fixed in a
chopping block, and then before his sister. Without
lifting her peering gaze from her book she meekly
dropped two pebbles in the plate, and the boy passed
on, lightly moaning, to the clothes-line post and a cock
scooping in some dust.

'Ah, the little impets!' cried Harvey Witlow. 'Here,
Toby! Here, Margaret!' He took two pennies from
his pocket and lobbed them from the window to the
astonished children. As they stooped to pick up the
coins Harvey heard the hoarse voice of neighbour
Nathan, their father, bawl from his kitchen: 'Come on
in, and shut that bloody door, d'y'ear!'

Harnessing his moody horse to the gig Harvey was
soon bowling away to Shag Moor, and as he drove along
he sung loudly. He had a pink rose in his buttonhole.
Mrs. Sadgrove received him almost affably, and though
Mary was more shy than ever before Harvey had determined to make an impression. During the dinner he
fired off his bucolic jokes, and pleasant tattle of a more
respectful and sober nature; but after dinner Mary sat
like Patience, not upon a monument but as if upon a
rocking-horse, shy and fearful, and her mother made
no effort to inspire her as the higgler did, unsuccessful
though he was. They went to the pens to look at the
pigs, and as they leaned against the low walls and poked
the maudlin inhabitants, Harvey began: 'Reminds me,
when I was in the war . . .'

'Were you in the war!' interrupted Mrs. Sadgrove.

'O yes, I was in that war, ah, and there was a pig . . .
Danger? O lord bless me it was a bit dangerous, but

you never knew where it was or what it 'ud be at next; it was like the sword of Damockels. There was a bullet once come 'ithin a foot of my head, and it went through a board an inch thick, slap through that board.' Both women gazed at him apprehendingly. 'Why I might 'a been killed, you know,' said Harvey, cocking his eye musingly at the weather vane on the barn. 'We was in billets at St. Gratien, and one day a chasseur came up — a French yoossar, you know — and he began talking to our sergeant. That was Hubert Luxter, the butcher: died a month or two ago of measles. But this yoossar couldn't speak English at all, and none of us chaps could make sense of him. I never could understand that lingo somehow, never; and though there was half a dozen of us chaps there, none of us were man enough for it neither. "Nil compree", we says, "non compos." I told him straight: "You ought to learn English", I said "it's much easier than your kind of bally chatter." So he kept shaping up as if he was holding a rifle, and then he'd say "Fusee — bang!" and then he'd say "cushion" — kept on saying "cushion". Then he gets a bit of chalk and draws on the wall something that looks like a horrible dog, and says "cushion" again.'

'Pig,' interjected Mary Sadgrove, softly.

'Yes, yes!' ejaculated Harvey, 'so 'twas! Do you know any French lingo?'

'O yes,' declared her mother, 'Mary knows it very well.'

'Ah,' sighed the higgler, 'I don't, although I been to France. And I couldn't do it now, not for luck nor love. You learnt it, I suppose. Well, this yoossar wants to borrow my rifle, but of course I can't lend him. So he taps on this horrible pig he'd drawn, and then he taps on his own head, and rolls his eyes about dreadful! "Mad?" I says. And that was it, that was it.

He'd got a pig on his little farm there what had gone mad, and he wanted us to come and shoot it; he was on leave and he hadn't got any ammunition. So Hubert Luxter he says, "Come on, some of you", and we all goes with the yoossar and shot the pig for him. Ah, that was a pig! And when it died it jumped a somersault just like a rabbit. It had got the mange, and was mad as anything I ever see in my life; it was full of madness. Couldn't hit him at all at first, and it kicked up bobs-a-dying. "Ready, present, fire!" Hubert Luxter says and bang goes the six of us, and every time we missed him he spotted us and we had to run for our lives.'

As Harvey looked up he caught a glance of the girl fixed on him. She dropped her gaze at once and, turning away, walked off to the house.

'Come and take a look at the meadow,' said Mrs. Sadgrove to him, and they went into the soft smooth meadow where the black pony was grazing. Very bright and green it was, and very blue the sky. He sniffed at the pink rose in his buttonhole, and determined that come what may he would give it to Mary if he could get a nice quiet chance to offer it. And just then, while he and Mrs. Sadgrove were strolling alone in the soft smooth meadow, quite alone, she suddenly, startlingly, asked him: 'Are you courting anybody?'

'Beg pardon, ma'am?' he exclaimed.

'You haven't got a sweetheart, have you?' she asked, most deliberately.

Harvey grinned sheepishly: 'Ha ha ha,' and then he said, 'No.'

'I want to see my daughter married,' the widow went on, significantly.

'Miss Mary!' he cried.

'Yes,' said she; and something in the higgler's veins

began to pound rapidly. His breast might have been a revolving cage and his heart a demon squirrel. 'I can't live for ever,' said Mrs. Sadgrove, almost with levity, 'in fact, not for long, and so I'd like to see her settled soon with some decent understanding young man, one that could carry on here, and not make a mess of things.'

'But, but,' stuttered the understanding young man, 'I'm no scholar, and she's a lady. I'm a poor chap, rough, and no scholar, ma'am. But mind you . . .'

'That doesn't matter at all,' the widow interrupted, 'not as things are. You want a scholar for learning, but for the land . . .!'

'Ah, that's right, Mrs. Sadgrove, but . . .'

'I want to see her settled. This farm, you know, with the stock and things are worth nigh upon three thousand pounds.'

'You want a farmer for farming, that's true, Mrs. Sadgrove, but when you come to marriage, well, with her learning and French and all that . . .!'

'A sensible woman will take a man rather than a box of tricks any day of the week,' the widow retorted. 'Education may be a fine thing, but it often costs a lot of foolish money.'

'It do, it do. You want to see her settled?'

'I want to see her settled and secure. When she is twenty-five she comes into five hundred pounds of her own right.'

The distracted higgler hummed and haa-ed in his bewilderment as if he had just been offered the purchase of a dubious duck. 'How old is she, ma'am?' he at last huskily inquired.

'Two and twenty nearly. She's a good healthy girl for I've never spent a pound on a doctor for her, and very quiet she is, and very sensible; but she's got a

strong will of her own, though you might not think it
or believe it.'

'She's a fine creature, Mrs. Sadgrove, and I'm very
fond of her, I don't mind owning up to that, very fond
of her I am.'

'Well, think it over, take your time, and see what you
think. There's no hurry I hope, please God.'

'I shan't want much time,' he declared with a laugh,
'but I doubt I'm the fair right sort for her.'

'O, fair days, fair doings!' said she inscrutably, 'I'm
not a long liver, I'm afraid.'

'God forbid, ma'am!' His ejaculation was intoned
with deep gravity.

'No, I'm not a long-living woman.' She surveyed
him with her calm eyes, and he returned her gaze.
Hers was a long sallow face, with heavy lips. Sometimes she would stretch her features (as if to keep them
from petrifying) in an elastic grin, and display her
dazzling teeth; the lips would curl thickly, no longer
crimson, but blue. He wondered if there was any sign
of a doom registered upon her gaunt face. She might
die, and die soon.

'You couldn't do better than think it over, then, eh?'
she had a queer frown as she regarded him.

'I couldn't do worse than not, Mrs. Sadgrove,' he
said gaily.

They left it at that. He had no reason for hurrying
away, and he couldn't have explained his desire to do
so, but he hurried away. Driving along past the end
of the moor, and peering back at the lonely farm where
they dwelled amid the thick furze snoozing in the heat,
he remembered that he had not asked if Mary was
willing to marry him! Perhaps the widow took her
agreement for granted. That would be good fortune,
for otherwise how the devil was he to get round a girl

who had never spoken half a dozen words to him! And never would! She was a lady, a girl of fortune, knew her French; but there it was, the girl's own mother was asking him to wed her. Strange, very strange! He dimly feared something, but he did not know what it was he feared. He had still got the pink rose in his buttonhole.

IV

At first his mother was incredulous; when he told her of the astonishing proposal she declared he was a joker; but she was soon as convinced of his sincerity as she was amazed at his hesitation. And even vexed: 'Was there anything the matter with this Mary?'

'No, no, no! She's quiet, very quiet indeed I tell you, but a fine young woman, and a beautiful young woman. O, she's all right, right as rain, right as a trivet, right as ninepence. But there's a catch in it somewheres, I fear. I can't see through it yet, but I shall afore long, or I'd have the girl, like a shot I would. 'Tain't the girl, mother, it's the money, if you understand me.'

'Well, I don't understand you, certainly I don't. What about Sophy?'

'O lord!' he scratched his head ruefully.

'You wouldn't think of giving this the go-by for Sophy, Harvey, would you! A girl as you ain't even engaged to, Harvey, would you!'

'We don't want to chatter about that,' declared her son. 'I got to think it over, and it's going to tie my wool, I can tell you, for there's a bit of craft somewheres, I'll take my oath. If there ain't, there ought to be!'

Over the alluring project his decision wavered for

days, until his mother became mortified at his inexplicable vacillation.

'I tell you,' he cried, 'I can't make tops or bottoms of it all. I like the girl well enough, but I like Sophy, too, and it's no good beating about the bush. I like Sophy, she's the girl I love; but Mary's a fine creature, and money like that wants looking at before you throw it away, love or no love. Three thousand pounds! I'd be a made man.'

And as if in sheer spite to his mother; as if a bushel of money lay on the doorstep for him to kick over whenever the fancy seized him; in short (as Mrs. Witlow very clearly intimated) as if in contempt of Providence, he began to pursue Sophy Daws with a new fervour, and walked with that young girl more than he was accustomed to, more than ever before; in fact, as his mother bemoaned, more than he had need to. It was unreasonable, it was a shame, a foolishness; it wasn't decent and it wasn't safe.

On his weekly visits to the farm his mind still wavered. Mrs. Sadgrove let him alone; she was very good, she did not pester him with questions and entreaties. There was Mary with her white dress and her red hair and her silence; a girl with a great fortune, walking about the yard, or sitting in the room, and casting not a glance upon him. Not that he would have known it if she did, for now he was just as shy of her. Mrs. Sadgrove often left them alone, but when they were alone he could not dish up a word for the pretty maid; he was dumb as a statue. If either she or her mother had lifted so much as a finger then there would have been an end to his hesitations or suspicions, for in Mary's presence the fine glory of the girl seized him incontinently; he was again full of a longing to press her lips, to lay down his doubts, to touch her bosom —

though he could not think she would ever allow that! Not an atom of doubt about *her* ever visited him; she was unaware of her mother's queer project. Rather, if she became aware he was sure it would be the end of him. Too beautiful she was, too learned, and too rich. Decidedly it was his native cunning, and no want of love, that inhibited him. Folks with property did not often come along and bid you help yourself. Not very often! And throw in a grand bright girl, just for good measure as you might say. Not very often!

For weeks the higgler made his customary calls, and each time the outcome was the same; no more, no less. 'Some dodge,' he mused, 'something the girl don't know and the mother does.' Were they going bankrupt, or were they mortgaged up to the neck, or was there anything the matter with the girl, or was it just the mother wanted to get hold of him? He knew his own value if he didn't know his own mind, and his value couldn't match that girl any more than his mind could. So what *did* they want him for? Whatever it was Harvey Witlow was ready for it whenever he was in Mary's presence, but once away from her his own craftiness asserted itself; it was a snare, they were trying to make a mock of him!

But nothing could prevent his own mother mocking him, and her treatment of Sophy was so unbearable that if the heart of that dusky beauty had not been proof against all impediments, Harvey might have had to whistle for her favour. But whenever he was with Sophy he had only one heart, undivided and true, and certain as time itself.

'I love Sophy best. It's true enough I love Mary, too, but I love Sophy better. I know it; Sophy's the girl I must wed. It might not be so if I weren't all dashed and doddered about the money; I don't know. But I do know that Mary's innocent of all this craftiness; it's her mother trying to mogue me into it.'

Later he would be wishing he could only forget Sophy and do it. Without the hindrance of conscience he could do it, catch or no catch.

He went on calling at the farm, with nothing said or settled, until October. Then Harvey made up his mind, and without a word to the Sadgroves he went and married Sophy Daws and gave up calling at the farm altogether. This gave him some feeling of dishonesty, some qualm and a vague unhappiness; likewise he feared the cold hostility of Mrs. Sadgrove. She would be terribly vexed. As for Mary, he was nothing to her, poor girl; it was a shame. The last time he drove that way he did not call at the farm. Autumn was advancing, and the apples were down, the bracken dying, the furze out of bloom, and the farm on the moor looked more and more lonely, and most cold, though it lodged a flame-haired silent woman, fit for a nobleman, whom they wanted to mate with a common higgler. Crafty, you know, too crafty!

v

The marriage was a gay little occasion, but they did not go away for a honeymoon. Sophy's grandmother from a distant village, Cassandra Fundy, who had a deafness and a speckled skin, brought her third husband, Amos, whom the family had never seen before. Not a very wise man, indeed he was a common man, stooping like a decayed tree, he was so old. But he shaved every day and his hairless skull was yellow. Cassandra, who was yellow too, had long since turned into a fool; she did not shave, though she ought to have done. She was like to die soon, but everybody said old Amos would live to be a hundred; it was expected of him, and he, too, was determined.

The guests declared that a storm was threatening, but Amos Fundy denied it and scorned it.

'Thunder p'raps, but 'twill clear; 'tis only de pride o' der morning.'

'Don't you be a fool,' remarked his wife, enigmatically, 'you'll die soon enough.'

'You must behold der moon,' continued the octogenarian; 'de closer it is to der wheel, de closer der rain; de furder away it is, de furder der rain.'

'You could pour that man's brains into a thimble,' declared Cassandra of her spouse, 'and they wouldn't fill it — he's deaf.'

Fundy was right; the day did clear. The marriage was made and the guests returned with the man and his bride to their home. But Fundy was also wrong, for storm came soon after and rain set in. The guests stayed on for tea, and then, as it was no better, they feasted and stayed till night. And Harvey began to think they never would go, but of course they couldn't and so there they were. Sophy was looking wonderful in white stockings and shiny shoes and a red frock with a tiny white apron. A big girl she seemed, with her shaken dark hair and flushed face. Grandmother Fundy spoke seriously, but not secretly to her.

'I've had my fourteen touch of children,' said Grandmother Fundy. 'Yes, they were flung on the mercy of God — poor little devils. I've followed most of 'em to the churchyard. You go slow, Sophia.'

'Yes, granny.'

'Why,' continued Cassandra, embracing the whole

company, as it were with her disclosure, 'my mother had me by some gentleman!'

The announcement aroused no response except sympathetic, and perhaps encouraging, nods from the women.

'She had me by some gentleman — she ought to ha' had a twal' month, she did!'

'Wasn't she ever married?' Sophy inquired of her grandmother.

'Married? Yes, course she was,' replied the old dame, 'of course. But marriage ain't everything. Twice she was, but not to he, she wasn't.'

'Not to the gentleman?'

'No! O no! He'd got money — bushels! Marriage ain't much, not with these gentry.'

'Ho, ho, that's a tidy come-up!' laughed Harvey.

'Who was the gentleman?' Sophia's interest was deeply engaged. But Cassandra Fundy was silent, pondering like a china image. Her gaze was towards the mantelpiece, where there were four lamps — but only one usable — and two clocks — but only one going — and a coloured greeting card a foot long with large letters KEEP SMILING adorned with lithographic honeysuckle.

'She's hard of hearing,' interpolated Grandfather Amos, 'very hard, gets worse. She've a horn at home, big as that . . .' His eyes roved the room for an object of comparison, and he seized upon the fire shovel that lay in the fender. 'Big as that shovel. Crown silver it is, and solid, a beautiful horn, but' — he brandished the shovel before them — 'her won't use 'en.'

'Granny, who was that gentleman?' shouted Sophy. 'Did you know him?'

'No! No!' declared the indignant dame. 'I dunno ever his name, nor I don't want to. He took hisself off the Ameriky, and now he's in the land of heaven. I never seen him. If I had, I'd a given it to him properly; O, my dear, not blay-guarding him, you know, but just plain language! Where's your seven commandments?'

At last the rain abated. Peeping into the dark garden you could see the fugitive moonlight hung in a million raindrops in the black twigs of all sorts of bushes and trees, while along the cantle of the porch a line of rain drops hung, even and regular, as if they were nailheads made of glass. So all the guests departed, in one long staggering, struggling, giggling and guffawing body, into the village street. The bride and her man stood in the porch, watching, and waving hands. Sophy was momentarily grieving: what a lot of trouble and fuss when you announced that henceforward you were going to sleep with a man because you loved him true! She had said good-bye to her Grandmother Cassandra, to her father and her little sister. She had hung on her mother's breast, sighing an almost intolerable farewell to innocence — never treasured until it is gone — and thenceforward a pretty sorrow cherished more deeply than wilder joys.

Into Harvey's mind, as they stood there at last alone, momentarily stole an image of a bright-haired girl, lovely, silent, sad, whom he felt he had deeply wronged. And he was sorry. He had escaped the snare, but if there had been no snare he might this night have been sleeping with a different bride. And it would have been just as well. Sophy looked but a girl with her blown hair and wet face. She was wiping her tears on the tiny apron. But she had the breasts of a woman and decoying eyes.

'Sophy, Sophy!' breathed Harvey, wooing her in the darkness.

'It blows and it rains, and it rains and it blows,' chattered the crumpled bride, 'and I'm all so be-scambled I can't tell wet from windy.'

'Come, my love,' whispered the bridegroom, 'come in, to home.'

VI

Four or five months later the higgler's affairs had again taken a rude turn. Marriage, alas, was not all it might be; his wife and his mother quarrelled un-endingly. Sometimes he sided with the one, some-times with the other. He could not yet afford to instal his mother in a separate cottage, and therefore even Sophy had to admit that her mother-in-law had a right to be living there with them, the home being hers. Harvey hadn't bought much of it; and though he was welcome to it all now, and it would be exclusively his as soon as she died, still, it was her furniture and you couldn't drive any woman (even your mother) off her own property. Sophy, who wanted a home of her own, was vexed and moody, and antagonistic to her man. Business, too, had gone down sadly of late. He had thrown up the Shag Moor round months ago; he could not bring himself to go there again, and he had not been able to square up the loss by any substantial new connections. On top of it all his horse died. It stumbled on a hill one day and fell, and it couldn't get up, or it wouldn't — at any rate, it didn't. Harvey thrashed it and coaxed it, then he cursed it and kicked it; after that he sent for a veterinary man, and the veterinary man ordered it to be shot. And it was shot. A great blow to Harvey Witlow was that. He had no money to buy another horse; money was tight with him, very tight; and so he had to hire at fabulous cost a decrepit nag that ate like a good one. It ate — well it would have astonished you to see what that creature disposed of, with hay the price it was, and corn gone up to heaven nearly. In fact Harvey found that he couldn't stand the racket much longer, and as he could not possibly buy another it looked very much as if he was in queer street once more, unless he could borrow the money from some friendly person. Of course there were plenty of friendly persons but they had no money, just as there were many persons who had the money but were not what you might call friendly; and so the higgler began to reiterate twenty times a day, and forty times a day, that he was entirely and absolutely damned and done. Things were thus very bad with him, they were at their worst — for he had a wife to keep now, as well as a mother, and a horse that ate like Satan, and worked like a gnat — when it suddenly came into his mind that Mrs. Sadgrove was reputed to have a lot of money, and had no call to be unfriendly to him. He had his grave doubts about the size of her purse, but there could be no harm in trying so long as you approached her in a right reasonable manner.

For a week or two he held off from this appeal, but the grim spectre of destitution gave him no rest, and so, near the close of a wild March day he took his desperate courage and his cart and the decrepit nag to Shag Moor. Wild it was, though dry, and the wind against them, a vast turmoil of icy air strident and baffling. The nag threw up its head and declined to trot. Evening was but an hour away, the fury of the wind did not retard it, nor the clouds hasten it. Low down the sun was quitting the wrack of storm, exposing a jolly orb of magnifying fire that shone flush under eaves and through the casements of cottages, casting a pattern of lattice and tossing boughs upon the interior walls, lovelier than dreamed-of pictures. The heads of mothers and old dames were also imaged there, recognizable in their black shadows; and little children held up their hands between window and wall to make five-fingered shapes upon the golden screen. To drive on the moor then was to drive into blasts more dire. Darkness began to fall, and bitter cold it was. No birds to be seen, neither beast nor man; empty of everything it was, except sound and a marvel of dying light, and Harvey Witlow of Dinnop with a sour old nag driving from end to end of it. At Prattle Corner dusk was already abroad: there was just one shaft of light that broached a sharp-angled stack in the rickyard, an ark of darkness, along whose top the gads and wooden pins and tilted straws were miraculously fringed in the last glare. Hitching his nag to the palings he knocked at the door, and knew in the gloom that it was Mary who opened it and stood peering forth at him.

'Good evening,' he said, touching his hat.

'O!' the girl uttered a cry, 'Higgler! What do you come for?' It was the longest sentence she had ever spoken to him; a sad frightened voice.

'I thought,' he began, 'I'd call — and see Mrs. Sadgrove. I wondered . . .'

'Mother's dead,' said the girl. She drew the door further back, as if inviting him, and he entered. The door was shut behind him, and they were alone in darkness, together. The girl was deeply grieving. Trembling, he asked the question: 'What is it you tell me, Mary?'

'Mother's dead,' repeated the girl, 'all day, all day, all day.' They were close to each other, but he could not see her. All round the house the wind roved lamentingly, shuddering at doors and windows. 'She died in the night. The doctor was to have come, but he has not come all day,' Mary whispered 'all day, all day. I don't understand; I have waited for him, and he has not come. She died, she was dead in her bed this morning, and I've been alone all day, all day, and I don't know what is to be done.'

'I'll go for the doctor,' he said hastily, but she took him by the hand and drew him into the kitchen. There was no candle lit; a fire was burning there, richly glowing embers, that laid a gaunt shadow of the table across a corner of the ceiling. Every dish on the dresser gleamed, the stone floor was rosy, and each smooth curve on the dark settle was shining like ice. Without invitation he sat down.

'No,' said the girl, in a tremulous voice, 'you must help me.' She lit a candle: her face was white as the moon, her lips were sharply red, and her eyes were wild. 'Come,' she said, and he followed her behind the settle and up the stairs to a room where there was a disordered bed, and what might be a body lying under the quilt. The higgler stood still staring at the form under the quilt. The girl, too, was still and staring. Wind dashed upon the ivy at the window and hallooed like a grieving multitude. A crumpled gown hid the body's head, but thrust from under it, almost as if to greet him, was her naked lean arm, the palm of the hand lying uppermost. At the foot of the bed was a large washing bowl, with sponge and towels.

'You've been laying her out! Yourself!' exclaimed Witlow. The pale girl set down the candle on a chest of drawers. 'Help me now,' she said, and moving to the bed she lifted the crumpled gown from off the face of the dead woman, at the same time smoothing the quilt closely up to the body's chin. 'I cannot put the gown on, because of her arm, it has gone stiff.' She shuddered, and stood holding the gown as if offering it to the man. He lifted that dead naked arm and tried to place it down at the body's side, but it resisted and he let go his hold. The arm swung back to its former outstretched position, as if it still lived and resented that pressure. The girl retreated from the bed with a timorous cry.

'Get me a bandage,' he said, 'or something we can tear up.'

She gave him some pieces of linen.

'I'll finish this for you,' he brusquely whispered, 'you get along downstairs and take a swig of brandy. Got any brandy?'

She did not move. He put his arm around her and gently urged her to the door.

'Brandy,' he repeated, 'and light your candles.'

He watched her go heavily down the stairs before he shut the door. Returning to the bed he lifted the quilt. The dead body was naked and smelt of soap. Dropping the quilt he lifted the outstretched arm again, like cold wax to the touch and unpliant as a sturdy sapling, and tried once more to bend it to the body's side. As he did so the bedroom door blew open with a crash. It was only a draught of the wind, and a loose latch — Mary had opened a door downstairs, perhaps — but it awed him, as if some invisible looker were there resenting his presence. He went and closed the door, the latch had a loose hasp, and tiptoeing nervously back, he seized the dreadful arm with a sudden brutal energy, and bent it by thrusting his knee violently into the hollow of the elbow. Hurriedly he slipped the gown over the head and inserted the arm in the sleeve. A strange impulse of modesty stayed him for a moment: should he call the girl and let her complete the robing of the naked body under the quilt? That preposterous pause seemed to add a new anger to the wind, and again the door sprang open. He delayed no longer, but letting it remain open, he uncovered the dead woman. As he lifted the chill body the long outstretched arm moved and tilted like the boom of a sail, but crushing it to its side he bound the limb fast with the strips of linen. So Mrs. Sadgrove was made ready for her coffin. Drawing the quilt back to her neck, with a gush of relief he glanced about the room. It was a very ordinary bedroom, bed, washstand, chest of drawers, chair and two pictures — one of deeply religious import, and the other a little pink print, in a gilded frame, of a bouncing nude nymph recumbent upon a cloud. It was queer: a lot of people, people whom you wouldn't think it of, had that sort of picture in their bedrooms.

Mary was now coming up the stairs again, with a glass half full of liquid. She brought it to him.

'No, you drink it,' he urged, and Mary sipped the brandy.

'I've finished — I've finished,' he said as he watched her, 'she's quite comfortable now.'

The girl looked her silent thanks at him, again holding out the glass. 'No, sup it yourself,' he said; but as she stood in the dim light, regarding him with her strange gaze, and still offering the drink, he took it from her, drained it at a gulp and put the glass upon the chest, beside the candle. 'She's quite comfortable now. I'm very grieved, Mary,' he said with awkward kindness, 'about all this trouble that's come on you.'

She was motionless as a wax image, as if she had died in her steps, her hand still extended as when he took the glass from it. So piercing was her gaze that his own drifted from her face and took in again the objects in the room, the washstand, the candle on the chest, the little pink picture. The wind beat upon the ivy outside the window as if a monstrous whip were lashing its slaves.

'You must notify the registrar,' he began again, 'but you must see the doctor first.'

'I've waited for him all day,' Mary whispered, 'all day. The nurse will come again soon. She went home to rest in the night.' She turned towards the bed. 'She has only been ill a week.'

'Yes?' he lamely said. 'Dear me, it is sudden.'

'I must see the doctor,' she continued.

'I'll drive you over to him in my gig.' He was eager to do that.

'I don't know,' said Mary slowly.

'Yes, I'll do that, soon's you're ready. Mary,' he fumbled with his speech, 'I'm not wanting to pry into your affairs, or anything as don't concern me, but how are you going to get along now? Have you got any relations?'

'No,' the girl shook her head, 'No.'

'That's bad. What was you thinking of doing? How has she left you — things were in a baddish way, weren't they?'

'O no,' Mary looked up quickly. 'She has left me very well off. I shall go on with the farm; there's the old man and the boy — they've gone to a wedding to-day; I shall go on with it. She was so thoughtful for me, and I would not care to leave all this, I love it.'

'But you can't do it by yourself, alone?'

'No. I'm to get a man to superintend, a working bailiff,' she said.

'O!' And again they were silent. The girl went to the bed and lifted the covering. She saw the bound arm and then drew the quilt tenderly over the dead face. Witlow picked up his hat and found himself staring again at the pink picture. Mary took the candle preparatory to descending the stairs. Suddenly the higgler turned to her and ventured: 'Did you know as she once asked me to marry you?' he blurted.

Her eyes turned from him, but he guessed — he could feel that she *had* known.

'I've often wondered why,' he murmured, 'why she wanted that.'

'She didn't,' said the girl.

That gave pause to the man; he felt stupid at once, and roved his fingers in a silly way along the roughened nap of his hat.

'Well, she asked me to,' he bluntly protested.

'She knew,' Mary's voice was no louder than a sigh, 'that you were courting another girl, the one you married.'

'But, but,' stuttered the honest higgler, 'if she knew that why did she want for me to marry you?'

'She didn't,' said Mary again; and again, in the pause, he did silly things to his hat. How shy this girl was, how lovely in her modesty and grief!

'I can't make tops or bottoms of it,' he said, 'but she asked me, as sure as God's my maker.'

'I know. It was me, I wanted it.'

'You!' he cried, 'you wanted to marry me!'

The girl bowed her head, lovely in her grief and modesty: 'She was against it, but I made her ask you.'

'And I hadn't an idea that you cast a thought on me,' he murmured. 'I feared it was a sort of trick she was playing on me. I didn't understand, I had no idea that you knew about it even. And so I didn't ever ask you.'

'O, why not, why not? I was fond of you then,' whispered she. 'Mother tried to persuade me against it, but I was fond of you — then.'

He was in a queer distress and confusion: 'O, if

you'd only tipped me a word, or given me a sort of look,' he sighed, 'O, Mary!'

She said no more but went downstairs. He followed her and immediately fetched the lamps from his gig. As he lit the candles: 'How strange,' Mary said, 'that you should come back just as I most needed help. I am very grateful.'

'Mary, I'll drive you to the doctor's now.'

She shook her head; she was smiling.

'Then I'll stay till the nurse comes.'

'No, you must go. Go at once.'

He picked up the two lamps, and turning at the door, said: 'I'll come again to-morrow.' Then the wind rushed into the room: 'Good-bye,' she cried, shutting the door quickly behind him.

He drove away in deep darkness, the wind howling, his thoughts strange and bitter. He had thrown away a love, a love that was dumb and hid itself. By God, he had thrown away a fortune, too! And he had forgotten all about his real errand until now, forgotten all about the loan! Well; let it go; give it up. He would give up higgling; he would take on some other job; a bailiff, a working bailiff, that was the job as would suit him, a working bailiff. Of course, there was Sophy; but still — Sophy!

Fishmonger's Fiddle (1925)

DUSKY RUTH

AT the close of an April day, chilly and wet, the traveller came to a country town. In the Cotswolds, though the towns are small and sweet and the inns snug, the general habit of the land is bleak and bare. He had newly come upon upland roads so void of human affairs, so lonely, that they might have been made for some forgotten uses by departed men, and left to the unwitting passage of such strangers as himself. Even the unending walls, built of old rough laminated rock, that detailed the far-spreading fields, had grown very old again in their courses; there were dabs of darkness, buttons of moss, and fossils on every stone. He had passed a few neighbourhoods, sometimes at the crook of a stream, or at the cross of debouching roads, where old habitations, their gangrenated thatch riddled with bird holes, had been not so much erected as just spattered about the places. Beyond these signs an odd lark or blackbird, the ruckle of partridges, or the nifty gallop of a hare, had been the only mitigation of the living loneliness that was almost as profound by day as by night. But the traveller had a care for such times and places. There are men who love to gaze with the mind at things that can never be seen, feel at least the throb of a beauty that will never be known, and hear over immense bleak reaches the echo of that which is no celestial music, but only their own hearts' vain cries; and though his garments clung to him like clay it was with deliberate questing step that the traveller trod the single street of the town, and at last entered the inn, shuffling his shoes in the doorway for a moment and striking the raindrops from his hat. Then he turned into a small smoking-room. Leather-lined benches, much worn, were fixed to the wall under the window and in other odd corners and nooks behind mahogany tables. One wall was furnished with all the congenial gear of a bar, but without any intervening counter. Opposite a bright fire was burning, and a neatly-dressed young woman sat before it in a Windsor chair, staring at the flames. There was no other inmate of the room, and as he entered the girl rose up and greeted him. He found that he could be accommodated for the night, and in a few moments his hat and scarf were removed and placed inside the fender, his wet overcoat was taken to the kitchen, the landlord, an old fellow, was lending him a roomy pair of slippers, and a maid was setting supper in an adjoining room.

He sat while this was doing and talked to the barmaid. She had a beautiful but rather mournful face as it was lit by the firelight, and when her glance was turned away from it her eyes had a piercing brightness. Friendly and well spoken as she was, the melancholy in her aspect was noticeable — perhaps it was the dim room, or the wet day, or the long hours ministering a multitude of cocktails to thirsty gallantry.

When he went to his supper he found cheering food and drink, with pleasant garniture of silver and mahogany. There were no other visitors, he was to be alone; blinds were drawn, lamps lit, and the fire at his back was comforting. So he sat long about his meal until a white-faced maid came to clear the table, discoursing to him about country things as she busied about the room. It was a long, narrow room, with a sideboard and the door at one end and the fireplace at the other. A bookshelf, almost devoid of books, contained a number of plates; the long wall that faced the windows was almost destitute of pictures, but there were hung upon it, for some inscrutable but doubtless sufficient reason, many dish-covers, solidly shaped, of the kind held in such mysterious regard and known as 'willow pattern'; one was even hung upon the face of a map. Two musty prints were mixed with them, presentments of horses having a stilted extravagant physique and bestridden by images of inhuman and incommunicable dignity, clothed in whiskers, coloured jackets, and tight white breeches.

He took down the books from the shelf, but his interest was speedily exhausted, and the almanacs, the county directory, and various guide-books were exchanged for the *Cotswold Chronicle*. With this, having drawn the deep chair to the hearth, he whiled away the time. The newspaper amused him with its advertisements of stock shows, farm auctions, travelling quacks and conjurers, and there was a lengthy account of the execution of a local felon, one Timothy Bridger, who had murdered an infant in some shameful circumstances. This dazzling crescendo proved rather trying to the traveller; he threw down the paper. The town was all as quiet as the hills, and he could hear no sounds in the house. He got up and went across the hall to the smoke-room. The door was shut, but there was light within, and he entered. The girl sat there much as he had seen her on his arrival, still alone, with feet on fender. He shut the door behind him, sat down, and crossing his legs puffed at his pipe, admired the snug little room and the pretty figure of the girl, which he could do without embarrassment, as her meditative head, slightly bowed, was turned away from him. He could see something of her, too, in the mirror at the bar, which repeated also the agreeable contours of bottles of coloured wines and rich liqueurs — so entrancing in form and aspect that they seemed destined to charming histories, even in disuse — and those of familiar outline containing mere spirits or small beer, for which are reserved the harsher destinies of base oils, horse medicines, disinfectants, and cold tea. There were coloured glasses for bitter wines, white glasses for sweet, a tiny leaden sink beneath them, and the four black handles of the beer engines.

The girl wore a light blouse of silk, a short skirt of black velvet, and a pair of very thin silk stockings that showed the flesh of instep and shin so plainly that he could see they were reddened by the warmth of the fire. She had on a pair of dainty cloth shoes with high heels, but what was wonderful about her was the heap of rich black hair piled at the back of her head and shadowing the dusky neck. He sat puffing his pipe and letting the loud tick of the clock fill the quiet room. She did not stir and he could move no muscle. It was as if he had been willed to come there and wait silently. That, he felt now, had been his desire all the evening; and here, in her presence, he was more strangely stirred in a few short minutes than by any event he could remember.

In youth he had viewed women as futile, pitiable things that grew long hair, wore stays and garters, and prayed incomprehensible prayers. Viewing them in the stalls of the theatre from his vantage-point in the gallery, he always disliked the articulation of their naked shoulders. But still, there was a god in the sky, a god with flowing hair and exquisite eyes, whose one stride with an ardour grandly rendered took him across the whole round hemisphere to which his buoyant limbs were bound like spokes to the eternal rim and axle, his bright hair burning in the pity of the sunsets and tossing in the anger of the dawns.

Master traveller had indeed come into this room to

be with this woman, and she as surely desired him, and for all its accidental occasion it was as if he, walking the ways of the world, had suddenly come upon what, what so imaginable with all permitted reverence as, well, just a shrine; and he, admirably humble, bowed the instant head.

Were there no other people within? The clock indicated a few minutes to nine. He sat on, still as stone, and the woman might have been of wax for all the movement or sound she made. There was allurement in the air between them; he had forborne his smoking, the pipe grew cold between his teeth. He waited for a look from her, a movement to break the trance of silence. No footfall in street or house, no voice in the inn but the clock, beating away as if pronouncing a doom. Suddenly it rasped out nine large notes, a bell in the town repeated them dolefully, and a cuckoo no further than the kitchen mocked them with three times three. After that came the weak steps of the old landlord along the hall, the slam of doors, the clatter of lock and bolt, and then the silence returning unendurably upon them.

He arose and stood behind her; he touched the black hair. She made no movement or sign. He pulled out two or three combs and, dropping them into her lap, let the whole mass tumble about his hands. It had a curious harsh touch in the unravelling, but was so full and shining; black as a rook's wings it was. He slid his palms through it. His fingers searched it and fought with its fine strangeness; into his mind there travelled a serious thought, stilling his wayward fancy — this was no wayward fancy, but a rite accomplishing itself! (*Run, run, silly man, y'are lost!*) But having got so far he burnt his boats, leaned over, and drew her face back to him. And at that, seizing his wrists, she gave him back ardour for ardour, pressing his hands to her bosom, while the kiss was sealed and sealed again. Then she sprang up and picking his scarf and hat from the fender said:

'I have been drying them for you, but the hat has shrunk a bit, I'm sure — I tried it on.'

He took them from her and put them behind him; he leaned lightly back upon the table, holding it with both his hands behind him; he could not speak.

'Aren't you going to thank me for drying them?' she asked, picking her combs from the rug and repinning her hair.

'I wonder why we did that?' he asked, shamedly.

'It is what I'm thinking too,' she said.

'You were so beautiful about ... about it, you know.'

She made no rejoinder, but continued to bind her hair, looking brightly at him under her brows. When she had finished she went close to him.

'Will that do?'

'I'll take it down again.'

'No, no, the old man or the old woman will be coming in.'

'What of that?' he said, taking her into his arms. 'Tell me your name.'

She shook her head, but she returned his kisses and stroked his hair and shoulders with beautifully melting gestures.

'What is your name? I want to call you by your name,' he said. 'I can't keep calling you Lovely Woman, Lovely Woman.'

Again she shook her head and was dumb.

'I'll call you Ruth then, Dusky Ruth, Ruth of the black, beautiful hair.'

'That is a nice-sounding name — I knew a deaf and

dumb girl named Ruth; she went to Nottingham and married an organ grinder — but I should like it for my name.'

'Then I give it to you.'

'Mine is so ugly.'

'What is it?'

Again the shaken head and the burning caress.

'Then you shall be Ruth; will you keep that name?'

'Yes, if you give me the name I will keep it for you.'

Time had indeed taken them by the forelock, and they looked upon a ruddled world.

'I stake my one talent,' he said jestingly, 'and behold it returns me fortyfold; I feel like the boy who catches three mice with one piece of cheese.'

At ten o'clock the girl said:

'I must go and see how *they* are getting on,' and she went to the door.

'Are we keeping them up?'

She nodded.

'Are you tired?'

'No, I am not tired.' She looked at him doubtfully.

'We ought not to stay in here; go into the coffee room and I'll come there in a few minutes.'

'Right,' he whispered gaily, 'we'll sit up all night.'

She stood at the door for him to pass out, and he crossed the hall to the other room. It was in darkness except for the flash of the fire. Standing at the hearth he lit a match for the lamp, but paused at the globe; then he extinguished the match.

'No, it's better to sit in the firelight.'

He heard voices at the other end of the house that seemed to have a chiding note in them.

'Lord,' he thought, 'is she getting into a row?'

Then her steps came echoing over the stone floor of

the hall; she opened the door and stood there with a lighted candle in her hand; he stood at the other end of the room, smiling.

'Good night,' she said.

'O no, no! come along,' he protested, but not moving from the hearth.

'Got to go to bed,' she answered.

'Are they angry with you?'

'No.'

'Well, then, come over here and sit down.'

'Got to go to bed,' she said again, but she had meanwhile put her candlestick upon the little sideboard and was trimming the wick with a burnt match.

'O, come along, just half an hour,' he protested. She did not answer but went on prodding the wick of the candle.

'Ten minutes, then,' he said, still not going towards her.

'Five minutes,' he begged.

She shook her head, and picking up the candlestick turned to the door. He did not move, he just called her name: 'Ruth!'

She came back then, put down the candlestick and tiptoed across the room until he met her. The bliss of the embrace was so poignant that he was almost glad when she stood up again and said with affected steadiness, though he heard the tremor in her voice:

'I must get you your candle.'

She brought one from the hall, set it on the table in front of him, and struck the match.

'What is my number?' he asked.

'Number six room,' she answered, prodding the wick vaguely with her match, while a slip of white wax dropped over the shoulder of the new candle. 'Number six . . . next to mine.'

The match burnt out; she said abruptly 'Good-night,' took up her own candle and left him there.

In a few moments he ascended the stairs and went into his room. He fastened the door, removed his coat, collar, and slippers, but the rack of passion had seized him and he moved about with no inclination to sleep. He sat down, but there was no medium of distraction. He tried to read the newspaper which he had carried up with him, and without realizing a single phrase he forced himself to read again the whole account of the execution of the miscreant Bridger. When he had finished this he carefully folded the paper, and stood up, listening. He went to the parting wall and tapped thereon with his finger tips. He waited half a minute, one minute, two minutes, there was no answering sign. He tapped again, more loudly, with his knuckles, but there was no response, and he tapped many times. He opened his door as noiselessly as possible; along the dark passage there were slips of light under the other doors, the one next his own, and the one beyond that. He stood in the corridor listening to the rumble of old voices in the farther room, the old man and his wife going to their rest. Holding his breath fearfully he stepped to *her* door and tapped gently upon it. There was no answer, but he could somehow divine her awareness of him; he tapped again; she moved to the door and whispered 'No, no, go away.' He turned the handle, the door was locked.

'Let me in,' he pleaded. He knew she was standing there an inch or two beyond him.

'Hush,' she called softly. 'Go away, the old woman has ears like a fox.'

He stood silent for a moment.

'Unlock it,' he urged; but he got no further reply, and feeling foolish and baffled he moved back to his own room, cast his clothes from him, doused the candle and crept into the bed with soul as wild as a storm-swept forest, his heart beating a vagrant summons. The room filled with strange heat, there was no composure for mind or limb, nothing but flaming visions and furious embraces.

'Morality . . . what is it but agreement with your own soul?'

So he lay for two hours — the clocks chimed twelve — listening with foolish persistency for *her* step along the corridor, fancying every light sound — and the night was full of them — was her hand upon the door.

Suddenly, then — and it seemed as if his very heart would abash the house with its thunder — he could hear distinctly someone knocking on the wall. He got quickly from his bed and stood at his door, listening. Again the knocking was heard and having half-clothed himself he crept into the passage, which was now in utter darkness, trailing his hand along the wall until he felt her door; it was standing open. He entered her room and closed the door behind him. There was not the faintest gleam of light, he could see nothing. He whispered 'Ruth!' and she was standing there. She touched him, but not speaking. He put out his hands, and they met round her neck; her hair was flowing in its great wave about her; he put his lips to her face and found that her eyes were streaming with tears, salt and strange and disturbing. In the close darkness he put his arms about her with no thought but to comfort her; one hand had plunged through the long harsh tresses and the other across her hips before he realized that she was ungowned; then he was aware of the softness of her breasts and the cold naked sleekness of her shoulders. But she was crying there, crying silently with great tears, her strange sorrow stifling his desire.

'Ruth, Ruth, my beautiful dear!' he murmured soothingly. He felt for the bed with one hand, and turning back the quilt and sheets he lifted her in as easily as a mother does her child, replaced the bedding, and, in his clothes, he lay stretched beside her comforting her. They lay so, innocent as children, for an hour, when she seemed to have gone to sleep. He rose then and went silently to his room, full of weariness.

In the morning he breakfasted without seeing her, but as he had business in the world that gave him just an hour longer at the inn before he left it for good and all, he went into the smoke-room and found her. She greeted him with curious gaze, but merrily enough, for there were other men there now, farmers, a butcher, a registrar, an old, old man. The hour passed, but not these men, and at length he donned his coat, took up his stick, and said good-bye. Her shining glances followed him to the door, and from the window as far as they could view him.

Adam and Eve and Pinch Me (1921)

SPEAKING LIKENESSES

ONCE upon a time there was a man in a beaver hat who lived to a ripe old age in a market town where they sold geese and hot pies on Tuesdays. He had a most beautiful name, but his name does not signify because he himself had grown old and ugly. It is well known that when beautiful people have ugly names like Offal or Bootsole or Maggotty they do not care to have such words repeated to them because it might spoil the flavour of their own beauty, and so I do not care to repeat this ugly man's beautiful name, in case it should spoil his appearance. Well, this man died — I forget what he died of, but I think it was something difficult to mention — and was put to rest in the churchyard, just by the bridge where the arbutus tree is bending over the river. A white stone stands there with his name carved upon it in one long important line; I won't tell you what it is, even now, but it begins with an A and has two Xs in it.

At the proper time another man in a beaver hat who was what is called an attorney-at-law came along and ordered the dead man's belongings to be sold up. He was a very wise man and I believe his name was Jones. Amongst the belongings in a cupboard he found the usual things you always find in such places, kettle-cosies, fiddlesticks, baskets for keeping onions carefully in, and a little something wrapped up in tissue paper bound round with a thread of green silk.

'Now what can this be?'

The attorney saw that it had a white label hanging down, and on the label was written in the best copy-hand style the one word WHISTLE. When he opened it he found it was a whistle, a wooden one with a pea in it.

The attorney put the whistle to his lips and blew so roughly on it that the little pea popped up out of the hole in the whistle and disappeared.

'Bless me to goodness!' the attorney cried. 'Where has the stupid thing gone?'

He searched and he searched but could not find it and so he gave it up.

'Anyway,' said the attorney, 'the pea cannot be of any value now, for it must have become shrivelled and useless for any musical purpose.'

Then the attorney came across an old book of the most rare kind, nearly a hundred years old but not quite, which had four coloured pictures in it.

At once he cried: 'Ho! ho! I like this, yes, I like it.' And when he had taken a glance round to see that nobody was watching him he put the book in his pocket and took it home to his house which had KNUTE painted on the gate. KNUTE was a house with a bent roof and a crooked chimney; it was so small that saucy boys often crossed out the word KNUTE and wrote KNAT instead, until the attorney swore to have the law of any more such ruffians. But whatever you called the house, it certainly had diamond windows and a garden of old-fashioned flowers like the watch-horn, the cornspingle, and the kill-me-tailor, which are very rare and seldom seen nowadays. The gate itself was so happy that it screamed with delight when it was opened, and the path of gravel stones gurgled with joy at every step of your foot upon it.

The attorney went into his house. He took off his hat. He laid it upon the table. And, do you know, there was the lost pea lodged in the brim of his beaver hat! He did not want the pea any more so he flipped it off with his finger, and away it flew again, clean out of the open window, and fell into the garden bed. Then he took the book out of his pocket and gazed upon the pictures again. They were small, but beautiful, four in all; one of a flower, one of a bird, one of a lady, one of a tiger, and at the bottom of each was engraved its name:

ROSE

GOLDSPINK

AMARYLLIS

TIGER

They were what are called speaking likenesses, and the colours of all of them were so wonderfully painted by hand that each glowed as though it was alive and real. That was partly because the book had seldom been opened and thus the colours had been preserved. The attorney cut the four little pictures out of the book and took them to a man.

'Can you frame these pictures for me?'

'Yes,' answered the man.

'In gold frames?'

The man said: 'Yes.'

'How much will you charge?'

The man told him what his charges would be.

'Done!' said the attorney. 'And as quickly as you can, please.'

When the man had finished framing the pictures the attorney took them home and hung them on the wall of his room. How splendidly they glowed! He clapped his hands in admiration.

'Beautiful!' he cried. 'So rich and real! And yet how much nicer than real, for the flower will never fade, the bird cannot fly away, the lady is for ever young, and the tiger recalls the infinite mysteries of creation.'

Day by day the sun shone upon the wall where they

reposed, and day by day the attorney clasped his hands under his coat tails and rocked on his heels and toes, murmuring with happiness: 'Yah, how interesting it is.'

Now the little pea had fallen into a furrow in the ground below the window, and taking root it sprouted and began to grow into a plant of much promise, swaying graciously with delicate airs, growing taller and taller, and in the course of time sprays of white flowers appeared on its stem, shaking a tender odour around and enticing the bees, until one day it managed to peep over the sill of the open window and observed the four little pictures on the wall.

'My dears!' exclaimed the pea plant in a merry tone, 'How do you do?'

Now you must understand that a sad thing had been happening; although the attorney had not noticed it, the colours of the pictures had faded in the sunlight. The once bright rose was pale, the goldspink was now no prettier than a common sparrow, the lady's cheeks were sallow as though she suffered from jaundice, and the striped tiger looked like a white cat with twenty black ribs. Each picture saw that the other three were faded; but it did not realize its own similar plight, and so they all held their heads as proudly as before, though their souls were dejected and they often quarrelled among themselves.

'Who are you?' they asked, and the pea plant replied: 'Do you not remember me? When we all lived together? In the old days? With our master who had so many fiddlesticks he didn't know what to do?'

They answered: 'No, we do not remember.'

'Well, well.' The pea plant smiled a compassionate smile: 'You were only pictures, of course, printed and coloured and shut up in a book of our master's who was a genius.'

'We never noticed that.'

'Genius is never noticed,' said the pea plant, 'it is only believed in. He was a musician. So was I. We loved each other so dearly that at one kiss from his lips I always burst into song — ah, finer than any bird.'

'Good heavens! Hark at that!' muttered the goldspink. 'I could surely crunch some peas now!' And the others made rude remarks, declaring that their position in life compared with a mere vegetable's was of superior importance and universally admired.

'Pooh!' The pea plant jeered at them. 'You have no memories, you are dull.' And it turned its back on them and gazed away at the cornspingles and the kill-me-tailors.

Rose was indignant. Ever since receiving her golden frame she had been ambitious, preening herself and trying to grow into a real blossom. She even looked down upon her companions, and annoyed them by her lofty disdain. Now she sighed morosely and exclaimed aloud:

'What is the use of a bird that cannot sing?'

'I have wings, lovely wings,' the goldspink ventured to reply.

'I can only see *one*,' sneered the rose.

'That's because I am painted sideways,' the bird explained. 'You should see me on the other side!'

'Can't you turn round?'

'No. Neither can you, if it comes to that.'

'And you can't fly? O, stupidest, you cannot even fly!'

'Well, but neither can I fall down, or be shot, or be eaten by cats,' the bird retorted brusquely.

The tiger now half-opened its horrid jaws, but no sound came from them. Chuckling demurely the pea plant slyly poked its head in at the window and asked: 'What is the use of a flower that has no perfume?'

But in bobbing back again it scratched its little chin on the window sill so sharply that it cried out: 'O! O!'

'I have my colour,' the rose proudly replied, 'and a most distinguished figure.'

'That's paint,' muttered the bird. 'O, how I could crunch some peas!'

'Quarrelling again!' exclaimed the lady Amaryllis. 'I am sure you have nothing much to quarrel about compared with poor me. Observe: I am only a head and shoulders — what is the use of that? I declare I feel my limitations most keenly. I do not know whether I am intended to be skinny or plump . . .'

The tiger opened its jaws again and emitted a faint sigh; a sigh so soft that it was scarcely heard, although the puff of its breath beclouded the whole glass of its picture frame.

'. . . I have no hands,' the lady went on, 'I cannot dress my hair when it gets awry, I haven't even a pocket handkerchief. I don't want any wings, I'm sure, but I *should* like some feet and legs. I fancy my figure would be as distinguished as anyone's.'

Again the tiger opened its jaws; the rose became quite enraged with it.

'What is that creature trying to do? Look at the stupid wretch! What is the use of a tiger that can neither rend nor roar?'

'Why, pardon me,' Amaryllis protested, 'that is surely the best *kind* of tiger!'

The pea plant popped its head in at the window again. 'Boh!' it said, 'you should have stayed where you were bright and happy. You have no memories, you are dull.'

Each little picture fumed with annoyance, even the tiger fumed, and the rose actually hissed. At that moment they all heard the garden gate scream with delight as it swung on its hinges and the gravel stones gurgle happily as some feet trampled upon them. It was the attorney. He paused in the garden, just outside the window, and the four little pictures could see the half of him, all the way up and down from the silver buckle on his beaver hat to the fob in his embroidered waistcoat.

'Heigho!' How happily he sighed. He stood clasping his hands under his coat tails, and rocked on his heels and toes. Amaryllis almost smiled, and even the tiger looked sweet. But suddenly, without warning, the attorney flung up his arms and uttered a screech of fury:

'Zounds, what do I see!'

The four little pictures very nearly shivered. The attorney's eyes flashed fire, he gnashed his teeth:

'By my father's hat! what is this common pea thing doing in my garden? Pah! Come out, you holy cossack!'

With one wrench he tore the pea plant up out of the sunny bed, crushing it cruelly, and flung it into a bin amongst a lot of low bottles and the bones of a sheep's head.

Coughing and hawking, he spat so fiercely that the very cornspingles flinched. He brushed his hands, muttering as he did so: 'Bah! Brrrr!'

The scentless rose, the bird with only one wing, the tiger with a sigh, and the agreeable portion of lady, were all hushed into silence and never spoke again.

Ninepenny Flute (1937)

SILVER CIRCUS

HANS SIEBENHAAR, a street porter, is basking on his stool in a fine street of Vienna, for anybody to hire for any sort of job. He is a huge man with a bulbous hairless face that somehow recalls a sponge, and this sponge is surmounted by a flat peaked hat encircled by a white band bearing these words in red: *Wiener Dienstmann*. His voice, which we shall hear later on, is a vast terrifying voice, that seems to tear a rent in Space itself. At fifty years of age Hans is a conspicuous man. But, a street porter! Not a profitable way of life, yet it must serve, and must continue to serve. It is a hot July morn, tropical; there are many noises but no one speaks. The fruit-stall women are silent and hidden; they have pinned newspapers around the edges of their big red umbrellas. It is stifling, languorous; one thinks of lilac, of cool sea, of white balloons; the populace tears off its hat, fans itself desperately, sips ice in the cafés, and still perspires. The very street sounds are injurious to the mind. The drivers of carts wear only their breeches, their bodies are brown as a Polynesian's and lovely to behold.

Just such a day it was as the day twelve months gone when Mitzi Siebenhaar, his second wife, had run away with that Julius Damjancsics. Yes, please very much, she had left him. Hans took off his hat. After contemplating its interior as though it was a coffer of extraordinary mystery, he sighed huskily into it. How was it possible to understand such an accident? Smoothing his brown bald skull with the other hand he collected so much sweat upon his hairy freckled fingers that as he shook them the drops simply splashed upon the pavement. Young Mitzi! It was her youth. Ah, God bless, she had the pull of him there, a whole fifteen years, fifteen years younger; youth as well as beauty, beauty as well as youth. At thirty-five she was as lovely as a girl, fitful and furious just like a girl, so he was only able to keep her for one little year; that is to say, keep her faithful, to himself. One little year! That is not long, but for a man of fifty it is so difficult, yes; but then Julius Damjancsics was just as old. And she had gone off with him! What could she see in Julius Damjancsics! How was it possible to understand such an accident! They had all been friends together, and Julius could play the mandolin, but Hans could pound him into dust. What could she see in Julius Damjancsics? He could crush him in one fist, like a gherkin. If he had caught them — but that was difficult too. Belgrade he had gone to, for Julius Damjancsics was a Serbian, and Buda-Pesth he had gone to, for Mitzi was Hungarian, but this Julius was a wandering fellow and very deceitful. So. Well, it was pitiful to think of in such hot weather, there was nothing to be done, he had come back to Vienna. And now here he was brooding, here he was groaning; pitiful to think of. At last he said to himself: 'Let us wipe our tears and forget that Christ died. Gloria Patri et Filio et Spiritu Sancto', he murmured, for he was a good catholic man, as Father Adolf of Stefans Dom could testify.

'Porter!' cried a voice.

Hans looked up quickly and put on his hat.

'Sir,' said he.

A big man, with a big important foreign face, and fat and flourishing appearance, and shiny black boots with grey cloth tops, stood as it were examining the porter. Although the boots were fastened with what appeared to be pearl buttons, they were rather uncared for, but to offset this a large gold watchchain was lavishly displayed, with jewelled tiepin and studs. The man's fists were in his trousers pockets; he twirled a long thin cigar between his rich red lips. Immense and significant, he might have been a Turk or a Tartar, but he was neither; he was the boss of a Roumanian Circus.

'Come with me, I want you,' and the huge Hans followed the circus man to a *bier garten* where another man was waiting who might have been a Tartar or a Turk. He called him Peter, he was certainly his brother, and Peter called him Franz. All three sat down and drank together.

'Tell me, Hans Siebenhaar,' said Franz, 'you are a strong man?'

'Yes, I am a strong man, that is so.'

'You have a good voice?'

'Please ...' Hans paused. 'I am no singer, not much.'

'Ah! No, no, no. You have a strong voice to speak, to shout, you can make great sounds with your voice?'

'O ay,' Hans agreed. 'I have a strong voice, that is so, very strong, I can make a noise.' And there and then he accorded them a succession of hearty bellows in testimony. There was only one other occupant of the *bier garten*, a man with an Emperor Franz-Josef sort of face and white whiskers like the wings of an easy chair, who sat smoking a china pipe under an acacia tree. And he seemed to be deaf, for he did not take the slightest notice of the appalling outcry. Two waiters rushed with alarm into the garden, but Franz waved them away.

'Good,' said Franz reflectively. 'Listen now.' And sitting there between the brothers Hans heard them propound to him a scheme that smote him with amazement and bereft him of sympathy; it filled him indeed with any and every emotion but that of satisfaction. They wanted him, in brief, to become a tiger.

'No,' Hans was indignant, and he was contemptuous. 'I do not understand, but I do not do this.'

Not at once — they cried — not to-day. No, no. Plenty of time, a week's time in fact. And they would instruct him in the art of impersonating a tiger, they would rehearse him, and for a single performance, one night only, they would give him two hundred Austrian shillings. Peter the Turk declared it was far too much money. Franz the Tartar invoked his God.

There is more in this — thought Hans — than strokes my ear; I have to beware of something. Aloud he inquired: 'Two hundred shillings?'

'Two hundred,' said Peter.

'Shillings,' echoed Franz, scratching the table with a wooden toothpick.

'And, please very much, I am to do?'

They told him what he was to do. He was to be sewn up in the skin of a tiger; he was to enact the part of a tiger in their menagerie; he was to receive two hundred shillings. Very, very simple for a strong man. Hans Siebenhaar was to be sewn up in the tiger's hide for two hundred shillings; he was to prance and fight and hideously roar in the best way he knew so that the hearts of the audience be rocked within them and fly into their throats — and the two hundred shillings was his. It was his voice, it was because of his great bellowing tigerish voice that they had come to him. Such a voice was worth some riches to them, and so they were going to pay two hundred shillings for his services.

'Two hundred shillings?' murmured Hans.

'Two hundred,' said Peter, and Franz said, 'Two hundred.'

It is not — thought Hans — to be sneezed at, but

there is more in this than strokes my hearing; I must be wary.

'Why do you not have,' he asked them, 'a real tiger?'

'But we had!' they both cried.

'And now he is dead,' said Peter.

'A real proper tiger,' Franz declared.

'But now he is dead,' repeated his brother. 'Ah, he had paws like a hassock.'

'And the ferocity!'

'Beautiful,' said Peter. 'He died of grief.'

'No, no, no,' objected Franz. 'I would not say that of this tiger.'

'But yes,' affirmed Peter. 'Of grief. He loved me, and lately I married again.'

'The heart was broken, yes, perhaps,' Franz admitted.

'His voice died away like a little whistle,' there was sorrow in Peter's eyes. 'No fury.'

'Two hundred shillings,' said Franz.

'Brrr-o-o-o-owh!' Hans suddenly roared, and skipping up he began capering and pawing madly about the garden. 'Ookah, pookah, boddle, oddle, moddle, miowh!' he roared.

The deaf old gentleman with the Franz-Josef whiskers gently laid his china pipe on the table before him; he neither observed nor heeded Hans, he only put his fingers into his mouth and extracted his false teeth. These he calmly examined, as though they were a foreign substance he had never noticed before and was wondering how it came to be there. Hans began crashing over the tables and chairs; waiters rushed into the garden and, flinging themselves upon the perspiring maniac, rolled him over into a corner.

'That is good,' cried Franz, 'very good!'

'Absolutely,' Peter said, 'absolutely!'

Three waiters clung to Hans Siebenhaar with the clear intention of throttling him.

'Enough!' shouted Franz. 'Let him go,' and with his powerful hands he dragged two of the waiters from the prostrate body of Hans as you would draw two pins from a pin-cushion, and likewise did Peter do with the other waiter.

'It is all right,' said Franz and Peter said it was quite all right. They gave the waiters a few coins and soothed them. In the meantime Hans had resumed his seat, and the deaf old gentleman was replacing his teeth.

To Hans the brothers said: 'Listen,' and Hans listened. Their circus-menagerie was now on view in The Prater, and at the festival next week they had contemplated to stage a novel performance, nothing less than a combat between a lion and a tiger — ah, good business! — but just at this critical moment what does their tiger do?

'It dies,' suggested Hans.

'Dies,' agreed Franz. 'It dies. So now!'

'Yes, now?' Hans said, and nodded.

'You must be our tiger, that is the simple fact of the business. You have the voice of a tiger, and the character. You will get the two hundred shillings. Hooray! It is like lapping honey, yes.'

'But what is this?' cried Hans. 'To fight a lion!'

'Pooh,' Peter said. 'It is more friendly and harmless than any kitten.'

'No,' said Hans, 'No.'

'Yes,' said Franz. 'Yes. It is, it is but a caterpillar, I tell you.'

'No!' shouted Hans.

'It has no teeth.'

'Not I,' cried the intended victim.

'It has been in our family for a hundred years.'

'Never,' declared Hans with absolute finality, and he got up as if to go. But the brothers seized each an arm and held him down in his chair.

'Have no fear, Mr. Siebenhaar; it will love you. Two hundred and fifty shillings!'

'No, I will not—ha!'

'Mr. Siebenhaar, we can guarantee you. Three hundred shillings,' said Peter.

'And fifty,' added Franz.

'Three hundred and fifty!' repeated Hans. 'So? But what? I cannot fight a lion. No, no. I am not a woman, I have my courage, but what is three hundred and fifty shillings for my life's blood and bones?' In short, a lion was not the kind of thing Mr. Siebenhaar was in the habit of fighting.

'Ach! Your blood and bones will be as safe as they are in your trousers. You will not have to fight this lion . . .'

'No, I will not—ha!'

'. . . you have only to play with it. This lion does not fight, Mr. Siebenhaar; it will not, it cannot.'

'Why so?'

'It is too meek, it is like a lamb in a meadow that cries baa. You have only to prance about before it and roar and roar, to make a noise and a fuss. It will cringe before you. Have no fear of him. A show, you understand, make a show.'

'I understand a show,' said Hans, 'but, please very much, permit me, I will not make a spectacle of my blood and bones.'

'So help me heaven!' shouted Franz, exasperated, 'do you think we want your bones!'

'Not a knuckle!' cried Hans.

Peter intervened. 'You misunderstand us, Mr.

Siebenhaar; we desire only entertainment, we do not want a massacre.'

'You do not want a massacre!'

'A massacre is very well in its way, perhaps, in its time and place,' Peter continued, 'but a massacre is one thing, and this is another.'

'Thank you,' said Hans, 'it is very clear, that is very good.'

And Franz and Peter intimated that they were simple men of business whose only care it was to bring joy and jollity into the life of the Viennese populace; that the fury of the lion was a figment, its courage a mockery, its power a profanation of all men's cherished fears. If there was one animal in the world more deserving the kindness and pity of mankind, more subservient, more mercifully disposed than any other — Franz assured him — it was a lion. And if there was one lion among all lions more responsive to the symptoms of affection — added Peter — it was this identical lion. Was three hundred and fifty shillings nothing to him?

'No,' Hans conceded.

'Is it a bunch of beans?'

'No, no.'

'Three hundred and fifty shillings is three hundred and fifty shillings, is it not?' Peter questioned him; and Hans replied: 'For what is past, yes; but for what is yet to come, no. The future — pardon, gentlemen — does not lie in our behinds.'

'Three hundred and fifty shillings is three hundred and fifty shillings, it is not a bunch of beans,' said Franz severely. They had men in their employ who implored him on their knees to be honourably permitted to enact the part of this tiger, but they had not the physique, they had not the voice, and, if Mr. Siebenhaar would pardon him, they had not the artist's delicate touch. One thing he, Franz, was certain of: he knew an artist when he saw one, hence this three hundred and fifty shillings.

At the end of it all Hans once more determined to wipe his tears and forget that Christ died. In effect, he agreed to be sewn up on such and such a date in the tiger's hide and to make a manifestation with Messrs. Franz and Peter's ingenuous lion, on the solemnest possible undertaking that no harm should befall his own blood and bones.

'Thunder and lightning! What could harm you?'

'Good.'

And after parting from Hans, and when they were well out of hearing, Mr. Franz said, 'Ha, ha!' and Mr. Peter said, 'Ho, ho!'

II

Hans Siebenhaar had several rehearsals before the eventful day. Submitting himself to be sewn up in the tiger's skin, he dashed his paws upon the floor, pranced, gnashed, snarled, whirled his mechanical tail, and delivered himself of a gamut of howls eminently tigerish. Perfectly satisfactory.

'Where,' Hans would ask, 'do you keep this old lion?'

'Yes,' the brothers always replied, 'he is not well, he is sleeping; you see him next time.'

And thus it happened that Hans did not see his adversary until they met in the cage of battle. The morning of that day was dull and Hans too was dull, for on awaking he felt so strange, so very unwell, that he greatly feared he would have to send Franz word that he could not come to perform his tiger; but as the day wore on and brightened, Hans, sitting on his stool in the sunny street, brightened with it, and while thinking of the three hundred and fifty shillings his sickness left him. A nice sum of money that! And what would he do with it? Ah, please very much, what would he not have done if Mitzi, the shameless one, had not forsaken him! They might have gone again, as they had gone of old, on one of those excursions to the Wiener Wald. He liked excursions, they were beautiful. With their happy companions they could climb the mountains, prowl in the forest for raspberries and mushrooms, and at noon they would sit under the chestnuts in the *bier garten* at The Hunter's Meadow and lap the rich soup and gulp lager and talk of love and wealth and food and childhood. That was life, that was wonderful! Then they would all go and loaf in the grass and Mitzi would throw off her frock and lie half naked, browning her sleek shining body, while Julius Damjancsics thrummed his mandolin and they all murmured songs. Ah, such music! She loved it. She had a dimple behind each shoulder, a rare thing, very beautiful. In the cool of the evening there would be dancing, and they would be at Dreimarkstein in time to see the fireworks go up from The Prater — he liked fireworks, lovely. Or to the trotting races, they might go and win some more money, for when luck was on you the fancy could never deceive; beautiful horses, he loved horses. Or to the baths at Gänse-haufel — the things one could do with a little money! But there was no longer any Mitzi, she had gone with Julius Damjancsics. Gone wife, gone friend; there were no more journeys now. But a man with three hundred and fifty shillings need never lack companions, there was a lot of friendship in three hundred and fifty shillings. But that Mitzi — she was very beautiful, that little Mitzi.

So the day wore on and the evening came and The Prater began to sparkle with the lights of its many booths and cafés, to throb with its much music, for youth was gallant and gay and there was love and money in the world. It was the hour at last. Hans had been sewn up in the tiger's skin. Now he crouched in a corner of a shuttered cage, alone, trembling in darkness, seeing no one and seen of none. There was a door in the side of his cage that led into a large empty lighted cage, and beyond that was another like his own in which walked a lion. At a certain moment the doors of the end cages would be opened and he would have to go into that central cage and face that other beast. But no, he could not, he was limp with fear. To the stricken man came the excited voices of the people coming in to witness his calamity, and the harsh tones of the trumpeting band playing in pandemonium outside on the platform, where there was a large poster of a combat between a tiger and a lion. Hans recalled that the lion's teeth were buried in the tiger's belly amid the gushing blood, and it seemed that his very heart violently cried: 'No! No! Let me out!'

Beating upon the walls of his cage he gasped: 'In Christ's name, let me out!' but nobody heeded, no one replied, and although he tore at his tiger skin his paws were too cumbersome for him to free himself. He was in a trap, he knew now he had been trapped. For an eternal anguishing time the clamour went on, then that dreadful side door which led into the central cage slid quietly open. Hans saw that this cage was yet empty, the lion's door was still closed, he was to be the first to enter. But he averted his eyes, he lay in the corner of his trap and would not budge from it. Almighty heaven! was he going to sacrifice himself for a few pitiful pieces of silver that he had never seen and never would see! He was not fit to do it, he was an old man, even his wife Mitzi had left him for another man — did they not know that! And all day long he had been unwell, sick as a dog. As he lay in his corner, refusing to budge and sweating most intensely, a sharp iron spear came through the bars and pricked him savagely in the behind. With a yell he leaped up, trying to snatch the spear. He would use it, it would save him — but he could not grasp it with his giant paws. Then came bars of red hot iron searing him, and more spears; he was driven screaming into the central cage. The door closed behind him and he was left alone behind those terrible bars with a vast audience gazing at him. Then, ah then, in a frenzy, an epilepsy of fear, he dashed himself so violently against the bars that the crowd was spellbound. The band played riotously on, drowning his human cries. The other side door slid open, there was silence in that other cage, but he dared not turn to meet whatever was there; he crouched half swooning, until he caught sight of a face in the audience that he knew. Wonder of God! It was Mitzi, she herself! O but there was something to fight for now and he turned resolutely. As he did so there was a titter in the audience that surged into general laughter — the lion had come into the cage. Truly, it was a cadaverous lion. Without the least display of ferocity or fear it stepped quietly into that cage and fixed its strong eyes upon the eyes of its enemy. Not a leap did it make, not a roar did it give, it padded forwards quietly, and the tiger retreated before it. Thus they circled and circled round the cage. Would that mocking laughter never stop?

God! Hans could bear it no longer, he turned and faced the lion, in appearance bold though trembling in his soul. The lion paused too.

'Pater noster qui es in coelis,' Hans gasped involuntarily.

To his unspeakable astonishment he heard the lion
answer:

'Et ne nos inducas in tentationem. Sed libera nos a
malo.'

In an incredible flash Hans realized that the lion
also was a spurious creature like himself; his fears
vanished, he knew now the part he had to play, and he
hurled himself upon the lion, howling:

'Brrr-o-o-owh! Ookah, pookah, boddle, oddle,
moddle, miowh!'

Over they rolled, lion and tiger, together, and the
onlookers shook with mirth.

'Not so rough, brother!' cried a voice from inside the
lion, and the tones struck a strange echo in the mind of
Hans Siebenhaar. They disengaged and stood up on
all fours facing each other. From the moment's silence
that ensued there issued a piercing cry of fear from a
woman in the audience. Hans turned. The lion turned.
It was Mitzi, shrieking 'Julius! Watch out!' Hans'
throbbing mind caught at that fatal name, Julius. By
all the gods, was it possible! Heaven and hell, he would
tear the heart out of *that* lion! *Not so rough, brother!*
Ha, ha, he knew it now, that voice! Ho, ho! and with
a cruel leap he jumped with his heels savagely in the
middle of the lion's back, the back of Julius Damjancsics, thief of Mitzi the beloved of Hans, and down sank
the lion with the tiger tearing at its throat as fearfully
as any beast of the jungle. Ah, but how the people
applauded; this was good in spite of the deception!
They had paid to see a real lion and a real tiger con-
tending, and they felt defrauded, insulted; but this was
good, yes, it was very comical, good, good. When they
noticed a man's hand appear outside the flapping paw
of the tiger their joy was unbounded.

'Tear him!' they cried, as one cries to a hound with

a fox. 'Ha, ha, tear him!' And Hans' loosened hand ripped up the seam in the lion's neck, and his hand went searching within the rent for a throat to tear. At once the teeth of Julius ground themselves upon it; in a trice Hans' smallest finger was gone, severed. But Hans never uttered a cry, he gripped the throat with his wounded hand and crushed everlastingly upon it, moment after moment, until he knew that Julius Damjancsics was gone, and for ever, to hell or glory, whatever destiny had devised for him. The lion moved no more, it lay on its back with its hind legs crooked preposterously, its forelegs outspread like one cruci- fied. The people hushed their laughter as Hans slunk trembling and sweating from that droll oaf wrapped in a lion's skin. He was afraid of it now and he crawled on all fours to the bars of the cage. The thing behind him was awfully still. The onlookers were still. They were strange, as strange as death. Mitzi was there, craning forward, her face as pale as snow. Hans caught hold of the cage bars and lifted himself to his feet. The onlookers could hear wild tormenting sobs bursting from the throat of the tiger as it hung ridiculously there. The door of Hans' first cage now slid open again, it was finished, he could go. But Hans did not go.

Silver Circus (1928)

DOE

THE Reverend Phalarope Doe, fondly referred to by his choir as Sammy, was vicar of a village in the South Country. His church and his vicarage, hung over by pastoral elms, were hunched beside a lucid stream near a bridge of stone; the water smiled under its arches, the fish hung dreaming in its tide. Just beyond the bridge the road forked at a triangle of grass where two vast lime trees towered above a tiny tiled hut with a padlocked door; the hut, never opened, and plastered with bills of circuses long remote in time and place, harboured a sort of fire-engine that had never been used, that only a few old men had ever seen. Then you came to the village on the flank of a small hill. It was an undistinguished heap of houses with a burden, no doubt easily assimilated, of the frequent traffic of trains; two long chimney shafts projected from a lime kiln that had died in its own pit and an iron-works that was decaying into rust. The place itself looked rusty, harassed alike by the roar of passing trains and the poverty of its trade.

Here, where incentives to virtue were not impressive, though vice seldom ogled with its alluring eye — at least, not observably — for forty years the Reverend Phalarope Doe, portly and ruddy, had ministered, and seldom had a vicar conferred so fair a lustre on so mean a village.

> His sermon never said or showed
> That Earth is foul, that Heaven is gracious.

For he was kind and wise, and, he was *so* forgiving — he could forgive anything. A pat on the shoulder, and something, somehow — *you* know.

'Now tell me,' he would ask some erring maiden, 'why were you so careless?'

'Oh, sir, he decaptivated me!'

'There, there; you shouldn't have done it. I shouldn't do it again, you know, not that kind of thing, if I were you. It's wrong; at least, it's not quite right, you know. I shouldn't do it again, not if I were you.'

Sammy's pleasant home was a little too big and his income a little too small. Too big for what? Too small for what? Well, he was a bachelor for one thing, and the vicarage — to say nothing of the garden — was larger than the church, and as he could afford neither curate nor gardener, he revelled personally in both activities at the expense of muscle and high-mindedness. Kindness was his hobby, his pastime; he played for the pleasure of giving — and, in his turn, taking — as one played bridge or golf. And what a player he was! When his wristbands became frayed he cut off the ends of his shirt-sleeves. Concealed in his study, behind an almanac of 'The Light of the World', there hung a certain map of his own neighbourhood, which he had marked with different coloured spots, each spot denoting the homes of agreeable souls on whom he could rely when rambling afoot. A green spot signified a place where he could be sure of a bed, a red spot meant lunch, blue merely tea, and so forth.

'Ah, splendid souls!' And, as it were, his very heart would give them a smile as he took his stick again to trudge the homeward path. At the first tree he came to he might pause awhile. These beautiful leaves! They grew and they died. The trees became bald, like himself, like the aged; their beauty was but skin deep; yet the *idea* of tree, the spirit manifested in its passion for continuity, its beaming leaves, was eternally beautiful.

How unlike man, whose idea here and now, was not in life alone, but whose destiny was assured!

One day he received a letter from a man with a vaguely familiar name, who lodged in apartments at Twickenham. Rowfant? Ellis Rowfant? It turned out to be an old college chum he had known forty years ago at Oxford. They had had rooms in the same college, the same scout had served them on the same stair, they had swotted for a degree together, taken it, and had gone down together. And then no more. That was all. Doe had been ordained and disposed of; Rowfant had vanished quite away and he had not heard from him, or of him, until now. The two men began a cordial correspondence, and the long lost friend soon came to pay Doe a visit of several days.

On the appointed afternoon Doe walked along to the small parched railway station, whose stationmaster had a permanently dazed appearance caused probably by the ignoring rush past of so many trains that never stopped. Its grey granite design seemed to invite the meeting of extremes, for when the weather was at all cold it was colder there than it could decently have been elsewhere, although if warmth were the order of the day it was here that the temperature multiplied.

'What a fine day!' exclaimed Mr. Doe.

'Ah,' retorted the stationmaster, 'we want plenty of this, and more of it.'

'It is sumptuous indeed,' said Mr. Doe.

The parson idled up the platform and down the platform, reading every placard quite seriously, even the notice which declared the railway company's resolve to transmit explosives only under the most stringent conditions, and that coal, coke, shoddy manure and statuary would be carried only on similar terms.

'Well, well! But really, you know . . .' the parson was reflecting as the train came in.

There could be no doubt that that queer figure was Rowfant. He was the only passenger to emerge, and he came peeringly up to Mr. Doe.

'My dear friend, do I see you! Good heavens, yes; do you know me?'

'I see you,' Doe assured him. 'We have trebled the years, but there is little change.'

'I fear we shall treble the change in vastly fewer years!' Rowfant rejoined.

'None of your pessimistic whim-whams now, Ellis. I remember you, O, I remember you very well. You were always a regular Hamlet.'

'Deplorable!' grinned Hamlet. 'I hope you don't mind me appearing like this? I've come straight off the river — must change directly we get to your place.'

'Come on,' said the parson. 'Come on.' And he picked up the traveller's bag.

Ellis Rowfant was an amiably vigorous gentleman in the sixties, with a slight round-shouldered stoop and a large clean-shaven magisterial face. But when you caught his gaze through the round spectacles, you saw that he had quite childish blue eyes. A small pink cap with a monogram was clapped upon his head in a way that seemed to fasten it there; his jacket of navy blue was flashing with buttons, and a pink tie adorned his throat. His trousers of blankety flannel were of such voluminous vastness that they fluttered audibly as he walked along.

'I've no car,' explained Doe, 'but it is only about ten minutes' walk to the vicarage. I hope you had a pleasant journey down?'

'Most exciting! We had a fellow in our compartment reeking with asthma, and he kept on snorting and spitting out of the window until a lady sitting opposite to him couldn't bear it any longer and complained.'

'Dear me. How? What?'

'She asked him to control himself. Ha! Ha!'

'Well, but really . . . ?' the parson said.

'Oh, he was a regular hard-boiled case. He just argued with her.'

'Argued! He should have left the carriage.'

'That's just what he would *not* do. She hinted at it, then she suggested it, then she bluntly requested him to, but he replied — and very politely, I *must* say — that that alternative was hers.'

'By Jove!' the parson said.

'So then she told him that he was the rudest man she had ever met, *and* the most disgusting! But he sat tight, he would not budge, and I am bound to say it got more provoking than ever. At last she burst out again: "This is insupportable! *Cannot* you control yourself?" "Madam," he says, "I can no more control myself than you can control your appearance. There are many things in life we have to put up with, afflictions and inflictions all very disagreeable. We are both suffering from the defects of nature. For instance, I do not care for your appearance" — he said — "I do not like it at all, it is repellent to me. But do I complain about it? Do I beg you to do something for it, or ask you to leave this compartment? I do *not*" — he said — "Heaven forbid! I just mutely suffer." "Well, I wish you would suffer a little *more* mutely," says she. "Madam" — he says — "it is impossible to suffer mutely from asthma." And they were still wrangling when I got out here. Ha! ha! By George, he *was* a rascal, he gave her such a dressing-down. I — do you know — I positively rejoiced at it!'

'Oh, but really, Ellis!'

'Can't help it. I'm sure you would have been the same — though I'm not much of a Christian these days. Anyhow, I'd almost bet they are very good friends before they get to their destination.'

'Of course, my dear Ellis. I'm sure they will be.'

'I wouldn't be too sure — it didn't strike me as a very promising beginning for romance.'

'Romance!' echoed the puzzled parson.

'Oh, she wasn't bad looking,' Rowfant explained.

They turned the corner by the lime trees and in a few moments there was the church with its untiring spire, the vicarage trees, the lawn garlanded with peonies and hedged with may, and in the water under the bridge the fish were gliding. A little bow-legged maid with a squint in her eyes took the visitor's bag. Ten minutes later they were drinking tea on the lawn, and Rowfant, admiring the old red wall with its top-knots of saxifrage, the squat house and its bow windows, the simple peace of the garden, murmured in envious tones his appreciation.

'You are most welcome here,' his host assured him with a beaming look.

'I'm not much of a religieux these days, I'm afraid,' Rowfant went on.

'Well . . . of course . . .!' Doe smilingly sipped his tea.

'It was never quite in my line, you know,' explained Rowfant.

'And I,' Doe responded, 'I'm a professional. Forty years, my boy. And I rejoice in it. I would not change, I could not.'

'Nor could I,' said Rowfant, 'but I love your home. You never married?'

And Doe answered: 'No. That was not in *my* line.'

'Nor mine,' said Rowfant abruptly.

For many days Rowfant abode there, lingering on and on under pressure from his friend. He soon learned that the parson's familiar name was Sammy, and he too used it fondly. Their old affection had bloomed once more and they were happy. Time and again they rambled in company to spots that were marked red or blue on the vicar's map, and when the parson was otherwise engaged Ellis would lounge for hours in the garden. On Sunday morning he sat there in a dream by the old red wall; the bells had chimed cheerfully, the voices and footsteps of assembling worshippers could be heard passing by. Then there was silence, a silence that itself seemed holy despite the chirping of birds, until the chanting of the choir stole across the road, threaded through the odour of the may, and filled him with melancholy joy. Mysterious melancholy, inexplicable joy! He had not once been into the church during his stay — such a sweet old church! He ought to have gone, at the very least he ought to have gone once. They sang well in there. He would go to-night, it would please Sammy.

When Doe returned Rowfant warmly praised the singing of the choir.

'Pretty good,' the vicar agreed. 'Two fine tenors, you know. Jerry has a glorious voice, perfectly topping. Arnold's tone is not so pure perhaps, but it's a shade more ineffable. I like that.'

Listening with affectionate amusement to his old friend, Rowfant would forget that there was no disparity of years between them; even when a parishioner came with some trouble, preposterous or profound, Rowfant, noting old Sammy's anxious care, would laugh to see him as a boy might laugh at his funny uncle. When he went visiting in his parish Sammy's pockets bulged with little gifts, the deuce knows what;

peppermints for a child, it might be, some crochet cotton for a dame, or a packet of quassia chips for cleaning Sergeant Tullifant's roses. Was Doe working in the garden? Then he would be in his shirt-sleeves and heavy boots, humming as he hoed and sweating as he dug.

'Ellis!' he would bawl across the lawn, 'Do you think that poet was sincere when he said: "The cut worm forgives the plough?"'

'I think he was ignorant.'

'Not ignorant, Ellis.'

'Well, he can't have known anything about the psychology of worms.'

'O! Should you think that worms have a psychology, Ellis?'

'They ought to have, Sammy, to carry their forgiveness to such extremes.'

'I don't know. It strikes me as a very profound utterance. I do hope it applies to spades, in gardens.'

Surely he was a happy man? He had his little life, so neat, so simple; his little desires, so pure, so few; and his little dreams of a very large heaven — while he, Rowfant, what had he got? Even his tragic memories had grown dull, posthumous heaven was a forlorn mirage, he lived in some rooms in Twickenham.

With all his asceticism old Sammy was man enough to enjoy his food to the uttermost — at night — in that low-pitched dining-room with the four Arundel prints on the walls — desperately devout *they* were — and photographs of college teams — *not* so immaculately pious — including one of Rowfant and Doe in a Corpus Christi torpid of eighteen hundred and . . . Good God, how incredible! No rugs encumbered the polished floor, no cloth the table and not even a clock on a shelf anywhere, for why have a clock when you've always a watch in your pocket? But there was a huge block of wood in one corner of the room that served as a stand for a tray.

'What *is* that lump of timber?'

'That, Ellis? Oh, that is quite unique. I got hold of it years ago. Do you like it? It's an ancient butcher's block.'

'Sweet!' grinned Rowfant.

'Don't you like it?'

'I might — in years to come. I must present you with a pole-axe to go with it.'

'Oh, forbear, Ellis! My dear chap, forbear!'

Dinner at night was a ritualistic indulgence by a soul that deserved every hope of the punctual benediction. Each forkful the reverend gentleman shovelled into his mouth caused him to close his eyes and smile. Paradise! He took a gulp of wine, and whispered to himself. Having consumed his heap of spaghetti, his piece of mutton, his apple and his orange, he settled down with a pair of crackers to the nuts and his second glass of wine — white this time in place of red. Selecting the nuts with care he would rattle them with a frown against his ear, and discard some; later, his toothpick came into play, raking his hollow teeth with the felicity of a rapier.

'And now, my dear Ellis, what about a game of draughts? Or dominoes? Any little excitement of that kind?'

And they would play on until the nightingales began.

These homely days exercised so beguiling a pressure that Rowfant almost forgot his own creeping age. Though youth was dead and gone, though the future had got all his destiny slyly tucked in its fob, wise old Sammy was friendship's mellowing sign, simple, steady and devoted, and the prospect of leaving him again for Twickenham's barren complexities filled Rowfant with many qualms. The years ahead of him might be few, or they might be many — one could not live for ever — and this lodging alone was a trashy affair; but one could live well with Sammy. Why *not*? Rowfant had a small income that freed him from the embarrassments and futilities of work. The parson's home was large but his income was small, smaller even than Rowfant's own, and with their resources pooled the two of them might dwell in ease for Sammy and some grace and harmony for himself. One night after dinner he spoke of this:

'Sammy, would you care to put up with me?'

'Put up with you?'

'For good. Could you do with a lodger here?'

'A lodger!'

'Yes, me! Tell me truly if the idea fills you with hatred, but I am making you a proposal, Mr. Doe. I want to live with you, to live here, always, and all my worldly goods on thee endow.'

The Reverend Phalarope listened intently while his friend dilated, outlining his resources and propounding his hopes.

'What do you think? Would it be possible?'

'It would be terrific!' cried Sammy. 'Nothing could be more terrific. It is ... good gracious, my *dear* Ellis ...' — he jumped up to grasp his friend's hand — 'a superb idea.'

'But could you really bear it?'

'My dear boy! Say no more, it shall be exactly as you wish.'

'No, Sammy, it is to be exactly as *you* wish; just as we are now, and you must throw me into the river as soon as you grow sick of it — poison me, pole-axe me, and dump me in a sack!'

'A sack!' shouted Sammy. 'I couldn't put you in a sack!'

'Then don't bother about the sack.'

'And you really mean it?'

'From the bottom of my heart.'

'It is settled then.'

'Settled it is, old friend.'

Again they clasped hands upon it. The parson stood for a few moments with closed eyes and Rowfant knew that some blessing had been invoked on their renewed alliance.

'I must go back to Twickenham, Sammy, for a couple of days, to clear up everything, and then . . .'

'Then you'll come?'

'I'll come. You don't mind harbouring such a barbarian?'

Doe gazed wildly at his friend. 'What do you mean by that, I wonder?'

'My not being a church-goer.'

'Pooh! You don't object to *my* going!'

'You see — I never could stand that holy capital letter of Holiness.'

'Ellis, that is merely a printer's fad.'

'Really, my dear Sammy! You'll shock me, you know.'

'If I could, my boy, you would be more than half-way to grace!'

'To grace!' Rowfant shook his head sadly. 'No, Sammy, I don't think so — ever. But there *is* something I must tell you if I am coming to live with you down here. It is only right that you should know all about it beforehand. I've been going to tell you . . . but . . . don't you see . . . ?'

'What *is* it?'

'Well, it will take some little time — shall we sit down?'

'Ellis!' cried the parson protestingly. 'Are you going to relate the story of your life?'

'More or less.'

'Have you a hideous past?'

'Yes.'

'O Lord! O dear!' Sammy wrung his hands and emitted a whimsical sigh.

'I *must* tell you,' Rowfant insisted. 'And you've *got* to hear it. So just squat down, there's a good chap.'

Down they sat, and Rowfant began his story.

II

'When I went down from Oxford forty years ago I lived with an aunt in Gloucestershire. I was an orphan, you know, and my Aunt Susie was a widow; she had looked after me since I was five years old, in fact, she was a mother to me and she adored me. I suppose I was fond of *her* — I hope I was, for she was the soul of goodness — but I am sure that my feeling for her *now* is stronger than it was *then*, all that long time ago. And it isn't exactly love, either; it is more like admiration. Or perhaps it is only gratitude? She gave so much and got so little; somehow there is nothing *inevitable* about such a situation, it is not *always* conducive to love and possibly not very often — what do *you* think?'

'I find it rather hard to think that, Ellis.'

'But it *is* so, I am sure. She was not what you call rich — just comfortably off — and we had a small house and garden and one servant maid named Elizabeth — Lizzy Lee. I was supposed to be going into the Government service but there were all sorts of difficulties and I made a mess of one or two exams. I was a pretty ineffectual sort of creature in those days; my aunt thought I had weak lungs or a heart or something like that, but the truth is it was laziness. I was *born* like it, really lazy. Do you know she never employed a gardener, and the two women — she and Lizzy Lee — managed the garden by themselves, digging and hoeing, and so on all at the proper times, and I never stirred a leg or lifted an arm to help them. I love a garden, but I dislike gardening, and they seemed to revel in it. Of course there was nothing physically the matter with me at all — never has been — I've rowed all my life, and still do — but at that time I was reading a lot of poetry and things and I fancied I could make some sort of a shot at composing a poetic drama. There was quite a vogue at that time for poetic dramas, and I went floundering about with my head in a fuzz of fatuous dreaminess which my Aunt Susie thought was a sign of genius! So did I, but it wasn't — it was mere cheek. Well, after about a year of this my aunt died, and *that* wiped my eye pretty thoroughly because most of her income came from a marriage settlement which ceased on her death. She left me the house though, and a block of shares in some African gold mines which had brought her in about two hundred a year, and she bequeathed thirty pounds to Elizabeth. Of course, I ought to have buckled to, then, and begun some sort of a career for myself, but I didn't. I decided to carry on the house and write my poetic plays. O, dear! I soon got a shock — two shocks, in fact. One came when I found out what wages my aunt had been paying Lizzy Lee — Elizabeth. It was fifteen pounds a year. At that time I was imbued with a lot of radical notions and it seemed to me dreadful to pay anyone such a miserable pittance, especially as Elizabeth was a model domestic. She was young, about my age, and rather pretty, but I assure you it wasn't *that* that did it — it was my socialism. I was really *shocked*, and I doubled her wages at once.'

'Humph! That was rather a jump,' exclaimed the vicar.

'O, she took it quite as a matter of course; it didn't make any difference, she was as near perfection as a servant could be; but I soon got my second shock. The dividends that year, my dividends on aunt's gold mine shares, were cut down by a half, and in the end I was only getting a bare hundred pounds. Still, I didn't regret having doubled Lizzy Lee's wages — I was very bigoted in my views in those days — but quite soon, as you may imagine, I was in desperate straits for money, got into debt all round for household necessaries and so on, and at last it came to the point where I decided to *sell* the house, *move* into a cottage somewhere cheap, and get rid of Lizzy Lee. Had I had any sense, I would have told her the truth, but I was too stuck-up to do *that*, I couldn't bring myself to do it, I could *not*, so she knew nothing at all about my financial bust-up, and managed the house in the same style she had always done. And I was absolutely on the rocks! So at last I had to tell her that I had arranged to move to a cottage in the Cotswolds and that I shouldn't require her services there. I told her the cottage was very small, that I intended to do all the work myself, in fact I talked a lot of Tolstoyan nonsense — even to her! And I gave her a month's notice. She said "Very good, sir". I can remember it even now. But before the month was up she offered to stay on, at her old wages, and seemed quite anxious to come to the cottage with me. That was out of the question, of course, and besides I simply could not afford to keep her on — though I didn't tell her *that*. She asked me if she had "done anything wrong", but you can understand that as I had donned the high hat by doubling her wages, I was too cocky to own up that I couldn't afford her at any price *now*. Worst of all, it never occurred to me — I was *such* a numskull in those days; I am still, I suppose — it didn't occur to me to ask her what she was going to do, not until the very last day when she was packed up and about to leave.

' "Where shall I send your letters?" I asked her. She said there wouldn't be any. I said I'd better have her address in case anything turned up. She said she was going to London, she didn't quite know whereabouts until she got there.

' "Where's your regular home?" I asked her.

'She answered, "I haven't got one!"

'That was the whole truth of it: her parents were both dead, she had nowhere to go. I hadn't known that, you see, and here was I, throwing her out on to the world! Not intentionally, of course, but still, I was a thoughtless ass, oozing with fatuous blank verse and having no notion of responsibility. She was about my own age, twenty-four or five, and — did I tell you? — she was really quite beautiful. There were tears in her eyes, but she kept a stiff upper lip and didn't suffer them to fall — not while I was looking. I could see though, and I simply *had* to ask her to stay on. I told her I had had no idea of her circumstances, that of course I could not let her go off like that, and she had better stop with me until she found another situation. O, a lot of palaver! But she was rather a proud young woman and her pride wouldn't let her accept my belated offer, and though I wasted a lot of words and remorse on her I could not induce her to change her mind. Away she went, after promising most solemnly to write and let me know how she got on in London. Of course she never kept that promise.'

'Didn't she?' asked the parson with a dubious frown.

'No. Well, within a week I moved to my new cottage. I took what I wanted of my aunt's furniture and sold the remainder with the house. And it turned out to be quite a good stroke of business. In a month or two I paid off all my debts and was left with a couple of hundred pounds in the bargain. I saw I had been altogether too hasty. I wished I had had more foresight and kept Lizzy Lee to look after me. I could have managed it easily after all, but as I say, I did not hear from her, she did not keep her promise to write. By that time she was very much on my mind or my conscience — I don't know which; I expect they are the same thing? It's no use having a conscience unless your mind directs it aright, it's a boat without a compass. I remembered that she was a woman, young, good-looking, though possibly my romantic fancy endowed her with ethereal glamours at times, for poetry does really play the deuce with you in your salad days. Quite often I had a cranky notion of trying to find her — goodness knows how! for she did not keep her promise to write to me — but if I could have got into touch with her again I *would* have had her back, for it is not all honey looking after yourself when you're lazy like I was. Besides, I'd got enough money after selling the house to go on paying her her proper wages. What made it more annoying still, in a way, was the fact that in a couple of years those confounded gold mine shares went soaring up again, so that I could even have kept on my aunt's old house, had I but foreseen it.'

Rowfant paused, and fixed a musing gaze on the print of some martyred saint who was being cauterized by demons with a few red-hot harpoons. 'It was very tantalizing, you know.'

'Well, but Ellis,' said the smiling parson, 'you have nothing to *reproach* yourself for.'

'O, haven't I!' exclaimed Rowfant. 'I haven't told you yet.'

'O! Indeed, O!' Mr. Doe said.

Rowfant went on to describe his efforts to compose poetic dramas, efforts which were frustrated time and again by such trivial impediments. His cottage was on the side of a Cotswold hill, it overlooked a woody valley and a stream. There were horizons too, threaded as it were by long belts of beech trees, a lofty, uplifting view which so stimulated him that he found it pleasanter to work sitting in his tiny garden rather than at the desk in his room. In that serene and open purview thoughts seemed to flow in him, ideas bubbled, and his imagination became as frisky and glittering as a fountain. But the fountain will not play for ever; bubbles are merely bubbles. The thoughts, although they flowed and flowed, did not flow *out* of him; they swirled, and then they subsided to depths he could never fathom. Ideas came, but they came and went untamed. He imputed this defeat to the languorous airs of summer, the distractions of birds, of bees, of clouds — to anything but his own want of genius. To-morrow would do, it would go better to-morrow. Every passing cloud or sign of shower was an interruption of his mind's aery play; their exquisite designs were invitations to dally, to postpone. To-morrow would be time, it would be better to-morrow. When autumn came along he felt a revival of vigour, a glow of renewal, but on the other hand the sharp air made it no longer agreeable to meditate out of doors, and the chill of life got into his mind when the rigour of the season got into his bones and drove him back into his cottage. There with his books he would sit by a drowsing fire, lying in wait for in-

spiration as a fox waits for a hare, until the idleness
bemused him and the tick of the clock became a noisy
nuisance past all bearing; he would stop the clock,
forget the time, and snooze.

'Ho, ho, my dear fellow!' cried Doe. 'You will be
able to write *here*. My, yes! Play after play. I believe
I could write a play. We must do one together, for the
village school.'

Rowfant smiled wryly. 'You know, Sammy, I might
have done a real good play if it hadn't been for those
infernal shares. You see — they had caused me to do a
mean thing, sacking Lizzy Lee, and then they turned on
me and gave me all I wanted. It was very significant.'

'I don't quite see the ... er ... significance?'
remarked the other.

'Don't you! Well, I was selfish — selfish enough,
God knows! — but I never really wanted anything at
that time except to write my plays. When the shares
slumped and I sacked Lizzy Lee I did her a great
wrong, it was a vile thing to do. If I had not done that
all would have come right in a few months; but I
hadn't the sense, I did the dire thing, and then those
shares waxed fat again as though they approved of
what I had done. They were certainly cursed; they
made me do things I should *not* have done, and they
prevented me doing the things I ought to have done.
It was over twenty years before I got rid of the brutes
— and it was too late then. I sold them in a boom year,
I may tell you.'

'Well, ah,' Mr. Doe blandly commented, 'I'm all
for castigating Mammon, but it sounds rather as
though you were biting the hand that fed you, Ellis!'

'Wait, Sammy, wait. Let me finish my story!'

'Haven't you finished yet?'

'Good Lord, no. Listen. I went on dithering in the

Cotswolds for six or seven years. By then I had got a regular lump of money in the bank; the shares paid hand over fist, and I spent little. I got into the way of dodging up to London fairly often to see plays, and on one such occasion I put up at a private boarding house in one of those squares just off Holborn. I had been to the theatre and I had gone home to bed. It was one of those places you just blunder upon, goodness knows how. Fate, I suppose. I've never been there since. And I was fast asleep when something woke me up with a great start. It was a cry, a loud cry, it was like the cry of some . . . well, of some lost soul! I sat up in bed and listened. The room was in darkness, pitch-black. I heard the shriek again. I lit the candle. It was two o'clock. My watch I remember was ticking very loudly and I watched it, almost breathless, for five solid minutes actually, but there wasn't another sound. So I blew out the candle and snuggled down in bed again.

'At that very moment I heard something more, and I half rose up and listened; you know — I listened *furiously*. I heard a voice wailing aloud: "O, won't somebody give me a match? I'm all in the dark and I'm terrified. Can't you hear me? For Christ's sake someone *give* me a match. I want to get up to my own *bed*. I'm all in the *dark*! For God's sake give me a match, can't you! I'm all alone in the dark and I'm frightened. Can't you hear, someone? For Christ's sake give me a match." Just like that, on and on, and very loud. I could not make out where the voice was coming from, upstairs or downstairs, man or woman, but it was certainly somebody in the house. I waited and trembled and waited, to hear what would come of it, for something to be done, but nobody took any notice. Nobody else seemed to hear it, and that awful wailing went on until I could not bear it a second longer. I *had* to get up and light the candle again, and pull on my dressing-gown. When I opened my door I could hear that the noise was downstairs, so I got hold of my candle and crept down the first flight. No one there, so I crept down the second flight to the hall. The crying had stopped directly my light appeared and half-way down I couldn't see anybody, in fact at first I only saw a grey skin mat at the foot of the stairs and a pot of very white geraniums shoved under the hatstand, but when I held the candle up high I could see a lady sitting all lopsided on the doormat with her hat cocked askew. And she was tipsy! *That* was it. A handsome woman and elegantly dressed, but tipsy! She said "Hullo, I've been here *such* a long time. What the devil's the matter with you all? Nobody ever takes *any* notice in this rotten house. You don't, do you? Who are you?" She seemed to think I was one of the servants. I put the candle on the hatstand and helped her to her feet. Her breath stank of rum and she tottered a little, but she just picked up the candle and made for the stairs. Of course I followed close behind her. She pulled herself together and held the candle up to look at me. "Rather nice," she said. "Haven't seen you before!" She had on a sort of cape, and she walked quite jauntily, carrying the candle in one hand and lifting her skirt with the other. I followed her as she stumbled up two flights of stairs. She opened a door quite close to my own.

' "Come in," she said; but I stopped in the doorway. She flung off her hat and cape, kicked off her shoes and then she began to undress. I called out: "If you've got a candle of your own here I'll light it for you." "Don't you trouble, my dear," she said! In a minute or two she got her own candle alight and brought mine to the door. I said: "Thank you, good night," and was walking off with my candle when she hissed out: "Are you all alone?" I thought it best not to answer, but she bawled: "*Are* you?" So I replied: "Yes, I am, thank you." "*Too* bad!" she said. "*So* sorry. Au revoir!" or something like that.

'I didn't get off to sleep again for a very long time. The sight of anybody intoxicated always distresses me, but a young woman beautiful and boozed is simply shocking. I couldn't help wondering who she was, and what she had been doing to get like it, and why no one had answered her cries, for I thought the whole house *must* have heard her. As a matter of fact I found out later that nobody *had* heard her. She had been staying there for quite a long time and had a latch-key. This night she had been out to a party, got fuzzy with rum, and had fallen down in the pitch-dark hall.

'I met her the next morning. I was all alone in the breakfast room when she came in, looking *radiant*. I didn't quite know whether I ought to greet her in such circumstances, but directly she saw me she came bang up to my table and said, "Thank you for last night." "A pleasure!" I said. "May I sit here?" she asked. "Do," I said; "what will you have for breakfast?" She sat down, she stared at me, and she suddenly exclaimed: "Mr. Rowfant!" And then I saw it was our Lizzy Lee, dressed in the pink of fashion and looking like a lady. Of course you could have split me with a paper knife. Such a surprise! "Why, whatever are you doing here, Elizabeth?" I said. For a long time I couldn't get much information out of her except that she was now a Mrs. Robinson, but we talked and talked and she became quite fascinating, you know. It is extraordinary what nurture and dress does for some women.

'At last, I asked what she had to do that morning.

She said she had no engagements. "Shall we go out?" I asked and she said, "Yes." "Where shall we go?" "I don't mind." So off we went and took a hansom as far as the Royal Academy. "Shall we go in?" "Yes," said she. I can remember the details of that visit perfectly, though I have forgotten all about the pictures we looked at. When we got into the courtyard of the Academy there was a baker's cart standing outside the door of the Astronomical Society. The horse had got its nosebag on and some sparrows were waiting and chippering at the horses' feet and Elizabeth had to stop and watch them. It made her laugh because the birds would chirrup and the horse would sneeze, and every time he sneezed he blew a handful of oats out of his nosebag, and the sparrows would snap up the grains and go on chippering encouragingly for more.

'Well, we saw some of the pictures and then we sat down in one of the galleries. I asked her about her marriage and so on, and then it all came out with a vengeance; she wasn't married, she had never been married at all, but, you understand, she *ought* to have been.

'The Mrs. Robinson name was just assumed for propriety's sake and convenience, but she wasn't married. Gradually I got the whole story. It appeared that when she left me and went off to London she was unlucky and could not find another situation. She tried for months and months, until her savings came to an end, and she was absolutely on her uppers. Then, of course, the inevitable happened — she was a handsome creature — she went as housekeeper to a certain man who was quite unscrupulous, although he was kind to her in a way. I think he died, and then there were one or two other episodes of that kind. Once — she said — she was an actress, but I discovered that she had only posed in some suggestive tableaux for a threepenny gaff travelling round the fairs. At last she had become the mistress of a rich man who was already married. All this filled me with dreadful remorse, but at the same time I was very angry with her. "Why in the name of all that's sacred didn't you write to me?" "Write to *you*?" said she. "Yes," I said, "as you promised?" "What do you take me for?" she answered (and with a good deal of spirit, by Jove!) "You had thrown me out, homeless." "No, no! I didn't," I said, "and you promised faithfully to write."

' "Well, it was all your fault," was her reply, "but it doesn't matter now."

'I couldn't believe it of our innocent Lizzy Lee, not for some time. I was appalled to think I had been the unwitting instrument to send her into such a way of life. She was quite insistent that it *was* my fault and of *course* it was, I *saw* that it was — it was only too awfully true.

'She sat on one of those lounges, looking really beautiful, better than any of the paintings I saw, and no one looking at her would have dreamed she had been drunk on the doormat at two o'clock that very morning. She asked me why I had been so anxious to get rid of her and I told her, then, the reason, the proper reason. That seemed to puzzle her. "You were hard up! I had no idea," she said. "Why didn't you tell me? I did not think it was anything like that at all." "What *did* you think it was?" I asked her. "O," she said, "I've forgotten now, but I'd have stayed on, of course I would, for nothing if I had known. Instead of that — you just threw me out!" She repeated that it was all *my* fault, as of course it *was*, this mess she was in.

'My fault, my helpless fault! And as I deeply realized it then, my guilt, my imagined guilt if you like, affronted me and I felt it was my solemn duty to get her out of it; I could not rest with a thing like that on my conscience. I told her that I had wanted to get her back again as soon as my affairs had recovered, but that I hadn't known where to find her. "Do you want me back now?" she ventured. "Would you come?" I asked. She laughed: "What wages would you pay me?" Saucy, wasn't it? We didn't say any more about it just then, we just dropped the subject, because in spite of everything she had become a very charming companion. For the next week we were inseparable, went about day after day together, and she behaved well, very well indeed. To cut a long story short I stayed on in that boarding house. I got very fond of her and didn't want to leave her, but it wasn't *only* that. I felt overwhelmingly that some reparation had to be made to her, from me, absolute reparation for the hideous harm I had done. Not intentional, of course; I had been careless, and it had brought this disaster on her. I felt I had to make amends — if only to redeem myself — and the best way as it seemed to me then would be to marry her.

'I began by asking her to give up this man who was keeping her. That made her look sad, so sad, I can't describe *how* mournful, yet when I asked her to marry me she just laughed aloud! But she soon realized I was not joking. I was serious, very serious, and I kept on at her until at last she agreed to marry me. And she did marry me, yes, absolutely! I gave up my Cotswold cottage and we took a little house at Brighton. I made Lizzy destroy every stitch she possessed in the way of clothing and personal belongings. She had heaps, but I was very squeamish about her retaining any of those things, and to do her justice she agreed with me. I spent a heap of money on refitting her, and the only thing she retained was a Bible her mother had given her; it had her name inscribed in it: "To Elizabeth, from her distracted mother on the day of the operation by Dr. Fuller to her nose." '

'Her nose!' echoed the parson. 'What was the matter with her nose?'

'O, it wasn't her nose,' Rowfant explained. 'Hers was fine, sort of Grecian, and she had an abundance of bright hair and the bluest eyes. No, it was her mother's nose — a polypus, I think. Lizzy was splendid and for over a year we seemed to be living in Eden itself, but after that things began to go wrong. It may have been my own stupidity, it may have been the cussedness of nature, or it may have been a conflict in myself that betrayed us, for I do know that the more deeply I loved her the more I came to loathe the thought of that awful life she had once led. I thought I had accepted all that, I had taken my share of the blame and supposed I could dismiss it from my mind, but that was very far from being so — it became a dreadful canker. And Lizzy, too, she had grown used to some of the extremer luxuries, was extravagant, ran into debt, began to drink again. Once more I found it difficult to make ends meet; my savings were all gone, my income was inadequate, and in short I did not know which way to turn. I could not give Lizzy the sack this time, even if I had wished to and I didn't wish that, though I was horribly hurt by some of the things she was doing, but a climax came when I found out that she was once more corresponding with her old paramour, had actually seen him again, and I guessed she had resumed relations with him. When I taxed her with this, she admitted it, and left me and went back to him. Yes, that's what Lizzy did. Ah, well, I can't describe the horrible bitterness of it, indeed I couldn't if I wanted to, for thirty years is too long a time to remember a grief. I know that I wanted a divorce. Now divorces are most expensive affairs, though it *is* so cheap to get married, but I still wanted to get Lizzy on to the right path again. I wanted that very much. This man was a widower now, and I imagined he would be very glad to marry her if she were free as well. Perhaps he would have done so, but as it turned out he did not. For three years I stinted and starved myself to get money enough to launch proceedings, for I was determined to pay the costs myself, no matter what was the award; it seemed a ghastly immorality to win her redemption — and mine too — with *his* money. Idiot! Fool! Blind besotted owl that I was! Well, at last I got my decree, but it was a sorry business for her man entered a defence and the case lasted several days and those confounded news-butchers made a great to-do in their newspapers. I got my decree, but it didn't avail poor Lizzy very much; within a week of its being absolute she died.'

Rowfant stopped at last. Apparently he was finished with his story.

'Dear me,' said the parson, 'how very sad that is.'

Rowfant blew his nose, using his handkerchief meticulously. The parson coughed. There was a silence lasting several moments. The parson coughed again. At length he said:

'You have had a very sad time, Ellis, a very sad time. But you behaved splendidly. There is something wrong about it all, somewhere, I feel. I don't know. But you behaved splendidly, Ellis, you did, indeed.'

'No,' said Rowfant. 'No. All that starving and stinting to pay the costs was monstrously Quixotic, and it was thrown away, wasted in the end. I didn't mind for myself, but for poor Lizzy I *did* mind. Don't you see? If I had been less of a fool, if I had thought more of her and less of my own precious scruples the poor

girl would have been divorced and free a couple of
years earlier at least. And she could have been married
to that man and it would have put things right for her
in a sort of way. But my stupidity prevented even that.
And she died, and — well — what about *her*?'

Soon the parson came and bent over his friend:

'All is well, my dear boy, all is well. Believe that.
Now — ah — just forget all about it. I wonder,' said
he, glancing around the room, 'I wonder, Ellis —
would you care to play a little game of dominoes?'

'Why, yes,' Ellis responded brightly, 'Yes, I should
love to.'

'Very well then.'

They played.

III

A few days later Rowfant was installed at the vicarage with his pink cap, his waterproof tobacco pouch,
and a lot of books that Sammy declared he would certainly have to look at — some time, later on. From the
day he turned his back upon the blandishments of
Twickenham and was inducted as it were into the pale
of the church Rowfant's heart was aware of revivals and
renewals he had not thought to experience again. And
there was no betrayal this time. The two old men in
friendly bondage shared a home, a life; and they shared
their thoughts, snoozing and brooding in the garden
under the leaning trees while the sun-inspired brook
inched warily by. In some half-maudlin mood Rowfant perhaps would ask 'What is Life?' And Sammy
would tell him.

Or Sammy would bridle with domestic ambition:

'We might put up a little greenhouse here, Ellis. I
am very partial to cucumbers — do they disturb you?'

Or there would be intimate wanderings over the sleepy fields, for the parson was no longer a lover of the open road.

'I really regret the dust, Ellis, the dust of the old highway. It often gave me real pleasure, thirty years ago, before the roads were so hardened and polished and thousands of wheels going where there were only ten before. Traffic was so small then, and it was genial, too; just a wagon, a butcher's cart, the squire's barouche, or a fleet of bicycles. And you could pad along so softly in the roads with a luxurious inch of fine dust under your footsoles; rich historical dust, too, gloating over ancient Britain and Julius Caesar, and the sun flaring at you while the sweat oozed and ran. And then, to come to some bosky chestnut tree at the corner of some turn with a pond and a goose deliberating on it! O dear, O dear; the tree and the pond may be there still, but the goose is gone!'

And Rowfant found that he too lamented the dust that had gone to dust indeed. He found that his own divergent thoughts were often of the same cast as his friend's, though *he* seemed to use them as stepping stones to directions Rowfant had always shunned. Despite his secular bigotries he found that he liked hearing his comrade pronounce the benediction at their meals together. One day Sammy said: 'Will *you* say grace, Ellis?' and stood with his venerable head piously bowed, never doubting his friend's response. Rather than grieve him, Rowfant submissively invoked a blessing in which he had no belief. He found that it pleased him immensely to please Sammy; he had no belief in God, but he believed in his friend.

Once he had asked Rowfant to be a good chap and go with him to the church and ring the bell for the evening service.

'Why, what is the matter with the sexton?' Rowfant inquired.

'Drunk,' replied Sammy. 'He is imperiously drunk.'

It seemed such an agreeable quandary for a parson to be in that Rowfant was delighted to oblige — just for once. But somehow things were never done 'just for once' with the inexorable Sammy. You were taken for granted, you were inveigled, you were roped in.

'We ought to do a Nativity Play at Christmas,' declared Sammy. 'Yes, to be performed in the church. And that's just your line, Ellis, isn't it? You could write something extraordinarily good, it's a beautiful theme, one of the finest the world has ever known — O, immeasurably! You just knock off the words, not too much spouting, you know, but action and simple piety, and I will find the performers — as many as you like, the more the merrier.'

It was a waste of time for Rowfant to plead his entire unfitness; he had to renew his acquaintance with the Gospel according to St. Luke and to plan his Christmas pageant. Naturally, this required — and it was somehow quite, *quite* natural — his occasional attendance in the church where a robin had once had the cheek to build its nest in a hole in Sammy's lectern and put five eggs in it. It ended in Rowfant's becoming a sort of lay clerk to the implacable Mr. Doe, in his sitting below his pulpit and responding to his Amens in no browbeaten manner.

'Wouldn't you like to read the lessons, Ellis?'

'No. You must excuse me, Phalarope.'

'I should like you to do that, Ellis.'

'I could not do that. I would not *mind*, but I do not feel myself *fitted*, you understand — *fitted*. I am interested in it all, you know that, but the fact remains that I am entirely insusceptible to any sort of religious emotion, utterly and entirely. The ceremonies are quite agreeable, they are pleasant, but beyond that they *mean* nothing to me.'

'Why should they? Ellis, what are you afraid of?'

'Afraid! I'm not afraid of anything. But I do miss something, I want some clue. I can't break through the crust of all these ceremonies and contradictions and find the thing I'm after, the thing which sometimes I find in myself, which satisfies *me*. I suppose I can't *find* what you call God. I can't believe in him.'

'It is all very simple, Ellis. The Kingdom of God is within you.'

'No, Sammy. The soul is not really man's identification with God, it is merely the possibility of such identification. Now suppose — just listen to me for a moment, Sammy — suppose there is a great Jehovah sitting in the skies, or wherever you like to have Him. That may be true, I won't argue about it, just suppose it. But even then it is quite easy and natural to suppose that this life of ours is the beginning and the end of things for mankind, isn't it? And what then?'

'Suppose! Suppose!' The Reverend Phalarope Doe wagged his head and smiled indulgently. 'I am not able to suppose any such thing, Ellis. And you have forgotten Jesus, haven't you?'

'I have not. Even he envisages this world as the centre of the universe.'

'Why not?'

'Why not! Don't you realize that our world is but a gnat in the galaxy of a million worlds?'

'I do.'

'He had no conception of any other world save Heaven.'

'Nor have I, Ellis, nor have you. To apprehend omniscience one must have an omniscient mind. All else is impertinence. You could put out your tongue at the Lama of Tibet, but even he would disdain to take notice of the gesture.'

'The Lama of Tibet?'

'Yes, you believe in him, although you have never seen him and never will.'

'But I *know* of his existence. I have read of him.'

'I have read of Jack the Giant Killer.'

'And do you believe in him!'

'No. But I have read of God, and his blessings confront me day by day. God's miracles are numberless, but in face of them all, Ellis, I am sometimes tempted to think that mankind's one stupendous miracle is greater than any of His. I mean the Miracle of Unbelief.'

'That's no miracle, Sammy!'

'To me it is. And I would like you to read the Lesson sometimes. You could do it beautifully. You read the Bible to yourself and it gives you pleasure, isn't that so? To put it at its lowest it gives you great pleasure. Now?'

Rowfant sighed. 'It's a duodecimo emotion, Sammy; not like yours, a folio in full calf.'

'Never mind the binding. Penny plain is no less than twopence coloured, which costs twice as much and means no more. Don't be selfish, Ellis, I'm not asking you to take a Sunday School class!'

So Rowfant read out the Word of God and feared no evil. He wrote his play, he rang the bell, he did whatever Sammy required him to do. There was no end to their exchanges of belief and unbelief, but there was no division between them; their differences were no more than a crude brush across a surface of velvet, as marked as the advance of a harrow across a pasture — and as fugitive. Sometimes while listening to Sammy's exhortations Rowfant would fall asleep and when he awoke Sammy would be gone away somewhere, to the garden, to his study, or into the church. 'Ah,' Rowfant would despondently sigh, 'he disapproves of me!' But it was not so, never so. The two old friends were in bondage to an affection that time and thought had no wish to subvert.

'Why did you never get married, Sammy? Don't you care for women?'

'I love mankind.'

'But women, Sammy?'

'And their children too.'

'Humph! I don't think I love man, really.'

'I do.'

'Not in the proper human way, not in any *wide* sense. I don't accept him as an equal, I'm afraid, but still I am content with him.'

'I am not content with him, Ellis, but I love him.'

What would have been impossible to Rowfant, or absurd in him, was so firm and beautiful and appropriate in old Doe, who was so fond and ever faithful, that Rowfant could not find it in his heart to oppose him. Against Sammy he could somehow advance his reasoning only with small shuffling steps, like a man on a tight rope balancing a rod that was no security against a fall. The multitudinous permutations of man's mind, its diversity of measure, its warp that would plait only with the woof of its self-sown views, left Rowfant without hope of ever sharing his dear friend's belief and bliss, but he lived gratefully in its reflected beam. The beam might be a mirage and lead no further than the grave — but what then? What pangs and what misery had such innocence avoided!

The autumn faded upon them and winter eves approached with the wild cries of those wounded winds that harried every obstruction, thorn, gulley, barn, garner, fold and fence. The sere skeletons of dead herbage were snapped on their fields and scattered. The clouds that hung above the firmament's meek frill of light were coloured like the inside of a shell. The surfaces of flat objects, such as the top of a well or the bar of a gate, had a grey doubtful lustre, but a rare planet sparkled aloft with a benignity bland as a prophet's faith. But the heart of a prophet — thought Rowfant — hears only the echo of its own sighing.

Dunky Fitlow (1933)

LUXURY

EIGHT o'clock of a fine morning in the hamlet of
Kezzal Predy Peter, great horses with chains clinking
down the road, and Alexander Finkle rising from his
bed singing: 'O lah soh doh, soh lah me doh', timing
his notes to the ching of his neighbour's anvil. He
boils a cupful of water on an oil stove, his shaving brush
stands (where it always stands) upon the window ledge
('Soh lah soh do-o-o-oh, soh doh soh la-a-a-ah!') but
as he addresses himself to his toilet the clamour of the
anvil ceases and then Finkle too becomes silent, for the
unresting cares of his life begin again to afflict him.

'This cottage is no good,' he mumbles, 'and I'm no
good. Literature is no good when you live too much
on porridge. Your writing's no good, sir, you can't
get any glow out of oatmeal. Why did you ever come
here? It's a hopeless job and you know it!' Stropping
his razor petulantly as if the soul of that frustrating
oatmeal lay there between the leather and the blade,
he continues: 'But it isn't the cottage, it isn't me, it
isn't the writing — it's the privation. I must give it up
and get a job as a railway porter.'

And indeed he was very impoverished, the living he
derived from his writings was meagre; the cottage had
many imperfections, both its rooms were gloomy, and
to obviate the inconvenience arising from its defective
roof he always slept downstairs.

Two years ago he had been working for a wall-paper
manufacturer in Bethnal Green. He was not poor
then, not so very poor; he had the clothes he stood up
in (they were good clothes) and fifty pounds in the
bank besides. But although he had served the wall-
paper man for fifteen years that fifty pounds had not

been derived from clerking, he had earned it by means of his hobby, a little knack of writing things for provincial newspapers. On his thirty-first birthday Finkle argued — for he had a habit of conducting long and not unsatisfactory discussions between himself and a self that apparently wasn't him — that what he could do reasonably well in his scanty leisure could be multiplied exceedingly if he had time and opportunity, lived in the country, somewhere where he could go into a garden to smell the roses or whatever was blooming and draw deep draughts of happiness, think his profound thoughts and realize the goodness of God, and then sit and read right through some long and difficult book about Napoleon or Mahomet. Bursting with literary ambition Finkle had hesitated no longer: he could live on nothing in the country — for a time. He had the fifty pounds, he had saved it, it had taken him seven years, but he had made it and saved it. He handed in his notice. That was very astonishing to his master, who esteemed him, but more astonishing to Finkle was the parting gift of ten pounds which the master had given him. The workmen, too, had collected more money for him, and bought for him a clock, a monster; it weighed twelve pounds and had a brass figure of Lohengrin on the top, while the serene old messenger man who cleaned the windows and bought surreptitious beer for the clerks gave him a prescription for the instantaneous relief of a painful stomach ailment. 'It might come in handy,' he had said. That was two years ago, and now just think! He had bought himself an inkpot of crystalline glass — a large one, it held nearly half a pint — and two pens, one for red ink and one for black, besides a quill for signing his name with. Here he was at 'Pretty Peter' and the devil himself was in it!

Nothing had ever been right, the hamlet itself was poor. Like all places near the chalk hills its roads were of flint, the church was of flint, the farms and cots of flint with brick corners. There was an old milestone outside his cot, he was pleased with that, it gave the miles to London and the miles to Winchester; it was nice to have a milestone there like that — your very own.

He finished shaving and threw open the cottage door; the scent of wallflowers and lilac came to him as sweet almost as a wedge of newly-cut cake. The may bloom on his hedge drooped over the branches like crudded cream, and the dew in the gritty road smelled of harsh dust in a way that was pleasant. Well, if the cottage wasn't much good, the bit of a garden was all right.

There was a rose bush too, a little vagrant in its growth. He leaned over his garden gate; there was no one in sight. He took out the fire shovel and scooped up a clot of manure that lay in the road adjacent to his cottage and trotted back to place it in a little heap at the root of those scatter-brained roses, pink and bulging, that never seemed to do very well and yet were so satisfactory.

'Nicish day,' remarked Finkle, lolling against his doorpost, 'but it's always nice if you are doing a good day's work. The garden is all right, and literature is all right — only, I live too much on porridge. It isn't the privation itself, it's the things privation makes a man do. It makes a man do things he ought not want to do, it makes him mean, it makes him *feel* mean, I tell you, and if he feels mean and thinks mean he writes meanly, that's how it is.'

He had written topical notes and articles, stories of gay life (of which he knew nothing), of sport (of which he knew less), a poem about 'hope', and some cheerful pieces for a girls' weekly paper. And yet his outgoings still exceeded his income, painfully and perversely after two years. It was terrifying. He wanted success, he had come to conquer — not to find what he *had* found. But he would be content with encouragement now even if he did not win success; it was absolutely necessary, he had not sold a thing for six months, his public would forget him, his connection would be gone.

'There's no use though,' mused Finkle, as he scrutinized his worn boots, 'in looking at things in detail, that's mean; a large view is the thing. Whatever is isolated is bound to look alarming.'

But he continued to lean against the doorpost in the full blaze of the stark, almost gritty sunlight, thinking mournfully until he heard the porridge in the saucepan begin to bubble. Turning into the room he felt giddy, and scarlet spots and other phantasmagoria waved in the air before him.

Without an appetite he swallowed the porridge and ate some bread and cheese and watercress. Watercress, at least, was plentiful there, for the little runnels that came down from the big hills expanded in the Predy Peter fields and in their shallow bottoms the cress flourished.

He finished his breakfast, cleared the things away, and sat down to see if he could write, but it was in vain — he could not write. He could think, but his mind would embrace no subject, it just teetered about with the objects within sight, the empty, disconsolate grate, the pattern of the rug, and the black butterfly that had hung dead upon the wall for so many months. Then he thought of the books he intended to read but could never procure, the books he had procured but did not like, the books he had liked but was already, so soon, forgetting. Smoking would have helped and he wanted to smoke, but he could not afford it now. If ever he had a real good windfall he intended to buy a tub, a little tub it would have to be, of course, and he would fill it to the bung with cigarettes, full to the bung, if it cost him pounds. And he would help himself to one whenever he had a mind to do so.

'Bah, you fool!' he murmured, 'you think you have the whole world against you, that you are fighting it, keeping up your end with heroism! Idiot! What does it all amount to? You've withdrawn yourself from the world, run away from it, and here you sit making futile dabs at it, like a child sticking pins into a pudding and wondering why nothing happens. What *could* happen? What? The world doesn't know about you, or care, you are useless. It isn't aware of you any more than a chain of mountains is aware of a gnat. And whose fault is that — is it the mountain's fault? Idiot! But I can't starve and I must go and get a job as a railway porter, it's all I'm fit for.'

Two farmers paused outside Finkle's garden and began a solid conversation upon a topic that made him feel hungry indeed. He listened, fascinated, though he was scarcely aware of it.

'Six-stone lambs,' said one, 'are fetching three pounds apiece.'

'Ah!'

'I shall fat some.'

'Myself I don't care for lamb, never did care.'

'It's good eating.'

'Ah, but I don't care for it. Now we had a bit of spare rib last night off an old pig. 'Twas cold, you know, but beautiful. I said to my dame: "What can mortal man want better than spare rib off an old pig? Tender and white, ate like lard." '

'Yes, it's good eating.'

'Nor veal, I don't like — nothing that's young.'

'Veal's good eating.'

'Don't care for it, never did, it eats short to my mind.'

Then the school bell began to ring so loudly that Finkle could hear no more, but his mind continued to hover over the choice of lamb or veal or old pork until he was angry. Why had he done this foolish thing, thrown away his comfortable job, reasonable food, ease of mind, friendship, pocket money, tobacco? Even his girl had forgotten him. Why had he done this impudent thing? It was insanity, surely. But he knew that man has instinctive reasons that transcend logic, what a parson would call the superior reason of the heart.

'I wanted a change, and I got it. Now I want another change, but what shall I get? Chance and change, they are the sweet features of existence. Chance and change, and not too much prosperity. If I were an idealist I could live from my hair upwards.'

The two farmers separated. Finkle staring haplessly from his window saw them go. Some schoolboys were playing a game of marbles in the road there. Another boy sat on the green bank quietly singing, while one in spectacles knelt slyly behind him trying to burn a hole in the singer's breeches with a magnifying glass. Finkle's thoughts still hovered over the flavours and satisfactions of veal and lamb and pig until, like Mother Hubbard, he turned and opened his larder.

There, to his surprise, he saw four bananas lying on a saucer. Bought from a travelling hawker a couple of days ago, they had cost him threepence halfpenny. And he had forgotten them! He could not afford another luxury like that for a week at least, and he stood looking at them, full of doubt. He debated whether he should take one now; he would still have one left for Wednesday, one for Thursday, and one for Friday. But he thought he would not, he had had his breakfast and he had not remembered them. He grew suddenly and absurdly angry again. That was the worst of poverty, not what it made you endure, but what it made you want to endure. Why shouldn't he eat a banana? Why shouldn't he eat *all* of them! And yet bananas always seemed to him such luxuriant, expensive things, so much peel, and then two, or not more than three, delicious bites. But if he fancied a banana — there it was. No, he did not want to destroy the blasted thing! No reason at all why he should not, but that was what continuous hardship did for you, nothing could stop this miserable feeling for economy now. If he had a thousand pounds at this moment he knew he would be careful about bananas and about butter and about sugar and things like that; but he would never have a thousand pounds, nobody had ever had it, it was impossible to believe that anyone had ever had wholly and entirely to themselves a thousand pounds. It could not be believed. He was like a man dreaming that he had the hangman's noose around his neck; yet the drop did not take place, and it would not take place. But the noose was still there. He picked up the bananas one by one, the four bananas, the whole four. No other man in the world, surely, had ever had four such fine bananas as that and not wanted to eat them? O, why had such stupid mean scruples seized him again? It was disgusting and ungenerous to himself, it made him feel mean, it *was* mean! Rushing to his cottage door he cried: 'Here y'are!' to the playing schoolboys and flung two of the bananas into the midst of them. Then he flung another. He hesitated at the fourth, and tearing the peel from it he crammed the fruit into his own mouth, wolfing it down and gasping: 'So perish all such traitors.'

When he had completely absorbed its savour, he stared like a fool at the empty saucer. It was empty, the bananas were gone, all four irrecoverably gone.

'Damned pig!' cried Finkle.

But then he sat down and wrote all this, just as it appears.

Clorinda Walks in Heaven (1922)

NIXEY'S HARLEQUIN

I MUST explain about Sally and me before I tell you the terrible thing that happened. I ought to tell you about the terrible thing first, I ought to begin with that because it is what the story is about, and desperately tragic, I can tell you. But as it happens there are two men named Wilson concerned, one of them very wickedly concerned, and my name is Wilson. It is a common enough name, you couldn't have anything commoner than Wilson, and I have told everybody that I am not the guilty Wilson; I am indeed as innocent as a newborn lamb, but nobody believes me, they just grin.

And why grin? In *any* case, why grin? Suppose I *were* the guilty Wilson, is that anything to grin at? Would they grin then? I suppose they would; it seems natural to some razor-faced individuals to grin at pain and shame — but why! I told the police it must be the other Wilson who was to blame, and they told me that that was just what *he* said about *me*! You see, my name is Thomas and his name is also Thomas. I cannot think why people are allowed to have similar names at all; your name ought to be sacred to you, as private as your own fingernails, but here is this fellow born certainly ten years later than me ... And at the age of forty, let me tell you, one has come to respect one's name; I mean one's name is one's own title and I like to preserve a good title — I don't mean merely being praised by inconspicuous clergymen ... And here's this fellow has taken my name, the same in every letter, what is called my cognomen, and dragged my character in the mire. What is more, he has fobbed off a dreadful responsibility on me. He is married, I am not. They seem to think that makes all the difference, in his favour. Now I ask you, what difference could that really make when you know the facts? Not an inch! Man is man, as I'm almost tired of telling them. And I am not that kind of man at all, in fact, I enjoy rather poor health, always did.

I can remember one day I was in the shop where Sally worked when this very Wilson came in, this other Tom Wilson. I admit I had been there some little while passing the time o' day to Sally, but what of it! She was one of the handsomest young women ever seen behind a counter; short fair hair that curled a little, cheeks as pink as roses, healthy as a wild bird. In came this Wilson, one of your hearty, cocksure, unpleasant sort of men, and when Sally asked: 'What would you like, Mr. Wilson?' he out and said: 'A kiss, and the afternoon off with you!' Just like that. Of course I suppose it was the perfect answer to make to pretty Sally, it consorted so with her charming primness and her general bloom. In a way it was genius. Or, though I don't know, it may have been a mere common tag, the sort of thing that men like that are always saying to girls in shops like that, but I *do* know that *I* could never bring myself to utter such fancies, or so blatantly either. I would *like* to, mind you. O please, very much! Make no mistake about that, I certainly would like; but there you are, I . . . can . . . not. I have plenty of words and things I *could* say to girls like Sally, but not that sort of thing. For instance: the india-rubber mat on the glass counter was half worn out by the coins of customers who never bought anything but tobacco; well, I could have asked if she never grew tired of seeing the same oafs buy the same brand of tobacco for the same price at the same hour daily, giving them exactly the same change from exactly the same coins, and all to be stuffed in the same pipes or be chewed by the same rotten teeth.

I use tobacco myself, of course. Men are alike, very much alike in habit and instinct; I am in some ways much like other men, and I haven't the moral imagination to wish myself any better than I am. Still, I have always preferred cigarettes, and I daresay shall continue that form as long as it suits me; in fact, I have no doubt about it at all at present.

You know, men of a certain type imagine things about girls like Sally, and . . . and . . . and there you are! I could never have said that sort of thing to her, but I confess that afterwards I sometimes imagined myself to ask her:

'What would you like, Sally?'

And she was to reply:

'A kiss, and the afternoon off with you, Mr. Wilson.'

Or perhaps she would say 'Tom'.

Of course I never never never *did* ask her any such thing; pardon, it is quite out of keeping with my character; but, I did have a feeling, often and very often, that that was what she *would* have said if I had ever put it so to her. Yes, exactly; but of course I did not. I had — indeed, I don't mind confessing it — an idea that the poor girl was really rather fond of me in a tobacconist-shop sort of way, but I never made up to her at all, never stroked her fingers as she gave me my change — it is — you will pardon me — I honestly do not think myself capable of such a thing.

And yet I got tangled up in the whole matter, one of the most frightful affairs a man could possibly be mixed up with, extremely repellent to me, and all because my name is Wilson — and not only that, but Thomas besides. You know, you will never be able to persuade me that such things are the mere *accidents* of life: I don't know what they *are*, but they are not that. I had known Sally Burden for at least a year, perhaps nearly two years, when she died suddenly while on a visit to a relative in London. Very mysterious it was, an inquest and all that was found to be necessary. Believe me, I did not hear of the poor girl's death, I did not even know about the inquest, until I heard my barber talking of that to Filkins the ironmonger two days after it had taken place. In London it was. I seldom read newspapers, in any case we have no local sheet; and though our town is a small town, there are at least fifty persons you do *not* know for every one you *do*, and so it was in no way surprising that I had remained so completely in the dark about a matter that was destined to concern me so seriously. Poisoning it was, the girl had died of poisoning, and I gathered it could not have been suicide because a man had been arrested, so the poor thing must have been murdered. That was the conclusion I came to. I bought newspaper after newspaper but I could not find any reference to Sally's case. I went up and down all the columns, but I need not have wasted my time and pence on the stupid things, for inquests, it seems, are as common in the metropolis as prayer meetings. I was to hear all — or nearly all — in the course of a few hours, and even that was much more than I wanted to hear, or had ever thought of hearing. To be brief — for I detest those people who beat about the bush, trying to beguile you into sympathizing with them before they reveal to you the crime they have committed — I myself was visited by the police, and interrogated about my relationship with that poor dead girl, closely and pointedly questioned. Most disagreeable and unnerving it was.

Perhaps you have already guessed the mystery?

Poor lamb, she had been seduced. I am sorry to say that is the whole explanation. Now when a girl finds herself in such a plight she generally ends by marrying the man in a right and proper way, but poor Sally *could not* marry the man, even if they had both been willing, because she had a husband already!

I tell you, that *was* a startler to begin with, the revelation that Sally was a wedded wife; but there was more to come — O, I'll not deceive you, that was nothing. A Mrs. Burden she was — not Miss at all, her maiden name had been Golightly — and married to a soldier, this Burden, who had gone abroad on foreign service, Seringapatam or some such place — I couldn't tell you, really — but he had been gone for two years and looked like staying for ever. He'll never come back now, that's certain.

One of the most extraordinary things is that difference — I can't tell what it is, I wish I could — between a woman who is married and a woman who is not, when you do not know *which* she is; but there are men who *do* seem to know and Sally, poor lamb, had fallen in love again with one, the wretch who had soon brought this trouble upon her. I am not going to defend her, nor am I going to blame him: I am not in a position to do so, for my ignorance on subjects of this nature is reasonably profound, and I hope will continue to be so: but I do feel there was something rather too casual about this Seringapatam marital arrangement. Even so, I'm not going to hold her entirely blameless. Having a husband somewhere in the offing she ought to have refrained from associating with this other person; but the reasons why women fall in love with some particular men are inscrutable; men with the faces of mice and the hearts of centipedes, indecently hairy men, or razor-faced men who blather to them about the right to self-fulfilment. Some such oaf had caught Sally's fancy, and the soldier in Seringapatam was betrayed.

And what had I to do with all this? A moment, please; I am coming to that.

The poor lamb was dead. Up in London she privily visited some quack in the underworld who throve on such cases, and he sold her something to remove the disgrace. In two days she was dead. The quack was traced and arrested. They could not find Sally's guilty lover; they did not know who he was, though there was plenty of suspicion; indeed to God there was altogether too much! That secret died with the girl, but she left a whole bushel of other secrets lying about. Because, the strange thing is, she had kept a diary — though that is not strange in itself — which was found by the police, and it told them all about her secret life and love ever since the departure of her husband. There was a great deal of it, with very intimate details. Why do some people delight to confess to themselves in secret those things they would rather die than out-face in public — as Sally did indeed die? Beauty like hers is glory, but it is a peril too, for her diary revealed the story of her illicit amours, not merely with the defaulting lover but with twenty-two different men, at various times and places. She had left an almost complete record, and she had left their names. In truth she was one of the most beautiful creatures in the bright world, and yet she had to do with some queer men, ugly fellows rather, and low characters, although one of them, I assure you, was the mayor of the town — but *he* had a wooden leg. Holy God, there is wicked-ness everywhere! I am a man of independent means myself, though I fraternize with the poorer orders and others because, of course, I realize that education is merely the means of enabling you to do easily the things you find difficult or do not care so much about; yet it is hard for me to understand that book. Still, many new ideas are born into God's world, and I am told it is not very hard to explain.

One of these men had brought her to her death. Which one? Several of the episodes in her diary implicated Tom Wilson, and, as I have already told you, there are two Thomas Wilsons in our town. I swear I am not the one referred to in the diary. I am *not*, I know my innocence as well as that viper with my name must know his own bitter sin, but there was nothing else to guide the police beyond those names written in the book of a girl who was dead and couldn't explain, and so we *both* had to go. The other names did not give any trouble; they, too, were common enough, like Meakins, Hoar, Tuckwell, Cox, Rowbotham — every man jack of them came from our town — and all were traced home and all, like the two Thomas Wilsons, protested their ignorance of the case. Nevertheless, we were all cited to appear and answer if called upon at the trial of this quack who had killed our Sally. For such a large party it was obviously possible, as well as wise, to make special arrangements; there were twenty-four all told, including the police inspector and me, and so we chartered a charabanc and rode up to London together.

I am not likely to forget a journey so noted in my memory, from that calm peerless morn down by the harbour, where I joined the charabanc, a cockily-painted motor-coach christened 'Nixey's Harlequin', until night, when it brought me back again — a marked man. The coach was but half full when I entered, the detective-sergeant stood at the door, and those within sat moodily staring seawards while we waited there for stragglers. There is no harbour really, nothing but a few stone piers left of a project abandoned before I was born — a hurricane killed it, I fancy. The giant mast that gives such a nautical air to the open space fronting the sea was only designed to support a flag on the king's birthday. Two black, speckled pigeons were bobbing on the pavement outside the fishmonger's. There were lilacs out in that garden next door to the blind umbrella-maker's. In so soft and warm an air, by so genial a sea, at so placid an hour, it seemed a world without end. People strolled on indolently with one hand on their hips and the old postman with blue spectacles on rambled unhurriedly in and out of shops and gardens. Upon the flat sea long slender rolls of water, smooth and soft as a bosom, would arise and slowly glide, and then begin to hurry as if tiptoeing to the shore, but they soon tired and subsided and never curled into rich waves.

The last arrival was this man Wilson, wearing a geranium in his buttonhole and carrying an umbrella and a suitcase. He was always noted for a sort of vile affability, and as he came into the coach he grinned expansively at us all and bawled:

'Now then, naughty boys, whad yeh all bin up to, eh?'

Nobody answered, all were stricken with consternation, for most of them were endeavouring by a gloss of unconcerned detachment to impress their fellow travellers with the sense that they were there by the purest of accidents and not at all as culprits.

'Ha, ha,' gurgled Wilson, as he found a seat and sat down. Pulling a green silk handkerchief from his breast, he smeared his mouth with it.

'Naughty boys! Whad yeh gunna do about it, eh?'

The detective looked round and delivered what I think in the circumstances was a correct and perfectly proper rebuke to him:

'If you please, we don't want any of that.'

'O, all right,' sneered Wilson, 'pass me the password, Reginald. That's all I want.'

The audacity of the fellow! And the sergeant's name was not Reginald at all. But I am bound to say he was quiet for the remainder of the journey.

The sergeant counted us, and as we were all aboard he gave the signal to start. But I felt my soul sicken at going where I was going with such men, sharing their wretched plight, and, remembering that they had all embraced her, breathing in their shame. For the shame, somehow, was not in her at all, it was in *them*, and they were going to deny her. It did not seem to matter a bit that she had been ... well ... had been ... unusual; to have seen her and enjoyed her beauty was a thing to be grateful for. I looked to see who amongst them had honoured her memory with a sign of mourning; there were only three or four wearing black ties, and these I perceived were the unmarried ones — they had nothing to fear from wives! Nearly all were of the artisan class, a carpenter, a fishmonger, a dairyman, an engineer, a clerk, the driver Nixey himself; Wilson was an insurance agent, and of course you could tell the mayor by his wooden leg. And it seemed as if all these men, except the sergeant and me, had had a hand in this crime. Perhaps it was the burden of that reflection that kept them all furtively mute until we got to London and disembarked at the court.

I can never make out why justice is chambered in such uncouth shape, in courts of absurd proportions, gloomy, unsavoury, moth-eaten, the concrete distillation of inconvenience, and staffed by attendants who seemed to have served their apprenticeship at some low menagerie. Nothing is in accord with the honour of justice, there is only a purposeless harmony with the misery of the delinquent. For hour after hour we sat in two rows at the back of the court, listening to the accusation and the denial and the examination of witnesses who infuriated the judge because they did not 'speak up'. A young woman in the witness-box, rather a pretty creature as things go, kept pressing her handkerchief to her mouth; the poor wretch was sweating with emotion. And at last the judge, whose face had the complexion of sliced ham, addressed her in lofty tones:

'Have you by any chance got toothache, or a cough, or a sore throat, or what? No! Then put that handkerchief away,' he bellowed. 'If your tonsils are not in a state of decay I want to hear them *booming* at me, you understand.'

The girl's replies to the next two or three questions were uttered in such a mere waif of sound that his lordship dashed his pen upon his desk and glared at her.

'O, this is intolerable! Shout at me, please, witness!'

The witness hung her head as if in tears.

'Will you do me the favour,' he roared, 'of shouting at me. Shout! Shout as if you were at one end of a telephone speaking to someone in the north of Scotland who couldn't hear you.'

Then, quite audibly, the voice of the witness rose: 'I don't know anybody in Scotland, sir.'

'That's right. Much better. Keep it up, now.'

But a few moments later he was again admonishing her:

'O, if you would only *scream* at me!'

So the case went on, and although time was consumed in trivialities and by a clerk who wrote down reams of evidence very slowly in a fair copyright hand, the hours passed so speedily that the end of the day was almost upon us before counsel reached the vital question of the diary.

'Where is it?' asked the judge.

The book was handed up to him and he perused it for some minutes, while the barrister folded his hands behind him under his black gown and engaged in confident meditation with the ceiling.

'How many did you say?'

Counsel sank upon his brief with alacrity:

'Er . . . twenty-two, my lord.'

'Have you any testimony to put forward in regard to this book. Were you proposing to call these men?'

'That is for you to decide, my lord. They are in attendance here' — and he waved a bland hand in our direction — 'all of them.'

And the judge said he didn't want to hear us; the judge actually said we were nothing to do with the case! He gave a sort of ruling — though I must say I do not understand the law — he gave a ruling (*a*) that the diary was *said* to have been written by the woman who was now dead, but there was no proof forthcoming that it had *indeed* been written by Mrs. Burden; in any case she could not be cross-examined about it. (*b*) The entries might or might not be true, but counsel was unable to substantiate them. (*c*) Even if counsel had been in a position to do so, the entries themselves had no bearing whatever on the charge he was trying. So he said he must rule it out. And he ruled it out! Yes, we were ruled out just as if nothing of this had the slightest relation to a person who had died.

We all waited until the court rose, but nothing more happened because the trial was not concluded; in fact, I was told, it lasted most of the following day. All my time and expense had been wasted, to say nothing of the trouble, for I was not given a chance of clearing myself of this odious suggestion. Things were left just as they were, just as, in fact, they are now, for I have never been able to make plain to anybody, public or private, that I was taken there under a misapprehension. No one would listen to me, no one paid me the slightest attention. I might have been a child complaining of a lost rattle. But I am a man not easily baulked, I determined to say my say and uphold my character. I have a natural regard for honest conduct, and I resolved to speak to the judge if I could, or if not him, then somebody else in authority, and so when I saw the prosecuting barrister passing out of the hall I ran after him and told him everything. He stopped whistling and said:

'Well, what do you want *me* to do?'

'Can't you see, sir, I am entirely innocent of all this?'

'No one has said otherwise,' he answered.

'But the police brought me here!'

'They will take you back again,' he said.

'I am not the T. Wilson referred to in the diary,' I told him.

'Still,' he says, 'you have not been charged with anything, have you?'

'No, but I come of a family that has always been esteemed,' I explained. 'My father was a master apothecary; he patented a cure for palsy and owned his own property. People do not like these millstones to be hung round their necks.'

'Neither do I,' says he; and off he struts, whistling again.

I shouted after him: 'It is a *most despicable, most* despicable business.' For though I am certainly not easily baulked, and with me difficulties come only to be *over*come, when it comes to being baffled by sheer absence of comprehension it is not so simple; you are baulked or baffled not by a difficulty so much as a complete void. And what do you do with a void? I could do nothing, I could do nothing then, I have been able to do no more to this very day.

Do you know, not a word was spoken about the case during the whole return journey. Would you believe it! We stopped at a public house half-way home to wet the whistle, as they say; one of those places of bloated service where the piano plays for a penny, and there I tried to wrestle out the mistake with this T. Wilson, but he was impervious. I kept saying to him: 'Look here, you know,' but I've no care to make a public show, my wish is to live and die private. He stood in the midst of that saloon-crowd holding a glass of whisky up in his right hand; the bloom of the geranium in his coat had been shattered to its sprigs.

'Not my drink, boys, by rights. I guarantee to say I don't drink a bottle of whisky a year. You know what I mean, not of my own drinking. If I am out with the boys, good men, one of ourselves, that's different, but I guarantee to say I do not, *not* in a year, not a *bottle*, not on my own. I mean to say of course if I'm out with friendly men, that's another matter, that's ex gratia; we're all sports, or we hope we are, you know what I mean. But apart from that, taking it all round, year in and year out, I guarantee to say a bottle of whisky does not pass my sacred lips.'

'Look here,' I began again.

'And what's more,' said he, 'it won't neither.'

'Listen here,' I said. 'I want to you explain to

everybody here that I am not the T. Wilson mixed up in this.'

But he soothered me with a lot of odious verbiage, neither quite denial nor quite admission; what we know we *know*, and what we *don't* know is done with, and all that. Ah, the cockroach! You'd have thought *he* was the mistaken, the misunderstood, and *I* the bad one! It was impossible to counter the vile and tricky affability of that man, and the others applauded him.

It was the same at the melancholy end of the journey. The harbour was in a drift of haze, foul with insipid moonlight, and the twenty-two parted as though there was something they had all conspired to suppress, to deny, to ignore, to cast out and bury deeply. But whatever they thought or said or did, shame is shame and you can't hide it in your pocket. Like Cain's mark it is on the brow, and I — my God! — I've got my unlucky share of it.

Nixey's Harlequin (1931)

THE CHERRY TREE

THERE was uproar somewhere among the backyards of Australia Street, so alarming that people at their mid-day meal sat still and stared at one another. A fort-night before murder had been done in the street, in broad daylight, with a chopper; people were nervous. An upper window was thrown open and a startled and startling head exposed.

'It's that young devil, Johnny Flynn, again! Killing rats!' shouted Mrs. Knatchbole, shaking her fist to-wards the Flynn's backyard. Mrs. Knatchbole was ugly; she had a goitred neck and a sharp skinny nose with an orb shining at its end, constant as grief.

'You wait, my boy, till your mother comes home, you just wait!' screamed this apparition, but Johnny was gazing sickly at the body of a big rat slaughtered by the dogs of his friend George. The uproar was caused by the quarrelling of the dogs, possibly for honours, but more probably, as is the custom of victors, for loot.

'Bob down!' warned George, but Johnny bobbed up to catch the full anger of those baleful Knatchbole eyes. The urchin put his fingers promptly to his nose.

'Look at that for eight years old!' screamed the lady. 'Eight years old 'e is! As true as God's my maker, I'll . . .'

The impending vow was stayed and blasted for ever, Mrs. Knatchbole being taken with a fit of sneezing, whereupon the boy uttered some derisive 'Haw haws!'

So Mrs. Knatchbole met Mrs. Flynn that night as she came from work, Mrs. Flynn being a widow who toiled daily and dreadfully at a laundry and perforce left her children, except for their school hours, to their own devices. The encounter was an emphatic one, and the tired widow promised to admonish her boy.

'But it's all right, Mrs. Knatchbole, he's going from me in a week, to his uncle in London he is going, a person of wealth, and he'll be no annoyance to ye then. I'm ashamed that he misbehaves but he's no bad boy really.'

At home his mother's remonstrances reduced Johnny to repentance and silence; he felt base indeed; he wanted at once to do something great and worthy to offset it all; he wished he had got some money, he'd have gone and bought her a bottle of stout — he knew she liked stout.

'Why do ye vex people so, Johnny?' asked Mrs. Flynn wearily. 'I work my fingers to the bone for ye, week in and week out. Why can't ye behave like Pomony?'

His sister was a year younger than he; her baptismal name was Mona, but Johnny's elegant mind had disliked it and so one day he re-baptized her; Pomona she became and Pomona she remained. The Flynns sat down to supper. 'Never mind, Mum,' said the boy, kissing her as he passed, 'talk to us about the cherry tree!'

The cherry tree, luxuriantly blooming, was the crown of the mother's memories of her youth and her father's farm; around the myth of its wonderful blossoms and fruit she could weave garlands of romance, and to her own mind as well as to the minds of her children it became a heavenly symbol of her old lost home, grand with acres and delightful with orchard and full pantry. What wonder that in her humorous narration the joys were multiplied and magnified until even Johnny was obliged to intervene:

'Look here, how many horses *did* your father have, Mum . . . really, though?'

'O . . . lots, Johnny; any amount of 'em!'

'But what *sort* of horses, Mum?'

'Sort! O . . . they were . . . they were . . . piebald horses . . . like circus horses.'

Johnny looked fearfully unconvinced.

'But what did you *do* with them, Mum?'

'O,' Mrs. Flynn was very blithe, 'I used to drive out with them, Johnny. Every morning before breakfast I used to drive out with my piebald horses and sit on the front seat, 'long with the butler. And we had a plum-pudding dog too, to trot under the axle . . .' But here Mrs. Flynn became vague, cast a furtive glance at this son of hers and suddenly screamed with laughter. She recovered her ground with: 'Ah, but there *was* a cherry tree, Johnny, truly!'

'What sort of a cherry tree, Mum?'

'Well . . . a cherry tree, a beautiful cherry tree.'

'A big one?'

'It was nearly as big as the house, Johnny.'

'And cherries on it?'

'Cartloads, cartloads of cherries on that tree, Johnny. Cartloads! All sorts. Every kind of cherry you can think of. It *was* a lovely cherry tree.'

Well, they got on with their supper, and grand it was — a polony and four or five potatoes — because Johnny was going away shortly, and ever since it was known that he was to go to London they had been having something special, like this, or sheep's trotters, or a pig's tail. Mother seemed to grow kinder and kinder to him. He wished he had some money, he would buy her a bottle of stout — he knew she liked stout.

Johnny went away to live with his uncle, but alas,

he was only two months in London before he was
returned to his mother and Pomony. Uncle was an
engine-driver who disclosed to his astounded nephew
a passion for gardening. This was incomprehensible
to Johnny Flynn. A great roaring boiling locomotive
was the grandest thing in the world, Johnny had rides
on it, so he knew. And it was easy for him to imagine
that every gardener cherished in the darkness of his
disappointed soul an unavailing passion for a steam
engine, but how an engine-driver could immerse himself in the mushiness of gardening was a baffling
problem. However, before he returned home he discovered one important thing from his uncle's hobby,
and he sent the information to his sister:

Dear Pomona,
    Uncle Henry has got a alotment and grow veggut-
ables. He says what makes the mold is worms. You
know we puled all the worms out off our garden and
chukked them over Miss Natchbols wall. Well you
better get some more quick a lot ask George to help you
and I bring som seeds home when I comes next week
by the xcursion on Moms birthday
                    Your sincerely brother
                                John Flynn

On mother's birthday Pomona met him at the
station. She kissed him shyly and explained that
mother was going to have a half-holiday to celebrate
the double occasion and would be home with them at
dinner time.
    'Pomony, did you get them worms?'
    Pomona was inclined to evade the topic of worms
for the garden, but fortunately her brother's enthusi-
asm for another gardening project tempered the wind

of his indignation. When they reached home he unwrapped two parcels he had brought with him. One was a bottle of stout and the other a bag of cherries. He explained a scheme to his sister and he led her into the garden. The Flynn's backyard, mostly paved with bricks, was small and so the enclosing walls, truculently capped by chips of glass, although too low for privacy were yet too high for the growth of any cherishable plant. Johnny had certainly once reared a magnificent exhibit of two cowslips, but these had been mysteriously destroyed by the Knatchbole cat. The dank little enclosure was charged with sterility; nothing flourished there except a lot of beetles and a dauntless evergreen bush, as tall as Johnny, displaying a profusion of thick shiny leaves that you could split on your tongue and make squeakers with. Pomona showed him how to do this, and Pomona and he busied themselves in the garden until the dinner siren warned them that mother would be coming home. They hurried into the kitchen and Pomona quickly spread the cloth and the plates of food upon the table, while Johnny placed conspicuously in the centre, after laboriously extracting the stopper with a fork and a hair-pin, the bottle of stout brought from London. He had been much impressed by numberless advertisements upon the hoardings respecting this attractive beverage. The children then ran off to meet their mother and they all came home together with great hilarity. Mrs. Flynn's attention having been immediately drawn to the sinister decoration of her dining table, Pomona was requested to pour out a glass of the nectar. Johnny handed this gravely to his parent, saying:

'Many happy returns of the day, Mrs. Flynn!'

'O, dear, dear!' gasped his mother merrily. 'You drink first!'

'Excuse me, no, Mrs. Flynn,' rejoined her son, 'many happy returns of the day!'

When the toast had been honoured Pomona and Johnny looked tremendously at each other.

'Shall we?' exclaimed Pomona.

'O yes,' decided Johnny; 'come on, Mum, in the garden, something marvellous!'

She followed her children into that dull little den, and happily the sun shone there for the occasion. Behold, the dauntless evergreen bush had been stripped of its leaves and upon its blossomless twigs the children had hung numberless couples of ripe cherries, white and red and black.

'What do you think of it, Mum?' cried the children, snatching some of the fruit and pressing it into her hands. 'What do you think of it?'

'Beautiful!' said the poor woman in a tremulous voice. They stared silently at their mother until she could bear it no longer. She turned and went sobbing into the kitchen.

Clorinda Walks in Heaven (1922)

THE PRESSER

Two or three years after the first Jubilee of Queen Victoria a small ten-year-old boy might have been seen slouching early every morning along the Mile End Road towards the streets of Whitechapel. Johnny Flynn was a pale boy of pinched appearance — for although his black coat was a size too large for him, his black trousers were a size too small — he was not very well, and he was tired. Plodding along from his aunt's house miles away in Hackney, he sometimes drowsily ran into things; things like sauntering policemen (who were ductile and kind) or letter boxes (that were not). A policeman genially shook him.

'Ay! Where ye going?'

'Going to work, sir.'

'Work! What work do ye work at?'

'Mr. Alabaster's, a tailor, sir.'

'Oh, a tailor! Mind he don't put ye under a thimble and suffocate ye. Get along with it, and don't go knocking people down 's if ye was popping off to Buckingham Palace!'

Johnny wanly smiled as he said 'No,' and 'Good-morning, sir.'

It was generally a letter-box, though, and after such a mishap one day he had gone into a public lavatory. There he had seen a bad word chalked up on the wall — a very bad word. Johnny Flynn knew all about bad words although he had never uttered them; his mind shrank from them as a snail shrinks when you spit on it. But this time he went on his way with the bad word chanting in his mind — he could *not* but listen to it, he was absorbed by it; and the very next letter-box he came to he said it out boldly and loud seven times, to the letter-box. And one day he dropped his packet of dinner into the mouth of one of those letter-boxes.

Well, when he came to Whitechapel there was Leman Street, and off Leman Street there were other streets full of shops with funny names over the windows, like Greenbaum, Goldansky, Finesilver and Artzbashev, and shops full of foreign food that looked nasty and smelled, or full of objects that seemed vaguely improper. There were hundreds of clattering carts bedazing him, and women who were drunk at eight o'clock in the morning sat on doorsteps with their heads in their hands. And they smelled, too. Very soon now he reached a high dull building that hoarded a barracks of prolific Jewish families, and ascending one flight of its sticky stone stairs he came to a standstill outside a door in a dark passage. There he had to wait until Mr. Sulky, who was the presser and had the key, arrived. Mr. Sulky was a big dark young man with a pale pitted face, who lodged in an eating house, and went for long walks on Sundays, and passed for a misogynist. The rest of his time he spent in pressing trousers with a large hot-iron goose.

Johnny said: 'Good morning, sir.'

Mr. Sulky said: 'Huh!' but he always said it with a faint smile.

The first business in the tailor's workshop was to light the fire, a great fire maintained with coke. Then, to sweep the room clean of its countless fragments of cloth and cotton. Heaping these in a wooden box, the boy staggered with it across the dark passage into a smaller apartment with a window, the very symbol of gloom, looking down into a dank yard where he could see people all day long going to the privy. The room contained only a colossal pile of cloth clippings covering the whole floor, and it was his unending task to sort these into their various kinds. The pile never lessened, it seemed to grow with absorbent inexorable growth. Sometimes he could scarcely enter the door to get into the room; and the implacable mountain of rags was watered with the tears of his childish hungers and despairs. He emptied the box and returned to the workshop.

Eight or nine women came in and began their work of making trousers. A massive table stood in the middle; the women sat round three sides of the room on old empty boxes — these were less comfortable than chairs, but more convenient. The room was large and well lighted from two windows. In summer the windows were a blessing to the women, the hot fire an affliction; in winter it was otherwise. Sometimes they sweated, and sometimes they sneezed or they coughed, but they never shivered. Each woman had a pad of needles tacked to her bodice, a pair of scissors and skeins of thread in her lap, and her hands were busied with the garments of men she knew nothing about. Each had a wedding ring on her nuptial finger, the beginnings of a hump on her shoulders, and the deuce knows what emotions in her heart. They were mostly young women, but they looked old, whereas Mr. Sulky and Mr. Alabaster were young and looked young. It reminded Johnny of the question propounded by a famous advertisement:

> Why does a woman look old
> sooner than
> a man?

And the answer was something to do with soap.

His favourite was certainly Helen, she was handsomest. Johnny liked her, she had a pretty freckled face and a big bosom, and was tall and fair. Johnny admired her, though she was not kind to him and effusive like old Mrs. Grainger. Indeed, she was in some ways, he thought, rather unkind and slightly haughty, but her smile was lovely. She was married to a bottle-washer named Smithers, and they had a little girl Hetty, six or seven years old, with weak eyes and heavy boots, who often came and sat on the stairs waiting for her mother. Mrs. Grainger was a wrinkled crone who got drunk on Saturday nights in order to import cheer into her fading hours. Beer, she declared, was better than hot soup in her belly. When Johnny first came to work with them she catechized him.

'You're a weeny little chap. What's your age?'

Her hands were shiny and lumpy; she was thin, but she had a plump behind.

'I'm ten years,' replied the flustered boy.

'God's my mercy! You ought to be at school, your age. Why don't you go to school?'

'I'm not well,' said Johnny.

'Nobody's well in this world. We're all alike.'

The old woman hawked and spat into her snuffy handkerchief. 'What's the matter with you?'

'I don't know,' Johnny Flynn confessed.

'How d'ye know you're not well then?'

'I can feel,' said Johnny.

'What can you feel?'

'In my liver,' the boy whispered. 'Inch and half lower than it ought to be, and we can't alter it. My mother's a widow.'

'So your father's dead?'

'Yes; she lives in the country.'

'And where do you live?'

'With my aunt and uncle. Down at Hackney. He's an engine-driver.'

'That's grand! D'ye like it?'

The boy reflected. 'I don't know,' he said slowly.

'Well, God's my mercy!' tittered the old woman. 'You must go out in the fresh air all you can.'

In the corner a girl sat machining seams. Mr. Sulky took a hot goose from the fire to the table and pressed trousers under a damp rag that soon rotted the air with the odour of steaming cloth. This was a necessary evil, for although all the others were engaged in cutting out, preparing, stitching, binding, button-holing, and generally compounding trousers, the art of finishing the garment lay with the presser, the prince of a tailor's workshop — and that was Mr. Sulky. No civilian, from a bookbinder to a bishop, would dream of donning a pair of trousers that had not been pressed. A Hottentot might, or a skipjack — yes, conceivably even a bookbinder might — but certainly not a bishop. Let it have buttons of gold, fabulous fabric, silky seams, and trimmings of rapture, fused in a noble equilibrium of cut, but until it had been baptized with a wet rag and punched with a hot iron it is nothing.

Mr. Sulky (who passed for a misogynist) whistled airily as he bumped and hissed with his iron, and then began to chaff the women.

'Well, ladies!'

Heavy scarlet lips gave him the pout of a sardonic man, but his face was a kind face, very pale and very bare. Not a hair or the sign of it was to be seen on his chin. Or on his arms. At work he cast off his coat, waistcoat and collar, and wore only a striped shirt and a belt round his trousers. He kept on his neat buttoned boots, turned up his stiff cuffs, and his cuff-links tinkled as he jerked his arms.

'What devilry have you all been at since yesterday?'

The ladies glanced at each other, and tittered.

'Nothing, Ernie, so help me God,' cackled Mrs. Grainger. 'Ask Helen.'

'Bah!' The presser clouted his goose down upon some innocent trousers.

'O dear, ladies,' cried the provoking old woman, 'he's got a wink over his eye this morning.'

Mr. Sulky, somewhat baffled, stuttered: 'Born devils! And you're the worst of the lot.'

'No, Ernie, no.' The old woman's glasses twinkled reassuringly at him. 'I had my dues, thank God, years ago.'

'Your dues!'

'Many a time, and I can't deny it,' said the old woman.

'Ah, devils born, I tell you,' groaned the presser.

'And the men! Dear Lord!' Mrs. Grainger shot at him, 'You can't even make your own trousers.'

Mr. Sulky made a rude reply, and the women laughed quietly though they pretended not to. It made Johnny laugh, but at the same time he was ashamed to laugh — and he pretended not to. Once, a boy at school had told him a rude joke, and it was such a cunning comical joke that he had to tell it in a whisper to his father. Father had giggled. 'Don't tell mother,' implored the boy. And father had said: 'Pooh, no. No fear!' But Johnny was sure that he had gone and told mother at once, and he could not bear to think of it.

There was no more joking after Mr. Alabaster came in, for he was the master. Mr. Alabaster had short bow legs, a pink face, and florid hair that curled dandily. So did his voice, for he lisped. Very cheerful he looked, and was seldom harsh to anyone. At the table opposite Mr. Sulky he stood with a measuring tape around his shoulders, a pair of shears or a piece of pipeclay in his right hand; and having made chalk marks on whatever piece of cloth was before him, he cut trousers out of serge, flannel, duck, vicuna, tweed, any mortal cloth you could think of, all day long. A very clever fellow. A thoughtful man, too. He would never allow Johnny Flynn to stay in the workshop during the dinner hour. Summer or winter, rain or shine, out he had to go.

'You muth get the fresh air into you,' Mr. Alabaster said. 'Itth good for the lining of the stomach, or I shall have the poleeth on me. You can go under the railway arch if it rainth.'

No one but Mr. Sulky had the privilege of staying in the workshop during dinner time; that was the edict, the injunction, the fixed rule. Then how was it that Mrs. Smithers stayed there sometimes; Johnny would like to know. Mr. Alabaster did not know of it, but Johnny knew and the women knew; what was more, although they never enjoyed that favour themselves, they were glad when Helen did. Johnny was glad too, in a way, because of course her husband was a nasty cruel man who slogged her about, and it was best for her not to go home more often than she had to.

Mrs. Grainger used to advise her about Smithers:

'Give him in charge, my gal, turn him out, or sling your hook. He's a dirty foul thing, and the Lord gave him to you for a walking wickedness.'

'How can I do that?' asked Helen. 'I'm married to him, and there's little Hetty.'

'Oh, God's my mercy!' Mrs. Grainger was baffled, but still emphatic. 'Give him in charge and sling your hook. What with the men and their women and the holy marriage bells, you can't tell your head from your elbow. It ought to be made impossible, and then there'd be some sense in Christianity.'

Well, the boy would go and walk in the streets. Unless it rained he avoided the railway arch because someone had done murder there, and someone else had painted a white skeleton on the wall; so he walked about. There was the dreadful den where the Jews brought their fowls to be strangled; knots of gabbling women dangling dead birds or birds that were going to be dead, the pavement dribbling blood, and feathers falling, sticking in the blood. And in the bakehouse next door you could watch a man flinging limp motzas, like pieces of white velvet, into a big oven, and another man drawing them out as stiff as china plates. Soon he opened his package of food — wedges of bread and slips of meat folded in a sheet of newspaper. Scrupulously he sniffed the meat, and not caring for that smell he dropped the meat into a gutter and chewed the bread with resentment. Yesterday it was pickled pork, and the day before; it would be pickled pork to-morrow, and the day after, and the day after that. Whatever it was he had it for a week; six days it savoured, and did all that it was not expected to do. His aunt was a wise and busy woman who could not prepare a fresh meal for him every day; it was not to be thought of and it was not necessary. Every Saturday night she bought for his separate and sole consumption a little joint of meat, cooking it specially for him on Sundays; and every week his stomach turned sour on it after a day or two. This image of that evil ort of flesh reposing undiminishably in the larder tormented him even in dreams. It never entered his mind to complain to his aunt, and if it had done so he had little of the spirit of complaint. If he was not exactly a Spartan, he was, you might say, spartanatical. Things happened to you; they were good, or they were bad — and that was the truth about everything.

Now this neighbourhood was full of little Jew boys, and it was the custom of little Christians to submit such heathens to mockery, often to ill-treatment. In the early days there Johnny Flynn had called after some of them, 'Sheeny! Sheeny!' Sweet knowledge, how we live and learn! It was no joke to be the one pure Christian boy in a street full of belligerent bloody-minded Hebrew serpents who pretended to run away when you made a face at them, but who, as soon as you pursued them, turned diabolically upon you and dashed your Christianity into discomfiture and blood. Perhaps it was these very misfortunes that made Johnny Flynn so fond of evangelical hymns. Whenever he experienced any joy — and that was not seldom — he would lift up his heart and sing to himself that he was

Sweeping through the gates of the New Jerusalem,
Washed in the blood of the Lamb.

Or if it were sorrow that he felt — and that, too, was not seldom — he would murmur the

Sweetest carol ever sung:
Jesus, blessed Jesus.

But maybe it was really an emotional gift from his mother. Always on Sunday eve she had taken him to an undenominational chapel run by some hooded sisters and a preacher with gaunt eyes who sometimes preached himself into a fit. At some stage of the service the sisters would come round and interrogate the worshipper.

'Are you saved?'

'Yes, ma'am, thank you,' Mrs. Flynn would reply.

'Praise God. Is your little boy saved?'

'Yes, ma'am,' said mother, with bright hope in her eyes, 'I *think* he is.'

'Praise God, sister.'

But when the lady had passed on Johnny would bend and growl at his mother:

'What d'you tell her that for?'

'Well, you *must* be saved, Johnny, you know you must.'

'I ain't going to be,' he would say wretchedly; 'never, I won't be.'

'Now don't you be a bad boy, Johnny, or you'll go to the fire. Of course you must be saved; whatever next!'

Then, seeing him so cross, she would press his hand fondly and he would love her again, so that when they stood up to sing 'Sweeping through the gates', he would join in quite happily and admire her sweet voice.

Ah, in such matters he was on the side of his father. Father was an atheist, he had even joined the Skeleton Army — a club of men who went about in masks or black faces, with ribald placards and a brass band, to make war upon the Salvation Army. Yet when his father had died — twelve months ago — and a friend had made a small wooden cross, painted black, to put on his grave, Johnny had painted his name and dates on the cross in white paint with a thin brush that vexed him to madness, for the hair of the brush kept sticking out at the angle of the pressure applied and looked like an L. Moreover, Johnny had decided that his father should have an epitaph; so he cut up a piece of a cardboard box, gave it a border of black ink, composed a verse, and tacked the card to the cross with some little nails.

I am not gone I am only a sleep.
   Where Jesus heavenly mansions keep.
Grieve not for long nor trouble be
   And love each other because of me.   J. F.

He wept while he composed this piece of deathly poetry, and whenever he recalled it afterwards he wept again. His mother, too, liked it so very much that tears came into her eyes. In a few weeks rain had soaked the card on the cross; the sun had bleached it and discoloured the ink so that it could hardly be read. When some of the tacks came out the card curled over and exposed an advertisement on its back of somebody's baking powder.

Long ere day was over the boy regretted his rash disposal of the meat; devastating hunger assailed him and he yearned for any scrap, even a dog's. At such times it was the joy of heaven to him if Mrs. Grainger beckoned at tea-time.

'Johnny, I want you to go and get me a ha'p'orth of tea, a ha'p'orth of sugar and a farthingsworth of milk. There's threeha'pence — you can have the farthing for yourself.'

Nice, nice old woman! With his farthing he would buy a few broken biscuits; and he would borrow a pinch of her sugar and dip his biscuits in her milk. That did not happen every day. At other times it was a desperate joy to stand in front of a grocer's window, to divide the display in half, and to ponder long and exquisitely which half he would have if a choice were given him. Would you have marmalade, potted tongue, cocoa, and condensed milk — things like that — or would you have pineapple, corn beef and split peas — candles being no good? Desperate schemes for obtaining any of these, or anything else eatable, simply assaulted his longing, but he had no courage to test them again after he had once stolen a salted gherkin that made him vomit. He would turn away and glare along the pavements and gutters, hoping to find an apple-core or a rotten orange. Once he had the odd chance to pick up a playing-card, which he tore in pieces. Mother had warned him against the sin of card-playing; she had warned him against everything immoderate and immodest — strong drink, little girls, stealing, smoking, swearing and such like. Yet whenever Mr. Alabaster or Mr. Sulky sent him out in the evening for a can of beer he could not resist taking a stealthy gulp or two of the liquid. Hunger was awful. In a daze he soaped seams for Mr. Sulky or sewed buttons for Helen and Mrs. Grainger. If there was nothing else to be done he had to go to the rag-room and sort clippings from that maddening pile. Kneeling down beside his box among the soft rags he would dream over the fine doings he had had on Queen Victoria's Jubilee day. That *was* a day! All the scholars went to school in the morning to pray, to implore God to confound and frustrate certain nameless nations, to receive a china mug with the Queen's face twice on it, a medal with her face again — in case the mug got broken — and a paper bag containing half a sausage-pie and a great piece of cake. Lord, how grand! He ate them all over again and again. Then you marched out to the park with flags, and the park was full — millions of kids. There were clowns and jokers and sports, and you had your mug filled with tea from a steam-roller. Hundreds of steam-rollers. And then he forgot everything and fell asleep sprawling amongst the rags until the was awakened by angry Mr. Alabaster.

'Hi! hi! Thith won't do, you know. I don't pay you for thleeping, it will bankrupt me. It won't do at all. You and I muth part. God bleth, aren't you well?'

'Yes, sir.'

'Well, then! God bleth, do you think I am a million-aire with hundredth of pounds. I can't understand you, and it won't do. You and I will part, my man.'

But at the end of the day the kind Mr. Alabaster would sometimes give him a penny to ride part of the way home in a tram. With his penny Johnny hurried off to buy a cake or a pie, and thereafter walked cheerfully home. Often that penny became such a mighty necessity to him that as he knelt alone among the rags in the gloomy room, the pose, the quiet, and the need induced a mood in which he mumbled dozens of prayers.

'O God, make him give me a penny to-night, only a penny; make him give me a penny, please God. Amen.'

As if to impregnate his pleas with suitable flavour, he crooned over the hymns he knew. Then again: This once, like you did before, and I won't ask again. Amen.'

Not often were these prayers answered, and directly their failure became apparent he would descend weakly to the street, his whole body burning with ferocity against so frightful, so callous, so unseeing a god; and he would gasp out horrible blasphemies, until he came to a shop window where he could pause for a long rest, divide up its delicacies, and mystically devour them. In such delight he always forgot his anger against Jehovah.

One morning Helen came to the workroom at a very late hour. Mr. Alabaster regarded her sternly as she came in, until he saw she had a black eye horribly bruised, and knew she had been crying. She whispered a few words to Mr. Alabaster before going to her seat, and he lisped: 'O yeth, yeth. Dear me! Itth dreadful, yeth. Dear, dear me. All right.'

Mr. Sulky did not utter a sound, not one terrible word, and the whole room became silent. After his first and only glance at the disfigured woman, Mr.

Sulky pounced upon his task with a fermenting malignity, the wrath of one whose soul has been split by a shock that drained him of charity and compunction, and his hot iron crashed upon the apparel before him as though it contained the body of a loathed enemy. Windows trembled at each mighty jar, implements on the table spitefully clattered, and paper patterns fluttered off the walls as if casting themselves to perdition. Mr. Alabaster looked across protestingly.

'My word, Ernie! I thay!'

The presser ignored him. Snatching the iron from its stand, he flashed across the room, flung the cooling goose into the heart of the fire, took another in its place, tested it with a spit of saliva that ticked and slid into limbo, and resumed his murderous attack on the trousers.

'Stheady, Ernie! God bleth, you'll have the theiling down on uth!'

Mr. Alabaster's pipeclay was jolted from the table by the next concussion. Mr. Alabaster was master there, but he was a timid man; Sulky could eat three of him, and Sulky was a pearl amongst pressers; so Mr. Alabaster put on his coat. If Sulky was going mad he could go mad in peace and comfort.

'Muth go up the town this morning. Be back after dinner. Look after everything, Ernie. You know. Don't . . . ah . . . don't break anything, Ernie.'

The ignoring Mr. Sulky signalized his master's departure by a volley of ferocious clouts upon the garment he was handling. Then he stopped. Although the sewing-machine whirred in its corner, the quietness of the women was perceptibly tense. Helen bent low over her work. Johnny knew that she was still crying, and he could not bear to see this, so he tiptoed away from the workshop into the room across the passage and flung himself into the melancholy business of sorting the clippings. Canvas, buckram, silesia, cotton, silk, tweed, serge, flannel and vicuna all fetched different prices in the rag market and had to be separated into heaps. The main heap was impregnable; it was a job that never could be finished, for the pieces always accumulated faster than the boy could sort them. It was a tide that ebbed lightly and flowed greatly, and the spirit of the boy was drowned in it. Once he had read a fairy tale about a prince in captivity who was given a barn full of canary seed to sort out in a single night or else he was to be turned into a donkey. But the prince had a fairy godmother who set some earwigs on the job, and they finished it while the prince went off to a ball and married a poor girl who was lovely and good and had cured the fairy godmother of toothache. But there were no fairy godmothers in Whitechapel, and earwigs were no use — not with cloth. And Johnny's head behaved strangely nowadays. Sometimes his head would go numb and he would feel as if he were falling out of his body and sinking into the void. Or if he only heard the ping of an omnibus bell in the city, even that gave him a horrible blow in his heart, and his heart would rattle madly. The sound of the bells was so shocking to him that when he went up to the city he always stuffed pieces of wadding in his ears. And the sight of the room full of rags affected him in much the same way: his head swam, his knees trembled, and his heart rocked.

Suddenly the door was dashed open and Mr. Sulky appeared.

'O,' he said, seeing Johnny there. Then: 'Get out of this!'

The boy slunk out into the dark passage. Helen stood at the door; she held a handkerchief to her eyes.

'Come,' said Mr. Sulky, and Helen followed him into the rag room. They did not fasten the door. Johnny lingered outside; he did not know what else to do, he was a stupid boy. Hearing nothing within the room and being somewhat bewildered, he pushed open the door. Helen and Mr. Sulky were folded tightly in each other's arms, silent.

'Where shall I go?' the boy timidly whispered.

The presser turned his white face towards him and with his great teeth bared he snarled:

'Go away, you idiot!'

Out shot his foot and the door slammed in Johnny's face. The boy felt that his indiscretion had been vulgar. There was something in the surprising embrace of the two people — the figure of the piteous Helen and her tender cherishing by Mr. Sulky — that seemed almost holy. He crept back to the workroom where the women were talking aloud.

'Here, Johnny,' cried Mrs. Grainger. 'Just run out and get me a pennyworth of pills at the post office. My consumption's so bad this morning, it's murdering me. Ask them for rhubarb pills. I don't suppose they'll do me any good — the only cure for me is a dose of poison; but God Almighty made the medicine, and I might be lucky. A pennyworth of rhubarb pills, Johnny. And tell the man with the crooked nose they're for a lady that's got a delicate stomach. Don't forget that, there's a good boy.'

When he returned from this errand of mercy Helen and Mr. Sulky were back in the workshop again, looking as if nothing particular had occurred. Helen seemed cheerful. Mr. Sulky whistled softly and did not bang his irons about very much.

This was one of the days on which silly Johnny had thrown his dinner away, and as time wore on the old hunger brought him to his old despair. At seven o'clock Mr. Alabaster and Mr. Sulky tossed up to see who should pay for supper, and Mr. Sulky won — he always did. Johnny fetched them a small loaf, some cheese, a tin of lobster, and a can of beer. He tore off as much of the loaf's crust as he dared, if he could only have got at the lobster he would have gone to prison for it. He placed the food on the table.

'Good night, sir. Good night, Mr. Sulky,' then he said, moving slowly towards the door. The two men were laughing and cracking jokes.

'Hi! Here, Johnny, hereth a penny for the tram!'

O my, it was very blissful then! Fatigue and despair left him; down the stairs he went leaping and fled to a cookshop in the Mile End Road. It was some distance away, but it was there you could buy such marvellous penny cakes, of a size, of a succulence, reeking with sweet fat and crusted with raisins. Never a thought of the Lord, never a thanksgiving prayer. Johnny unwrapped the cake and stood gazing at it, seeking the loveliest corner of entry, when a large boy came to him from an alley near by and accosted him.

'Give us a bite, young 'un.'

'Gives nothing.' Master Flynn was positive to the point of heartlessness.

'I've had nothing to eat all day,' the large boy said mournfully.

Johnny intimated that he was in the same unfortunate case himself.

'Give us half of it, d'ye hear,' the other demanded in truculent tones, 'or I'll have the lot.'

Johnny shook his head and hiked a shoulder. 'No you won't.'

'Who'd stop me?' growled the bandit.

'Inky,' replied young Flynn. And then, as he lifted

the cake to his mouth and prepared to bite a great gap in it, the absolute and everlasting end of the world smote him clump on the ridge of his chin. He heard the rough fellow grunt: 'There's the upper cut for yer'; the cake was snatched from his paralysed grasp. 'And there's another for civility.' Again the end of the world crashed upon his face from the other side. Johnny felt no pain, not the faintest scruple of a physical twinge, but there was such a frantic roaring in his ears that he had to bend down with his head in his hands and stare abstractedly at the pavement. Scores of people were passing, but none seemed to have noticed this calamity; and when he looked up the fellow was gone, and the cake was gone. Dazed Johnny, after an interval for recovery, and after imprinting upon his mind the exact spot of the occurrence and the situation of that darksome alley, walked on grinding his teeth and registering a vow. He would train for a whole week on puddings made of blood — and then! Arabs gave their horses cakes made with mutton fat and they would fly over the desert, mad, all day long; but for people it had to be blood — and then you could blind anyone. He'd get some blood, a lot.

The next day was cold, with a frozen mist niggling in the streets, and when Johnny returned from an afternoon journey to the city it was almost dark. As he ascended the stairs he could just discern the little girl Smithers sitting there.

'Hullo, Hetty,' he said; and she said, 'Mind where you're coming!' She was nursing a black kitten.

'Your mother ain't done yet, Hetty, not for hours.'

The child hugged her kitten more closely, making no reply.

'Why don't you go home?' Johnny asked.

The child looked up at him, as if wondering at his foolishness.

'Somebody 'ull kick you,' he went on, 'sitting down. What you sitting there for?'

A voice from the head of the stairs called 'Hoi!'

Johnny looked up. 'It's me,' he said.

Down came Mr. Sulky. 'Is that Hetty?'

The child stood up and the man put an arm round her shoulders. 'Hallo, Hetty. Cold, aren't you? Want some tea?'

Hetty tucked the kitten under her arm and said, 'Yes', very softly. So Mr. Sulky put his hand in his pocket and jingled some money. Then he turned to Johnny. 'You want some tea?'

'No, not much,' lied the boy.

'Well, here's sixpence. Take Hetty out to some coffee-shop and give her a good tea, anything she likes, and have some yourself if you want any. Will you do that?'

'Yes,' said the boy.

'There you are, Hetty,' Mr. Sulky said; 'you go along of Johnny. He'll take you. And then come back here with him.' Bending down, Mr. Sulky astonishingly kissed the child.

She and Johnny clattered down the stone stairs together and out into the street.

'You can't bring that kitten,' Johnny pointed out, 'not in a shop.'

'Why?' asked the little girl.

'They won't serve you, not in a shop.'

Dully the child answered: 'Yes, they will.'

'They'll laugh at you,' protested Johnny. 'They'll . . . they'll cut its head off.'

'No, they won't,' Hetty said.

And in point of fact they did not, although the first

thing they saw on entering the coffee-house was a man in a white apron sharpening a long thin knife — a very large man. They sat down in a compartment, rather like a church pew, and the large man soon came up to them and tapped on the table with his ferocious knife.

'Well?' said he, very affably.

'Two cups of coffee, please, and two dorks, please,' young Flynn timidly ordered.

Soon the large man returned with these things.

'Two coffee, two slices,' he said, and pushed a basin of brown sugar towards them. Johnny thereupon gave him the sixpence, and the man gave him threepence change.

'It's nice in here, ain't it?' said Johnny. And indeed it was; warm and savoury, with the mingled odours of fish and bacon and the sawdust on the floor. Most of the other compartments had men in them, but they took no notice at all of the children or the kitten. Hetty dropped some spoonfuls of coffee into her saucer and stood the kitten on the table. It lapped a few drops and then sat upon its haunches to gaze at the ceiling.

'Going to have some more coffee?' inquired the boy.

Hetty nodded her head and said, 'You?'

'Na!' Johnny was contemptuous. 'I don't want any more coffee. What else d'you want?'

'Jam turnover,' replied the child.

The boy made a wry face. 'You don't want that. Nothing in 'em,' he declared. 'If I was you I'd have a lump of Tottenham cake. Have some Tottenham cake?'

Hetty picked the kitten off the table. 'Ernie said I could have what I like. . . .'

Johnny took her empty cup and walked off to the counter, returning with the cup refilled, a jam turnover, and a triangle of cake that had a pink bile-provoking veneer upon it. 'Tottenham,' said Johnny. They lingered on for some time until everything had disappeared, and Johnny had to explain to incredulous Hetty that all the money was gone.

'Where d'you live?' he asked her, and she replied that she lived in Bermondsey, that her father was a bottle-washer.

'I ain't got no father,' said Johnny Flynn dismally.

'He gets drunk every day,' continued Hetty.

'I ain't got no father at all,' repeated the boy, leaning his elbows on the table and looking mournful.

'And slashes mum,' said she.

'What for?' The boy was awed, but curious.

'He keeps on trying to kill us.'

'Yes, but what for?'

'I dunno,' said the little girl. 'Mum says he's gone into bad habits.'

'When my father got drunk,' Johnny Flynn expanded, 'he was grand.'

'And 'e's a noremonger,' Hetty added.

'What's that?'

'I dunno,' Hetty went on, stroking her kitten. 'I wish we'd got another one; I don't like him. More does mum.'

'But you can't have another father! Course you can't, silly,' commented Johnny Flynn.

'Yes, you can; and mum says we will, soon. We'll have to.'

Just then a quarrel arose in a compartment near them, between a man with a peg-leg and a man with a patch over one eye. They were sitting opposite each other.

'You're a liar!' bawled the wooden-leg man.

'O! Am I!'

'Yes. There you are. Now you know. I don't care

what company I'm in, or what company I ain't in, that's straight from my bloody heart.'

'I'm a liar, am I?' Patch-eye shouted.

'Yes, there you are!'

'And there *you* are!' cried the other, and he walloped his accuser over the head with a jar of salt.

The large man in the white apron dropped his knife and rubbed his hands together, yelling: 'Hi! Drop it. Devil and hell, where d'ye think you are — in the bull ring?'

And he hurled himself competently upon the brawlers.

'Drop it, d'ye hear! Or I'll have the guts out of you for my garters. Drop it!'

Both combatants subsided into their benches.

'D'ye see where he hit me?' said the peg-leg man, pointing with his finger to a spot on his head. 'Feel that!'

The fat host plunged his fingers amongst the greying hair. 'Jesus wept!' he murmured. 'There's a lump like St. Paul's Cathedral. I'm surprised at you, Patchy.'

'Called me a liar,' the aggressor explained callously.

'Pooh, that's only his ignorance!'

'Ignorance!' moaned the afflicted one. 'He's broken my brainpan. That's done me a lot of good, ain't it?'

'Ay, it's just his playful heart, that's all! Now behave yourselves,' the host went on, with emollient raillery, '. . . or! You know what I'll do to you — ha, ha! You know that, don't you? I'm the king of the castle here, and an Englishman's castle's his birthright all the world over. A king can do no wrong.'

'Why not?'

'It's just a law, like everything else,' mine host explained, 'but of course it's kept private.'

'O,' said the one-eyed man resignedly, 'give him another cup of cawfee!'

During this tumult Hetty trembled fearfully, and at last Johnny had to usher her out of the place.

'I don't like these dark streets,' said she, clutching Johnny's hand and tucking the kitten under her arm.

'That's nothing,' Master Flynn assured her. 'I like fighting. Don't you like fighting? I had a scrap with a bloke last night in the Mile End Road, and I split his head open in six places. Do you know what Peter Jackson does when he trains himself? He's the champion of the world, he is.'

Miss Smithers did not know.

'He drinks blood,' Johnny informed her.

When they approached the workshop they met Hetty's mother standing in the doorway at the foot of the stairs, so Johnny told her of the grand tea they had had. And while he was also telling her about the quarrel Mr. Sulky came tripping down the stairs.

'Hallo!' he cried, greeting them, as if he had just met them for the first time. 'Here we are then. This way, Nell. Good night, Johnny. Come on, Hetty.' And before Johnny could explain how he had spent the whole sixpence Mr. Sulky took Helen's arm and Hetty's hand, and the three of them walked off together. And Johnny heard Hetty exclaiming:

'Mum! Look at the dear little kitten!'

Johnny never saw Helen again. Apparently she had gone away, and she would be happier now. At the end of the week the women had a 'whip round' and collected a small sum of money to buy Mr. Sulky a teapot. He was setting up housekeeping — Mrs. Grainger said. And when she gave him the teapot she said God bless him, and wished him the best of luck.

In a little while Johnny's tribulation came to a happy

end. His mother wrote that she could not bear to be parted from him any longer; he had been away a year; he must come home to her now. His aunt was deeply annoyed at such ingratitude and wanted him to refuse to go home; but Johnny gave his notice in to Mr. Alabaster, who said he was very sorry to part with him, and declared that he 'wath the beth boy he ever had'. When the joyous last day came Mr. Alabaster wished him good-bye and gave him some good advice. Mr. Sulky did the same and presented him with sixpence as well.

'Good-bye, little Johnny,' whispered old Mrs. Grainger — and she gave him two new pennies. Johnny kept them sacredly in a box for many a long day.

Silver Circus (1928)

NINEPENNY FLUTE

HARRY DUNNING sold me his flute for ninepence. I didn't pay him the money all at once because at that time I was working for two horrible blokes and they didn't do me right. One was a Scotchman, and very Scotch, and the other a Jew, one of these 'ere Jews, and a credit to his race I must say. So I give Harry Dunning a tanner down and promised him the other as soon as I could. And this flute — I mean it was a fife — had a little crack in it near the top, only Harry Dunning said that didn't injure the tune at all because the crack was above the mouth-hole and the noise had to come out the bottom end. He said he'd get me into his fife and drum band if I bought it and as it was no good him getting me in the band if I hadn't got any flute I said I'd give him all the ninepence as soon as I could. So that's how I began to get real musical. My ma was very musical and after our dad pegged out she used to sing in the streets along of the Salvation Army. I didn't care much about that but she wanted me to get musical too, so I bought this fife and practised on 'The Wild Scottish Bluebells' till Harry Dunning took me one night to the instructor's class in Scrase's basement, after I'd paid him twopence more off the ninepence.

Mrs. Scrase always used to go out on the practice nights. She was a fat woman and their sitting-room wasn't very big and when old Scrase got the big drum in there she said it overpowered her. I suppose that's only woman-like, but all the same I really reckon it was because she didn't care much about music, in fact I don't think she liked it. Well, there was about a dozen of us there besides old Scrase; one of 'em had a kettle drum all polished up like gold and a lot of little screw taps on it to screw the skin up tighter or not. But it cost a fearful lot and it was only such chaps as Hubert Fossdyke could go in for a drum, his father being a master butcher as sold his own meat and cooked sheeps' heads and had a horse and cart. Old Scrase instructed Hubert some way I couldn't get the gauge of. 'Daddy — Mummy' he used to keep on saying to him, 'Daddy — Mummy', and Hubert would make a roll on the kettle drum that blooming near deafened you. Daddy meant tap it one way with one stick and Mummy meant tap it some other way — I couldn't cotton on to it — and it was a treat to hear. I'd much rather have had a kettle drum, they've got more dash than these flutes, only they cost such a fearful lot. And it's Eyes Front for drummers, always, none of your looking to the right or left — Eyes Front! The fifers had little brass gadgets to fit on the flutes and put the music cards in, and old Scrase comes up to me. He was a paperhanger by trade, with a cast in his eye. Not half the size of his missus and he'd got a medal pinned on his lapel for life-saving somebody out of the sea that was drowning, and I made up my mind I'd have a go at learning to swim too, because it's healthy for you and I like medals. There's something about medals, especially when you've got four or five all in a row. And Scrase says to me:

'Can't you read music?'

'I ought to,' I says, 'I was in a church choir once.'

'Yah, but can you *play* it? Let's hear you.'

I had a go at some card he give me, but as a matter of fact I was absolutely bamfoozled, because as a matter of fact I never could make anything of this old notation. So I told him I could really play anything if only I heard it once or twice. I'd a good ear for music.

'O!' he says; 'how'd you get in the church choir if you couldn't read music?'

'I got in all right,' I told him.

'Yes, but how?'

'I dunno — I did. But it's this flute, I can't do with it yet, not properly.'

'No,' he says, 'you can't.'

'I never played before.'

'No,' he says, 'you ain't.'

All the same, after about an hour, off we all goes out for a route march slap up the High Street playing hallelujah on the Wild Scottish Bluebells, Hubert in front blurring away on his kettle drum (grand it was) and old Scrase bringing up the rear — whump, whump — on the big 'un. Half the time I didn't know what else we was playing, but I give 'em Bluebells, and we kept in step, everybody on the pavements stopping and staring at us and some bits of kids stepping out behind whistling the tune.

I dunno what it is, but there's something in a band makes you want to sock anybody that sauces you, and there was a couple of chaps as gave us a nasty bit of lip. They did; but you mustn't step out of the ranks when you're playing on the march, not without orders. You're all together, doing your best, and you get no thanks for it, no thanks at all. There was these two chaps I made a note of — I know 'em — and when I sees 'em again . . . ! I wonder what they'll have to say then! I shall stipulate for one at a time, of course.

After we had done our route march we finished up outside Scrase's and he give us the dismiss.

'But step inside a minute, boys, will you?' he said. 'Just a minute, I'm not satisfied; there's something wrong to-night.'

So in we goes. 'Shan't keep you a minute,' he says,

and we all tumbled after him down the basement stairs, and there was Mrs. Scrase frying something hot for supper.

'My God!' she says. 'Albert, you ain't going to bring that ruddy drum in here again, are you?'

'No,' he says, 'I ain't going to do that, Min.' And half of us was already in the sitting-room when she says: 'What's all these blooming mohawks want here for?'

It was enough to make poor old Albert set about her, but he only said: 'They don't want anything to eat, Min. There was something not quite all si-garney about 'em to-night, and I'm just a-trying 'em. Now boys, I want a bar or two of "The Wild Scottish Bluebells".'

So we ups and tootles a few.

Poor old Albert shook his blooming head. 'Damme, whatever is it? Play it again, right through.'

We does so.

'God!' he says then. 'Play it singly.'

So Fashy played it by himself, and Billy Wigg played it, and then it came to my turn and I played it.

'Ar! I thought so!' says Albert. 'It's you, is it!'

And so it was. My flute was a different pitch to theirn; not much, only half a note or so, but it properly upset Albert. He grabbed hold of my flute and unscrewed it.

'It's cracked!' he said. 'Where'd you get this thing?'

I told him I bought it off Harry Dunning. Harry Dunning said it was quite all right when he sold it to me. I said no it wasn't. 'It was cracked,' I said, 'and you said that didn't matter as I could play alto on it.' But Harry Dunning denied that; he denied it. And it surprised me a lot and I didn't like him any the more. I never did like him much, he was only a plasterer's boy though he always made out to be apprenticed to a mason, and I never did like the shape of his nose, it looked bad somehow. He denied it.

'Well, it's no good,' Albert said. 'Don't you come here with that thing any more.'

I tell you, I went red in the face about it, and then, when we got outside again, Harry Dunning asked me for the penny I still owed him on it.

'Not much!' I says. 'It's broke, it's out of tune, and Albert says it's no good — you heard him.'

'That flute's all right,' Harry Dunning says. 'Only you can't play it yet.'

'I could play it,' I says, 'if it was a good 'un.'

He said: 'No, you couldn't do that even. And what do you expect for eight penn'orth?'

'You take it,' I says, 'and give me back my eightpence.'

'Gives nothing,' he says. 'It cost two and ninepence original — what could you have better than that? Two bob I'm giving you! The flute's perfect. All you got to do is poke a bit of wood up in the top of the mouthpiece part and that will make the pitch same as all ours.'

Of course I didn't like him at all, but he was bigger than me. Next day I cut out a round piece of wood and shoved it up in the top of the mouthpiece part. It sounded worse than awful. I must have put up too much. And the worst of it was I couldn't get it down again, so there I was, dished. But I didn't give Harry Dunning the penny I owed him. Not me!

I couldn't afford no more on fifes and drums then so I didn't go again, I give it up, but my ma was struck more than ever on me getting musical ideas. She even wanted me to be confirmed, but that was the doings of some old priest called Father Isinglass. She'd gone up very high church all of a sudden and chucked the Salvation Army for the Roman Catholics because she liked confessing her sins. Well, I don't, but she did — only she was very forgetful. She wrote out what she was going to tell Father Isinglass on a little bit of paper, just to remind herself at the end of the week, only she would leave this bit of paper knocking about all over the room, and when I used to read it I couldn't help laughing. Poor old ma! I'm blessed if she didn't forget to take it with her sometimes!

So she wanted me to be confirmed and she wanted me to get some musical ideas, but I said I couldn't contend with 'em both. She said I ought to do one or the other, and I said music was as good as confirmation any day. She said it wasn't *quite* as good, but still it *was* very good and so she let me off being confirmed. To tell you the truth I did not much care for this holy father she was struck on; his breath smelt rotten, and he brought us some Jerusalem artichokes once that nearly did me in. I got rather keen on the volunteers, only I wasn't grown up enough to join them. They used to go round about our town lugging four great cannons behind some horses and chaps on 'em dressed up like soldiers. They didn't look *quite* like soldiers, not quite, but the drivers had whips and helmets and jackboots with spurs on; and there'd be a squad of volunteers on foot, all dressed up like soldiers, only as it happened our town was a garrison town and had a barracks full of regulars like the Inniskilling Dragoons or the Lancers, and you couldn't help noticing the difference. Especially on Sunday mornings when the proper army turned out from the barracks to go to St. Martin's Church for the service, with the band playing. Hundreds of 'em, all of 'em with swords and spurs and tight trousers with yellow stripes down the

leg, dead in step from the front rank to the back one
— plonk, plonk, plonk, plonk! When you watched
'em sideways from behind it looked like one long
scorpion with thousands of legs. Going under the
railway arch by the pill factory you couldn't hear
yourself speak, especially if there was a train going
over. And when any of 'em died they did have some
grand funerals. Grand and solemn, the poor corpse on
the gun carriage leading the regiment for the only
time, Union Jack on the corpse, his helmet on top of
that, and his old horse walking behind him without a
rider. Ma always cried when she saw the horse.
There'd be all the regiment following, very slow step,
carbines upside down, and the 'Dead March'. Lord,
it made you feel good! And when they'd finished
burying him in the cemetery on the hill they'd fire a
few shots up in the air and blow on the bugles. So
long, old pal, so long. Then they'd all turn home
again, quick march, quick as you like now, with the
band playing something lively, like 'Biddy McGrah':

> Biddy McGrah, the colonel said,
> Would you like a soldier made of your son Fred,
> With a sword by his side and a fine cocked hat —
> Biddy McGrah, how would you like that?

and everybody would be laughing — nearly everybody
— whistling and laughing and jolly like.

Still, the volunteers was quite nice. They was all
right. One of the volunteers' wives (he was a sergeant)
knew my ma and knew I was musical, so her husband
asked us if I would like to join them as a bugle boy.
Course, there wasn't any chance of ever going to any
wars — I shouldn't have cared a lot for that sort of
thing — but I thought it 'ud be grand to have red
stripes and a bugle with white cord and tassels. My!

So I told my ma to say as I wouldn't mind being a bugler boy as long as there wasn't anything to pay, because I tell you straight you can't keep on for ever buying, buying, buying these here instruments. So this sergeant comes along one evening and takes me with him down to the drill hall to try and see how I could get on with bugles. It was a big hall where these four cannon was kept, but the sergeant took me up some wooden steps to a loft where the practice was going on and set me down on a box and left me there among a lot of chaps dressed anyhow in their ordinary clothes, but they had all got helmets on and I watched 'em blowing on bugles enough to deafen a Greek. Then they had a go on some trumpets made of brass, larger than the bugles and very pretty. I liked 'em much better; there's more music in a trumpet, you know; it makes a nicer kind of noise, much grander and looks more nice. It's the proper thing you have to blow before the king when he goes out, or these judges when they go to assizes, not like these fat little bugles which only give a kind of a moo — there's no comparison.

After about an hour the bandmaster come up to me and asked me what I wanted. Of course, I didn't really know, because the sergeant hadn't told me what to say — they do mess you about, these chaps, and all for nothing. This bandmaster was a posh fellow, all got up with black braid on his tunic and a quiff. Well, I told him something, and he says:

'You're not very big.'

'But I'm tough,' I says.

'How old are you?'

I told him, and he said I wasn't old enough, but anyway, he went and fetched me a bugle to try on. I wasn't half surprised when I found I couldn't blow the thing at all, not a sound, not in five minutes! I hurt my face trying. So then he gets me a trumpet, and the trumpet was no better than the bugle — not for me. And it looked so easy! Well, the result was he said I was too young (of course I knew that already) and too little, and said I should have to eat a lot more pudden for a year or two and then try again. I tell you, I was ashamed about the whole blessed lot of these volunteers. I was quite angry, too. It gets you that way, messing about over sizes and ages when you been left school and out to work for nearly two years. If a chap's old enough to go out to work he's old enough to go bugling. I should say so, and you couldn't expect a nipper like me to play 'Annie Lorry' on the thing the very first time. I should say not. Anyhow, I gives him a salute and says: 'Good night, sir.'

I couldn't find the sergeant, he'd mizzled, so I started off home by myself. It was dark outside and the gas lamps were all alight. Mind you, I was in a great wax, but it somehow made me feel as if I wanted to cry. My ma's a bit that way too, only she cries about nothing at all. This drill hall was in a quiet street, but not far off I sees a crowd where there was a row on. I like a bit of a shindy so I wedges my way in. The row was over a couple of drunken soldiers out in the middle of the road challenging anyone to fight, and nobody 'ud take 'em on! There they was, the crowd all standing on the pavement each side, and the two soldiers prancing up and down the middle of the road offering to pay anyone who'd fight 'em. They'd got forage caps on and spurs and canes in their hands, both of 'em half canned, but one of 'em a bit more mad than the other. He kept on yelling out:

'Come on, ye bastards, I'm the ten stone champion of Belfast! Forty men I've killed and I've eaten tigers alive!'

Not a soul in that crowd said a word or blinked an eye — he sounded too awful. The second soldier walked behind the other and kept swishing his own leg with his cane and asking everybody very quiet-like: 'D'ye want to fight? D'ye want to fight? He's the cock of the world.'

As if they would! But it made you feel angry though, it does make you get angry, that kind of thing. I could feel my savage blood surging up, but I thought I'd better keep quiet. Nobody wanted to tackle this champion and he got angrier and angrier, going up to fellows and grabbing them by the lapel of their coats:

'Come on, come on,' he said, 'it 'ull do ye the world of good.' But the chaps all dodged away from him.

'Almighty God!' the soldier yells, 'I must kill somebody. Come on, ye yeller guts, all of ye!' And he picked hold of another chap and spit in his face. Then the people in the back of the crowd started calling out: 'Send for the picket. Where's the police?' And I'm blessed if this champion didn't come up to me and say: 'D'ye want a bit of a brish?'

I thought to myself: 'Lord, shall I have just one good sock at his eye!' but before I knew what I was thinking of I said: 'No, thank you, sir,' and he passed on to someone else. We all stood silent there like a flock of sheep waiting to be pole-axed and not daring to say a word. I was ashamed, but still, if anyone had tried to move away he'd a been pounced on by this soldier and corpsed straight there. And this pal of his kept swishing his own leg with his cane: 'D'ye want to fight? He's the cock of the world.'

Now standing just by the crowd was a deaf and dumb bloke known as Dummy — but I didn't know his right name. Everybody knew him because he *was* dumb and couldn't speak or hear, but these two soldiers didn't know him. Old Dummy stood there with his bowler hat on, but he couldn't a known much about what was going on, being deaf, and anyway, he couldn't say anything 'cause he couldn't speak, and this fighting soldier seemed to take a regular fancy to Old Dummy.

'Come on,' he roars out at him: 'Come on, you'll do!' and prances in front of him, wagging his fists. Old Dummy never said a thing — well, he couldn't, you see. But this soldier didn't know that and kept prancing at him till some woman at the back shrieks out:

'Don't you hit him! He's dumb, he is. Let him alone, you dirty coward!'

When the soldier heard that he stopped still and looked all over the crowd. Everybody shivered in their shoes, you could a heard a pin drop.

'What did I hear? Me? Who said that? Who said it?' And he didn't half swear. He chucked his cane to his pal and marched right into the crowd and banged poor Dummy's hat hard down on his ears.

'Will ye fight?' he says, and poked his ugly face out to Dummy and tells him: 'Come on, hit me, hit me here.'

Old Dummy could only make a funny noise with his mouth — Mum ... um ... um ... um ... um — and he put up his hands to save his hat. That only made the soldier madder still. He rushed at Dummy and fetched him a terrible slosh across the jaw with his right and followed it up with another biff in the neck with his left. Talk about wallop, I never seen anything like it — and really, there's something grand about this scientific art of boxing. Poor old Dummy went down like a sow, full stretch on his side with his nose in the gutter. The blood was coming out of his face. He didn't move and he didn't say a word — well, of course, he couldn't. And that did seem to stir up one or two of these people. They began shouting at the soldiers and some picked Dummy up and carried him across into a pub called the Corporation Arms — I could see its gold letters shining sideways because of the gas lamp further up. When the two soldiers saw the damage they done and the crowd getting so threatening they went to clear off. The champion got his cane from his pal and marched away like a lord, but his pal stopped to argue with some of the people, and while he was arguing who should come out of the Corporation Arms but Arthur Lark! He was a tough nut was Arthur Lark, a carriage cleaner up at the railway; only just left off work, because he still had his uniform on, green corduroys, and was having a drink when they took Dummy in the pub where Arthur was. He come walking up to the crowd very quiet and says: 'Is this him?'

They says: 'That's one of 'em,' they says, and without any more ado Arthur knocked the soldier's pal senseless with one punch. O gosh!

'Where's the other?' says Arthur.

Of course he'd gone off, but we all pelted after him, this champion one, and except for a couple of women no one took any notice of that blooming soldier lying in the road like a dead 'un. We soon saw the champion of Belfast staggering along and wagging his cane about, but just then a bobby pops round a corner, sees our crowd, and steps in the road and stops us. A big chap, fifteen stone I bet he was, and I could tell you his number only that wouldn't do! Stops us: 'What's all this? What's going on here?'

Arthur Lark never budged an inch. He up and told the bobby what was on and what had happened, what the soldier had done to Dummy. The bobby said: 'I'll run the bleeder in.'

'That's no good, no,' says Arthur, 'what's the use a doing that! Soon as you got him the picket 'ull come and fetch him away! You let me have a word or two with him now, just five minutes. Shan't want any more. You turn your eyes another way, you go on up the street for a walk, it's a nice evening, ain't it?'

I can see old Arthur now, a fine bloke with a funny bent face. After a bit more palaver the bobby did a grin: 'All right, go on,' he says, 'but hurry up, and don't forget — I ain't *seen* you, I ain't seen *anything*!'

We went off with a whoop again, and the bobby shouted: 'Not so much noise there, please!'

Coughdrop, he was.

When that soldier heard us all coming after him he turned and gave one look and then bolted for his life. We youngsters headed him off a side turning. Arthur got up with him at the bottom of the street where there's a row of houses with gardens and iron railings facing you. The soldier didn't know whether to run to the right or the left, and Arthur caught him wallop in the gutter. I never saw such a blow in my life, right in the guts, and lifted him fair across the pavement bang into the iron railings. And so help me God, the railings cracked and broke, fair crumbled up, and when the soldier fell the bits fell all over him. He lay down there quiet as a lamb. We gathered round and picked up the bits of iron railing.

'Get up!' says Arthur.

But the soldier wouldn't get up, he said he couldn't, he said it was a foul blow: 'It's damn near killed me!'

'Foul!' Arthur says, and he shoved his fist right in front of this soldier's nose: 'D'ye see that! Was it a foul blow? Was it?'

'You let me alone,' the soldier said, 'or you'll be sorry for it.' And you could see he was real bad.

'You got that for striking a harmless dumb man what couldn't help hisself,' said Arthur.

'How did I know he was dumb?' the soldier said.

'How did you *know*! Couldn't you *see* it? And deaf, too!'

'How did I know he was deaf?' the swaddy said. He was sweating like a stoker and his face was the colour of suet. Anyone could see he was real bad. So Arthur said: 'Here, some of you chaps, just fold him up and put him in a tram for the barracks. With my compliments, say.' And off goes Arthur as calm as a cucumber! He left us to it. That's what I liked so much about Arthur; so quiet with his old bent face, and no fuss; he just put this soldier out of mess and left us to it. Presently we saw the policeman coming towards us again.

'Come on, soldier,' we says, 'here's a rozzer coming, you better get up now.'

He managed to sit up all right after a bit, and then he says: 'Go away or I'll blind the lot of ye to hell!' So we mooched off and left him, because of this rozzer. But I think he was all right — anyways I never heard no more about him nor any of 'em. I suppose he must have been all right, because you don't half cop it for killing a soldier. He was supposed to be the true champion of Belfast, but he didn't like the way Arthur cooked his eggs for him. My God! But there's no doubt about it, boxing is the most patriotic thing after all. To my mind it's absolutely noble. I mean what's the good of these here bugles, blowing your insides out? Give me a pair of dukes like Arthur Lark.

Well, after all my blooming trouble this musical business didn't come to anything again, so I give up the idea altogether. Somebody showed me a pipe called a oboe, but it cost a fearful lot. Besides, I couldn't make any sound come out of it. I dunno why everything you wants to go in for costs so much. I can't make it out and I can't stand it neither, so I give up these musical ideas and bought a rabbit off a fellow as said he was going to learn me all the doings of the noble art of self-defence.

Ninepenny Flute (1937)

THE GREEN DRAKE

In the village of So-and-so lived an old woman, Rebecca Cracknell, who had a dog with an odd eye and the name of Jack, a kitten with an odd tail and the name of Jack, and a green drake with odd ambitions that was called Jack. The old woman's only son was young Jack, and her husband, long since dead, had been known as old Jack. They began by having different names, every one of them, but the forces of habit were so strong in the good old woman that she always called everything and everybody by that one name. The drake was a middle-aged duck, cooped up in a yard as dry as the deserts of Egypt. Sometimes it tried to go sporting out into the great wet world of gutters and puddles and pools, but Rebecca could not bear to see it behaving so untidily so she confined it, and there in the dry yard it pined and lived.

One day her son Jack tucked the drake under his arm.

'Jacky, my lad, I do believe to-day is your birthday!' And off he went with the drake under his arm for a mile or more until he came to a field with a barn in it and a pond beside, whose grassy banks, so moist and green, sloped gently into the water. The water itself was only a dark bronze liquid that stank, but there were three or four chestnut trees close by just casting their pure blooms into it. How bright the day! And how the wind blew!

Into this pond the young man Jack threw Jack the drake, and the drake became demented with joy. It heaved the water up with its beak and cast it over its back. It trod and danced, or flew skimming the pond from shore to shore. It tried to bury itself in the waters, to burst down through them into that duck paradise that lies at the bottom of all ponds, but half of him — and the worst half — always remained quivering in the common world above.

The lad Jack said he would leave him there to enjoy himself, because it was his birthday, and he would come again and fetch him before nightfall. So the drake was left alone on the pond, and swam about quacking incessantly in his pride and excitement. How bright the day and how the wind blew, dashing among the chestnut trees until their heavy foliage seemed a burden to them and they snowed their white petals upon the bosom of the pond! A crow came chattering in the trees, to scoff at the buffoonery and bad manners of the drake. Intoxicated it was!

Later on a man in the prime of life with a brown face and a weather-coloured hat came passing by. He'd a moleskin suit on with the breeches belted below the knees, and a wicker bag slung across his shoulder. He had drunk ale in the sweetness of the morning. One hand rested in the broad belt round his belly, with the other he took out his pipe — and spat fulsomely.

'Hey, my cocky!' he cried when he saw the drake, and he stood viewing its antics with meditative eyes.

The drake replied, 'Quack.'

'Quack to me!' cried the man in surly tones. 'Where's your manners?'

So the drake knew he was not conversing with a common creature, but one who might be a god or a gentleman, and he answered him then with care and addressed him with respect.

'Hey, my hearty!' the man exclaimed, 'you's as fine a young feller of a duck as ever I see.'

It was — the drake informed him — his birthday.

'Hi up!' cried the man, and at once he squatted down upon a hump on the bank of the pond, a great castle of a place that some ants had built — ants are such ambitious creatures.

'Hi up!' repeated the man, and he said it was his birthday too. 'Allecapantho!' Now wasn't that curious?

'So I stops me at home this morning,' he continued, 'but my old woman kept growling and groaning until I had to ask her, very civil-like: "Whatever's come over you?" — I asks her — "on my birthday? You're like a dog with a sore nose" — I says — "and I can't do with you and I can't stand your company, not on my birthday. You're nought but a bag o' mutton" — I says — "you go and pick the fleas out of your tail" — I told her — and I went off to my allotment and cultivated a few chain of the earth. And now my neck's as stiff as a crust a beeswax. Cold winds and sweat, I suppose. Misfortune was ever following me, I tell you. Misfortune was my downfall, and so it is, I can tell you. If you wants to know my history I can tell you: I was born honest, so I shall die poor.'

The drake snoozed upon the water, blinking with affability and deep enjoyment. Never had anybody taken so much notice of him before, or flattered him with so much kindly attention. And here he was now! The man sat on the ant-hill dividing his attention in three parts: by puffing at a cold pipe, by trying to light it again, by talking genially to the duck on the pond.

'You's as pretty a little duck as ever I seed. I couldn't say no fairer if I'd a mind to.'

'But,' the drake sorrowfully sighed, 'I am only an orphan.'

'Pooh! What about it? Anyone can be an orphan

if they like. Anyone. 'Cept royalty. You mustn't run away with any funny notions, young feller,' the bluff man declared. 'What part are you from?'

The drake told him that he came from the village of So-and-so.

The man knew the place very well. 'Hi up! yes,' he said, 'but there's not a mortal thing in that village to attract a sunny soul, neither bliss nor blessing. There's not a man of that sort nor a woman of that sort; there's not a house of that sort, nor an inn of that sort, not a child, pony, hog, dog, or hen of that sort. All poor bred-uns they be.'

The drake confessed that life there was very dull, yes; often it had desired to change its habitation.

'Dull!' roared the other. 'Why, I could not bear to live in that hole, not if the streets was paved with crystal and there was gold on every floor. No, I live in a better place nor that.'

'Pardon me, sir,' said the polite little drake. 'I do not know your name, or where you dwell.'

'Ha, ha! Allecapantho!' returned the man. 'Appercrampus! You would like to know my pedigree? There's a touch of Muscovy about you, I should say, with a brush of Indian blood. O, I can see it, you're a good bred-un. So am I; there's few can trace their ancestors back to history like me, not straight forward they can't. That's sound truth, speak it or be shamed. Two stones in Barclay Buttle churchyard — d'ye know it? No! Two stones in Shimp churchyard — d'ye know it? No! There used to be four in Shimp but two on 'em fell over (or was pushed over, if truth be known), and Fiddler Kinch stole 'em for his hog-pen, but he never had no more luck with a pig till the day he died after it. Bolted his food, he did. It's true; everyone can tell you truth as knows it, but if it ain't known it can't be revealed. Two stones in Shimp, two stones in Barclay Buttle, brass plate with a skull's head on it in Tooby chancel. What's amiss in that for pedigree? Tooby, Shimp, and Barclay Buttle? Came over with the king of the Busbys and we're still hereabouts. William Busby.' Here the man smote his bosom with pride, and thus the duck learned that his friend's name was W. Busby, and not allecapantho or appercrampus.

'When Fiddler died the reverend Saxby discovered they stones where they were — course he'd known all along. Parson took 'em up in the dead a night and transferred them. If you want to see they stones you just lift up the cloth and you'll see 'em on top of the altar in Shimp church, all fixed and fast and consecrated upside down. What's amiss in our tribe? You never heard nothing against the family of Busby — not as a family. I could show you the stone now, if you had the time, of the Busby twins, Hezekiah and Joseph, who met untimely ends (just what it says) from the sting of a viper coming from church after being confirmed. 1766. Hi up! God bless us, I remember my old great grandfather as used to tell me about William the Conqueror, all about that man he told me, every word. The Busbys are a great nation of chaps, they're everywhere, high up and well-breeched, please God. I heard a one up in the county of Nottinghamshire as owns a row of houses with a shaving-shop at one end and a coastguard station at the other! And all belongs, all belongs — a master man, ye know. He used to stuff birds and fishes and one thing and another, could stuff 'em well, like life. Used to stuff for the Duke of Whatevers-the-name-of-the-feller, and for royalty. Years and years — rows of houses — till his eyes give out and he got old and his spirits sunk. Kidneys, I shouldn't wonder; I be troubled the same myself. Master man! They've got it up here.'

With his finger Busby indicated a position in the middle of his forehead, and then appeared to swallow something. 'Appercrampus!' he added mystically.

The little drake smiled, and quacked his delight at the conversation of Mr. Busby, who now stood up, surveyed the surrounding field with deliberation, and then sat down upon the ant-hill again, drawing a tobacco box from his pocket. A pipe was filled and ignited, and for a while Mr. Busby puffed and gazed dreamily at the pond and the drake, and listened to the wind threshing in the chestnut trees. Ah, a lovely day!

'Who do you live with in So-and-so?' the man inquired.

'I live with Jack Cracknell,' answered the gentle duck, 'do you know him?'

'Know him! Allecapantho! I knew his father; we were at school together. He always said he was younger than me, but I can't understand how that could be because he left school afore I did and went and drove plough for the sleepy girl's husband. I kept on at school for another six months, and then I became a thatcher. All the Busbys be master men. They got it up here.' The man took his pipe from his mouth and pointed with it to his forehead again, and then spat richly over his shoulder to defeat the play of the wind.

The drake asked him another question: 'Who was the sleepy girl?'

'Eli Sadler's daughter,' replied Busby. 'She dropped off to sleep one day and she slept so's they couldn't rouse her no more. There were two girls and Eli and their mother. Of course Eli died, and there was Mary and there was this Annie. Mary was in service at the squire's, but Annie went to sleep and didn't wake up for seven years. She lay in her bed for seven unconscious years, and she didn't wake up and she did not die. People came from all parts of the world to look at her and stick pins in her — dukes and schoolmasters and members of parliament — but they could not wake her up, nobody couldn't. Seven years is a long time, ye know. Mystery. Her mother made a fortune a money out a that girl, a fortune, sacks of it. But of course the mother died, and everyone said to Mary: "Mary, you'll have to come home and look arter your sleepy sister." Mary said no, she wouldn't have that caper. "Why not?" they says to her, "she's your sister," they says, "helpless and dependent on your care." "Because," says Mary, "I shall damn soon wake her up." And that's what she did do — woke her up! And Annie went and got married and had ten children in next to no time. Never went to sleep no more. Sleeping beauty, they called her. Huh. She was the biggest fraud as ever stepped on England's ground, the biggest fraud within forty thousand miles. And old Jack Cracknell began work for the sleepy girl's husband. Well, upon my soul, there's all sorts a dodges for getting a living, and if you wants a thing in this world you must get it by force or by fudge. Force and fudge rule this sinful world, my cocky; everything's for someone's selfish pleasure — never your own. D'ye know what my advice is to you? My advice to you, sir, is this: if your pleasure brings more harm to another than it brings in joy to you — and it very often will — then you must do the best you can with your pleasure. If' — Busby pointed with his pipe straight at the attentive little duck — 'if so be you are the sort as don't stop to think, you won't know of the harm you do, and you won't pause, and you won't care. Mind you, if you are of the other sort, the sort that *do* care as man to man, my advice would be wasted —

for of course you wouldn't follow it, you could not. Such is human nature,' Busby said, applying yet another match to his pipe, 'and such' (puff) 'is life.'

'Yes, that is very true,' sighed the happy drake.

'And another thing,' continued the philosophizing thatcher. 'We may not get all we asks for, but you may lay your life we'll get all that's coming to us, and I shan't be far away from my own funeral. Nor will you, my cocky. Force and fudge, I tell you, rule this sinful world. If you can tell the tale, grief will never be your master. Take Jack Cracknell, as worked for sleepy girl's husband: I never did trust that man Cracknell. For one thing, he'd talk the skin off your nostrils! I never trusted anyone from the village of So-and-so, I never liked 'em; poor bred-uns, all. Young Jack's the same. And my advice to you is: don't return there any more, preserve your independence now you've got it, and don't own him, don't listen to him, don't follow him. Never let misfortune be your downfall. My lad, I like you, I will be your friend for life. There's my hand on it.'

Busby stood up, surveyed the landscape with care, spat a good spit, rubbed his right hand upon his haunch, and went to the water's edge. So the little drake swam in to accept of his friendship.

'Hey, my cocky!' The man's hand closed tightly round the duck's neck, and the bird was snatched from the water. In a few moments its neck was limp; it fluttered no more, it spake no more, it lived no more.

'Nice li'l bird,' commented Busby, feeling its breast and back, 'beautiful bird.' And putting the body in his bag he slung the bag over his shoulder again.

'Appercrampus!' he joyously murmured as he walked away. 'Allecapantho!'

Nixey's Harlequin (1931)

ARABESQUE—THE MOUSE

In the main street amongst tall establishments of mart and worship was a high narrow house pressed between a coffee factory and a bootmaker's. It had four flights of long dim echoing stairs, and at the top, in a room that was full of the smell of dried apples and mice, a man in the middle age of life had sat reading Russian novels until he thought he was mad. Late was the hour, the night outside black and freezing, the pavements below empty and undistinguishable when he closed his book and sat motionless in front of the glowing but flameless fire. He felt he was very tired, yet he could not rest. He stared at a picture on the wall until he wanted to cry; it was a colour print by Utamaro of a suckling child caressing its mother's breasts as she sits in front of a blackbound mirror. Very chaste and decorative it was, in spite of its curious anatomy. The man gazed, empty of sight though not of mind, until the sighing of the gas jet maddened him. He got up, put out the light, and sat down again in the darkness trying to compose his mind before the comfort of the fire. And he was just about to begin a conversation with himself when a mouse crept from a hole in the skirting near the fireplace and scurried into the fender. The man had the crude dislike for such sly nocturnal things, but this mouse was so small and bright, its antics so pretty, that he drew his feet carefully from the fender and sat watching it almost with amusement. The mouse moved along the shadows of the fender, out upon the hearth, and sat before the glow, rubbing its head, ears and tiny belly with its paws as if it were bathing itself with the warmth, until,

247

sharp and sudden, the fire sank, an ember fell, and the mouse flashed into its hole.

The man reached forward to the mantelpiece and put his hand upon a pocket lamp. Turning on the beam, he opened the door of a cupboard beside the fireplace. Upon one of the shelves there was a small trap baited with cheese, a trap made with a wire spring, one of those that smashed down to break the back of ingenuous and unwary mice.

'Mean — so mean,' he mused, 'to appeal to the hunger of any living thing just in order to destroy it.'

He picked up the empty trap as if to throw it in the fire.

'I suppose I had better leave it though — the place swarms with them.' He still hesitated. 'I hope that little beastie won't go and do anything foolish.' He put the trap back quite carefully, closed the door of the cupboard, sat down again and extinguished the lamp.

Was there anyone else in the world so squeamish and foolish about such things! Even his mother, mother so bright and beautiful, even she had laughed at his childish horrors. He recalled how once in his childhood, not long after his sister Yosine was born, a friendly neighbour had sent him home with a bundle of dead larks tied by the feet 'for supper'. The pitiful inanimity of the birds had brought a gush of tears; he had run weeping home and into the kitchen, and there he had found the strange thing doing. It was dusk; mother was kneeling before the fire. He dropped the larks.

'Mother!' he exclaimed softly. She looked at his tearful face.

'What's the matter, Filip?' she asked, smiling too at his astonishment.

'Mother! What are you doing?'

248

Her bodice was open and she was squeezing her breasts; long thin streams of milk spurted into the fire with a little plunging noise.

'Weaning your little sister,' laughed mother. She took his little inquisitive face and pressed it against the delicate warmth of her bosom, and he forgot the dead birds behind him.

'Let me do it, mother,' he cried, and doing so he discovered the throb of the heart in his mother's breast. Wonderful it was for him to experience it, although she could not explain it to him.

'Why does it do that?'

'If it did not beat, little son, I should die and the Holy Father would take me from you.'   .

'God?'

She nodded. He put his hand upon his own breast. 'Oh, feel it, Mother!' he cried. Mother unbuttoned his little coat and felt the gentle *tick tick* with her warm palm.

'Beautiful!' she said.

'Is it a good one?'

She kissed his upsmiling lips. 'It is good if it beats truly. Let it always beat truly, Filip, let it always beat truly.'

There was the echo of a sigh in her voice, and he had divined some grief, for he was very wise. He kissed her bosom in his tiny ecstasy and whispered soothingly: 'Little mother! little mother!' In such joys he forgot his horror of the dead larks; indeed he helped mother to pluck them and spit them for supper.

It was a black day that succeeded, and full of tragedy for the child. A great bay horse with a tawny mane had knocked down his mother in the lane, and a heavy cart had passed over her, crushing both her hands. She was borne away moaning with anguish to the surgeon who cut off the two hands. She died in the night. For years the child's dreams were filled with the horror of the stumps of arms, bleeding unendingly. Yet he had never seen them, for he was sleeping when she died.

While this old woe was come vividly before him he again became aware of the mouse. His nerves stretched upon him in repulsion, but he soon relaxed to a tolerant interest, for it was really a most engaging little mouse. It moved with curious staccato scurries, stopping to rub its head or flicker with its ears; they seemed almost transparent ears. It spied a red cinder and skipped innocently up to it ... sniffing ... sniffing ... until it jumped back scorched. It would crouch as a cat does, blinking in the warmth, or scamper madly as if dancing, and then roll upon its side rubbing its head with those pliant paws. The melancholy man watched it until it came at last to rest and squatted meditatively upon its haunches, hunched up, looking curiously wise, a pennyworth of philosophy; then once more the coals sank with a rattle and again the mouse was gone.

The man sat on before the fire and his mind filled again with unaccountable sadness. He had grown into manhood with a burning generosity of spirit and rifts of rebellion in him that proved too exacting for his fellows and seemed mere wantonness to men of casual rectitudes. 'Justice and Sin,' he would cry, 'Property and Virtue — incompatibilities! There can be no sin in a world of justice, no property in a world of virtue!' With an engaging extravagance and a certain clear-eyed honesty of mind he had put his two and two together and seemed then to rejoice, as in some topsy-turvy dream, in having rendered unto Caesar, as you might say, the things that were due to Napoleon! But this kind of thing could not pass unexpiated in a world of men having an infinite regard for Property and a pride in their traditions of Virtue and Justice. They could indeed forgive him his sins but they could not forgive him his compassions, so he had to go seek for more melodious-minded men and fair unambiguous women. But rebuffs can deal more deadly blows than daggers; he became timid — a timidity not of fear but of pride — and grew with the years into misanthropy, susceptible to trivial griefs and despairs, a vessel of emotion that emptied as easily as it filled, until he came at last to know that his griefs were half deliberate, his despairs half unreal, and to live but for beauty — which is tranquillity — to put her wooing hand upon him.

Now, while the mouse hunts in the cupboard, one fair recollection stirs in the man's mind — of Cassia and the harmony of their only meeting, Cassia who had such rich red hair, and eyes, yes, her eyes were full of starry inquiry like the eyes of mice. It was so long ago that he had forgotten how he came to be in it, that unaccustomed orbit of vain vivid things — a village festival, all oranges and houp-la. He could not remember how he came to be there, but at night, in the court hall, he had danced with Cassia — fair and unambiguous indeed! — who had come like the wind from among the roses and swept into his heart.

'It is easy to guess,' he had said to her, 'what you like most in the world.'

She laughed. 'To dance? Yes, and you . . .?'

'To find a friend.'

'I know, I know,' she cried, caressing him with recognitions. 'Ah, at times I quite love my friends — until I begin to wonder how much they hate me!'

He had loved at once that cool pale face, the abundance of her strange hair as light as the autumn's clustered bronze, her lilac dress and all the sweetness about her like a bush of lilies. How they had laughed at the two old peasants whom they had overheard gabbling of trifles like sickness and appetite!

'There's a lot of nature in a parsnip,' said one, a fat person of the kind that swells grossly when stung by a bee, 'a lot of nature when it's young, but when it's old it's like everything else.'

'True it is.'

'And I'm very fond of vegetables, yes, and I'm very fond of bread.'

'Come out with me,' whispered Cassia to Filip, and they walked out in the blackness of midnight into what must have been a garden.

'Cool it is here,' she said, 'and quiet, but too dark even to see your face — can you see mine?'

'The moon will not rise until after dawn,' said he, 'it will be white in the sky when the starlings whistle in your chimney.'

They walked silently and warily about until they felt the chill of the air. A dull echo of the music came to them through the walls, then stopped, and they heard the bark of a fox away in the woods.

'You are cold,' he whispered, touching her bare neck with timid fingers. 'Quite, quite cold,' drawing his hand tenderly over the curves of her chin and face. 'Let us go in,' he said, moving with discretion from the rapture he desired. 'We will come out again,' said Cassia.

But within the room the ball was just at an end, the musicians were packing up their instruments and the dancers were flocking out and homewards, or to the buffet which was on a platform at one end of the room. The two old peasants were there, munching hugely.

'I tell you,' said one of them, 'there's nothing in the world for it but the grease of an owl's liver. That's it, that's it! Take something on your stomach now? Just to offset the chill of the dawn?'

Filip and Cassia were beside them, but there were so many people crowding the platform that Filip had to jump down. He stood then looking up adoringly at Cassia, who had pulled a purple cloak around her.

'For Filip, Filip, Filip,' she said, pushing the last bite of her sandwich into his mouth, and pressing upon him her glass of Loupiac. Quickly he drank it with a great gesture, and, flinging the glass to the wall, took Cassia into his arms, shouting: 'I'll carry you home, the whole way home, yes, I'll carry you!'

'Put me down!' she cried, beating his head and pulling his ears, as they passed among the departing dancers. 'Put me down, you wild thing!'

Dark, dark was the lane outside, and the night an obsidian net, into which he walked carrying the girl. But her arms were looped around him, she discovered paths for him, clinging more tightly as he staggered against a wall, stumbled upon a gulley, or when her sweet hair was caught in the boughs of a little lime tree.

'Do not loose me, Filip, will you, do not loose me,' Cassia said, putting her lips against his temple.

His brain seemed bursting, his heart rocked within him, but he adored the rich grace of her limbs against his breast. 'Here it is,' she murmured, and he carried her into a path that led to her home in a little lawned garden where the smell of ripe apples upon the branches and the heavy lustre of roses stole upon the air. Roses and apples! Roses and apples! He carried her right into the porch before she slid down and stood close to him with her hands still upon his shoulders. He could breathe happily at the release, standing silent and looking round at the sky sprayed with wondrous stars but without a moon.

'You are stronger than I thought you, stronger than you look, you are really very strong,' she whispered, nodding her head to him. Opening the buttons of his coat she put her palm against his breast.

'O, how your heart does beat: does it beat truly — and for whom?'

He had seized her wrists in a little fury of love, crying: 'Little mother, little mother!'

'What are you saying?' asked the girl, but before he could continue there came a footstep sounding behind the door, and the clack of a bolt. . . .

What was that? Was that really a bolt or was it . . . was it . . . the snap of the trap? The man sat up in his room intently listening, with nerves quivering again, waiting for the trap to kill the little philosopher. When he felt it was all over he reached guardedly in the darkness for the lantern, turned on the beam, and opened the door of the cupboard. Focusing the light upon the trap he was amazed to see the mouse sitting on its haunches before it, uncaught. Its head was bowed, but its bead-like eyes were full of brightness, and it sat blinking, it did not flee.

'Shoosh!' said the man, but the mouse did not move. 'Why doesn't it go? Shoosh!' he said again, and suddenly the reason of the mouse's strange behaviour was made clear. The trap had not caught it completely, but it had broken off both its forefeet, and the thing crouched there holding out its two bleeding stumps humanly, too stricken to stir.

Horror flooded the man, and conquering his repugnance he plucked the mouse up quickly by the neck. Immediately the little thing fastened its teeth in his finger; the touch was no more than the slight prick of a pin. The man's impulse then exhausted itself. What should he do with it? He put his hand behind him, he dared not look, but there was nothing to be done except kill it at once, quickly, quickly. O, how should he do it? He bent towards the fire as if to drop the mouse into its quenching glow; but he paused and shuddered, he would hear its cries, he would have to listen. Should he crush it with finger and thumb? A glance towards the window decided him. He opened the sash with one hand and flung the wounded mouse far into the dark street. Closing the window with a crash he sank into a chair, limp with pity too deep for tears.

So he sat for two minutes, five minutes, ten minutes. Anxiety and shame filled him with heat. He opened the window again, and the freezing air poured in and cooled him. Seizing his lantern he ran down the echoing stairs, into the empty street, searching long and vainly for the little philosopher until he had to desist and return to his room, shivering, frozen to his very bones.

When he had recovered some warmth he took the trap from its shelf. The two feet dropped into his hand; he cast them into the fire. Then he once more set the trap and put it back carefully into the cupboard.

Adam and Eve and Pinch Me (1921)

THE MAN FROM KILSHEELAN

IF you knew the Man from Kilsheelan it was no use saying you did not believe in fairies and secret powers; believe it or no, but believe it you should — there he was! It is true he was in an asylum for the insane, but he was a man with age upon him so he didn't mind; and besides, better men than himself have been in such places, or they ought to be, and if there is justice in the world they will be.

'A cousin of mine,' he said to old Tom Tool one night, 'is come from Ameriky. A rich person.'

He lay in the bed next him, but Tom Tool didn't answer so he went on again: 'In a ship,' he said.

'I hear you,' answered Tom Tool.

'I see his mother with her bosom open once, and it stuffed with diamonds, bags full.'

Tom Tool kept quiet.

'If,' said the Man from Kilsheelan, 'if I'd the trusty comrade I'd make a break from this and go seek him.'

'Was he asking you to do that?'

'How could he an' all and he in a ship?'

'Was he writing fine letters to you then?'

'How could he, under the Lord? Would he give them to a savage bird or a herring to bring to me so?'

'How did he let on to you?'

'He did not let on,' said the Man from Kilsheelan.

Tom Tool lay long silent in the darkness; he had a mistrust of the Man, knowing him to have a forgetful mind; everything slipped through it like rain through the nest of a pigeon. But at last he asked him: 'Where is he now?'

'He'll be at Ballygoveen.'

'You to know that and you with no word from him?'

'O, I know it, I know; and if I'd a trusty comrade I'd walk out of this and to him I would go. Bags of diamonds!'

Then he went to sleep, sudden; but the next night he was at Tom Tool again: 'If I'd a trusty comrade,' said he; and all that and a lot more.

' 'Tis not convenient to me now,' said Tom Tool, 'but to-morrow night I might go wid you.'

The next night was a wild night, and a dark night, and he would not go to make a break from the asylum, he said: 'Fifty miles of journey, and I with no heart for great walking fcats! It is not convenient, but to-morrow night I might go wid you.'

The night after that he said: 'Ah, whisht wid your diamonds and all! Why would you go from the place that is snug and warm into a world that is like a wall for cold dark, and but the thread of a coat to divide you from its mighty clasp, and only one thing blacker under the heaven of God and that's the road you walk on, and only one thing more shy than your heart and that's your two feet worn to a tissue tramping in dung and ditches. . . .'

'If I'd a trusty comrade,' said the Man from Kilsheelan, 'I'd go seek my rich cousin.'

'. . . stars gaping at you a few spans away, and the things that have life in them, but cannot see or speak, begin to breathe and bend. If ever your hair stood up it is then it would be, though you've no more than would thatch a thimble, God help you.'

'Bags of gold he has,' continued the Man, 'and his pockets stuffed with the tobacca.'

'Tobacca!'

'They were large pockets and well stuffed.'

'Do you say, now!'

'And the gold! large bags and rich bags.'

'Well, I might do it to-morrow.'

And the next day Tom Tool and the Man from Kilsheelan broke from the asylum and crossed the mountains and went on.

Four little nights and four long days they were walking; slow it was for they were oldish men and lost they were, but the journey was kind and the weather was good weather. On the fourth day Tom Tool said to him: 'The Dear knows what way you'd be taking me! Blind it seems, and dazed I am. I could do with a skillet of good soup to steady me and to soothe me.'

'Hard it is, and hungry it is,' sighed the Man; 'starved daft I am for a taste of nourishment, a blind man's dog would pity me. If I see a cat I'll eat it; I could bite the nose off a duck.'

They did not converse any more for a time, not until Tom Tool asked him what was the name of his grand cousin, and then the Man from Kilsheelan was in a bedazement, and he was confused.

'I declare, on my soul, I've forgot his little name. Wait now while I think of it.'

'Was it McInerney then?'

'No, not it at all.'

'Kavanagh? the Grogans? or the Duffys?'

'Wait, wait while I think of it now.'

Tom Tool waited; he waited and all until he thought he would burst.

'Ah, what's astray wid you? Was it Phelan — or O'Hara — or Clancy — or Peter Mew?'

'No, not it at all.'

'The Murphys — the Sweeneys — the Moores.'

'Divil a one. Wait while I think of it now.'

And the Man from Kilsheelan sat holding his face

as if it hurt him, and his comrade kept saying at him: 'Duhy, then? Coman? McGrath?' driving him distracted with his O this and O that, his Mc he's and Mc she's.

Well, he could not think of it; but when they walked on they had not far to go, for they came over a twist of the hills and there was the ocean, and the neat little town of Ballygoveen in a bay of it below, with the wreck of a ship lying sunk near the strand. There was a sharp cliff at either horn of the bay, and between them some bullocks stravaiging on the beach.

'Truth is a fortune,' cried the Man from Kilsheelan, 'this it is!'

They went down the hill to the strand near the wreck, and just on the wing of the town they saw a paddock full of hemp stretched drying, and a house near it, and a man weaving a rope. He had a great cast of hemp around his loins, and a green apron. He walked backwards to the sea, and a young girl stood turning a little wheel as he went away from her.

'God save you,' said Tom Tool to her, 'for who are you weaving this rope?'

'For none but God himself and the hangman,' said she.

Turning the wheel she was, and the man going away from it backwards, and the dead wreck in the rocky bay; a fine sweet girl of good dispose and no ways drifty.

'Long life to you then, young woman,' says he. 'But that's a strong word, and a sour word, the Lord spare us all.'

At that the rope walker let a shout to her to stop the wheel; then he cut the rope at the end and tied it to a black post. After that he came throwing off his green apron and said he was hungry.

'Denis, avick!' cried the girl. 'Come, and I'll get your food.' And the two of them went away into the house.

'Brother and sister they are,' said the Man from Kilsheelan, 'a good appetite to them.'

'Very neat she is, and clean she is, and good and sweet and tidy she is,' said Tom Tool. They stood in the yard watching some white fowls parading and feeding and conversing in the grass; scratch, peck, peck, ruffle, quarrel, scratch, peck, peck, cock-a-doodle-doo.

'What will we do now, Tom Tool? My belly has a scroop and a screech in it. I could eat the full of Isknagahiny Lake and gape for more, or the Hill of Bawn and not get my enough.'

Beyond them was the paddock with the hemp drying across it, long heavy strands, and two big stacks of it beside, dark and sodden, like seaweed. The girl came to the door and called: 'Will ye take a bite?' They said they would, and that she should eat with spoons of gold in the heaven of God and Mary. 'You're welcome,' she said, but no more she said, for while they ate she was sad and silent.

The young man Denis let on that their father, one Horan, was away on his journeys peddling a load of ropes, a long journey, days he had been gone, and he might be back to-day, or to-morrow, or the day after.

'A great strew of hemp you have,' said the Man from Kilsheelan. The young man cast down his eyes; and the young girl cried out: '' Tis foul hemp, God preserve us all!'

'Do you tell me of that now.' he asked; but she would not, and her brother said: 'I will tell you. It's a great misfortune, mister man. 'Tis from the wreck in the bay beyant, a good stout ship, but burst on the rocks one dark terror of a night and all the poor sailors tipped in the sea. But the tide was low and they got ashore, ten strong sailor men, with a bird in a cage that was dead drowned.'

'The Dear rest its soul,' said Tom Tool.

'There was no rest in the ocean for a week, the bay was full of storms, and the vessel burst, and the big bales split, and the hemp was scattered and torn and tangled on the rocks, or it did drift. But at last it soothed, and we gathered it and brought it to the field here. We brought it, and my father did buy it of the salvage man for a price; a Mexican valuer he was, but the deal was bad, and it lies there; going rotten it is, the rain wears it, and the sun's astray, and the wind is gone.'

'That's a great misfortune. What is on it?' said the Man from Kilsheelan.

'It is a great misfortune, mister man. Laid out it is, turned it is, hackled it is, but faith it will not dry or sweeten, never a hank of it worth a pig's eye.'

''Tis the devil and all his injury,' said Kilsheelan.

The young girl, her name it was Christine, sat grieving. One of her beautiful long hands rested on her knee, and she kept beating it with the other. Then she began to speak.

'The captain of that ship lodged in this house with us while the hemp was recovered and sold; a fine handsome sport he was, but fond of the drink, and very friendly with the Mexican man, very hearty they were, a great greasy man with his hands covered with rings that you'd not believe. Covered! My father had been gone travelling a week or a few days when a dark raging gale came off the bay one night till the hemp was lifted all over the field.'

'It would have lifted a bullock,' said Denis, 'great lumps of it, like trees.'

'And we sat waiting the captain, but he didn't come

home and we went sleeping. But in the morning the Mexican man was found dead murdered on the strand below, struck in the skull, and the two hands of him gone. 'Twas not long when they came to the house and said he was last seen with the captain, drunk quarrelling; and where was he? I said to them that he didn't come home at all and was away from it. "We'll take a peep at his bed," they said, and I brought them there, and my heart gave a strong twist in me when I see'd the captain stretched on it, snoring to the world and his face and hands smeared with the blood. So he was brought away and searched, and in his pocket they found one of the poor Mexican's hands, just the one, but none of the riches. Everything to be so black against him and the assizes just coming on in Cork! So they took him there before the judge, and he judged him and said it's to hang he was. And if they asked the captain how he did it, he said he did not do it at all.'

'But there was a bit of iron pipe beside the body,' said Denis.

'And if they asked him where was the other hand, the one with the rings and the mighty jewels on them, and his budget of riches, he said he knew nothing of that nor how the one hand got into his pocket. Placed there it was by some schemer. It was all he could say, for the drink was on him and nothing he knew.

'"You to be so drunk," they said, "how did you get home to your bed and nothing heard?"

'"I don't know," says he. Good sakes, the poor lamb, a gallant strong sailor he was! His mind was a blank, he said. "'Tis blank," said the judge, "if it's as blank as the head of himself with a gap like that in it, God rest him!"'

'You could have put a pound of cheese in it,' said Denis.

'And Peter Corcoran cried like a loony man, for his courage was gone, like a stream of water. To hang him, the judge said, and to hang him well, was their intention. It was a pity, the judge said, to rob a man because he was foreign, and destroy him for riches and the drink on him. And Peter Corcoran swore he was innocent of this crime. "Put a clean shirt to me back," says he, "for it's to heaven I'm going." '

'And,' added Denis, 'the peeler at the door said "Amen".'

'That was a week ago,' said Christine, 'and in another he'll be stretched. A handsome sporting sailor boy.'

'What . . . what did you say was the name of him?' gasped the Man from Kilsheelan.

'Peter Corcoran, the poor lamb,' said Christine.

'Begod,' he cried out as if he was choking, ' 'tis me grand cousin from Ameriky!'

True it was, and the grief on him so great that Denis was after giving the two of them a lodge till the execution was over. 'Rest here, my dad's away,' said he, 'and he knowing nothing of the murder, or the robbery, or the hanging that's coming, nothing. Ah, what will we tell him an' all? 'Tis a black story on this house.'

'The blessing of God and Mary on you,' said Tom Tool. 'Maybe we could do a hand's turn for you; me comrade's a great wonder with the miracles, maybe he could do a stroke would free an innocent man.'

'Is it joking you are?' asked Christine sternly.

'God deliver him, how would I joke on a man going to his doom and destruction?'

The next day the young girl gave them jobs to do, but the Man from Kilsheelan was destroyed with trouble and he shook like water when a pan of it is struck.

'What is on you?' said Tom Tool.

'Vexed and waxy I am,' says he, 'in regard of the great journey we's took, and sorra a help in the end of it. Why couldn't he do his bloody murder after we had done with him?'

'Maybe he didn't do it at all.'

'Ah, what are you saying now, Tom Tool? Wouldn't anyone do it, a nice, easy, innocent crime? The cranky goossoon to get himself stretched on the head of it, 'tis the drink destroyed him! Sure there's no more justice in the world than you'd find in the craw of a sick pullet. Vexed and waxy I am for me careless cousin. Do it! Who wouldn't do it?'

He went up to the rope that Denis and Christine were weaving together and he put his finger on it.

'Is that the rope,' says he, 'that will hang my grand cousin?'

'No,' said Denis, 'it is not. His rope came through the post office yesterday. For the prison master it was, a long new rope—saints preserve us—and Jimmy Fallon the postman getting roaring drunk showing it to the scores of creatures would give him a drink for the sight of it. Just coiled it was, and no way hidden, with a label on it, "O.H.M.S." '

'The wind's rising, you,' said Christine. 'Take a couple of forks now, and turn the hemp in the field. Maybe 'twill scour the Satan out of it.'

'Stormy it does be, and the bay has darkened in broad noon,' said Tom Tool.

'Why wouldn't the whole world be dark and a man to be hung?' said she.

They went to the hemp so knotted and stinking, and begun raking it and raking it. The wind was roaring from the bay, the hulk twitching and tottering; the gulls came off the wave, and Christine's clothes stretched out from her like the wings of a bird. The hemp heaved upon the paddock like a great beast bursting a snare that was on it, and a strong blast drove a heap of it up on the Man from Kilsheelan, twisting and binding him in its clasp till he thought he would not escape from it and he went falling and yelping. Tom Tool unwound him, and sat him in the lew of the stack till he got his strength again, and then he began to moan of his misfortune.

'Stint your shouting,' said Tom Tool, 'isn't it as hard to cure as a wart on the back of a hedgehog?'

But he wouldn't stint it. ''Tis large and splendid talk I get from you, Tom Tool, but divil a deed of strength. Vexed and waxy I am. Why couldn't he do his murder after we'd done with him. What a cranky cousin! What a foolish creature! What a silly man, the devil take him!'

'Let you be aisy,' the other said, 'to heaven he is going.'

'And what's the gain of it, he to go with his neck stretched?'

'Indeed, I did know a man went to heaven once,' began Tom Tool, 'but he did not care for it.'

'That's queer,' said the Man, 'for it couldn't be anything you'd not want, indeed to glory.'

'Well, he came back to Ireland on the head of it. I forget what was his name.'

'Was it Corcoran, or Tool, or Horan?'

'No, none of those names. He let on it was a lonely place, not fit for living people or dead people, he said; nothing but trees and streams and beasts and birds.'

'What beasts and birds?'

'Rabbits and badgers, the elephant, the dromedary, and all those ancient races; eagles and hawks and cuckoos and magpies. He wandered in a thick forest for nights and days like a flea in a great beard, and the beasts and the birds setting traps and hooks and dangers for a poor feller; the worst villains of all was the sheep.'

'The sheep! What could a sheep do then?' asked Kilsheelan.

'I don't know the right of it, but you'd not believe me if I told you at all. If you went for the little swim you was not seen again.'

'I never heard the like of that in Roscommon.'

'Not another holy soul was in it but himself, and if he was taken with the thirst he would dip his hand in a stream that flowed with rich wine and put it to his lips, but if he did it turned into air at once and twisted up in a blue cloud. But grand wine to look at, he said. If he took oranges from a tree he could not bite them, they were chiny oranges, hard as a plate. But beautiful oranges to look at they were. To pick a flower it burst on you like a gun. What was cold was too cold to touch, and what was warm was too warm to swallow, you must throw it up, or die.'

'Faith, it's no region for a Christian soul, Tom Tool. Where is it at all?'

'High it may be, low it may be, it may be here, it may be there.'

'What could the like of a sheep do? A sheep!'

'A devouring savage creature it is there, the most hard to come at, the most difficult to conquer, with the teeth of a lion and a tiger, the strength of a bear and a half, the deceit of two foxes, the run of a deer, the . . .'

'Is it heaven you call it! I'd not look twice at a place the like of that.'

'No, you would not, no.'

'Ah, but wait now,' said Kilsheelan, 'wait till the Day of Judgment.'

'Well, I will not wait then,' said Tom Tool sternly.

'When the sinners of the world are called to their judgment, scatter they will all over the face of the earth, running like hares till they come to the sea, and there they will perish.'

'Ah, the love of God on the world!'

They went raking and raking, till they came to a great stiff hump of it that rolled over, and they could see sticking from the end of it two boots.

'O, what is it, in the name of God?' asks Kilsheelan.

'Sorra and all, but I'd not like to look,' says Tom Tool, and they called the girl to come see what was it.

'A dead man!' says Christine, in a thin voice with a great tremble coming on her, and she white as a tooth. 'Unwind him now.' They began to unwind him like a tailor with a bale of tweed, and at last they came to a man black in the face. Strangled he was. The girl let a great cry out of her. 'Queen of heaven, 'tis my dad; choked he is, the long strands have choked him, my good, pleasant dad!' and she went with a run to the house crying.

'What has he there in his hand?' asked Kilsheelan.

' 'Tis a chopper,' says he.

'Do you see what is on it, Tom Tool?'

'Sure I see, and you see, what is on it; blood is on it, and murder is on it. Go fetch a peeler, and I'll wait while you bring him.'

When his friend was gone for the police Tom Tool took a little squint around him and slid his hand into the dead man's pocket. But as he did so he was nearly struck mad from his senses, for he pulled out a loose dead hand that had been chopped off as neat as the foot of a pig. He looked at the dead man's arms, and there was a hand to each; so he looked at the hand again. The fingers were covered with the rings of gold and diamonds. Covered!

'Glory be to God!' said Tom Tool, and he put his hand in another pocket and fetched a budget full of papers and banknotes.

'Glory be to God!' he said again, and put the hand and the budget back in the pockets, and turned his back and said prayers until the peelers came and took them all off to the court.

It was not long, two days or three, until an inquiry was held; grand it was and its judgment was good. And the big-wig asked: 'Where is the man that found the body?'

'There are two of him,' says the peeler.

'Swear 'em,' says he, and Kilsheelan stepped up to a great murdering joker of a clerk, who gave him a book in his hand and roared at him: 'I swear by Almighty God . . .'

'Yes,' says Kilsheelan.

'Swear it,' says the clerk.

'Indeed I do.'

'You must repeat it,' says the clerk.

'I will, sir.'

'Well, repeat it then,' says he.

'And what will I repeat?'

So he told him again and he repeated it. Then the clerk goes on: '. . . that the evidence I give . . .'

'Yes,' says Kilsheelan.

'Say those words, if you please.'

'The words! Och, give me the head of 'em again!'

So he told him again and he repeated it. Then the clerk goes on: '. . . shall be the truth . . .'

'It will,' says Kilsheelan.

'. . . and nothing but the truth . . .'

'Yes, begod, indeed!'

'Say "nothing but the truth," ' roared the clerk.

'No!' says Kilsheelan.

'Say "nothing".'

'All right,' says Kilsheelan.

'Can't you say "nothing but the truth"?'

'Yes,' he says.

'Well, say it!'

'I will so,' says he, 'the scrapings of sense on it all!'

So they swore them both, and their evidence they gave.

'Very good,' his lordship said, 'a most important and opportune discovery, in the nick of time, by the tracing of God. There is a reward of fifty pounds offered for the finding of this property and jewels; fifty pounds you will get in due course.'

They said they were obliged to him, though sorrow a one of them knew what he meant by a due course, nor where it was.

Then a lawyer man got the rights of the whole case; he was the cunningest man ever lived in the city of Cork; no one could match him, and he made it straight and he made it clear.

Old Horan must have returned from his journey unbeknown on the night of the gale when the deed was done. Perhaps he had made a poor profit on his toil, for there was little of his own coin found on his body. He saw the two drunks staggering along the bay — he clove in the head of the one with a bit of pipe — he hit the other a good whack to still or stiffen him — he got an axe from the yard — he shore off the Mexican's two hands, for the rings were grown tight and wouldn't be drawn from his fat fingers. Perhaps he dragged the captain home to his bed — you couldn't be sure of that — but put the hand in the captain's pocket he did, and then went to the paddock to bury the treasure. But a blast of wind whipped and wove some of the hemp strand around his limbs, binding him sudden. He was all huffled and hogled and went mad with the fear struggling, the hemp rolling him and binding him till he was strangled or smothered.

And that is what happened him, believe it or no, but believe it you should. It was the tracing of God on him for his dark crime.

Within a week of it Peter Corcoran was away out of gaol, a stout walking man again, free in Ballygoveen. But on the day of his release he did not go near the ropewalker's house. The Horans were there waiting, and the two old silly men, but he did not go next or near them. The next day Kilsheelan said to her: 'Strange it is my cousin not to seek you, and he a sneezer for gallantry.'

' 'Tis no wonder at all,' replied Christine, 'and he with his picture in all the papers.'

'But he had a right to have come now and you caring him in his black misfortune,' said Tom Tool.

'Well, he will not come then,' Christine said in her soft voice, 'in regard of the red murder on the soul of my dad. And why should he put a mark on his family, and he the captain of a ship.'

In the afternoon Tom Tool and the other went walking to try if they should see him, and they did see him at a hotel, but he was hurrying from it; he had a frieze coat on him and a bag in his hand.

'Well, who are you at all?' asks Peter Corcoran.

'You are my cousin from Ameriky,' says Kilsheelan.

'Is that so? And I never heard it,' says Peter. 'What's your name?'

The Man from Kilsheelan hung down his old head and couldn't answer him, but Tom Tool said: 'Drifty he is, sir, he forgets his little name.'

'Astray is he? My mother said I've cousins in Roscommon, d'ye know 'em? the Twingeings . . .'

'Twingeing! Owen Twingeing it is!' roared Kilsheelan. ''Tis my name! 'Tis my name! 'Tis my name!' and he danced about squawking like a parrot in a frenzy.

'If it's Owen Twingeing you are, I'll bring you to my mother in Manhattan.' The captain grabbed up his bag. 'Haste now, come along out of it. I'm going from the cunning town this minute, bad sleep to it for ever and a month! There's a cart waiting to catch me the boat train to Queenstown. Will you go? Now?'

'Holy God contrive it,' said Kilsheelan; his voice was wheezy as an old goat, and he made to go off with him. 'Good-day to you, Tom Tool, you'll get all the reward and endure a rich life from this out, fortune on it all, a fortune on it all!'

And the two of them were gone in a twink.

Tom Tool went back to the Horans then; night was beginning to dusk and to darken. As he went up the ropewalk Christine came to him from her potato gardens and gave him signs, he to be quiet and follow her down to the strand. So he followed her down to the strand and told her all that happened, till she was vexed and full of tender words for the old fool.

'Aren't you the spit of misfortune! It would daunt a saint, so it would, and scrape a tear from silky Satan's eye. Those two deluderers, they've but the drainings of half a heart between 'em. And he not willing to lift the feather of a thought on me? I'd not forget him till there's ten days in a week and every one of 'em lucky. But . . . but . . . isn't Peter Corcoran the nice name for a captain man, the very pattern?'

She gave him a little bundle into his hands. 'There's a loaf and a cut of meat. You'd best be stirring from here.'

'Yes,' he said, and stood looking stupid, for his mind

was in a dream. The rock at one horn of the bay had a red glow on it like the shawl on the neck of a lady, but the other was black now. A man was dragging a turf boat up the beach.

'Listen, you,' said Christine. 'There's two upstart men in the house now, seeking you and the other. There's trouble and damage on the head of it. From the asylum they are. To the police they have been, to put an embargo on the reward, and sorra a sixpence you'll receive of the fifty pounds of it: to the expenses of the asylum it must go, they say. The treachery! Devil and all, the blood sweating on every coin of it would rot the palm of a nigger. Do you hear me at all?'

She gave him a little shaking for he was standing stupid, gazing at the bay which was dying into grave darkness except for the wash of its broken waves.

'Do you hear me at all? It's quit now you should, my little old man, or they'll be taking you.'

'Ah, yes, sure, I hear you, Christine; thank you kindly. Just looking and listening I was. I'll be stirring from it now, and I'll get on and I'll go. Just looking and listening I was, just a wee look.'

'Then good-bye to you, Mr. Tool,' said Christine Horan, and turning from him she left him in the darkness and went running up the ropewalk to her home.

The Black Dog (1923)

PURL AND PLAIN

At ten o'clock one summer night Father Corkery was in his study devouring a fine large governmental report on Population when his housekeeper tapped and told him that a gentleman was wanting to see him, and very anxious. Father Corkery was a good citizen of the world, a little plump now, a little bald now, a little lazy now, for at sixty you become more impressionable to the blandishments of Time, but he was also a good priest, so he received the gentleman at once, a rich young gentleman, and his name it was Robert Moriarty. It is your business to understand now that this Mr. Moriarty was not only an Irishman, he was an enthusiastic Irishman, his servants were Irish, and he had just now sought out Father Corkery because he was an Irish Priest. Mr. Moriarty was married to an agreeable English lady, a creature of beauty! and both she and her husband were newly come to the Borough of Clapham where Father Corkery was in holy orders. By the grace of God (and the connivance of Mr. Moriarty) this lady was even now being brought to bed of a child, so would his reverence come along at once to baptize the child as soon as it should be born. 'Will a duck swim!' says Father Corkery.

Off they went together to a new nice house in the Borough of Clapham, where they were let in by a pretty Irish servant, and her name it was Mary O'Sullivan. Her master inquired: had anything come along while he was away? 'No, Mr. Bob,' says she, 'not a finger of it yet.' So young Mr. Moriarty — a very nice affable fellow, a bit distracted, but who wouldn't be at such times — he bowed his reverence into a nice room and sat him in an arm-chair. He took his black bag away from him and put it under a sofa, but then he picked it up out of that again and set it on the piano. The room was used as a dining-room, or it was used as a drawing-room, but now it had the air of having temporarily suppressed its customary spirits. It smelled faintly of tomato sauce and was filled with dark heavy orderly furniture, a sideboard with a canopy reaching the ceiling, arm-chairs of leather, a grandfather's clock as big as a coffin, and a long rectangular table covered with a cloth of patterned rose and brown. The only frivolous objects in the room were the electric lights and a white elephant of china which stood on the mantelpiece where a clock ought to have been.

Father Corkery and Mr. Moriarty then conversed gently with each other as Mr. Moriarty told the story of his marriage. And this was the way of that. A year ago he had been married — to the finest woman in Ireland. He had been born and bred a good Catholic but he had been overpowered with love for a lady who was only a Protestant. It was a little bit of an obstacle, that difference of religion, but 'Jewel' — says he — 'my heart's in your pocket.' There could be no other obstacle, both of them being young and ripe for marriage, their incomes were agreeable and their relations obliging. 'I, Robert, take thee, Millicent, to my wedded wife.' And it was agreed there and then that any boys born of their marriage were to become good little Catholics (or they should), and any girls might become little Protestants, and so here they were now waiting for the first child to be born. The doctor was upstairs, the nurse was there, the priest was here. . .

'So if it's a girl,' said Father Corkery, 'my time is wasted and I'll not be wanted?'

Mr. Moriarty walked over the room, took the priest's black bag off the piano and put it on the whatnot.

'I was going to tell you about that, Father,' he began. He was deeply obliged to his reverence for coming; he had dearly wanted an Irish priest, for as his reverence knew there were only two sorts of people in the world — the Irish, and those others. 'I was going to tell you about that,' repeated Mr. Moriarty, when the door was knocked and Mary O'Sullivan came ushering in a young curate and said: 'Mr. Caspin, Mr. Bob.'

'Hey, hey, come along,' said Mr. Moriarty. The curate, who had the complexion of a fair girl, and the mouth of an old man, went up to Father Corkery very close, said 'Good evening', and shook him violently by the hand. And then, as he took off a light overcoat, revealing himself dressed in a cassock like Father Corkery, he remarked again that it was a pleasant evening. Like his reverend brother he, too, had brought a little black bag with him, and in this they both resembled the doctor, except that *he* was supervising the child's entry into this world while they were already concerning themselves about its entry into the next. Mr. Moriarty took Mr. Caspin's bag and went to put it on the whatnot, until he noticed another bag there, and so he bent down and shoved it under a chair.

'No, not yet,' said Mr. Moriarty to the curate, 'but almost any moment now. Will you seat yourself, sir? . . . Father Corkery, this is the Reverend Caspin against it's a girl — you mind what I told you. And Mr. Caspin, this is Father Corkery against it's a boy — you mind what I told you earlier on? Excuse me now, reverend gentlemen.'

Pressing a handkerchief to his brow the young man left the two clerics sitting opposite each other before the empty fireplace. Almost immediately Mr. Moriarty rushed in again, opened a cupboard and placed on the table a decanter of port and two glasses.

'Help yourselves, gentlemen, please,' said he, and rushed away again.

'I never touch it,' the curate said.

Father Corkery was pouring out a good glass.

'Forgive me, gentlemen!' cried Mr. Moriarty rushing in once more in great agitation, 'Cigars!' From the same cupboard he brought a box of cigars.

'I never touch them,' the curate said. Father Corkery said he would use his pipe, and he began to fill his pipe as Mr. Moriarty went away again.

'I suspect,' then said the one to the other, 'that we have a long wait before us.'

'Is the poor lady in difficulties?' inquired Mr. Caspin.

Father Corkery nodded into his tobacco pouch and replied: 'O, so so. A trying day, ye know, is the day of birth, and for a while the heart pines for oblivion. But in a very short time she will discover, what every mother discovers early or late, that she has been divinely chosen to give birth to one of the world's prodigies.'

To the Reverend Ferdinand Caspin, this homely and familiar notion sounded strange; perhaps it was because he thought Father Corkery used the word 'protégés', a word that at such a time, on such an occasion, had certain unnameable sectarian connotations. Pressing the tips of his fingers together in the immemorial symbol of curacy he leaned forward:

'Tell me, sir: do you approve of these family arrangements? Do you think it right for a child's religion to be decided by the mere accident of its sex?'

Father Corkery puffed his pipe in the immemorial grandeur of reflection. Then he said:

'For us to approve or not to approve makes devil a

bit of difference; it's like putting a lock on a cardboard door. On the other hand sex is no accident at all; it comes, I suppose, by the grace of God. All the important things of life are decided by sex, and maybe it's as good a guide as any other.'

'O come, I say,' Mr. Caspin almost gasped, 'really now!'

'Well,' laughed his reverence. 'I admit I have sometimes thought it would not be a bad thing if all men were Christians, and all women heathens. Indeed, I fancy Nature intended something of the kind and that we have blundered.'

'By Jove,' exclaimed the curate, 'do you know, sir — have you read the ninth volume of Thatchbason's Commentaries?'

Well, now, Father Corkery had never even heard of Thatchbason.

'Upon the Epistles!' the curate insisted. 'By Jove, really; he has something absolutely new to say about Saint Augustine, as well as Saint Paul. He propounds, expounds and defends a thoroughly new position, and a very brilliant position.'

'Something new? Ay?'

'Entirely. And, of course, sir, one is forced to recognize that the female sex is definitely inferior in moral stability — not to be trusted.'

'O, I like a woman to be reasonably unreliable,' said Father Corkery, replenishing his glass and pushing the decanter towards Caspin, who however reminded him that he never touched it.

'O,' said Father Corkery, 'I was thinking it was tobacco you never touched.'

'Tobacco, too,' confessed the curate, blushing.

'Ah, you don't touch tobacco! Humph. Yes,' continued Father Corkery, 'that is rather my own feeling about woman. I was in Venice once — were you ever in Venice?'

Mr. Caspin nodded enthusiastically. 'O, a fascinating place! I shall never forget . . .'

'Have you a match?' interrupted Father Corkery.

Mr. Caspin handed a box across to his confrère and repeated: 'I shall never forget . . .' when Father Corkery again slid the decanter towards him and ejaculated 'Port!'

'No, no, thank you,' Mr. Caspin replied, and was then silent.

After a few moments Father Corkery asked him *what* it was he would never forget.

'O, I only wanted to say,' the curate said, 'that I shall never forget the oleanders on the Lido and the charming little lizards flashing about under the dried seaweed.'

'O, I never saw them. While I was there,' Father Corkery proceeded, 'I once went into a great beautiful church, very quiet and lonely. As I went in at the door I heard voices singing, but sounding far away, as if in some chamber, muffled, but extraordinarily beautiful. I stood rapt and the saintly sound brought tears to my eyes. When I looked about I could not discover where the singing came from. Suddenly the door of the sacristy opened, and then it shut. For a moment I caught a full wave of that rich singing. Then I saw a young girl who had come out of that doorway, and she walked across to the high altar and fetched an armful of candlesticks. I could still hear the music, faintly, but the girl had got on those loose slippers the Italian women wear and the flapping of her heels made a very sharp clatter. When she reached the door again she could not open it because her arms were full of the candlesticks, so she kicked on it, crying angrily for it to be opened. I was quite near her so I went and pulled open the door, and then the song burst on me in great fulness. I could see a dozen women inside, old and young, sitting at a long bench cleaning the holy plate. But what smote me, like a cudgel on a drunken head, was the thing they were all singing, with the gusto of a happy choir in beautiful unison. Do you know what it was? I could hear it clearly, and I had heard it before. It was a song of the last conceivable bawdiness? Too wicked for anything.'

Ferdinand Caspin sighed 'Good heavens! Dear me!'

'And yet,' Father Corkery went on, lolling easily in his chair, 'I never think of Venice but I recall the sweet emotion that their fine singing gave me. O, they were happy innocent women. And I can see that young girl now, kicking the door, with her arms full of candlesticks, and calling harshly "open!" '

Father Corkery glanced across at the other, who was mute, and then he gurgled with laughter.

'Is that a box of dominoes I see over on the sideboard? If it is I will play you a game.'

Mr. Caspin thought it was not a box of dominoes. And in any case he did not play dominoes.

'I thought we might be here a long time,' said his reverence.

After Father Corkery had taken another swig at the wine Mr. Caspin said:

'I suppose you really approve this arrangement of the Moriartys about their children?'

Father Corkery took his pipe from his mouth: 'I am rather old now to approve things. At my time of life it is much easier to condemn anything, only condemnation so often upsets the kidneys, ye know.'

'Indeed, sir,' said the other, 'I thought age brought a . . . a . . . a more mellow wisdom.'

'It may bring wisdom,' Father Corkery agreed, 'but wisdom isn't mellow; what is mellow is one's indifference. Wisdom must be critical, or what is the use of having it at all? On the other hand, we often fall into the error of believing that criticism itself is wisdom when it may only be bad temper. It is impossible to exercise wisdom in regard to women, for instance, and to criticize them is merely bad taste. Woman is most prone to superstition — so she worships man. She is a great gambler — so she bears his children. It's a pity you don't play dominoes. What do you think; will it be a boy or a girl to-night?'

Mr. Caspin intimated that he could not tell, but they would be bound to know before very much longer.

'I bet you,' Father Corkery said, 'that it's a girl.'

'No, no,' the other shook his head. 'I never gamble.'

'Not! Why not?'

'To me,' said Mr. Caspin, but he made it plain that his present objection was quite impersonal, 'to me gambling is superstition, dissatisfaction, greed, and idolatry.'

'Well,' said Father Corkery, 'we are already dissatisfied and greedy and superstitious, all of us, women more so than men . . .'

'Exactly,' interjected the curate.

'And that,' his reverence continued, 'may be because they have more to fear — as observed by your Mr. Thatchbason. But now, give a guess; d'ye *think* it will be a boy, or d'ye *think* it will be a girl?'

Mr. Caspin was disinclined to prophesy, but he had an intuition. 'My intuitions,' he declared, 'very seldom fail me.'

'Ha, ha!' Father Corkery rallied him. 'Some people can't resist 'em; it's like cards and horse-racing.'

'Well, if you insist,' said the curate, 'my intuition is that the child will be a boy.'

'Is that so?' murmured Father Corkery. 'Now I will tell you my intuition. To-day is the seventh day of the seventh month, and as I walked here with Mr. Moriarty we passed very few people; all told there were seven — and all of them were women. Now what d'ye think of that for a female tip!'

Mr. Caspin was bound to laugh at him. 'I think,' he replied, looking at the clock, 'it is very likely that this child will be born on the eighth day. Now I will tell you something. After Mr. Moriarty called on me this evening about this matter I went to my study. In my brief absence somebody had been into my room and tidied up, for on the mantelpiece my own photograph stood confronting me — upside down!'

'Well,' temporized the other, 'what d'ye make of that?'

'Surely,' smiled the curate, 'that I am losing my time in this case, that the child will be a little boy.'

'That's a grave omen,' said Father Corkery with a twinkle. 'It probably will be little, but I bet you . . .' Pausing he raked in his pocket and inspected some coins he found there '. . . I bet you a solid two shillings that it's a female child.'

'No, certainly not,' Mr. Caspin replied, a little wanly.

'As you will,' retorted the other.

For some time both were silent, Father Corkery puffing imperturbably, Mr. Caspin clasping his knees with folded hands and gazing into anything but the present and at anything but the priest. The house grew so oppressive in its quiet that when the clock struck eleven the air boomed and oozed with its reverberations; they poured through door and ceiling, and burst upon the roof to shock the dreaming chimneys.

'I was interested in a case recently of a sailor,' then began Mr. Caspin, 'who fell off the rigging in the Bahamas. He was on a ship in the Bahamas, I think it was, but I'm not sure at the moment where it was — humph!'

Father Corkery chanted: 'Where the remote Bermudas ride.'

'No, it *was* the Bahamas,' continued Mr. Caspin, 'and broke his leg so badly that it had to be amputated and he had to be discharged. He came home and had to be an attendant in a men's public lavatory, one of those underground places, in the parish of a friend of mine, a man I know very well. The sailor's wife had disappeared; I don't know anything about that matter, but no one knew where or why she had gone, so the sailor had to lodge with his married daughter. Every day at one o'clock that young woman, a very respectable creature, had to take her father's dinner to him at that place. She had to stand at the top of the steps and call out "Father!" until he came up to her. Awful, you know. My friend was vicar of the parish and such a thing was most distasteful to him, as you can understand. Every day this young married woman was subject to all the ribald remarks of any men coming or going in such a place. So my friend had to take steps and he tried to put a stop to it one way and another, and at first he couldn't, though at last he succeeded. He arranged for one of his choir boys who lived in the same street to take the man's dinner every day. But the extraordinary thing was that the young woman was very angry and would never enter my friend's church again! Very touchy, these people,' concluded Mr. Caspin.

'Asperity has many friends,' Father Corkery conceded that it was a picturesque case. 'What did the sailor do about that?'

'O,' Mr. Caspin was confused, but he gloomily continued, 'he was a bad lot after all. Some quite unmentionable traffic went on between them, I never knew what, something indelicate, and it was found out.'

'Between whom?' asked Father Corkery.

'The sailor and the choir boy,' returned the other. 'Of course the man was discharged and the boy was sent to a home. Detestable! Why are men so weak? Tell me!' he cried, 'the past was heroic, why is our own age so vulgar?'

Father Corkery brushed his hand over his benignant baldness. 'Ah, my friend, we are superstitious and dissatisfied and greedy. We are endowed, you know, with far more prejudice than judgment. Man enjoys his sinful manhood until he comes to a conviction of sin. Then he reforms and enjoys his reformation until he comes to a conviction of foolishness. That's the way of his life, alternations, a sort of purl and plain woven into the figure of him.'

Mr. Caspin murmured that this was painfully true.

'It helps,' Father Corkery added, 'to make a pattern, just as it does in knitting. But what is that?' he asked sharply, 'Listen!'

They listened, and they heard the thin cry of a newborn babe. Father Corkery put down his pipe and crossed himself. Mr. Caspin jumped up, went to his bag, and wriggled into his surplice while the priest went on whispering a prayer. Then Father Corkery opened his own bag and put on his own surplice.

'This water I have here,' he said, 'is from the River Shannon; a colleague sent me a quart of it a little while ago. I've brought it specially because our friend is an enthusiastic Irishman. To him the Irish are the greatest people in the world.'

'Dear, dear, this racial pride is fantastic,' said Caspin. 'Do you know, the Japanese believe they are actually descended from the gods?'

'There is really nothing fantastic about that,' his reverence answered, 'for every devout Christian necessarily believes the same.'

At that moment young Mr. Moriarty came rushing in with a very happy look on him.

'It is a girl,' he shouted.

The two clerics looked at each other. 'There now!' laughed Father Corkery. 'I should have won my bet! Ah well, the blessing of God on it all, Mr. Moriarty; I congratulate you from the bottom of my soul. From the bottom of my soul,' he repeated, raising his arms and struggling to get out of his surplice. 'And may the wee thing grow up as beautiful as Helen, as wise as Pallas, and as chaste as, as . . . who was that other one, Caspin? Ah never mind! And is your wife doing well?'

'Splendid, Father, the cream of creation,' cried Mr. Moriarty with gleeful pride. 'Splendid! But don't be so hasty now, your reverence. It's what I have to tell you, I have to tell something to both of you and I don't know how to tell it to either of you. But it's about Milly — that's herself — she's renagged, at the last moment, of her own will. Yes, Father, will you keep your surplice on. There was the babe in the basket by her side, and she looking at it like a pot of gold, and I'm telling her you both were ready for the baptizing. "I'd forgotten about all that" — says she. "But you remember the arrangement, Milly" — says I — "the boys for me, the girls for you!" "Sure, I'd forgotten entirely", says she, "and now it's a girl after all." "Jewel" — I says — "I've the Protestant man downstairs." "No" — she says — "I was never cracked about religion, but 'twould be a sin for a child to be different from her father and her brothers." "Then it's Catholic, you mean" — says I. "Catholic it is" — says she.'

Mr. Moriarty could not conceal, even from Mr. Caspin, his glee at the way things turned out, but he said to him:

'A hundred thousand pardons for disturbing you, sir, and troubling you for nothing at all. It's the women, sir, are the queer creatures.'

Mr. Caspin put his clothes off and into the bag and begged him not to mention it. In a few moments he bade them both good-night.

'Mr. Moriarty,' Father Corkery said, 'God has blessed you with a very fine wife.'

'True for you,' the happy husband beamed, 'and you don't even know her like I do.'

'God has blessed you,' repeated his reverence, 'with the finest wife in the world.'

'True it is, Father; but you can't tell what they'd be wanting from one hour to another. The devil himself, saving your presence, don't know where he is with the creatures.'

'No,' asserted Father Corkery as they went upstairs together. 'God alone knows.'

Silver Circus (1928)

THE WATERCRESS GIRL

When Mary McDowall was brought to the assize court the place was crowded, Mr. O'Kane said, 'inside out'. It was a serious trial, as everybody — even the prisoner — well knew; twelve tons of straw had been thrown down on the roads outside the hall to deaden the noise of carts passing and such-like pandemoniums, and when the judge drove up in his coach with jockeys on the horses, a couple of young trumpeters from the barracks stiffened on the steps and blew a terrible fanfare up into heaven. 'For a sort of a warning, I should think,' said Mr. O'Kane.

The prisoner's father having been kicked by a horse was unable to attend the trial, and so he had enlisted Mr. O'Kane to go and fetch him the news of it; and Mr. O'Kane in obliging his friend suffered annoyances and was abused in the court itself by a great fat geezer of a fellow with a long staff. 'If you remained on your haunches when the judge came in,' complained Mr. O'Kane, 'you were poked up, and if you stood up to get a look at the prisoner when *she* came in you were poked down. Surely to God we didn't go to look at the judge!'

Short was her trial, for the evidence was clear, and the guilt not denied. Prisoner neither sorrowed for her crime nor bemoaned her fate; passive and casual she stood there at the willing of the court for a thing she had done, and there were no tears now in Mary McDowall. Most always she dressed in black, and she was in black then, with masses of black hair; a pale face with a dark mole on the chin, and rich red lips; a big girl of twenty-five, not coarsely big, and you could guess she was strong. A passionate girl, caring nothing or not much for this justice; unimpressed by the solemn court, nor moved to smile at its absurdities; for all that passion concerns with is love — or its absence — love that gives its only gift by giving all. If you could have read her mind, not now but in its calm before the stress of her misfortune, you would have learned this much, although she herself could not have formulated it: I will give to love all it is in me to give; I shall desire of love all I can ever dream of and receive.

And because another woman had taken what Mary McDowall wanted, Mary had flung a corrosive acid in the face of her enemy, and Elizabeth Plantney's good looks were gone, gone for certain and for ever. So here was Mary McDowall and over there was Frank Oppidan; not a very fine one to mislead the handsome girl in the dock, but he had done it, and he too had suffered and the women in court had pity for him, and the men — envy. Tall, with light oiled hair and pink sleepy features (a pink heart, too, you might think, though you could not see it), he gave evidence against her in a nasal tone with a confident manner, and she did not waste a look on him. A wood-turner he was, and for about four years had 'kept company' with the prisoner, who lived near a village a mile or two away from his home. He had often urged her to marry him, but she would not, so a little while ago he told her he was going to marry Elizabeth Plantney. A few evenings later he had been strolling with Elizabeth Plantney on the road outside the town. It was not yet dark, about eight o'clock, but they had not observed the prisoner, who must have been dogging them, for she came slyly up and passed by them, turned, splashed something in his companion's face and then walked on. She didn't run; at first they thought it was some stupid joke, and he was for going after the prisoner whom he had recognized.

'I was mad angry,' declared Oppidan, 'I could have choked her. But Miss Plantney began to scream that she was blinded and burning, and I had to carry and drag her some ways back along the road until we came to the first house, Mr. Blackfriar's, where they took her in and I ran off for the doctor.' The witness added savagely, 'I wish I *had* choked her.'

There was full corroboration, prisoner had admitted guilt, and the counsel briefed by her father could only plead for a lenient sentence. A big man he was with a drooping yellow moustache and terrific teeth; his cheeks and hands were pink as salmon.

'Accused,' he said, 'is the only child of Fergus McDowall. She lives with her father, a respectable widower, at a somewhat retired cottage in the valley of Trinkel, assisting him in the conduct of his business — a small-holding by the river where he cultivates water-cress, and keeps bees and hens and things of that kind. The witness Oppidan had been in the habit of cycling from his town to the McDowall's home to buy bunches of watercress, a delicacy of which, in season, he seems to have been — um — inordinately fond, for he would go twice, thrice and often four times a week. His visits were not confined to the purchase of watercress, and he seems to have made himself agreeable to the daughter of the house; but I am in possession of no information as to the nature of their intercourse beyond that tendered by the witness Oppidan. Against my advice the prisoner, who is a very reticent, even a remarkable, woman, has insisted on pleading guilty and accepting her punishment without any — um — chance of mitigation, in a spirit, I hope, of contrition, which is not — um — entirely unadmirable. My Lord, I trust . . .'

While the brutal story was being recounted, the prisoner had stood with closed eyes, leaning her hands upon the rail of the dock; stood and dreamed of what she had not revealed:

Of her father Fergus McDowall; his child she was, although he had never married. That much she knew, but who her mother had been he never told her, and it did not seem to matter; she guessed rather than knew that at her birth she had died, or soon afterwards, and the man had fostered her. He and she had always been together, alone, ever since she could remember, always together, always happy, he was so kind; and so splendid in the great boots that drew up to his thighs when he worked in the watercress beds, cutting bunches deftly, or cleaning the weeds from the water. And there were her beehives, her flock of hens, the young pigs, and a calf that knelt and rubbed its neck on the rich mead with a lavishing movement just as the ducks did when the grass was dewy. She had seen the young pigs, no bigger than rabbits, race across the patch of greensward to the blue-roan calf standing nodding in the shade; they would prowl beneath the calf, clustering round its feet, and begin to gnaw the calf's hoof until, full of patience, she would gently lift her leg and shake it, but would not move away. Save for a wildness of mood that sometimes flashed through her, Mary was content, and loved the life that she could not know was lonely with her father beside the watercress streams. He was uncommunicative, like Mary, but as he worked he hummed to himself or whistled the soft tunes that at night he played on the clarinet. Tall and strong, a handsome man. Sometimes he would put his arms around her and say, 'Well, my dear.' And she would kiss him. She had vowed to herself that she would never leave him, but then — Frank had come. In this mortal conflict we seek not only that pleasure may not divide us from duty, but that duty may not detach us from life. He was not the first man or youth she could or would have loved, but he was the one who had wooed her; first-love's enlightening delight, in the long summer eves, in those enticing fields! How easily she was won! All his offers of marriage she had put off with the answer: 'No, it would never do for me,' or 'I shall never marry', but then, if he angrily swore or accused her of not loving him enough, her fire and freedom would awe him almost as much as it enchanted. And she might have married Frank if she could only have told him of her dubious origin, but whether from some vagrant modesty, loyalty to her father, or some reason whatever, she could not bring herself to do that. Often these steady refusals enraged her lover, and after such occasions he would not seek her again for weeks, but in the end he always returned, although his absences grew longer as their friendship lengthened. Ah, when the way to your lover is long, there's but a short cut to the end. Came a time when he did not return at all and then, soon, Mary found she was going to have a child. 'Oh, I wondered where you were, Frank, and why you were there, wherever it was, instead of where I could find you.' But the fact was portentous enough to depose her grief at his fickleness, and after a while she took no further care or thought for Oppidan, for she feared that like her own mother she would die of her child. Soon these fears left her and she rejoiced. Certainly she need not scruple to tell him of her own origin now, he could never reproach her now. Had he come once more, had he come then, she would have married him. But although he might have been hers for the lifting of a finger, as they say, her pride kept her from calling him into the trouble, and she did not call

him and he never sought her again. When her father
realized her condition he merely said 'Frank?' and she
nodded.

The child was early born, and she was not prepared;
it came and died. Her father took it and buried it in
the garden. It was a boy, dead. No one else knew, not
even Frank, but when she was recovered her pride
wavered and she wrote a loving letter to him, still keeping her secret. Not until she had written three times
did she hear from him, and then he only answered that
he should not see her any more. He did not tell her
why, but she knew. He was going to marry Elizabeth
Plantney, whose parents had died and left her £500.
To Mary's mind that presented itself as a treachery to
their child, the tiny body buried under a beehive in the
garden. That Frank was unaware made no difference
to the girl's fierce mood; it was treachery. Maternal
anger stormed in her breast, it could only be allayed by
an injury, a deep admonishing injury to that treacherous
man. In her sleepless nights, the little crumpled corpse
seemed to plead for this much, and her own heart
clamoured, just as those bees murmured against him
day by day.

So then she got some vitriol. Rushing past her old
lover on the night of the crime she turned upon him
with the lifted jar, but the sudden confrontation dazed
and tormented her; in momentary hesitation she had
dashed the acid, not into *his* faithless eyes, but at the
prim creature linked to his arm. Walking away, she
heard the crying of the wounded girl. After a while
she had turned back to the town and given herself up
to the police.

To her mind, as she stood leaning against the dock
rail, it was all huddled and contorted, but that was her
story set in its order. The trial went droning on beside

her remembered grief like a dull stream neighbouring
a clear one, two parallel streams that would meet in the
end, were meeting now, surely, as the judge began to
speak. And at the crisis, as if in exculpation, she
suffered a whisper to escape her lips, though none
heard it.

' 'Twas him made me a parent, but he was never a
man himself. He took advantage; it was mean, I love
Christianity.' She heard the judge deliver her sentence:
for six calendar months she was to be locked in a gaol.
'O Christ!' she breathed, for it was the lovely spring;
lilac, laburnum, and father wading the brooks in those
boots drawn up to his thighs to rake the dark sprigs
and comb out the green scum.

They took her away. 'I wanted to come out then,'
said Mr. O'Kane, 'for the next case was only about a
contractor defrauding the corporation — good luck to
him, but he got three years — and I tried to get out of
it, but if I did that geezer with the stick poked me
down and said I'd not to stir out of it till the court rose.
I said to him I'd kill him, but there was a lot of peelers
about so I suppose he didn't hear it.'

II

Towards the end of the year Oppidan had made up
his mind what he would do to Mary McDowall when
she came out of prison. Poor Liz was marred for life,
spoiled, cut off from the joys they had intended together. Not for all the world would he marry her now;
he had tried to bring himself to that issue of chivalry,
of decency, but it was impossible; he had failed in the
point of grace. No man could love Elizabeth Plantney
now, Frank could not visit her without shuddering,

and she herself, poor generous wretch, had given him back his promise. Apart from his ruined fondness for her, they had planned to do much with the £500; it was to have set him up in a secure and easy way of trade, they would have been established in a year or two as solid as a rock. All that chance was gone, no such chance ever came twice in a man's lifetime, and he was left with Liz upon his conscience. He would have to be kind to her for as long as he could stand it. That was a disgust to his mind for he wanted to be faithful. Even the most unstable man wishes he had been faithful — but to which woman he is never quite sure. And then that bitch Mary McDowall would come out of her prison and be a mockery to him of what he had forgone, of what he had been deprived. Savagely he believed in the balance wrought by an act of vengeance — he, too! — eye for eye, tooth for tooth; it had a threefold claim, simplicity, relief, triumph. The McDowall girl, so his fierce meditations ran, miked in prison for six months and then came out no worse than when she went in. It was no punishment at all, they did no hurt to women in prison; the court hadn't set wrong right at all, it never did; and he was a loser whichever way he turned. But there was still a thing he could do (Jove had slumbered, he would steal Jove's lightning) and a project lay troubling his mind like a gnat in the eye, he would have no peace until it was wiped away.

On an October evening, then, about a week after Mary McDowall's release, Oppidan set off towards Trinkel. Through Trinkel he went and a furlong past it until he came to their lane. Down the lane too, and then he could hear the water ruttling over the cataracts of the cress-beds. Not yet in winter, the year's decline was harbouring splendour everywhere. Whitebeam was a dissolute tangle of rags covering ruby drops, the service trees were sallow as lemons, the oak resisted decay, but most confident of all were the tender-tressed ashes. The man walked quietly to a point where, unobserved, he could view the McDowall dwelling, with its overbowering walnut tree littering the yard with husks and leaves, its small adjacent field with banks that stooped in the glazed water. The house was heavy and small, but there were signs of grace in the garden, of thrift in the orderly painted sheds. The conical peak of a tiny stack was pitched in the afterglow, the elms sighed like tired old matrons, wisdom and content lingered here. Oppidan crept along the hedges until he was in a field at the back of the house, a hedge still hiding him. He was trembling. There was a light already in the back window; one leaf of the window stood open and he saw their black cat jump down from it into the garden and slink away under some shrubs. From his standpoint he could not see into the lighted room, but he knew enough of Fergus's habits to be sure he was not within; it was his day for driving into the town. Thus it could only be Mary who had lit that lamp. Trembling still! Just beyond him was a heap of dung from the stable, and a cock was standing silent on the dunghill while two hens, a white one and a black, bickered around him over some voided grains. Presently the cock seized the black hen and the white scurried away; but though his grasp was fierce and he bit at her red comb, the black hen went on gobbling morsels from the manure heap, and when at last he released her she did not intermit her steady pecking. Then Oppidan was startled by a flock of starlings that slid across the evening with the steady movement of a cloud; the noise of their wings was like showers of rain upon trees.

'Wait till it's darker,' he muttered, and skulking back to the lane he walked sharply for half a mile. Then, slowly, he returned. Unseen, he reached the grass that grew under the lighted window, and stooped warily against the wall; one hand rested on the wall, the other in his pocket. For some time he hesitated but he knew what he had to do and what did it matter! He stepped in front of the window.

In a moment, and for several moments longer, he was rigid with surprise. It was Mary all right (the bitch!), washing her hair, drying it in front of the kitchen fire, the thick locks pouring over her face as she knelt with her hands resting on her thighs. So long was their black flow that the ends lay in a small heap inside the fender. Her bodice hung on the back of a chair beside her, and her only upper clothing was a loose and disarrayed chemise that did not hide her bosom. Then, gathering the hair in her hands, she held the tresses closer to the fire, her face peeped through, and to herself she was smiling. Dazzling fair were her arms and the one breast he astonishingly saw. It was Mary; but not the Mary, dull ugly creature, whom his long rancour had conjured for him. Lord, what had he forgotten! Absence and resentment had pared away her loveliness from his recollection, but this was the old Mary of their passionate days, transfigured and marvellous.

Stepping back from the window into shadow again, he could feel his heart pound like a frantic hammer; every pulse was hurrying at the summons. In those breathless moments, Oppidan gazed as it were at himself, or at his mad intention, gazed wonderingly, ashamed and awed. Fingering the thing in his pocket, turning it over as a coin whose toss has deceived him, he was aware of a revulsion; gone revenge, gone rancour, gone all thought of Elizabeth, and there was left in his soul what had not gone and could never go. A brute she had been — it was bloody cruelty — but, but ... but what? Seen thus, in her innocent occupation, the grim fact of her crime had somehow thrown a conquering glamour over her hair, the pale pride of her face, the intimacy of her bosom. Her very punishment was a triumph; on what account had she suffered if not for love of him? He could feel that chastening distinction meltingly now; she had suffered for his love.

There and then shrill cries burst upon them. The cat leaped from the garden to the window-sill; there was a thrush in its mouth, shrieking. The cat paused on the sill, furtive and hesitant. Without a thought Oppidan plunged forward, seized the cat and with his free hand clutched what he could of the thrush. In a second the cat released it and dropped into the room, while the crushed bird fluttered away to the darkened shrubs, leaving its tail feathers in the hand of the man.

Mary sprang up and rushed to the window. 'Is it you?' was all she said. Hastily she left the window, and Oppidan with a grin saw her shuffling into her bodice. One hand fumbled at the buttons, the other unlatched the door. 'Frank.' There was neither surprise nor elation. He walked in. Only then did he open his fist and the thrush's feathers floated in the air and idled to the floor. Neither of them remembered any more of the cat or the bird.

In silence they stood, not looking at each other.

'What do you want?' at length she asked. 'You're hindering me.'

'Am I?' he grinned. His face was pink and shaven, his hair was almost as smooth as a brass bowl. 'Well, I'll tell you.' His hat was cumbering his hands, so he put it carefully on the table.

'I come here wanting to do a bad thing, I own up to that. I had it in my mind to serve you same as you served her — you know who I mean. Directly I knew you had come home, that's what I meant to do. I been waiting about out there a good while until I saw you. And then I saw you. I hadn't seen you for a long, long time, and somehow, I dunno, when I saw you . . .'

Mary was standing with her hands on her hips; the black cascades of her hair rolled over her arms; some of the strands were gathered under her fingers, looped to her waist; dark weeping hair.

'I didn't mean to harm her!' she burst out. 'I never meant that for her, not what I did. Something happened to me that I'd not told you of then, and it doesn't matter now, and I shall never tell you. It was you I wanted to put a mark on, but directly I was in front of you I went all swavy, and I couldn't. But I had to throw it, I had to throw it.'

He sat down on a chair, and she stared at him across the table: 'All along it was meant for you, and that's God's truth.'

'Why?' he asked. She did not give him an answer then, but stood rubbing the fingers of one hand on the finely scrubbed boards of the table, tracing circles and watching them vacantly. At last, she put a question:

'Did you get married soon?'

'No,' he said.

'Aren't you? But of course it's no business of mine.'

'I'm not going to marry her.'

'Not?'

'No, I tell you I wouldn't marry her for five thousand pounds, nor for fifty thousand, I wouldn't.' He got up and walked up and down before the fire. 'She's — aw! You don't know, you don't know what you done to her! She'd frighten you. It's rotten, like a leper. A veil on indoors and out, has to wear it always. She don't often go out, but whether or no, she must wear it. Ah, it's cruel.'

There was a shock of horror as well as the throb of tears in her passionate compunction. 'And you're not marrying her!'

'No,' he said bluntly, 'I'm not marrying her.'

Mary covered her face with her hands, and stood quivering under her dark weeping hair.

'God forgive me, how pitiful I'm shamed!' Her voice rose in a sharp cry. 'Marry her, Frank! Oh, you marry her now, you must!'

'Not for a million, I'd sooner be in my grave.'

'Frank Oppidan, you're no man, no man at all. You never had the courage to be strong, nor the courage to be evil; you've only the strength to be mean.'

'O, dry up!' he said testily; but something overpowered her and she went leaning her head sobbing against the chimneypiece.

'Come on, girl!' he was instantly tender, his arms were around her, he had kissed her.

'Go your ways!' She was loudly resentful. 'I want no more of you.'

'It's all right, Mary. Mary, I'm coming to you again, just as I used to.'

'You . . .' She swung out of his embrace. 'What for? D'ye think I want you now? Go off to Elizabeth Plantney . . .' She faltered. 'Poor thing, poor thing, it shames me pitiful; I'd sooner have done it to myself. O, I wish I had.'

With a meek grin Oppidan took from his pocket a bottle with a glass stopper. 'Do you know what that is?'

It looked like a flask of scent. Mary did not answer. 'Sulphuric,' continued he, 'same as you threw at her.'

The girl silently stared while he moved his hand as if he were weighing the bottle. 'When I saw what a mess you'd made of her, I reckoned you'd got off too light, it ought to have been seven years for you. I only saw it once, and my inside turned right over, you've no idea. And I thought: there's she — done for. Nobody could marry her, less he was blind. And there's you, just a six months and out you come right as ever. That's how I thought and I wanted to get even with you then, for her sake, not for mine, so I got this, the same stuff, and I came thinking to give you a touch of it.'

Mary drew herself up with a sharp breath. 'You mean — throw it at me?'

'That's what I meant, honour bright, but I couldn't — not now.' He went on weighing the bottle in his hand.

'O, throw it, throw it!' she cried in bitter grief, but covering her face with her hands — perhaps in shame, perhaps fear.

'No, no, no, no.' He slipped the bottle back into his pocket. 'But why did you do it? She wouldn't hurt a fly. What good could it do you?'

'Throw it,' she screamed, 'throw it, Frank, let it blast me!'

'Easy, easy now. I wouldn't even throw it at a rat. See!' he cried. The bottle was in his hand again as he went to the open window and withdrew the stopper. He held it outside while the fluid bubbled to the grass; the empty bottle he tossed into the shrubs.

He sat down, his head bowed in his hands, and for some time neither spoke. Then he was aware that she had come to him, was standing there, waiting. 'Frank,' she said softly, 'there's something I got to tell you.' And she told him about the babe.

At first he was incredulous. No, no, that was too much for him to stomach! Very stupid and ironical he was until the girl's pale sincerity glowed through the darkness of his unbelief: 'You don't believe! How could it not be true!'

'But I can't make heads or tails of it yet, Mary. You a mother, and I were a father!' Eagerly and yet mournfully he brooded. 'If I'd 'a' known — I can't hardly believe it, Mary — so help me God, if I'd 'a' known . . .'

'You could done nothing, Frank.'

'Ah, but I'd 'a' known! A man's never a man till that's come to him.'

'Nor a woman's a woman, neither; that's true, I'm different now.'

'I'd 'a' been his father, I tell you. Now I'm nothing. I didn't know of his coming, I never see, and I didn't know of his going, so I'm nothing still.'

'You kept away from me. I was afraid at first and I wanted you, but you was no help to me, you kept away.'

'I'd a right to know, didn't I? You could 'a' wrote and told me.'

'I did write to you.'

'But you didn't tell me nothing.'

'You could 'a' come and see me,' she returned austerely, 'then you'd known. How could I write down a thing like that in a letter as anybody might open? Any dog or devil could play tricks with it when you was boozed or something.'

'I ought 'a bin told, I ought 'a bin told.' Stubbornly he maintained it. ' 'Twasn't fair, you.'

''Twasn't kind, you. You ought to 'a' come; I asked you, but you was sick o' me, Frank, sick o' me and mine. I didn't want any help, neither, 'twasn't that I wanted.'

'Would you 'a' married me then?' Sharply but persuasively he probed for what she neither admitted nor denied. 'Yes, yes, you would, Mary. 'Twould 'a' bin a scandal if I'd gone and married someone else.'

When at last the truth about her own birth came out between them, O, how ironically protestant he was! 'God a' mighty, girl, what did you take me for! There's no sense in you. I'll marry you now, for good and all (this minute if we could), honour bright, and you know it, for I love you always and always. You were his mother, Mary, and I were his father! What was he like, that little son?'

Sadly the girl mused. 'It was very small.'

'Light hair?'

'No, like mine, dark it was.'

'What colour eyes?'

She drew her fingers down through the long streams of hair. 'It never opened its eyes.' And her voice moved him so that he cried out: 'My love, my love, life's before us; there's a many good fish in the sea. When shall us marry?'

'Let me go, Frank. And you'd better go now, you're hindering me, and father will be coming in, and . . . and . . . the cakes are burning!'

Snatching up a cloth she opened the oven door and an odour of caraway rushed into the air. Inside the oven was a shelf full of little cakes in pans.

'Give us one,' he begged, 'and then I'll be off.'

'You shall have two,' she said, kneeling down by the oven. 'One for you — mind, it's hot!' He seized it from the cloth and quickly dropped it into his pocket. 'And another, from me,' continued Mary. Taking the second cake, he knelt down and embraced the huddled girl.

'I wants another one,' he whispered.

A quick intelligence swam in her eyes: 'For?'

'Ah, for what's between us, dear Mary.'

The third cake was given him, and they stood up. They moved towards the door. She lifted the latch.

'Good night, my love.' Passively she received his kiss. 'I'll come again to-morrow.'

'No, Frank, don't ever come any more.'

'Aw, I'm coming right enough,' he cried cheerily and confidently as he stepped away.

And I suppose we must conclude that he did.

Fishmonger's Fiddle (1925)

CHRISTINE'S LETTER

CHRISTINE was vexed. A charming waitress; she wore a wedding ring, but she was the most attractive girl at the Café Tee To Tum, always deft and alert, with beauty that cheered you, good sense that satisfied, a gentle dignity that pleased; now she was vexed, fuming. The girl at the cash desk had given her a letter, it had come by the afternoon post, a fat letter, it had been re-directed once or twice, and Christine was anxious to read it. She had read snatches of it, she burned to read more, the whole of it, it was so long and beseeching, and it so gilded her triumph, because it was from her husband living in the country. Christine had not seen him for three or four months, she had not even heard from him since she had left him, this was the first letter that had reached her, and it began: 'Come, it was not nice of you to run away and leave me so, but I do not reproach you.' The phrases were in the very spirit of the namby unmasterful creature she had so unhappily married, but hating him though she did, she was eager to know how much her lightning severance of their bond had wounded him. Did he want her to return; was he sorry, or angry, or what? Not that she cared now: he was in the south, she was in the north, there were hundreds of miles between them. Sick to loathing she had run from him and put herself to work, mean work. Christine did not like working for her living, but it was heaven compared to living with *that*. She read: 'I wish I had never married you, it was my mother's fault, she urged me to it.'

'O, it is not true; how he enrages me! Lies, lies,

lies! He besieged me, swore he would kill himself with . . .'

'Some bread and butter,' said the clergyman she was called to attend. 'Household bread, and stale if you have got it.' His voice seemed to threaten the very food he was ordering. Old, tottery, and abrupt he was, with a vague warp of rufous hairs combed from left to right across his poll that was coloured like a pineboard.

'He is a hound, you know,' ruminated Christine. 'As if his mother had anything to do with it!'

At the buffet she filled a pot of tea, clapped bread and butter upon a plate, knife, spoon, milk, and conveyed her tray to the clergyman.

'China tea?' he inquired, peering up. 'No? I said China. I can't drink this.' He was very ugly for a man of God.

'I do not reproach you. Indeed! O, thanks!' and with a hoity-toity aria in her soul Christine replaced the Indian beverage with Chinese potion. 'He wants me back and promises not to grumble! Jam, sir? Pastry?'

'No. I detest pastry. O . . . I don't know, what else have you got; where's the card? I'd like to see it, though I shan't want anything else. Mum . . . mum . . . mum . . . bananas. I suppose there is no cream for threepence each? No. Yes, a banana.' And he pushed a fold of bread and butter into his mouth without offering a grace.

Christine served him with a small plump banana on a little white dish, and for some reason pushed a cruet towards him. But people continued to pour in and she could not find a corner or a moment in which to read another line of her letter. So distracting it was, she could hardly grasp what the customers said to her, and she gazed with a lost gaze through the great window with those white letters stamped upon it backwards:

ƎƎⱵⱭO TAⱭOϽO AƎT

Flittings of experience came to and fro in her mind: conjugal life in their hamlet, so quiet, so empty, so dull and therefore so exhausting; a husband who wanted to be a poet, whose pensive melancholy would have blackened the soul of an angel; their incompatible association, his serenity, her despair, and her suppressed fury at it all.

The tottery clergyman went, went without offering a God-bless-it, Christine was sure; a stout matron with a green parasol desired a glass of water, some cracknels and the loan of the time-table; a little fat-legged girl lolling with her toes on a table rail fell with her chair backwards and screamed.

'I hate the things you think, and the things you have done to me.' Well, it was his own fault; she had not loved him, she never could have loved him, for he stifled her, his very goodness mangled every fibre of her self-respect, so that, at last, to be in the same room with him submitted her to a sort of ghostly asphyxiation. They had never quarrelled, not really quarrelled, but O how often she had longed to shatter with some blasphemy the contentment of his eyes. The wild cat was in Christine, hidden, it had never been tamed, he had never known of it — how *was* he to know of it? — propriety had swamped him in such billows. And yet the place had been beautiful, ah, the hills, the woods, the sky like holy balm — if only, O, if only . . . !

Christine kept stealing the letter from her breast, it began: 'Beloved', but she could not win two moments of repose, it would have to wait, it was a long, long letter, pages and pages. So Christine went on serving; there was a shower of rain outside and the people lingered on. But the rain stopped at last and the people began to go, soon they were nearly all gone and then ... Then Arabella Barnes came up with her knuckle bleeding, to beg Christine to bind it up for her, and there and then Phyllis Wicks began to beguile them with stories of her own true love. He was a bus-conductor, and had violet eyes; they made Phyllis reckless, and she lavished her pocket-money upon him.

'What's mine is his,' Phyllis said to Arabella, 'and what's his is mine.'

'But not,' Arabella sniffed, 'not that boil on the back of his neck?'

'There's no such thing! His flesh is as sweet as a lamb.'

Faugh! Christine almost shrieked, but she only said 'Excuse me!' and ran off to the only place where she could be free from unceasing interruptions — the lavatory. O blessed inviolable refuge! Instantly she began to read her letter.

'Beloved,

'Come, it was not nice to run away and leave me so, but I will not reproach you. No, nor for anything. But still, why did you? Why did you? It is hard for me to account for your absence, you know, I am in a false position, a stupid position, I am a fish out of water, I am like a fish that some tidal wave has left upon an ironmonger's counter. People, the neighbours, your friends, the very tradesmen, imagine painful things. They must know, they can see it, they smirk and pity me. How am I to explain? It is not possible. Perhaps you have gone off with another man. Of course we had ceased to love each other, though we had only been married a year, a little long year; our life together was stifling, unbearable, though I never told you so — you would not have understood. We stung and annoyed each other — but, what of that? Excuse me, my dear, what of it?

This then is life,

This is what has come to the surface after so many throes and convulsions.

And you have gone, have gone without a good-bye, without a quarrel, without even a kiss-my-behind, and left me only some of your old shoes and a bottle of aspirin tablets. Did you think I suffered from headaches? I have never suffered from headaches. I shall throw them away soon and give the shoes to that girl with the blue eyes who brings the washing. After these months of silence what am I to think, or do? Why have you not written? I wish I had never married you, it was my mother's fault, she urged me to it. And you were pretty. I liked that, though I did not like your irreligion, or your ideas, or the friends you favoured. They were foolish people, they were, believe me, my dear, I know, I know, all of them unworthy of you. Was I too? And yet, without boasting, I could have done great and marvellous things if you had cared for them, yes in time I could; but you were restless, you were artistic I suppose, Bohemian, and the long slow months exhausted you. For myself I was content in the little house in this sweet country place, yet often I envied riches. O, my goodness, yes; you did not guess that! I envied riches for you, so that we could have gone, well, where *could* we have gone? Now, perhaps you are gone with some man. That is not right or fitting, but if you would come home again I should not say anything about it. One forgets, it is lonely here, foolish here, but I dare not go away lest you come suddenly home again. O, I wish you would. You were always wanting to travel, to blaze out, to "do" things; even on your last birthday you said bitterly, "A quarter of a century and nothing done". What is it you want to do? You will not have children. Let us travel together. We will give up this little house, it is too isolated and unspacious, there is not enough room in it for you and I together, it makes us melancholy and mean and full of evil. It is true, yes, though you did not believe there was any evil in me — and that used to annoy you. I'll take a mistress, I will, I swear it, and what will you say to that? O forgive me, my blessed one, I wish you would come back, it is lonely here, foolish here. Sometimes I am singing quite happily and loudly all by myself, and then in the midst of a song, without any reason at all I stop and burst into tears. Why, why is this? O tell me, dear one, come and tell. When first you left me, I did not mind, I was unmoved. It was summer, and in summer what is now monotony was almost ideal. Unless you lay and stared at the sky everything you saw was green leaves and grass, grass and leaves. The birds were all those friendly fellows of one or two notes, chiff-chaffs calling for hours, the tom-tit sawing, the magpie rattling a box of peas, and the cuckoo whose company always stirred the small birds to such rages. All gone now. And at night there were nightjars, and out on the down the curlew. The boughs of the trees would just float in the hot air and the leaves would hum like gnats. Time really existed, a thick accreting medium, without lapse. Pine needles filled our water shoot, there were cobwebs everywhere. And now the garden has run to waste, all except the bed of parsley, it *has* grown. I do not use it, but you were so fond of parsley. How it did annoy me when you sent me out at night into the dark garden to gather a sprig or two for some fish cakes or some-

thing! I would grope about and light matches end-
lessly in the wind until I'd picked a handful and then
I would bring it to you. The grass of the lawn is
getting long and rough. Do you remember one day
last April when it snowed and you stripped yourself
naked and went out on the lawn and danced in the
white flakes? So reckless of you, anybody passing
might have seen you, but I did not say anything. I did
not even watch you. I got out some towels and warmed
them for you, but somehow you did not like that. Why
not? It always pleased you greatly to be displeased. I
wish you believed in God. How can you not — there
is Christ? You believed only in the things that concerned you, you said: death was death and you knew
nothing about it and could not know. O, false, dreadful,
trivial spirit of the age, so flippant and so fleeting;
every year a new Abraham prepares to sacrifice a new
Isaac. The everlasting wanders in the void, for half the
truths we know can never be told, they are too divine
for speech. But God is freedom from evil — is it not
so? I told my mother that you were gone abroad with
friends, I have not told her the truth, I dare not tell
myself. Besides, it may not be true. Sometimes I have
a conviction, sweet and lovely one, that it is not true,
that it never can be true. Not to-day, alas, no, for it
rains, it rains all over the world. There is melancholy
in my mind and gloom in everything, in the straggled
forlorn briars and the scoops of dark leaves shrinking
from the wind on the common. I have just been walking there, along by the pond. The tiny pond shivered
as the lorn drops fell upon it, some sheep lay under the
blackthorn, the wind was cold. The misty hills with
their dying woods were far away, too far. There was a
horse tied to the white palings beside the inn, and it
lifted its head and neighed as I came by. I bowed my

own head and almost wept, wept for nothing save that life was gloomy and chill. And yet, a mile above those clouds that cling to the land the sunlight must be everlastingly beautiful; even in the next county the day may be bright and warm, and perhaps on some happy sea-coast, blue and golden a hundred miles away, little white yachts are gliding, and people sit and snooze and declare that life is splendid. Yet here my misery fits me as tightly as a new hat that I cannot discard, it is my clothing, my element, my doom. O, you are right, my darling, this is no place for a beautiful woman. You were a bright pin stuck in a cushion of mud, it was right to go and leave me. But I might find you again and take you far away. Every time I come home my glance leaps to the hallrack to see if your hat and coat are there. No, not to-day, certainly not to-day. I do not even know whether this letter will reach you. Perhaps I shall not send it after all. I have written others, many, and I have not sent them, so you do not reply; but I go on writing and writing, and perhaps some day I will show them all to you. But no, you are harsh and evil, I hate the things you think and the thing you have done to me — it is just crude cruelty. And there is hatred in me too, and evil, for I know you will never come back, never, never, never. You will find another lover who may deserve you more than I, though he could not love you better. But, however that may fall, you will deserve him as little as you deserved me, poor thing as I am. For you had no generosity of spirit, all you had was a beautiful alluring body, nothing more on which a man could anchor his deep feeling. I suppose I could go on abusing you for a long, long page. It is sad to have to say the last thing between us. I know I shall go on loving you. Perhaps I shall find a true friend who will love me better than you, and I shall love her — until I remember. Then I suppose I shall tell her of a lover I once had, far sweeter than she, who used me well, was beautiful beyond all, was forbearing and kind and understanding. Listening, she will vainly envy you, not, O not for your love of me, but because of your surpassing excellence.

'Christine, my wife, do not believe it ever. I am a bird in your heart that will sing when you remember me.'

'The hound! The hound!' gasped Christine, clenching the letter with fury. As for a moment she stood with it crushed between her hands her wry glance caught one word at the beginning of the letter. 'Beloved'. So she began to read it again, opening it until she came to the lines: 'I wish I had not married you, it was my mother's fault, she urged me to it.' Once more she crushed the detestable pages together, and this time she cast them into the lavatory. A gesture of the hand, and they were swirled away.

'I want,' called the girl in the cash desk when Christine returned, 'twopence from you.'

'Twopence?'

'Please. It was surcharged, that letter of yours. Didn't you notice the envelope? It had been redirected or something. I paid the postman. Twopence it was.'

'O, dear,' Christine said, 'It wasn't of the slightest consequence. I wish you hadn't. It was from . . . from someone I didn't know.'

The Field of Mustard (1926)

OLIVE AND CAMILLA

THEY had lived and travelled together for twenty years, and this is a part of their history: not much, but all that matters. Ever since reaching marriageable age they had been together, and so neither had married, though Olive had had her two or three occasions of perilous inducement. Being women they were critical of each other, inseparably critical; being spinsters they were huffy, tender, sullen and demure, and had quarrelled with each other ten thousand times in a hundred different places during their 'wanderings up and down Europe'. That was the phrase Camilla used in relating their maidenly Odyssey, which had comprised a multitude of sojourns in the pensions of Belgium, Switzerland, Italy and France. They quarrelled in Naples and repented in Rome; exploded in anger at Arles, were embittered at Interlaken, parted for ever at Lake Garda, Taormina and Bruges; but running water never fouls, they had never really been apart, not anywhere. Olive was like that, and so was her friend; such natures could nowise be changed. Camilla Hobbs, slight and prim, had a tiny tinkling mind that tinkled all day long, she was all things to little nothings. The other, Olive Sharples, the portly one, had a mind like a cuckoo-clock; something came out and cried 'Cuckoo' now and again, quite sharply, and was done with it. They were moulded thus, one supposes, by the hand of Providence; it could neither be evaded or altered, it could not even be mitigated, for in Camilla's prim mind and manner, there was a prim deprecation of Olive's boorish nature, and for her part Olive resented Camilla's assumption of a superior disposition. Saving a precious month or two in Olive's favour they were both now of a sad age, an age when the path of years slopes downwards to a yawning inexplicable gulf.

'Just fancy!' Camilla said on her forty-fifth birthday — they were at Chamonix then — 'we are ninety between us!'

Olive glowered at her friend, though a couple of months really is nothing. 'When I am fifty,' she declared, 'I shall kill myself.'

'But why?' Camilla was so interested.

'God, I don't know!' returned Olive.

Camilla brightly brooded for a few moments. 'You'll find it very hard to commit suicide; it's not easy, you know, not at all. I've heard time and time again that it's most difficult. . . .'

'Pooh!' snorted Olive.

'But I tell you! I tell you I knew a cook at Leamington who swallowed ground glass in her porridge, pounds and pounds, and nothing came of it.'

'Pooh!' Olive was contemptuous. 'Never say die.'

'Well, that's just what people say who can't do it!'

The stream of their companionship was far from being a rill of peaceful water, but it flowed, more and more like a cataract it flowed, and was like to flow on as it had for those twenty years. Otherwise they were friendless! Olive had had enough money to do as she modestly liked, for though she was impulsive her desires were frugal, but Camilla had had nothing except a grandmother. In the beginning of their friendship Olive had carried the penurious Camilla off to Paris where they mildly studied art, and ardently pursued the practice of water-colour painting. Olive, it might be said, transacted doorways and alleys, very shadowy and grim, but otherwise quite nice; and Camilla did streams with bending willow and cow on bank, really sweet. In a year or two Camilla's grandmother died of dropsy and left her a fortune, much larger than Olive's, in bank stock, insurance stock, distillery, coal — oh, a mass of money! And when something tragical happened to half of Olive's property — it was in salt shares or jute shares, such unstable friable material — it became the little fluttering Camilla's joy to play the fairy godmother in her turn. So there they were in a bondage less sentimental than appeared, but more sentimental than was known.

They returned to England for George V's coronation. In the train from Chamonix a syphon of soda-water which Camilla imported into the carriage — it was an inexplicable thing, that bottle of soda-water, as Olive said after the catastrophe: God alone knew why she had bought it — Camilla's syphon, what with the jolting of the train and its own gasobility, burst on the rack. Just burst! A handsome young Frenchwoman travelling in their compartment was almost convulsed with mirth, but Olive, sitting just below the bottle, was drenched — she declared — to the midriff. Camilla lightly deprecated the coarseness of the expression. How could *she* help it if a bottle took it into its head to burst like that! In abrupt savage tones Olive merely repeated that she was soaked to the midriff, and to Camilla's horror she began to divest herself of some of her clothing. Camilla rushed to the windows, pulled down the blinds and locked the corridor door. The young Frenchwoman sat smiling while Olive removed her corsets and her wetted linen; Camilla rummage d s feverishly in Olive's suitcase that the compartment began to look as if arranged for a jumble sale; there were garments and furbelows strewn everywhere. But at last Olive completed her toilet, the train stopped at a station, the young Frenchwoman got out. Later in the day, when they were nearing Paris, Olive's corsets could not be found.

'What did you do with them?' Olive asked Camilla.

'But I don't think I touched them, Olive. After you took them off I did not see them again. Where do you think you put them? Can't you remember?'

She helped Olive unpack the suitcase, but the stays were not there. And she helped Olive to repack.

'What am I to do?' asked Olive.

Camilla firmly declared that the young French-woman who had travelled with them in the morning must have stolen them.

'What for?' asked Olive.

'Well, what do people steal things for?' There was an air of pellucid reason in Camilla's question, but Olive was scornful.

'Corsets!' she exclaimed.

'I knew a cripple once,' declared Olive, 'who stole an ear trumpet.'

'That French girl wasn't a cripple.'

'No,' said Camilla, 'but she was married — at least, she wore a wedding ring. She looked as deep as the sea. I am positive she was up to no good.'

'Bosh!' said Olive. 'What the devil are you talking about?'

'Well, you should not throw your things about as you do.'

'Soda-water,' snapped Olive, with ferocious dignity, 'is no place for a railway carriage.'

'You mean . . . ?' asked Camilla with the darling sweetness of a maid of twenty.

'I mean just what I say.'

'Oh no, you don't,' purred the triumphant one; and she repeated Olive's topsy-turvy phrase. 'Ha, ha, that's what you said.'

'I did not! Camilla, why are you such a liar? You know it annoys me.'

'But I tell you, Olive . . .'

'I did not! It's absurd. You're a fool.'

Well, they got to England and in a few days it began to appear to them as the most lovely country they had ever seen. It was not only that, it was their homeland. Why have we stayed away so long? Why did we not come back before? It was so marvellously much better than anything else in the world, they were sure of that. So much better, too, than their youthful recollection of it, so much improved; and the cleanness! Why did we never come back? Why have we stayed away so long? They did not know; it was astonishing to find your homeland so lovely. Both felt that they could not bear to leave England again; they would settle down and build a house, it was time; their joint age was ninety! But, alas, it was difficult, it was impossible, to dovetail their idea of a house into one agreeable abode.

'I want,' said Olive Sharples, 'just an English country cottage with a few conveniences. That's all I can afford, and all I want.'

So she bought an acre of land at the foot of a green hill in the Chilterns and gave orders for the erection of the house of her dreams. Truly it was a charming spot, pasture and park and glebe and spinney and stream, *deliciously* remote, quite half a mile from *any* village, and only to be reached by a *mere* lane. No sooner had her friend made this decision than Camilla too bought land there, half a dozen acres adjoining Olive's, and began to build the house of *her* dreams, a roomy house with a loggia and a balcony, planting her land with fruit trees. The two houses were built close together, by the same men, and Camilla could call out greetings to Olive from her bedroom window before Olive was up in the morning, and Olive could hear her — though she did not always reply. Had Olive suffered herself to peer steadily into her secret thoughts, in order to discover her present feeling about Camilla, she would have been perplexed; she might even have been ashamed, but for the comfort of old acquaintance such telescopic introspection was denied her. The new cottage brought her felicity, halcyon days; even her bedroom contented her, so small and clean and bare it was. Beyond bed, washing-stand, mirror and rug there was almost nothing, and yet she felt that if she were not exceedingly careful, she would break something. The ceiling was virgin white, the walls the colour of butter, the floor the colour of chocolate. The grate had never had a fire in it; not a shovelful of ashes had ever been taken from it, and, please God — so it seemed to indicate — never would be. But the bed was soft and reposeful. O heavenly sleep!

The two friends dwelt thus in isolation; there they were, perhaps this was happiness. The isolation was tempered by the usual rural society, a squire who drank, a magistrate who was mad, and a lime-burner whose daughters had been to college and swore like seamen. There was the agreeable Mr. Kippax, a retired fellmonger, in whom Camilla divined a desire to wed somebody — Olive perhaps. He was sixty and played on the violin-cello. Often Olive accompanied him on Camilla's grand piano. Crump, crump, he would go; and primp, primp, Olive would reply. He was a serious man, and once when they were alone he asked Olive why she was always so sad.

'I don't know. Am I?'

'Surely,' he said, grinning, running his fingers through his long grey hair. 'Why are you?'

And Olive thought and thought. 'I suppose I want impossible things.'

'Such as . . .?' he interrogated.

'I do not know. I only know that I shall never find them.'

Then there were the vicarage people, a young vicar with a passionate complexion who had once been an actor and was now something of an invalid having had a number of his ribs removed for some unpleasant purpose; charming Mrs. Vicar and a tiny baby. Oh, and Mrs. Lassiter, the wife of a sea captain far away on the seas; yet she was content, and so by inference was the sea captain, for he never came home. There was a dearth of colour in her cheeks, it had crowded into her lips, her hair, her eyes. So young, so beautiful, so trite, there was a fragrant imbecility about her.

Olive and Camilla seldom went out together: the possession of a house is often as much of a judgment as a joy, and as full of ardours as of raptures. Gardens, servants and tradespeople were not automata that behaved like eight-day clocks, by no means. Olive had an eight-day clock, a small competent little thing; it had to be small to suit her room, but Camilla had three — three eight-day clocks. And on the top of the one in the drawing-room — and really Camilla's house seemed a positive little mansion, all crystal and mirror and white pillars and soft carpets, but it wasn't a mansion any more than Olive's was a cottage — well, on the mantelpiece of the drawing-room, on top of Camilla's largest eight-day clock, there stood the bronze image of a dear belligerent little lion copied in miniature from a Roman antique. The most adorable creature it was, looking as if it were about to mew, for it was no bigger than a kitten although a grown-up lion with a mane and an expression of annoyance as if

it had been insulted by an ox — a toy ox. The sweep
of its tail was august; the pads of its feet were beautiful
crumpled cushions, with claws (like the hooks of a tiny
ship) laid on the cushions. Simply ecstatic with anger,
most adorable, and Olive loved it as it raged there
on Camilla's eight-day clock. But clocks are not like
servants. No servant would stay there for long, the
place was so lonely, they said, dreadful! And in wet
weather the surroundings and approach — there was
only a green lane, and half a mile of that — were so
muddy, dreadful mud; and when the moon was gone
everything was steeped in darkness, and that was
dreadful too! As neither Camilla nor Olive could miti-
gate these natural but unpleasing features — they were,
of course, the gifts of Providence — the two ladies,
Camilla at any rate, suffered from an ever-recurrent
domestic Hail and Farewell. What — Camilla would
inquire — *did* the servants want? There was the village,
barely a mile away; if you climbed the hill you could
see it splendidly, a fine meek little village; the woods,
the hills, the fields, positively thrust their greenness
upon it, bathed it as if in a prism — so that the brown
chimney pots looked red and the yellow ones blue.
And the church was new, or so nearly new that you
might call it a good second-hand; it was made of brown
bricks. Although it had no tower, or even what you
might call a belfry, it had got a little square fat chimney
over the front gable with a cross of yellow bricks
worked into the face of the chimney, while just below
that was a bell cupboard stuffed with sparrows' nests.
And there were unusual advantages in the village —
watercress, for instance. But Camilla's servants came
and went, only Olive's Quincy Pugh remained. She
was a dark young woman with a white amiable face,
amiable curves to her body, the elixir of amiability in

her blood, and it was clear to Camilla that *she* only remained because of Luke Feedy. He was the gardener, chiefly employed by Camilla, but he also undertook the work of Olive's plot. Unfortunately Olive's portion was situated immediately under the hill and, fence it how they would, the rabbits always burrowed in and stole Olive's vegetables. They never seemed to attack Camilla's more abundant acreage.

Close beside their houses there was a public footway, but seldom used, leading up into the hills. Solemn steep hills they were, covered with long fawn-hued grass that was never cropped or grazed, and dotted with thousands of pert little juniper bushes, very dark, and a few whitebeam trees whose foliage when tossed by the wind shook on the hill-side like bushes of entangled stars. Half-way up the hill path was a bulging bank that tempted climbers to rest, and here, all unknown to Camilla, Olive caused an iron bench to be fixed so that tired persons could recline in comfort and view the grand country that rolled away before them. Even at midsummer it was cool on that height, just as in winter it took the sunbeams warmly. The air roving through the long fawn-hued grass had a soft caressing movement. Darkly green at the foot of the hill began the trees and hedges that diminished in the pastoral infinity of the vale, further and further yet, so very far and wide. At times Olive would sit on her iron bench in clear sunlight and watch a shower swilling over half a dozen towns while beyond them, seen through the inundating curtain, very remote indeed lay the last hills of all, brightly glowing and contented. Often Olive would climb to her high seat and bask in the delight, but soon Camilla discovered that the bench was the public gift of Olive. Thereupon lower down the hill, Camilla caused a splendid ornate bench of teak with a foot-rest to be installed in a jolly nook surrounded by tall juniper bushes like cypresses, and she planted three or four trailing roses thereby. Whenever Camilla had visitors she would take them up the hill to sit on her splendid bench; even Olive's visitors preferred Camilla's bench, and remarked upon its superior charm. So much more handsome it was, and yet Olive could not bear to sit there at all, never alone. And soon she gave up going even to the iron one.

Thus they lived in their rather solitary houses, supporting the infirmities of the domestic spirit by mutual commiseration, and coming to date occasions by the names of those servants — Georgina, Rose, Elizabeth, Sue — whoever happened to be with them when such and such an event occurred. These were not remarkable in any way. The name of Emma Tooting, for instance, only recalled a catastrophe to the parrot. One day she had actually shut the cockatoo — it was a stupid bird, always like a parson nosing about in places where it was not wanted — she had accidently shut the cockatoo in the oven. The fire had not long been lit, the oven was not hot, Emma Tooting was brushing it out, the cockatoo was watching. Emma Tooting was called away for a few moments by the baker in the yard, came back, saw the door open, slammed it to with her foot, pulled out blower, went upstairs to make bed, came down later to make fire, heard most horrible noises in kitchen, couldn't tell where, didn't know they came from the oven, thought it was the devil, swooned straight away — and the cockatoo was baked. The whole thing completely unnerved Emma Tooting and she gave notice. Such a good cook, too. Mrs. Lassiter and the lime-burner — that was a mysterious business — were thought to have been imprudent in Minnie

Hopplecock's time; at any rate, suspicion was giddily engendered then.

'I shouldn't be surprised,' Camilla had declared, 'if they were all the way, myself. Of course, I don't know, but it would not surprise me one bit. You see, we've only instinct to go upon, suspicion, but what else has anyone ever to go upon in such matters? She is so deep, she's deep as the sea; and as for men . . .! No, I've only my intuitions, but they are sufficient, otherwise what is the use of an intuition? And what *is* the good of shutting your eyes to the plain facts of life?'

'But why him?' inquired Olive brusquely.

'I suspect him, Olive.' Camilla, calmly adjusting a hair-slide, peered at her yellow carpet which had a design in it, a hundred times repeated, of a spool of cord in red and a shuttlecock in blue. 'I suspect him, just as I suspect the man who quotes Plato to me.'

Mr. Kippax that is — thought Olive. 'But isn't that what Plato's for?' she asked.

'I really don't know what Plato is for, Olive; I have never read Plato; in fact I don't read him at all; I can't read him with enjoyment. Poetry, now, is a thing I can enjoy — like a bath — but I can't talk about it. Can you? I never talk about the things that are precious to me; it's natural to be reserved and secretive. I don't blame Maude Lassiter for that; I don't blame her at all, but she'll be lucky if she gets out of this with a whole skin: it will only be by the skin of her teeth.'

'I'd always be content,' Olive said, 'If I could have the skin of my teeth for a means of escape.'

'Quite so,' agreed Camilla, 'I'm entirely with you. O, yes.'

Among gardeners Luke Feedy was certainly the pearl. He had come from far away, a man of thirty or thirty-five, without a wife or a home in the world, and now he lodged in the village at Mrs. Thrupcott's cottage; the thatch of her roof was the colour of shag tobacco; her husband cut your hair in his vegetable garden for twopence a time. Luke was tall and powerful, fair and red. All the gardening was done by him, both Olive's and Camilla's, and all the odd and difficult jobs from firewood down to the dynamo for electric light that coughed in Camilla's shed. Bluff but comely, a pleasant man, a very conversational man, and a very attractable man; the maids were always uncommon friendly to him. And so even was Olive, Camilla observed, for she had actually bought him a gun to keep the rabbits out of the garden. Of course a gun was no use for that — Luke said so — yet, morning or evening, Olive would perambulate with the gun, inside or outside the gardens, while Luke Feedy taught her the use of it, until one October day, when it was drawing on to evening — Bang! — Olive had killed a rabbit. Camilla had rushed to her balcony, 'What is it?' she cried in alarm, for the gun had not often been fired before and the explosion was terrifying. Fifty yards away, with her back towards her, Olive in short black fur jacket, red skirt, and the Cossack boots she wore, was standing quite still holding the gun across her breast. The gardener stalked towards a bush at the foot of the hill, picked up a limp contorted bundle by its long ears, and brought it back to Olive. She had no hat on, her hair was ruffled, her face had gone white. The gardener held up the rabbit, a small soft thing, dead, but its eyes still stared, and its forefeet drooped in a gesture that seemed to beseech pity. Olive swayed away, the hills began to twirl, the house turned upside down, the gun fell from her hands. 'Hullo!' cried Luke Feedy, catching the swooning woman against his shoulder. Camilla saw it all and flew to their aid, but by the time she had got down to the garden Feedy was there too, carrying Olive to her own door. Quincy ran for a glass of water, Camilla petted her, and soon all was well. The gardener stood in the room holding his hat against his chest with both hands. A huge fellow he looked in Olive's small apartment. He wore breeches and leggings and a grey shirt with the sleeves uprolled, a pleasant comely man, very powerful, his voice seemed to excite a quiver in the air.

'What a fool I am,' said Olive disgustedly.

'O, no,' commented the gardener. 'O no, ma'am; it stands to reason ...' He turned to go about his business, but said: 'I should have a sip o' brandy now, ma'am, if you'll excuse me mentioning it.'

'Cognac!' urged Camilla.

'Don't go, Luke,' Olive cried.

'I'll fetch that gun in, ma'am, I fancy it's going to rain.' He stalked away, found his coat and put it on (for it was time to go home), and then he fetched in the gun, Camilla had gone.

'Take it away, please,' cried Olive. 'I never want to see it again. Keep it. Do what you like, it's yours.'

'Thank you, ma'am,' said the imperturbable Feedy. Two small glasses of cognac and a long slim bottle stood upon a table in the alcove. Olive, still a little wan, pushed one towards him.

'Your very good health, ma'am,' Feedy tipped the thimbleful of brandy into his mouth, closed his lips, pursed them, gazed at the ceiling, and sighed. Olive now switched on the light, for the room was growing dimmer every moment. Then she sat down on the settee that faced the fire. An elegant little settee in black satin with crimson piping. The big man stood by the shut door and stared at the walls; he could not tell whether they were blue or green or grey, but the skirting was white and the fireplace was tiled with white tiles. Old and dark the furniture was though, and the mirror over the mantel was egg-shaped in a black frame. In the alcove made by the bow window stood the round table on crinkled legs, and the alcove itself was lined with a bench of tawny velvet cushions. Feedy put his empty glass upon the table.

'Do have some more; help yourself,' said Olive, and Luke refilled the glass and drank again amid silence. Olive did not face him — she was staring into the fire — but she could feel his immense presence. There was an aroma, something of earth, something of man, about him, strange and exciting. A shower of rain dashed at the windows.

'You had better sit down until the rain stops,' Olive poked a tall hassock to the fireplace with her foot, and Luke, squatting upon it, his huge boots covering quite a large piece of the rug there, twirled the half-empty glass between his finger and thumb.

'Last time I drunk brandy,' he mused, 'was with a lady in her room, just this way.'

Olive could stare at him now.

'She was mad,' he explained.

'O,' said Olive, as if disappointed.

'She's dead now,' continued Luke, sipping.

Olive, without uttering a word, seemed to encourage his reminiscence.

'A Yorkshire lady she was, used to live in the manor house, near where I was then; a lonely place. Her brother had bought it because it was lonely, and sent her there to keep her quiet because she had been crossed in love, as they say, and took to drink for the sorrow of it; rich family, bankers, Croxton the name, if you ever heard of them?'

Olive lolling back and sipping brandy, shook her head.

'A middling size lady, about forty-five she was, but very nice to look at — you'd never think she was daft — and used to live at the big house with only a lot of servants and a butler in charge of her, name of Scrivens. None of her family ever came near her, nobody ever came to visit her. There was a big motor-car and they kept some horses, but she always liked to be tramping about alone; everybody knew her, poor daft thing, and called her Miss Mary, 'stead of by her surname Croxton, a rich family; bankers they were. Quite daft. One morning I was going to my work — I was faggoting then in Hanging Copse — and I'd got my billhook, my axe and my saw in a bag on my back when I see Miss Mary coming down the road towards me. 'Twas a bright spring morning and cold 'cause 'twas rather early; a rare wind on, and blew sharp enough to shave you; it blew the very pigeons out the trees, but she'd got neither jacket or hat and her hair was wild. "Good morning, miss," I said, and she said "Good morning", and stopped. So I stopped, too; I didn't quite know what to be at, so I said, "Do you know where you are going?" '

'Look here,' interrupted Olive, glancing vacantly around the room. 'It's still raining; light your pipe.'

'Thank you, ma'am,' Luke began to prepare his pipe. ' "Do you know where you're going?" I asked her. "No," she says. "I've lost my way; where am I?" and she put' — Luke paused to strike a match and ignite the tobacco — 'put her arm in my arm and said, "Take me home." "You're walking away from home," I said, so she turned back with me and we started off to her home. Two miles away or more, it was. "It is kind of you," she says, and she kept on chattering as if we were two cousins, you might say. "You ought to be more careful and have your jacket on," I said to her.

"I didn't think, I can't help it," she says: "it's the time
'o love; as soon as the elder leaf is as big as a mouse's
ear I want to be blown about the world," she says. Of
course she was thinking to find someone as she'd lost.
She dropped a few tears. "You must take care of yourself these rough mornings," I said, "or you'll be
catching the inflammation." Then we come to a public-
house, The Bank of England's the name of it, and
Miss Mary asks me if we could get some refreshment
there. "That you can't," I said ('cause I knew about
her drinking), "it's shut", so on we went as far as
Bernard's Bridge. She had to stop a few minutes there
to look over in the river, all very blue and crimped with
the wind; and there was a boat-house there, and a new
boat cocked upside down on some trestles on the landing, and a chap laying on his back blowing in the boat
with a pair of bellows. Well, on we goes, and presently
she pulls out her purse: "I'm putting you to a lot of
trouble," she says. "Not at all, Miss," I said, but she
give me a sovereign, then and there, she give me a
sovereign.'

Olive was staring at the man's hands; the garden
soil was chalky, and his hands were covered with fine
milky dust that left the skin smooth and the markings
very plain.

'I didn't want to take the money, ma'am, but I had
to, of course; her being such a grand lady it wasn't my
place to refuse.'

Olive had heard of such munificence before; the
invariable outcome, the denouement of Feedy's stories,
the crown, the peak, the apex of them all was that
somebody, at some point or other, gave him a sovereign.
Neither more nor less. Never anything else. Olive
thought it unusual for so *many* people ...

'... and I says, "I'm very pleased, miss, to be a help

to anyone in trouble." "That's most good of you," she said to me. "That's most good of you; it's the time of year I must go about the world, or I'd die," she says. By and by we come to the manor house and we marched arm in arm right up to the front door and I rong the bell. I was just turning away to leave her there but she laid hold of my arm again. "I want you to stop," she says, "you've been so kind to me." It was a bright fresh morning, and I rong the bell. "I want you to stop. Scrivens," she says, "this man has been very kind to me; give him a sovereign, will you." Scrivens looked very straight at me, but I gave him as good as he sent, and the lady stepped into the hall. I had to follow her. "Come in," she says, and there was I in the dining-room, while Scrivens nipped off somewhere to get the money. Well, I had to set down on a chair while she popped out at another door. I hadn't hardly set down when in she come again with a lighted candle in one hand and a silver teapot in the other. She held the teapot up, and says, "Have some?" and then she got two little cups and saucers out of a chiffonier and set them on the table and filled them out of the silver teapot. "There you are," she says, and she up with her cup and dronk it right off. I couldn't see no milk and no sugar and I was a bit flabbergasted, but I takes a swig — and what do you think? It was brandy, just raw brandy; nearly made the tears come out of my eyes, 'specially that first cup. All of a sudden she dropped on a sofy and went straight off to sleep, and there was I left with that candle burning on the table in broad daylight. Course I blew it out, and the butler came in and gave me the other sovereign, and I went off to my work. Rare good-hearted lady, ma'am Pity,' sighed the gardener. He sat hunched on the hassock, staring into the fire, and puffing smoke.

There was attraction in the lines of his figure squatting beside her hearth, a sort of huge power. Olive wondered if she might sketch him some time, but she had not sketched for years now. He said that the rain had stopped, and got up to go. Glancing at the window Olive saw it was quite dark; the panes were crowded on the outside with moths trying to get in to the light.

'What a lot of mawths there be?' said Luke.

Olive went to the window to watch them. Swarms of fat brown furry moths with large heads pattered and fluttered silently about the shut panes, forming themselves into a kind of curtain on the black window. Now and then one of their eyes would catch a reflection from the light and it would burn with a fiery crimson glow.

'Good night, ma'am,' the gardener said, taking the gun away with him. Outside, he picked up the dead rabbit and put it in his pocket. Olive drew the curtains; she did not like the moths' eyes, they were demons' eyes, and they filled her with melancholy. She took the tall brandy bottle from the table and went to replace it in a cabinet. In the cabinet she saw her little silver teapot, a silver teapot on a silver tray with a bowl and a jug. Something impelled her to fill the teapot from the long slim bottle. She poured out a cup and drank it quickly. Another. Then she switched out the light, stumbled to the couch and fell upon it, laughing stupidly, and kicking her heels with playful fury.

That was the beginning of Olive's graceless decline, her pitiable lapse into intemperance. Camilla one May evening had trotted across to Olive's cottage; afterwards she could recall every detail of that tiniest of journeys; rain had fallen and left a sort of crisp humidity in the gloomy air; on the pathway to Olive's door she nearly stepped on a large hairy caterpillar solemnly confronting a sleek nude slug. That lovely tree by Olive's door was desolated — she remembered — the blossoms had fallen from the flowering cherry tree so wonderfully bloomed; its virginal bridal had left only a litter and a breath of despair. And then inside Olive's hall was the absurd old blunderbuss hanging on a strap, its barrel so large that you could slip an egg into it. Camilla fluttered into her friend's drawing-room: 'Olive could you lend me your gridiron?' And there was Olive lounging on the settee simply incredibly drunk! In daylight! It was about six o'clock of a May day. And Olive was so indecently jovial that Camilla, smitten with grief, burst into tears and rushed away home again.

She came back of course; she never ceased coming back, hour by hour, day after day; never would she leave Olive alone to her wretched debauches. Camilla was drenched with compunction, filled with divine energy; until she had dragged Olive from her trough, had taken her to live with her again under her own cherishing wings, she would have no rest. But Olive was not always tipsy, and though moved by Camilla's solicitude, she refused to budge, or 'make an effort', or do any of the troublesome things so dear to the heart of a friend. Fond as she was of Camilla she had a disinclination — of course she was fond of her, there was nothing she would not do for Camilla Hobbs — a disinclination to reside with her again. What if they had lived together for twenty years? It is a great nuisance that one's loves are determined not by judgment but by the feelings. There are two simple tests of any friendly relationship: can you happily share your bed with your friend, and can you, without unease, watch him or her partake of food? If you can do either of these things with amiability, to say nothing of joy, it is well between you; if you can do both it is a

sign that your affection is rooted in immortal soil.
Now Olive was forthright about food; she just ate it,
that was what it was for. But she knew that even at
breakfast Camilla would cut her bread into little cubes
or little diamonds; if she had been able to she would
surely have cut it into little lozenges or little marbles;
in fact the butter was patted into balls the same as you
had in restaurants. Every shred of fat would be
laboriously shaved from the rasher and discarded. The
cube or the diamond would be rolled in what Camilla
called the 'jewse' — for her to swallow the grease but
not the fat was a horrible mortification to Olive —
rolled and rolled, and then impaled by the fork. Snip
off a wafer of bacon, impale it; a triangle of white egg,
impale that; plunge the whole into the yolk. Then, so
carefully, with such desperate care, a granule of salt,
the merest breath of pepper. Now the knife must pursue with infinite patience one or two minuscular
crumbs idling in the plate, and at last wipe them
gloatingly upon the mass. With her fork lavishly
furnished and elegantly poised, Camilla would then
bend to peer at sentences in her correspondence, and
perhaps briskly inquire:

'Why are you so glum this morning, Olive?'

Of course Olive would not answer.

'Aren't you feeling well, dear?' Camilla would
exasperatingly persist, still toying with her letters.

'What?' Olive would say.

Camilla would pop the loaded fork into her mouth,
her lips would close tightly upon it, and when she drew
the fork slowly from her encompassing lips it would
be empty, quite empty and quite clean. Repulsive!

'Why are you so glum?'

'I'm not!'

'Sure? Aren't you?' Camilla would impound

another little cube or diamond and glance smilingly at her letters. On that count alone Olive could not possibly resume life with her.

As for sleeping with Camilla — not that it was suggested that she should, but it was the test — Olive's distaste for sharing a bed was ineradicable. In the whole of her life Olive had never known a woman with whom it would have been anything but an intensely unpleasant experience, neither decent nor comfortable. Olive was deeply virginal. And yet there had been two or three men who, perhaps, if it had not been for Camilla — such a prude, such a killjoy — she might ... well, goodness only knew. But Camilla had been a jealous harpy, always fond, Olive was certain, of the very men who had been fond of Olive. Even Edgar Salter, who had dallied with them one whole spring in Venice. Why, there was one day in a hayfield on the Lido when the grass was mown in May ... it was, oh, fifteen years ago. And before that, in Paris, Hector Dubonnel, and Willie Macmaster! Camilla had been such a lynx, such a collar-round-the-neck, that Olive had found the implications, the necessities of romance quite beyond her grasp. Or, perhaps, the men themselves ... they were not at all like the bold men you read about, they were only like the oafs you meet and meet and meet. Years later, in fact, not ten years ago, there was the little Italian count in Rouen. They were all dead now, yes, perhaps they were dead. Or married. What was the use? What did it all matter?

Olive would lie abed till midday in torpor and vacancy, and in the afternoon she would mope and mourn in dissolute melancholy. The soul loves to rehearse painful occasions. At evening the shadows cast by the down-going sun would begin to lie aslant the hills and then she would look out of her window, and seeing the bold curves bathed in the last light, she would exclaim upon her folly. 'I have not been out in the sunlight all day; it would be nice to go and stand on the hill now and feel the warmth just once.' No, she was too weary to climb the hill, but she would certainly go to-morrow, early, and catch the light coming from the opposite heaven. Now it was too late, or too damp, and she was very dull. The weeks idled by until August came with the rattle of the harvest reapers, and then September with the boom of the sportsman's gun in the hollow coombes. Camilla one evening was sitting with her, Camilla who had become a most tender friend, who had realized her extremity, her inexplicable grief; Camilla who was a nuisance, a bore, who knew she was not to be trusted alone with her monstrous weakness for liquor, who constantly urged her to cross the garden and live in peace with her. No, no, she would not. 'I should get up in the night and creep away,' she thought to herself, 'and leave her to hell and the judgment,' but all she would reply to Camilla was: 'Enjoy your own life, and I'll do mine. Don't want to burden yourself with a drunken old fool like me.'

'Olive! Olive! what are you saying?'

'Drunken fool,' repeated Olive sourly. 'Don't badger me any more, let me alone, leave me as I am. I . . . I'll . . . I dunno . . . perhaps I'll marry Feedy.'

'Nonsense,' cried Camilla shrilly. She turned on the light, and drew the blinds over the alcove window. 'Nonsense,' she cried again over her shoulder. 'Nonsense.'

'You let me alone, I ask you,' commanded her friend. 'Do as I like.'

'But you can't . . . you can't think . . . why, don't be stupid!'

'I might. Why shouldn't I? He's a proper man; teach me a lot of things.'

Camilla shuddered. 'But you can't. You can't, he is going to marry somebody else.'

'What's that?' sighed Olive. 'Who? O God, you're not thinking to marry him yourself, are you? You're not going . . .'

'Stuff! He's going to marry Quincy. He told me so himself. I'd noticed them for some time, and then, once, I came upon them suddenly, and really . . . ! Honest love-making is all very well, but, of course, one has a responsibility to one's servants. I spoke to him most severely, and he told me.'

'Told you what?'

'That they were engaged to be married, so what. . . .'

'Quincy?'

'Yes, so what can one do?'

'Do? God above!' cried Olive. She touched a bell and Quincy came in answer. 'Is this true?'

Quincy looked blankly at Miss Sharples.

'Are you going to marry Mr. Feedy?'

'Yes'm.'

'When are you going to marry Mr. Feedy?' Olive had risen on unsteady legs.

'As soon as we can get a house, ma'am.'

'When will that be?'

The girl smiled. She did not know; there were no houses to be had.

'I won't have it!' shouted Olive suddenly, swaying. 'But no, I won't, I won't! You wretched devil! Go away, go off. I won't have you whoring about with that man I tell you. Go off, off with you; pack your box!'

The flushing girl turned savagely and went out, slamming the door.

'O, I'm drunk,' moaned Olive, falling to the couch again. 'I'm sodden. Camilla, what shall I do?'

'Olive, listen! Olive! Now you *must* come to live with me; you won't be able to replace her. What's the good? Shut up the house and let me take care of you.'

'No, stupid wretch I am. Don't want to burden yourself with a stupid wretch.' With her knuckle Olive brushed a tear from her haggard eyes.

'Nonsense, darling!' cried her friend. 'I want you immensely. Just as we once were, when we were so fond of each other. Aren't you fond of me still, Olive? You'll come, and we'll be so happy again. Shall we go abroad?'

Olive fondled her friend's hand with bemused caresses. 'You're too good, Camilla, and I ought to adore you. I do, I do, and I'm a beast. . . .'

'No, no, listen. . . .'

'Yes, I am. I'm a beast. I tell you I have wicked envious feelings about you, and sneer at you, and despise you in a low secret way. And yet you are, O Camilla, yes, you are true and honest and kind, and I know it, I know it.' She broke off and stared tragically at her friend. 'Camilla, were you ever in love?'

The question startled Camilla.

'Were you?' repeated Olive. 'I've never known you to be. Were you ever in love?'

'O . . . sometimes . . . yes . . . sometimes.'

Olive stared for a moment with a look of silent contempt, then almost guffawed.

'Bah! Sometimes! Good lord, Camilla. O no, no, you've never been in love. O no, no.'

'But yes, of course,' Camilla persisted, with a faint giggle.

'Who? Who with?'

'Why, yes, of course, twenty times at least,' admitted the astonishing Camilla.

'But listen, tell me,' cried Olive, sitting up eagerly as her friend sat down beside her on the couch. 'Tell me — it's you and I — tell me. Really in love?'

'Everybody is in love,' said Camilla slowly, 'some time or another, and I was very solemnly in love . . . well . . . four times. Olive, you mustn't reproach yourself for . . . for all this. I've been . . . I've been bad, too.'

'Four times! Four times! Perhaps you will understand me, Camilla, now. I've been in love all my life. Any man could have had me, but none did, not one.'

'Never mind, dear. I was more foolish than you, that's all, Olive.'

'Foolish! But how? It never went very far?'

'As far as I could go.'

Olive eyed her friend, the mournful, repentant, drooping Camilla.

'What do you mean? How far?'

Camilla shrugged her shoulders. 'As far as love takes you,' she said.

'Yes, but . . .' pursued Olive, 'do you mean . . . ?'

'I could go no further,' Camilla explained quickly.

'But how — what — were you ever really and truly a lover?'

'If you must know — that is what I mean.'

'Four times!'

Camilla nodded.

'But I mean, Camilla, were you really, really, a mistress?'

'Olive, only for a very little while. O my dear,' she declined on Olive's breast, 'you see, you see, I've been worse, much worse than you. And it's all over. And you'll come back and be good too?'

But her friend's eagerness would suffer no caresses; Olive was sobered and alert. 'But . . . this, I can't understand . . . while we were together . . . inseparable we were. Who . . . did I know them? Who were they?'

Camilla, unexpectedly, again fairly giggled: 'Well, then, I wonder if you can remember the young man we knew at Venice . . .?'

'Edgar Salter, was it?' Olive snapped at the name. 'Yes.'

'And the others? Willie Macmaster and Hercules and Count Filippo!' Olive was now fairly raging. Camilla sat with folded hands. 'Camilla Hobbs, you're a fiend,' screamed Olive, 'a fiend, a fiend, an impertinent immoral fool. O, how I loathe you!'

'Miss Sharples,' said Camilla, rising primly, 'I can only say I despise you.'

'A fool!' shrieked Olive, burying her face in the couch; 'an extraordinary person with a horrible temper and intolerant as a . . . yes, you are. O, intolerable beast!'

'I can hardly expect you to realize, in your present state,' returned Camilla, walking to the door, 'how disgusting you are to me. You are like a dog that barks at every passer.'

'There are people whose minds are as brutal as their words. Will you cease annoying me, Camilla!'

'You imagine' — Camilla wrenched open the door — 'you imagine that I'm trying to annoy you. How strange!'

'O, you've a poisonous tongue and a poisonous manner; I'm dreadfully ashamed of you.'

'Indeed.' Camilla stopped and faced her friend challengingly.

'Yes.' Olive sat up, nodding wrathfully, 'I'm ashamed and deceived and disappointed. You've a coarse soul. O,' she groaned. 'I want kindness, friendship, pity, pity, pity, pity, most of all, pity. I cannot bear it.' She flung herself again to the couch and sobbed forlornly.

'Very well, Olive, I will leave you. Good night.'

Olive did not reply and Camilla passed out of the room to the front door and opened that. Then: 'O,' she said, 'how beautiful, Olive!' She came back into Olive's room and stood with one hand grasping the edge of the door, looking timidly at her friend. 'There's a new moon and a big star and a thin fog over the barley field. Come and see.'

She went out again to the porch and Olive rose and followed her. 'See,' cried Camilla, 'the barley is goose-necked now, it is ripe for cutting.'

Olive stood staring out long and silently. It was exquisite as an Eden evening, with a sleek young moon curled in the fondling clouds; it floated into her melancholy heart. Sweet light, shadows, the moon, the seat, the long hills, the barley field, they twirled in her heart with disastrous memories of Willie Macmaster, Edgar Salter, Hercules and Count Filippo. All lost, all gone now, and Quincy Pugh was going to marry the gardener.

'Shall I come with you, Camilla? Yes, I can't bear it any longer; I'll come with you now, Camilla, if you'll have me.'

Camilla's response was tender and solicitous.

'I'll tell Quincy,' said Olive. 'She and Luke can have this cottage, just as it is. I shan't want it ever again! They can get married at once.' Camilla was ecstatic. 'And then will you tell me, Camilla,' said Olive, taking her friend's arm, 'all about... all about... those men!'

'I will, darling; yes, yes, I will,' cried Camilla. 'O, come along.'

The Field of Mustard (1926)

ABEL STAPLE DISAPPROVES

A LITTLE harbour at the mouth of an Anglian river. On the far side, a mile away, a tiny town gleaming quietly in the sunset, with two church towers, an ecclesiastical college and a home for ancient mariners. On the near side, wharves, huts, sand dunes and a solitary inn called the Ferry which had some daffodils in its half-a-perch of front garden; beyond that, pastoral heaths, windmills, and hamlets.

Evening was placidly enfolding the harbour. A few rugged smacks nudged amiably at the wharves, fumes of tar and fish drifted from the blocks, cordage and tackle, and sea odours rose from the fallen tide in the river. A man by the name of Billings who was squatting on a bollard got up and slouched away into the bar of the Ferry Inn. There is no keeping some people out of some public-houses, and Billings had the mystical compulsion. He also had a seafaring hat with a red paper flower fastened at the corner of the peak, and gold rings in his florid ears; a fair man, a tall man, a man in a blue jersey, with brine in his voice and long wading boots up to his thighs — in short, a fisherman. Into the Ferry goes Billings, and 'Good evening' to him says the landlord Alan Starr, a fraternally dapper person with avid eyes and a waxed moustache; his white shirt sleeves were rolled up above his elbows.

'A pint,' replied Billings.

'Nice evening, Edward,' repeated the landlord, and Billings grunted 'Ah'! When he had taken a good quaff of ale he said: 'You ain't seen my brother-in-law yet?' And he lounged easily against the counter — he was the sort of man that always leans.

'No, bor; I ain't seen Abel for three or four days.'
'I'm expecting him by and by.'

It was a dim faded taproom and seemed too shy ever to have been painted — it had been cleaned so well. A couple of tables scrubbed to the bone, some hard chairs, and framed photographs on the walls of wedding groups twenty years ago, beanfeasts, and cricketers wherein Alan Starr might be guessed at as the knowing young man with cap cocked awry and a ball in his fist. But the worn linoleum on the floor, streaked grey and white, had a suggestion about it of the entrails of some glutinous leviathan. There was not a great deal of profit to be made out of the custom of the Ferry Inn, and Mr. Starr augmented his income by crafty deals in antique clocks and life-saving dogs.

Two flat-faced, tidy strangers sat at one table, stoutish, with pipes protruding from their faces. The landlord, addressing them, resumed an interrupted yarn:

'Well, it was in the time of the Fenians . . .'

'Just fill that mug again,' one of the stout strangers commanded.

'Yes, sir!' cried Alan with ferocious alacrity. As he gave the handle of the beer engine a coaxing pull he repeated: 'In the Fenian days it was . . .' He set the pot in front of the customer, who then asked to be obliged with a postage stamp. Alan disappeared into his private parlour in search of a postage stamp.

'It's a good tale, this Fenian tale,' the one man remarked to his companion.

'It *was*.' The other puffed at his pipe stolidly.

'But it wants telling, you must realize that. It wants *telling*, in a certain *way*, delicate.'

'Yes, yes; and I heard it twenty years ago,' said the other with an air of contempt.

'So've I. Five thousand times. But a good tale is worth hearing over and over again, Harry, so long as it's well told. It's the art of it.'

'That's right enough, Sam, and I had a queer experience once, I did. . . .'

'It *is* funny how experience keeps on cropping up!'

'A very funny experience. . . .'

'Wherever you go, experience is a great thing, Harry. It carries you through all the troubles and trials of life. And you never forget it.'

'I was there for three weeks once. . . .'

'Where?'

'Edinburgh.'

'Don't I know it! I been there. A noble city, wide streets — ain't they? — and very well educated I should say, such a lot of bookshops.'

'The streets are all blooming granite and the books are all religious, but I was only there for three weeks and three days, I was. . . .'

'Just long enough, Harry   Just long enough to love what you like. That's the main factor, ain't it?'

'I was ordered to go on guard. . . .'

'D'ye know, that's a duty I always liked when I was a soldier. Most chaps didn't, but I did. I liked being on guard.' Sam swilled down a hearty draught. 'Go on, you tell your tale, Harry, you tell it.'

'Well, it's a good 'un. Just give me half a chance, Sam; if you'll only listen, and my God it's good.'

Then Harry began to mumble so secretively to Sam that Billings could not overhear any more. Back came the landlord:

'There you are, sir!' he cried, and laid a postage stamp before the inquiring man, who thereupon tendered him sixpence. The two friends waited mutely until the change was brought. The landlord then, after a furtive glance round, rested his hands oratorically upon their table and began: 'As I was just about to tell you . . .'

A woman with a jug came in at the door and stepped up to the bar counter.

'It was in the time of the Fenians,' shouted the landlord, retreating to his lair. 'I'll tell you in a minute. Yes, ma'am?' He picked up the woman's jug and hovered over his handles. 'In the time of the Fenians . . . Beer, did you say, ma'am?'

'Stout,' answered the woman wearily, counting some coppers from her purse.

'Pint, ma'am? No — half a pint, of course.' He pulled and paused. 'Stout, I think you said, ma'am? Lumme, this cask is nearly empty; I must go and see to it.' And after serving the woman he trotted down into his cellar.

Harry resumed his colloquy with Sam, while Billings still leaned, watching for his brother-in-law, Abel Staple. Tap, tap, tap; the landlord was adjusting his barrels. His wife, an unpleasant woman with red hands and an agate brooch, came into the taproom and lit a hanging lamp. The two men ceased their whispering until she had finished. Then a labourer entered.

'A pint, missus,' he muttered.

As she was supplying the drink the labourer said quietly to her: 'I just been along to see Albert, and, O, he's dying fast; he can't last another hour.'

'Oh, oh,' the landlady intoned distressfully, and quickly put the pot on the counter. The man drew it towards him and laid down his pence. She pushed the money away. 'No, no, I could not take it. I'm very grateful to you for coming and telling me. I must run along at once and see the poor thing.'

She flung on a cloak and bonnet and called down to

her husband in the cellar that Cousin Albert was just dying. As she and the labourer left the taproom together, Alan Starr came up to the bar again.

'Poor old Albert!' he said to Billings. 'How that man have suffered! Operation after operation, in and out of hospital like a bee in a hive. It's a funny thing, though, but if your bladder's got a slit in it, it grows with a sort of selvedge edges and won't come together again. Stands to reason, flesh won't grow together unless it's raw. There's no arguing about that; you can put your two fingers side by side, like that, but they won't join up — not unless you skin 'em, mind you, and scrape the flesh raw and bind 'em tight together. *Then* they might, but not without. Poor Albert, it's a funny business! Dear me! Poor old Albert!'

Turning briskly towards Harry and Sam he cried: 'Well, gents, about these here Fenians . . .'

Both men instantly arose.

'Must bid you good evening,' said Sam.

'What! Are you off, gentlemen?'

'Yes, we are off.'

'We got to go,' added Harry.

'Aye, aye. Good evening,' Alan said, 'and thank you.'

In silence after their departure the landlord meditatively filled his pipe; having lit it, he marshalled his hopes once more with a sigh and leaned upon the counter:

'Did I ever tell you that tale about the Fenians, Ted? I don't think I did, did I?'

Billings slowly shook his head: 'I can't call to mind I ever heard it.' The landlord glanced at the clock.

'Well, it was in the time of the Fenians . . .'

'Just a bit,' the tall fisherman interposed. 'Give us another pint, will you?'

'Pint, Ted? Certainly.'

Billings drew some coins from his pocket and selected a shilling. The landlord pushed the filled pot towards him. 'Yes, it was in the Fenian days ...' But the coin slipped from Alan's wet fingers and went rolling and wriggling across the taproom floor as though escaping from some dire tyranny.

'Hoi! Hoi!'. The landlord trotted round after it. 'Now where are you gone to?' He stooped, peering under the hard chairs and the tables after the lost coin. 'Did you see where he went, Ted?'

No, Ted had not observed that. Alan sunk upon one knee and struck a match, searching here and there.

'Come out, you shameful thing!'

But the shilling lay low, and the landlord was soon exhausted by the pressure of his belt and the constriction of his breeches.

'Well, may I be boiled alive!' he cried. ''S gone hopping off like a frog in a tunnel. Must be here somewhere.'

'I di'n' see it go,' Billings said. 'You had it.'

'Yes, I had it, but I di'n' see it go neither. I'll find it,' he said, rising, 'to-morrow morning. It must be there, I know it's there.'

Returning to the bar, he composed himself once more. 'Well, I was going to tell you ...'

Again Billings interposed: 'What about my change?'

'Your change! Ah! What was it you give me, Ted?'

'I give you that shilling.'

'Oh, ah,' sighed Alan, 'that darned thing!' He glared into the dark corner of the room where the coin was last seen. 'I know it's just there, I see it go. Let me get a candle; I'll soon have him out of that.'

So with a lit candle he searched, and after much

gaping and groping and groaning he found the shilling just as the door was thrust open and Abel Staple came in.

Staple was a clean-shaven ruddy countryman, clad in fawn corduroy that reeked of sheep, and his shrill voice was so powerful that it produced tangible vibrations in the air. He lived in a village a few miles off, where his wife Fanny, a sister of Ted Billings, had died the year before.

'How goes it, Abel?' was the landlord's greeting as he returned to his counter.

'O . . . there's beef and butter, and the bread's none so bad!' grinned Abel.

'Ain't seen much of you lately.'

'Well, what with the time o' year and the time o' life and the time o' day I can't stand the pressure of these late nights. Five o'clock in the morning you'll see me in my bloom! A pint, please.'

'Pint? Five o'clock, eh? The Almighty never put it in my power to behave like that, Abel. I could not do it, not for the Emperor of China and fifteen pound a week.'

'You can always get up if you got anything to get up arter.'

'Pooh,' replied Alan, 'It's only a habit!'

Abel paid him from a leather purse, and then turned to his brother:

'I got a rabbit for you, Ted.'

'I got a dozen herring for you,' answered Ted.

'This rabbit ought a bin a hare.'

'They're longshore-uns, but half of 'em has tidy roes.'

The two men moved over to a table in the corner furthest from the bar counter and sat down side by side.

'What about my change, Alan?' Billings sternly called.

'Di'n' I give it you?'

'If you did I ain't seen it.'

'If you ain't seen it, Ted my boy, then I reckon I can't have given it to you.'

He brought the change and handed it to Billings: 'Nothing like honesty and a free mind.' Then he went humming away to sit in his private parlour.

Night had grown dark outside; there were no sounds from the harbour or the sea, for the wind was still. The old clock in the bar was ticking loudly.

'Have you thought of any little thing to put in the paper?' Abel asked in a lowered voice. 'Any little bit of a jink that's nice and proper?' And Billings, extracting two or three scraps of paper from somewhere under his jersey, replied: 'I got one or two snatches here.'

They were proposing to insert a joint notice in the 'In Memoriam' column of the local newspaper; Billings read out from one of his paper scraps:

> *In fond memory of Fanny Staple who fell asleep May 12. Gone but not forgotten. From her sorrowing husband Abel and her brother E. Billings.*

The sorrowing husband emitted a doubtful 'Humph!'

'I think that's a good one,' Billings declared. 'Don't you? It 'ull cost two shillings. Or you could have a verse of a hymn or a text from the Bible and that 'ull be half-a-crown.'

'I don't much like that fell asleep talk,' the widower commented.

'It's only a manner of speaking, Abel.'

'Yah. But sleeping is sleeping, and when you're in your grave it's something else or different. I go to sleep, but I get up again. Five o'clock of a morning, my angel, year in, year out.'

'It's only a manner of speaking.'

'I know that; but, dammit, she died, didn't she!'

'Well, all right; what about a hymn?' her brother suggested. 'Fanny was always partial to hymns — it runs in our family. I like a song myself.'

'God bless us and well I knows of it! She'd howl her eyes out over a hymn.'

'You mustn't forget she had a tender heart,' Billings maintained. 'Right from girlhood she had.'

'No call to! Not as I could ever see.'

'I dunno . . . I dunno . . . Some has a smile for one thing and a sob for another and you can't understand the reason for either.' Billings seemed to be mournfully affected by some recollection. 'If we could understand that, Abel, we should know a lot more than we do.'

'You's looking for the place where the cat put her paws, Teddy. You know she's bin and collared the cream, so what does it signify? Fanny was as good a wife as ever trod on this earth, cooking, washing, mangling, mending — every mortal thing the heart could wish for — except a child — and that she never had. That was her downfall. She come to me in her prime, pretty as a lamb, a laughing girl, but she soured early and took to other ways. I tell you honest, Ted, she gave me a fair sickener of hymns and tears. You can cry tears till your breast is wet and you dream of nothing else; you can drop your tears all over the furniture — I've seen the spatters, ah! — and then you can go and drop them all over the garden, but tears don't make the beans to grow. So much psalming is all very well and we has to put up with it, but out of season is out of reason, I say. I've been religious and soulful, too, in my day — we all of us have, ain't we? In my young time forty year ago, when I was a boy, Parson Froggett took me through my confirmation and he was a good old Christian vicar as ever tipped a shoe. I can remember him marching us all off from the schoolhouse one fine morning to go for the blessing of the lord bishop. (Just such another day, it was, as that fine Whitsun when Fanny and I got wed; lilacs, laburnums, and the grass sweet as an apple.) I can remember him now! Off we goes across the fields to the church, boys in front and the gals behind all dressed in their white muslins. And we boys got the devil in us somehow that morning, it was such a pink of a day, and the bell ringing, and we rooshed along over stiles and through hedges till the gals puffed and blowed and tore their frocks to tatters, and old Froggett — he was very fat, fine old face, stuttered a bit — he calls out: "S . . . s . . . s . . . steady boys, steady; n . . . n . . . n . . . not so fast in front there!" But we boys got the devil in us that morning and we made their backs sweat for 'em. He were a good old Christian man, Froggett; kept up a good house though he was never married hisself; cook, coachman, two maids, and Eva Martin's daughter cleaned his boots for years and got tuppence a week for it; but I'm blammed if he didn't go and poison hisself arter all. I liked old Froggett.'

The fisherman ruminated, with puff puff puff at his pipe.

' 'Twarn't so much the eyes,' he said, 'it was the mind weeping.'

'I shouldn't ha' said she was weakminded, Ted.'

'Nah, well,' Billings sighed. 'What are you going

to put in this notice? We got to put in something or other — or ain't you going to, arter all?'

'Sure!' cried Abel, 'I be game enough.'

' 'Cause if you ain't,' Billings declared, 'I'll put it in myself.'

'You've no call to say that,' Abel soothingly answered. 'You've got a brother's full heart, I know, I know you have, but she was my wife, whether or no, and I'm not renagging.'

'There's this one, then.' Billings fingered another paper scrap: '*Till we meet again.*'

'Well, ye know, that's pretty much of a hymn, too!'

'She was fond of hymns, very fond,' Billings steadfastly declared.

'She was, O she was, Ted; but my heart was never a crock for that sort of pickle. Let's have something cheerful and a bit different now it's all over. *Peace, perfect Peace*, I reckon is the best. We don't want a lot of palaver about a silent tear and that sort of chatter. It's all over. Let's have *Peace, perfect Peace.*'

The brother was silent. After waiting some moments Abel inquired:

'What do *you* say, Ted?'

And Ted said: 'O, have it your own way. I'm agreeable.'

'All right now,' Abel answered. 'That's settled then: *Peace, perfect Peace.* Of course, next year, if God spares us, you can put in whatever you've a mind to; that's only fair. Now you look arter it, Ted, will you, and see it goes in the paper the proper time. When *is* the date of it?'

'Week after next.'

' 'Course it is! Whatever was I thinking about! Time flies so. *Peace, perfect Peace* then. Landlord!'

349

Abel rapped loudly upon the table with his empty pot. Alan came forward: 'Give us a couple a pints.'

The beer was drawn. Alan Starr pocketed the money and lingered with a smile on his face as the men gulped deeply; then, suddenly leaning upon the table, he began once more: 'It was in the time of the Fenians.' It would be unmeet, however, to pursue that story to its close, though the prospects of impropriety, however reprehensible, are very alluring. At its conclusion the two men prepared to go home.

'Here's your herring,' said Ted to Abel.

'Aye, aye; here's your rabbit,' Abel replied.

'And what about paying for the memorial notice? Half and half you said, Abel.'

'That's right, I was near forgetting. Tell ye what, Ted: I don't mind tossing ye to see who pays the lot.'

'Call to me,' said Ted grimly.

Abel called and lost.

'My, if that ain't a blow from a pig's tail!' he cheerfully cried, as he handed Billings a two-shilling piece.

Dunky Fitlow (1933)